W9-CRP-069

PRAISE FOR *KEEPERS OF THE GATE*

"A strongly plotted, impressively solid new entry."
—*Kirkus Reviews*

"This is a big, complex mystery propelled by a genuinely compelling plot and its likable lead characters. We enjoy watching these smart, efficient detectives sort out what's what and we enjoy watching the author have fun with his bigger-than-life plot, carefully calculating how far he can go without turning his story into a cartoon. . . . A lively and well-told yarn, sure to please fans of high-concept thrillers."
—*Booklist*

"A labyrinthine tale of conspiracy and deception. . . . Land is adept at gauging the unique effects the Mideastern culture and history will have on the emotions and motivations of his protagonists."
—*Publishers Weekly*

"Land's pacing is masterful, giving the reader a sense that he is watching an action movie. And he depicts the very real Israeli-Palestinian conflicts with clarity and poignancy. . . . Another spectacular, fast-paced, suspense-filled thriller from Land, one that will keep you up at night turning the pages. *Keepers* is a keeper."
—*The Providence Sunday Journal*

"Land is coming into his own with the Ben Kamal series, reflecting a maturity of craft most authors struggle to convince us they have and fail. With *Keepers of the Gate* Land hits his stride. . . . Land stands head and shoulders above his competition in creating—down to the smallest detail—characters who provoke both our caring and interest. The devil is in the details, as they say, and in this case Jon Land has done better than give the devil his due—he's given us genre that manages to capture the elusive human factor."
—Gary Kadet, Crime editor *The Boston Book Review*

"Few writers capture the conflict and turmoil of the Middle East like thriller author Jon Land. Land has done it again in *Keepers of the Gate*, a novel of suspense about the Palestinian-Israeli conflict, murders, Nazi hunters, Holocaust survivors and biotech research. . . . Land captures the complex and tumultuous nature of the Arab-Israeli conflict without making sweeping indictments on either side. . . . Land gives the reader a little more in *Keepers of the Gate*, an engaging thriller with a more personal touch than his previous works."

—*The Charleston Post and Courier*

"Jon Land writes exciting and believable political thrillers in the tradition of Clancy and Cornwall. . . . The theme of *Keepers of the Gate* is universal, yet heartwrenching so that readers will understand the motives of the key players, whose flaws make them so human. Mr. Land is a great storyteller who enriches his audience with every novel he writes."   —*The Midwest Book Review*

"International intrigue and double feints are par for the course in this thrilling tale. Be advised, when you think you've figured it out, Land has more surprises in store. . . . A white-knuckled read. Land has packed eight days of action into this tersely written, well-plotted work which races towards its surprising conclusion."   —*BookSense*

"*Keepers of the Gate* keeps this powerful series alive and kicking, shimmering in its knowledgeable details, its awareness of Israeli-Palestinian confrontations, and its carefully crafted plot. The mysteries and the mayhem never let up, right until the final page. Land's new novel is a crackerjack of a tingling, constantly surprising, compulsively readable thriller."   —*Providence Monthly*

JON LAND

KEEPERS OF THE GATE

A TOM DOHERTY ASSOCIATES BOOK
NEW YORK

This is a work of fiction. All the characters and events portrayed in this book are either products of the author's imagination or are used fictitiously.

KEEPERS OF THE GATE

Copyright © 2001 by Jon Land

All rights reserved, including the right to reproduce this book, or portions thereof, in any form.

A Forge Book
Published by Tom Doherty Associates, LLC
175 Fifth Avenue
New York, NY 10010

www.tor.com

Forge® is a registered trademark of Tom Doherty Associates, LLC.

ISBN: 0-812-57003-0
Library of Congress Catalog Card Number: 00-049512

First edition: April 2001
First mass market edition: February 2002

Printed in the United States of America

0 9 8 7 6 5 4 3 2 1

April 20, 1999

For the students of Columbine High,
Those who survived, and those who didn't

Heroes all

ACKNOWLEDGMENTS

THINGS CERTAIN IN LIFE: death, taxes, and a new book by me every year! If you've taken this ride with me before, welcome back. If it's your first trip, welcome aboard and get ready to have fun.

My brilliant editor at Forge, Natalia Aponte, added more than a new book this year. She's now the proud mother of Victoria Jane, born this past September. Operators of our favorite restaurant, Bolo, have missed her lately and so have I. But her creative genius will be back to work on my next one before long.

The extended Forge family is headed by Tom Doherty, who's like a father to everyone associated with the company. His daughter, Linda Quinton, heads a team that still answers their own phones, including Jennifer Marcus and Jodi Rosoff in publicity, whom I'll try not to drive quite as crazy this time.

My wondrous agent, Toni Mendez, meanwhile, keeps me sane, and you'll find Ann Maurer's incredibly appreciated pursuit of perfection on every page that follows.

Rabbi Jim Rosenberg, fully recovered from hip surgery by now, was of great assistance on this one again. So too

Nancy and Moshe Aroche, Rita and Wiley Archer, Irv and Josh Schechter, David Macaulay for his brilliant book *Castle* (Houghton Mifflin, 1977), Uwe Anton, Justin Turner, and the still brilliant, busier-than-ever Emery Pineo.

It's funny. Every year when I sit down to write this page for one book, I've also just begun the next book. (Tentatively called *The Dragon at Sunset*. Like the title? You can e-mail me at jonlandauthor@netscape.net. Love to hear from you.) That means we'll be speaking again this time next year. I'm already looking forward to it.

Wide is the gate and broad is the
way that leadeth to destruction.

—MATTHEW 7:13

PROLOGUE

TESS SANDERSON RUSHED down the hallway, readying her access card for the swipe that would take her into the institute's most secure laboratory area. The call had reached her in her office at Hessler Industries, just a few blocks away. After waiting a few interminable minutes for a cab, she started to walk before settling into a near-jogger's pace. The exertion left her breathless and hot by the time she reached the interconnected complex of buildings that bore the name of the institute's founder, Paul Hessler.

Tess's hand trembled as she swiped her card through the slot. The metallic click sounded and she yanked back on the heavy door. Inside, she felt colder instantly, chilled by the humidity-free seventy-degree air of the research wing. The stark white walls and bare tile invariably made her expect a clinical antiseptic smell. But the air was utterly devoid of scent save for a stray whiff of someone's perfume or cologne that still lingered.

Tess continued past a series of knobless, electronically operated stainless steel doors, aware only peripherally of what was going on inside them. The institute was not her domain—at least it hadn't been until recent months, and her role even now remained strictly informational. Conduit for a project that had been officially shut down more than six months earlier.

She reached a door marked CLOSED FOR CONSTRUCTION and pressed the six-digit entry code into a keypad. The door popped open and Tess entered, closing it quickly behind her.

The lights in the antechamber sprang on automatically, and she pressed her right eye against a lens inset next to a second door. A soft light brightened before her as it scanned her iris, leading the inner door to slide open once she had been positively identified.

Will Nakatami, the project's chief researcher, stood directly before her, his thin wiry frame nearly bouncing in his shoes. Beyond him stretched a hundred-foot square laboratory partitioned into various cubicles where his assistants were busy analyzing data in the areas of their specific expertise. To assure total secrecy, each understood only those portions of the project relevant to his individual work. The entire scope remained a mystery to be pondered but never grasped.

"I'm not supposed to be here," Tess said by way of greeting. "You know that."

"You've got to see this for yourself," Nakatami told her.

"What?"

"The latest data and samples from the test cases. I haven't quite finished the analysis but—"

Tess grabbed Nakatami's forearm and squeezed. "Yes or no?"

Nakatami nodded. "Yes."

"You're sure?" Tess asked, already reaching for her cell phone as her heartbeat quickened.

"The data confirm it. This is beyond anything we expected or hoped for at this stage."

Tess finished dialing a phone number halfway across the

world in Israel, then waited for the signal to sound before speaking.

"Lot four-sixty-one works," she announced and pressed END.

ONE
MONTH
LATER
DAY ONE

CHAPTER 1

I'M SORRY FOR the intrusion," Danielle Barnea said to the woman seated on the couch before her.
"This won't take very long."

Layla Saltzman nodded stiffly, as if it were something
she had gotten quite used to doing in recent weeks. Her
face was expressionless, her eyes dry and cried out. Dull
brown hair hung over her face in stray locks she had given
up caring about. The house, squeezed amidst other modest
one- and two-story stucco-finished homes in the Jerusalem
suburb of Har Adar, smelled of stale coffee and burned
pastry.

Six days before, Layla Saltzman's seventeen-year-old
son Michael had committed suicide. Before the case could
be officially closed, a final interview was required to make
sure the facts in question were all in order. Normally this
would have been a matter for local authorities—in this
instance the Jerusalem police—but all cases involving a
firearm were automatically referred to National Police.
And Danielle's superior, the commissioner or *Rav nitzav*
Moshe Baruch, had elected not to refer it back even after
suicide became apparent.

Now, seated in the suicide victim's living room, Danielle found her eyes wandering to the framed pictures adorning the coffee table between her chair and the couch on which the boy's mother sat. All showed Michael Saltzman in various poses through the years. Tennis racquet in his left hand, wearing a summer camp T-shirt. Baseball glove and uniform. His Bar Mitzvah. There was still plenty of space atop the table, but there would be no more pictures to fill it.

Her gaze lingered for a time on one shot that pictured Michael between his parents, an arm tossed casually around both their shoulders. The angle of the room's light gave Danielle a clear view of her own face, in effect projecting herself into the picture. Now that she was pregnant once again, she found comfort in the thought she might fill her own coffee table with photos some day. The comfort was short lived, though, as she reflected that the child's father in her pictures would be missing.

Danielle studied herself in the glass, seeing a youngish thirty-five year old, her face unlined by wrinkles, athletic and robust. She wore her wavy brown hair the same way she had in college, because it framed her full face better than any of the more contemporary styles would. How strange. Despite her professional reputation as a progressive innovator, she was, in this respect anyway, truly a creature of the past.

"Chief Inspector?"

Distracted, Danielle shuffled the folder on her lap and the forensics photos spilled out onto the living room rug. She stooped to retrieve them and watched Layla Saltzman's expression waver as she peered at the pictures through the coffee table's glass top. Danielle noticed she was wearing on her wrist a man's watch with a broken face.

"I'm sorry," Danielle said, sticking the photos in the rear of the folder. "Just a few more questions, I promise."

Layla Saltzman nodded.

"You were away the day of . . . the incident."

"I was at work."

Danielle gazed again at the picture of Michael standing between his two parents, everybody smiling. "And your husband?"

"We're divorced. He moved back to the United States. Remarried a woman with three young children. He returned to them the day after the funeral."

"I'm sorry."

Layla Saltzman shrugged as if she were tired of hearing that.

Danielle continued scanning the case report. "So the last time you spoke to your son . . ."

"At breakfast the day he . . ." Layla Saltzman's voice trailed off and she cleared her throat. "He seemed fine."

Danielle nodded, returning her focus to the case.

"I need to ask you about the gun, Mrs. Saltzman."

"He knew where it was kept, how to use it. Just in case. My husband wanted him to know. With the crime rates what they are here now, well . . . I forgot we even had it. Maybe if I had remembered and gotten rid of the damn thing . . ."

Layla Saltzman laced her hands together and wrung them raw. Danielle looked at her, trying to relate. She would have been a single mother now too, had she not miscarried her first pregnancy. And she fully intended to raise her new baby by herself. But the sight of the woman on the couch across from her started Danielle thinking. Layla Saltzman was alone now and would more than likely stay that way. Her child's father had been six thousand miles away when the boy died.

The father of Danielle's unborn child lived barely thirty miles from Jerusalem, yet she had decided to keep him out of the child's life. She tried to imagine herself on the other side of an interview like this. Alone, with nothing but photos to remind her it had not always been that way.

Layla Saltzman raised her arm and twisted it around to show Danielle the watch with the broken face. "This was Michael's watch. A present from his girlfriend last year. I was thinking about giving it back to her. Do you think I should?"

"If it makes you feel better," Danielle tried lamely.

"Nothing makes me feel better, Chief Inspector. That's the point." Layla Saltzman's eyes gestured toward Danielle's folder. "Does it say in there what a wonderful student Michael was? Does it say he spent a semester at a special cooperative school for Israelis and Palestinians outside of Jerusalem in Abu Gosh? Does it say what a tremendous soccer player he was, that American universities were sending him letters to recruit him? I didn't want him to go because that meant he'd be closer to his father than to me. Does it say that in there?"

Danielle remembered her preliminary study of Michael Saltzman's file. "There was mention of the incident involving your son's friend," she said, imagining herself having to live in a world of stale coffee and forced smiles in eighteen years time. No one to sit next to her, thanks to the decision she thought she had finally put behind her.

Layla Saltzman nodded. "Yes, a girl named Beth Jacober from Tel Aviv. They were close. I don't know how close, you understand." Her voice broke slightly. "Michael met her at his new school, the cooperative. She was killed in a car accident a week before he . . ."

"Mrs. Saltzman, you don't have to—"

"Everyone thinks Michael did it because he was depressed about Beth. I guess the two of them could have been closer than I thought. Who can tell with kids these days?" She balled her hands into tight fists and cradled them in her lap. "I—I didn't go to Beth's funeral with him; he didn't want me to. Michael wasn't depressed. He was dealing with Beth's death, he was coping." She flashed her son's watch with the broken face again. "It doesn't work anymore, but I still wear it."

Danielle looked at Michael Saltzman's watch, at the pictures of him on the coffee table featuring a family that would never be together again, that had squandered its chances.

Was this the kind of life she wanted for herself and her child?

Danielle flipped through the folder once more, finding the crime scene photos and the report filed in obligatory fashion by the case officers. Studied the photo picturing the nine millimeter pistol just out of the grasp of the dead boy's fingers.

"He wasn't wearing the watch when he died," she said vacantly.

Layla Saltzman shook her head. "No. It was on his dresser. I forgot to put it on his wrist for the funeral, then threw it across the room when I got home. That's when it broke." Something that passed for serenity spread briefly over her expression. "No one asked me about that before."

Danielle felt a jolt of recognition as she realized something no one else must have. She looked back at the collection of pictures on the glass coffee table, past the one of Michael with his arms around both his parents' shoulders, to the picture of the boy tossing a tennis ball into the air for the serve. Focused on him holding his racquet, ready to swipe it down in a wide booming arc.

"Is something wrong, Chief Inspector?" Layla Saltzman asked her.

"No," Danielle said, knowing no sense lay in saying anything to the woman yet, not until she was sure. "Nothing at all."

CHAPTER 2

COMMAND TO POST One," Ben Kamal said into his walkie-talkie, ignoring its low-battery warning light.

"Post One, Command."

"Do you still have visual on the subject?"

"I have him, Command. Still in his damned front row seat. Hasn't moved an inch."

"Roger," Ben replied and mopped the sweat from his brow. He figured it was over a hundred degrees in the cavernous bowels of Jericho's brand new soccer stadium, situated in a naturally flat valley between Elisha's Spring and the Ein as-Sultan refugee camp. Someday this would be the well-ventilated home of souvenir and refreshment stands that were supposed to have been ready at the same time the stadium was completed. But the collapse of the peace process had brought construction to a screeching halt, the Palestinian workers having abandoned their tools for rocks, slingshots, and, increasingly, guns.

Around him Ben heard a cheer go up that shook the walls, tried to guess what might have transpired. Not the winning goal; that noise would have truly rattled his eardrums. Probably just a great save or defensive stop.

The inaugural game of Palestine's soccer team versus Greece was well into overtime now with neither team having scored a goal. Thirty thousand fans had packed the stadium, causing a traffic jam so massive that the Greek team had to walk to the stadium from its hotel. The game had started nearly two hours late; those who had arrived on time left were to roast in stands that had been built with no shade whatsoever.

Ben and his surveillance team had been among the first to arrive in order to stake out their assigned surveillance points. They were here because Colonel Nabril al-Asi had received a tip that a leading Hamas terrorist named Mahmoud Fasil was going to be making a delivery. What, to whom, and precisely when during the game, the colonel didn't know.

"Why not just handle it yourself?" Ben had asked him.

"Our president needs the support of Hamas right now, Inspector," al-Asi replied, unable to disguise the bitterness in his voice. "Thus, my Protective Security Service is under strict orders to avoid operations against any of its members."

"Which, of course, doesn't apply to us lowly police officers."

"You have the privilege of being able to plead ignorance, Inspector."

Ben nodded, understanding. "Use our incompetence to its best advantage."

Al-Asi had merely shrugged, not bothering to offer a denial.

Mahmoud Fasil claimed his front row seat late and had not budged from it since the start of the game. Besides the flat-faced henchmen on either side of him, Fasil had not spoken to a single soul. The twelve policemen Ben had placed throughout the stadium to cover every angle had seen nothing out of the ordinary.

If nothing else, this would serve as an excellent exercise in a part of police work for which the Palestinian force had little practice. Ben had been putting his dozen years as a Detroit cop to good use in the West Bank for six years now, responsible for much of the most advanced training the detective force had undergone. They still did not totally accept him but he had proven himself often enough that neither could they disregard his advice. And anyone who did risked facing the wrath of Jericho's acting mayor, and Ben's former chief, Fawzi Wallid.

"Anything?" Wallid asked, after Ben approached him in the future concessions area. The mayor was only thirty-one years old. But his ruddy, pockmarked complexion and hooded brown eyes made him look older.

"No, *sidi*."

"Perhaps Colonel al-Asi's intelligence was wrong."

"Colonel al-Asi's intelligence is never wrong."

The young acting-mayor frowned. "He's been trying to catch Fasil himself for months. The colonel would like nothing better than for someone else to be given the blame for failure. You know that."

"Or the credit for catching this asshole. I know that too, *sidi*."

"Post Four to Command," both of them heard over Ben's walkie-talkie.

"Where are you, Four?" Ben returned.

"Behind the goal. They're setting up for penalty shots."

"Can you see Fasil?"

"On his feet cheering with everyone else. Can I keep this camera when we're finished, Inspector?"

"Just keep your eye on him. I'm coming up."

"Hurry so you don't miss the finish."

"I'd better head back to my seat too," Wallid said, obviously disappointed.

"We haven't failed yet, *sidi*."

"The intelligence services always get the credit for the ones like Mahmoud Fasil, Inspector. This was a big opportunity for us. We know Fasil is planning to run soon. We won't get another."

"The game's not over."

"Have your team ready to help with the traffic detail once it is."

Ben followed Wallid up the ramp and stood under cover of the overhang beneath the stadium's second tier. With everyone in the crowd standing to watch the penalty kicks, he had no view of Fasil or any of the rows closest to the field.

The crowd fell silent as the first Greek kicker lined up and fired his penalty shot into the goal, then erupted when the first Palestinian shooter did the same, high to the opposite corner. Ben feared he had missed something, went over his strategy to see if there was anything he had neglected. No, he had covered every angle. Mahmoud Fasil had not been out of his surveillance team's sight since Fasil entered the stadium.

The first three rounds ended with each team having made all of its penalty kicks. The fourth was the same, but the Greek player kicking fifth had his shot deflected wide by the Palestinian goalie. That gave Palestine's leading scorer, Abdel Sidr, a chance to win the game.

Sidr placed the ball down dramatically, lengthening the moment of utter silence in the stands as he measured his steps away from it. Ben tried to picture the chaos that would follow this upset, if Sidr knocked the ball home. He had seen European soccer crowds in action, couldn't imagine the hysteria over victory here.

Ben felt a slight chill.

Chaos . . . hysteria . . .

If anything happened, it would be *now!*

Ben pushed his way down the aisle toward the box seats just above field level.

Abdel Sidr started forward, swooping toward the ball.

Ben caught a glimpse of Mahmoud Fasil before someone shifted sideways behind him. And then he realized. In the moment Sidr's foot drew backward and then retraced its arc, he realized.

What better time, what better place? . . .

"All Posts, move in on target. The exchange is going

down!" he said into his walkie-talkie. "Repeat, the ex—"

The rest of Ben's words were drowned out by cheers when Abdel Sidr cracked his foot solidly into the ball and drilled it straight into the right-hand corner of the net. Ben continued trying to raise the members of his team as he was jostled and shoved by joyous fans intent on storming the field. Ben let himself be swept up in the flow that drove him down the aisle and spilled him over the lowest row of box seats onto the sideline.

Ben landed atop three young men and pushed himself off them to his feet, walkie-talkie back against his lips. "This is Command. Does anybody have him? Repeat, does anybody have Fasil?"

"This is Post Four. Field level. I've got him, I've got him! A few yards in front of the net. I think, yes, that's Fasil hugging the hero Sidr."

"Keep your eyes on him! Everyone else, converge, but don't try to take him until you hear from me."

"He's moving away, pushing through the crowd," Post Four reported.

"I've got him now," announced an out-of-breath officer.

"Heading toward an exit," Post Four repeated. "Big bastard on either side of him."

"I've lost him," from the still out-of-breath officer.

"Post Four," said Ben. "Stay with him but don't approach. Repeat, don't approach."

Ben pushed his way through the mounting crowd, trying to see. The goal had spilled over and fans were tearing at the netting. Players elbowed their way forward to escape the frenzy. Ben thought he saw the game's hero, Abdel Sidr, being rushed toward the player's ramp by stadium security.

"Command, this is Post Four. I've got the target. Closing now!"

"No, just stay—"

The sound of firecrackers made Ben break off his words. At least, that's what they sounded like. But the panicked screams and sudden thrust of the crowd away from the noise told Ben they were gunshots.

"Post Four, Post Four, come in! Post Four, come in!"

Hoping for a reply, Ben drew his pistol and surged forward, no longer making any effort to be subtle.

"Police!" he screamed. "Police! Make way!"

The crowd scattered as best it could. Ben shoved people aside, saw Mahmoud Fasil change directions and sprint toward the other end of the field. His two bodyguards, meanwhile, continued toward the nearest exit, clearing a path with their drawn guns.

Ben lifted his walkie-talkie to order his men after them, but the warning light was flashing now, telling him the battery had died. Ben pocketed it, as he neared the fallen officer. Post Four was barely out of his teens. Blood pooled beneath the hands clutching his side. The officer looked up at Ben in shocked fear when Ben pushed the crowd away and scooped him up as gently as he could to stop him from being trampled.

"I'm sorry," the young officer muttered, lips trembling horribly.

"You're a hero. There's nothing to be sorry about."

"Rah a moot."

"You're not going to die. I'm going to help you." Ben laid the young officer down in the relative calm beyond the far sideline and used a hand to compress the man's wound. The blood was warm, almost hot. Ben could feel it pushing up against his palm, wanting to spread. "You're going to be fine."

Ben yelled to a pair of stadium guards when they passed and the men reluctantly took his place over the fallen officer.

"One of you stay with him," Ben ordered. "The other get an ambulance and bring it back here."

His tone left no room for argument. He swung around and spotted Mahmoud Fasil just past the center line, weaving his way through the crowd. Ben started after him across the worn center of the field. He eased bystanders from his path firmly, never taking his eyes off Fasil. Gun held low by his hip, hoping to remain unnoticed for as long as possible.

He was still twenty yards back when the terrorist turned and spotted him. Ben saw the gun coming up in Fasil's hand, certain he was going to open fire on him when the terrorist twisted back around and fired a series of shots forward instead. Ben watched three bodies fall, their backs arching horribly as the life was ripped from them.

"Fasil!" he screamed, as the chaos the terrorist had created converged from all directions.

Bodies slammed into him, ping-ponging left and right. Ben felt his breath sucked away. He remembered as a child being kicked by a pair of boys who had pushed him down on the schoolyard ground, how he'd fought to get up and couldn't. Today he fought to hold his feet, pressing on as he forced his pistol up and steadied it forward into the mad rush swirling before him.

Damn al-Asi! Of all the cases to pass on to the police . . .

Whatever fear Ben had been feeling was trumped by rage. He swept forward, impervious to the panic cresting around him. He picked up speed, clearing his own way and sprinting in the same path plowed by players just minutes before. Mahmoud Fasil had almost reached the far goal when Ben stopped and joined a second hand to his pistol.

"Police! Everybody down!" Then, *"Fasil, stop!"*

Screaming, the crowd in front of Ben dropped en masse. Still twenty yards before him, Mahmoud Fasil froze, pistol held low by his hip.

"Drop the gun, Fasil! Do it now!"

Twenty yards was a tough shot for anyone, and Ben was hardly an expert marksman to begin with. But right now he didn't care. Right now missing was the farthest thing from his mind.

"Drop the gun!" he repeated.

Fasil spun instead, and opened fire.

Ben began firing too. It happened so fast he never consciously willed himself to do it. There was a dim awareness of muzzle flashes glowing from the bore of Fasil's pistol, followed by a bubbling hollowness in Ben's ears that accompanied the sharp reports of his own gun. He drew his finger back on the trigger again and again as rapidly as he could. His shooter's stance kept the gun's kick to a minimum, and the clacking of the spent, ejected shells burned through the stench of cordite into the edges of his consciousness.

Whatever aim he managed came from instinct and practice, not measure or thought. He didn't so much outshoot Fasil as outlast him when the terrorist's pistol clicked empty. Ben saw his last few bullets punch the terrorist backwards into the goal where the netting snagged Fasil and held him up.

Ben kept hammering the trigger well after the slide had locked, ceasing only when the clinging of shells stopped echoing in his ears and the dull haze of bore smoke began to lift.

B EN MOVED THROUGH the crowded, rank locker room, battling the press and various proud Palestinian dignitaries for space as he headed for Abdel Sidr's locker. The air conditioning hadn't been installed down here yet, another casualty of the return to arms by Israelis and Palestinians, and the stifling heat led players to seek the quickest possible exit. Not Sidr, though. The smiling star, still bloodied and dirty from the nearly two-hour game, was between questions from reporters when Ben leaned over and whispered in his ear.

"Hand over what Mahmoud Fasil gave you and I won't arrest you until the press is gone."

The look in Sidr's eyes when he saw the dangling police badge told Ben his suspicion had been correct. Fasil hadn't waited around through the whole game for nothing. Sidr's dramatic, clinching penalty shot had provided the perfect opportunity for what would otherwise have taken place here in the locker room.

"Now," Ben added, meaning it.

Sidr barely missed a beat in answering questions, as he reached back into his locker and plucked a dirt- and sweat-smeared envelope from the shelf. He pressed it into Ben's waiting hand with a forced smile. Then he cast his gaze toward the door, perhaps weighing his chances of disappearing through it with the rest of the crowd.

"When you're finished with your adoring public," Ben told him, reading Sidr's eyes, "my men will be waiting outside the locker room."

CHAPTER 3

PAUL HESSLER STEPPED back into the shadows of the cavernous room as soon as the alarm began to sound.

"We have incoming!" a technician blared from behind her radar screen.

Hessler watched the general in charge of Israel's Air Force Defense Command hurry across the floor. "Identification!"

The technician studied the readouts streaming across the lower portion of her screen, while a neat white line streaked toward Israel's airspace above. "Height, seven point five kilometers! Trajectory, eighty-five by sixty! Course heading, zero point one-five at fifteen hundred nautical miles per hour. It's a Scud Four, sir."

"Origin!" the general blared, standing bent at the knees in order to study the screen himself.

The technician studied some additional readouts, dragging a trembling finger across the bottom of her screen. Then she turned to look up at the general.

"Iran, sir."

"I need targeting."

"It's Tel Aviv, sir," the technician reported, eyes back on her screen. "Eight minutes to impact."

"Sir!" Hessler heard another uniformed technician yell from the other side of the room, the schematics of the South Korean Scud Four missile displayed on his monitor. "The Scud Four was constructed to carry nuclear ordnance!"

Paul Hessler watched the general hurry to another section of the center. This was Hessler's first time inside Israel's Air Defense Command headquarters located in a bunker buried in the Negev Desert. A much smaller version of NORAD in the United States, Air Defense Command constantly monitored Israel's and surrounding airspaces to guard against the possibility of surprise attacks. Israeli ADC "shared" information from American satellites in orbit, eliminating the need to rely on standard and inferior ground-based radar systems for intelligence.

"Take us up to Joshua Alert Status and get the prime minister on the line for me," the general ordered a subordinate Paul Hessler couldn't see from his vantage point.

"Yes, sir."

"Switch your display to the Big Screen."

Instantly the huge wall before the room's personnel came alive with a computer simulation of Israel portrayed in three-dimensional virtual reality, so a shot of any part or all of the country could be displayed at any angle or from multiple perspectives. Much like watching a panoramic postcard come to life. Currently that was a downward view from the sky, as a white streak denoting the Scud Four missile, now over Jordan, inched closer to Israeli airspace.

The general moved to a distant corner of the room, set off from the rest of the frantic activity, where a quartet of technicians were busy working four separate computer stations in restrained, calm fashion.

"Arrow is on-line and tracking, General," one of the four announced.

"All system lights green," added a second.

"Awaiting your order, sir," from the first again.

"You have the go to launch intercept," the general instructed.

Their voices became a blur to Paul Hessler, as the words and seconds passed with the blip representing a nuclear weapon soaring ever closer to Israel on the Big Screen.

"Beginning countdown now!"

"System primed and ready!"

"Automated launch sequence activated!"

On one of the four technicians' screens, a portion of the Negev Desert floor seemed to recede. A large white missile sprouted from the ground affixed to a launching arm.

"We have a target lock! Thirty seconds to intercept launch!"

"All lights green. All systems nominal."

On the Big Screen, the blip representing the Scud Four missile entered Israeli airspace.

"Arrow fixed and ready."

"Fifteen seconds to intercept launch."

From a distance Paul Hessler watched information and data scrolling down computer screens far faster than the human eye could follow. He heard electronic beeps, saw flashing lights and notations.

"Seven, six, five, four..."

The Scud Four streaked over the West Bank on an elliptical course for Tel Aviv. It was a detonation-on-impact weapon, Hessler knew, compared to the more advanced ICBMs which actually detonated miles up in the atmosphere.

"We have Arrow launch!"

And on the monitor picturing the Negev, the white missile burst into the air, surging out of sight in a heartbeat.

"Arrow has firm target fix."

"Sir," a voice called to the general weakly, "I have the prime minister."

The general pressed a satellite phone against his ear. "I'm here, sir."

A second white streak appeared on the Big Screen, ris-

ing up out of the virtually realistic Negev Desert on an
angle designed to intersect with the Scud Four's course.

"Speed and angle of ascent within parameters!"

*"Final intercept coordinates programming. Impact ex-
pected in ten seconds, nine, eight, seven . . ."*

The Scud Four continued to soar over Israel, as the Arrow missile rose directly in line with it.

"Five, four, three . . ."

Paul Hessler tried to imagine Tel Aviv in the wake of
a direct nuclear hit, had to remind himself to breathe.

"Two, one . . ."

The paths of the two missiles crossed each other, the
white streaks merging into a single blinding flash.

*"We have successful intercept! We have a kill. Repeat,
enemy missile has been killed!"*

The personnel of Israel's Air Defense Command broke
into spontaneous cheers and applause. Hessler continued
to focus on the virtual sky over Israel that was now clear,
until the overhead lights in the operations center snapped
on. A large group of civilian, military, and government
officials emerged from the darkness, clapping as well.

"It works," Hessler heard Israel's foreign minister blare
excitedly from behind him. "The damn thing works."

"This completes the drill," a droning voice announced
over the loudspeaker. *"All personnel remain on station."*

The applause continued as David Turkanis, foreign minister of the State of Israel, stepped from the shadows. In
his early forties, Turkanis was considered a rising star in
Israel's Labor party and was already being groomed to fill
the role of prime minister someday.

"Ladies and gentlemen," Turkanis announced, barely
able to restrain his exuberance. "I give you Paul Hessler
of Hessler Industries, developer of the Arrow Two Missile
Defense Shield."

The clapping gave way to boisterous cheers, acknowledged by Hessler with a shy wave of his hand as he moved
forward to join Israel's foreign minister. Since the Arrow
Missile Shield fell into Turkanis's domain, the success of

today's test would help cement his place in the line of party succession. Coupled with his friend Paul Hessler's vast influence, in fact, his rise to prime minister within the decade was virtually assured.

"Thanks to Paul Hessler," Turkanis continued, making no effort to hide his excitement, "the Arrow Two system is now successfully deployed and the the State of Israel is the most safe and secure she has ever been."

Hessler smiled broadly and beckoned his son Ari to join him. The old man clapped his son on the back and closed both hands over Ari's as they shook in celebration. Father and son both acknowledged the crowd with courteous waves. Paul Hessler waited until the noise in the control room had abated before he finally spoke in a strong, deep voice that belied his years.

"My son and I are, of course, ecstatic with the results of today's test. But the credit lies more with people like you, and those in the design center, as well as the assembly line. People who refused to quit and never wavered in their commitment to a safer Israel. You are a credit to your nation, as well as your parents and grandparents, many of them refugees like myself who dreamed of the day all of us will now live to see."

The story of Paul Hessler, Nazi labor camp escapee, was well-known to all those gathered in the control room. They applauded again and Paul Hessler waited for them to stop before he continued.

"My role in this was small. I don't even understand how the system works. My God, I can't even program the clock on my VCR."

Laughter filtered through the room. Hessler turned to foreign minister David Turkanis.

"While I gratefully accept your thanks and your congratulations, I am mindful that what we have accomplished only magnifies the importance of the work that remains to be done. My son, myself, and everyone at Hessler Industries is thankful that the day has finally come when no Israeli need ever fear harm from an attack by an enemy missile. Whatever part I have played in it . . ."

Paul Hessler let his voice fade. He looked around at the reverent expressions on the faces transfixed before him, eased his arm over his son's shoulder again and let it stay there.

"Whatever part I have played in it," he resumed, "is the least I could do for my country."

CHAPTER 4

BACK IN HER OFFICE, Danielle was staring at Michael Saltzman's open file when the phone on her desk rang. The desk was metal with a thin wood veneer badly scratched by the office's previous occupant. A single window behind the desk overlooked the parking lot and provided enough sunlight to fade the topmost portion of the filing cabinet squeezed into the corner. Her own chair and another with frayed vinyl upholstery fronting her desk composed the remainder of the office's scant furnishings.

Danielle fumbled the receiver on the way to her ear and cleared her throat. "Barnea."

"The Rav nitzav would like to see you, Pakad," the familiar voice of her superior's assistant ordered.

"I'll be right up."

"Now, please. And bring your file on the Saltzman case."

Danielle pushed her chair away from her desk, knowing what awaited her in Moshe Baruch's office on the fourth floor. Assigning her cases like Michael Saltzman's suicide was meant as extra punishment for Danielle doing everything she could to prevent him from being named head of

Israel's National Police. The former number two man at Shin Bet, the country's internal security service, Baruch had taken over as commissioner on an interim basis following the stroke and subsequent death of Danielle's mentor, Hershel Giott. She had never expected Baruch to seek the job on a permanent basis, was convinced he had done so as much as anything to terrorize her.

After all, they hadn't gotten along when he was her direct superior at Shin Bet and he had taken offense at her request for a transfer back to National Police after her miscarriage two years earlier. Upon securing the commissioner's job, Baruch's first order of business had been to bypass Danielle for both of the high-ranking deputy slots that had been promised her. She remained a chief inspector, forced to be at the beck and call of a man who a few months earlier had gone from tense antagonist to sworn enemy.

Baruch wanted her to quit.

Danielle refused to give him the satisfaction.

"You wanted to see me, sir?" she asked, after being escorted from the elevator to the Rav nitzav's office. Baruch had had the bare walls repainted and most of the furniture replaced since taking over for Hershel Giott. All that remained of her beloved mentor was the hardwood desk that had so dwarfed Giott but seemed small when measured against Baruch's massive frame.

"Yes, Barnea," he said. His huge forearms were emphasized by the short-sleeve shirt he always wore. He was a bear of a man, thick and hairy on every visible inch of flesh. Baruch seemed to notice Danielle had come to his office empty-handed. "You were instructed to bring the Saltzman file with you."

"I haven't completed it yet."

He looked puzzled. "I thought your interview was this morning."

"It was. I have some loose ends to tie up, that's all."

"Loose ends? It was a suicide."

"I like to be thorough."

"Just so long as I have it by the close of business today," Baruch said indifferently, letting Danielle see just how little her work meant to him.

He delighted in giving Danielle cases that could more appropriately be handled by local authorities, especially involving children, no matter how trivial and superfluous the required work might be. Just routine, indeed. She hadn't headed up an actual case for almost four months now, and Baruch clearly had no intention of assigning her one anytime soon.

The head of National Police let his elbows settle on the desk. "Is there a problem, Pakad?"

"None."

"I would have expected there wouldn't be, considering that I've lightened your load in view of your condition."

"Have I forgotten to thank you?"

"Along with your manners, yes," Baruch said, gloating, since Danielle had not officially informed anyone at National Police or the government about her pregnancy. Clearly he wanted to show her not only that he knew but also the damage he could do as a result, should the identity of the child's father be released for public consumption. The knowledge Baruch kept tucked away in his pocket like an old bill assured an uneasy truce between them, keeping Danielle from doing any more against him than she had already done.

She had been one of the first women to be selected for service in the Sayaret, Israel's elite commando unit, and then the youngest woman ever to achieve the rank of chief inspector with National Police. Her brief tenure with Shin Bet had followed, during which time she was assigned to the case that had changed her life forever by pairing her with a Palestinian detective named Ben Kamal in the West Bank.

"Have you given any thought to how much longer you wish to stay on the job?" Baruch asked her coldly.

"No," Danielle replied.

"I think an extended leave could be arranged, considering the extenuating circumstances."

"I wasn't aware there were any," she said.

"Then just feel free to keep the offer in mind."

"Thank you."

Baruch's deepset, neanderthal-like eyes fixed on her with typical coldness. "Have that report on the Saltzman boy on my desk by the end of the day," he reminded her.

B ACK IN HER office, Danielle found her voice mail light flashing. She recognized the voice as that of her obstetrician and listened apprehensively to his request that she call him back at her earliest convenience.

"I'd like to see you this afternoon," Dr. Barr said, as soon as he came on the line.

"Can't you tell me over the phone?" Danielle asked, her heart starting to hammer in her chest harder.

"It would be better if we discuss this in person. How is this afternoon for you?"

"Well—"

"I have an opening at four o'clock."

"That's fine."

"I'll see you then," the doctor said, and hung up before Danielle could press him further.

CHAPTER 5

FAWZI WALLID, ACTING mayor of Jericho, arrived at the hospital waiting room a half hour after Ben.

"How is the young officer, Inspector?"

"They rushed him into surgery. We won't know for a while."

"It wasn't your fault. You mustn't blame yourself."

"He was too young to be part of the detail. I should have known that."

Wallid clapped Ben lightly on the shoulder. "You should know that a computer disc contained in the envelope Mahmoud Fasil passed to Abdel Sidr contained Fasil's entire network. The president will be most pleased. I'm sure commendations will be coming."

"What about Sidr?" Ben wondered.

"Our soccer star claims he was just a messenger, that Fasil threatened to kill his family if he didn't cooperate."

"He's probably telling the truth."

"We're checking out his story." Wallid noticed the blood staining Ben's shirt. "You're not hurt, are you, Inspector?"

"It's the young officer's blood. I'd rather it was mine."

"You'll call me as soon as you hear something."

"Of course."

Flanked by a pair of Palestinian policemen, Fawzi Wallid started for the door and then turned back around. "And please send the young officer my best."

"As soon as he's well enough to hear me."

Ben started walking down the hall to continue his vigil closer to the surgical wing on the second floor. The hospital building was a modern three-story complex with a white-stone finish that helped it blend in perfectly among the buildings around it. It was laid out in a rectangle around a centrally placed parking lot and courtyard hidden from casual view from the street. Ben hoped to find a chair by a window that faced the courtyard to avoid the stomach-knotting feelings of claustrophobia that struck him whenever he was inside a hospital.

He stepped out of the elevator on the second floor and nearly collided with a sobbing woman who held a damp handkerchief pressed against her nose and eyes.

"Excuse me," Ben said. "I'm sorry."

The woman looked up, saw Ben's police badge dangling from his neck and lunged at him, grabbing his shirt.

"Please, you must help me. My son!" the woman ranted, ringing Ben's sweat dampened-shirt with her fingers. *My son is dead!*"

Ben eased the sobbing woman away from him and gently pried her hands from his shirt. "I'm afraid I—"

"You're a *policeman*, aren't you? Then help me. Help me!"

"I can refer you to—"

"They brought him here," the woman persisted, grabbing hold of Ben again. "They did not tell me he was dead, only that he'd been hurt and I should come down immediately."

Ben nodded; that had been one of the procedures the Palestinian police had enacted on his advice.

"My phone wasn't working. He was here for hours before they reached me."

The woman dropped her handkerchief and Ben retrieved it from the floor.

"He goes to work in Israel, every day after school," the woman muttered in a voice muffled by the sobs and the handkerchief soaked with her tears. "Today he doesn't show up, so they call to ask me where he is. But then it is hours before I get another call to come to the hospital." She looked up again. "They found him on the side of the road."

"I'm truly sorry for your loss," Ben said, trying to sound soothing. "But accidents are investigated by—"

"This wasn't an accident!" the woman screamed, loud enough to draw the attention of all those in the hall. She grabbed Ben's wrist and yanked him closer. "My son was stabbed. *He was murdered!*"

CHAPTER 6

ARI HESSLER RODE in the backseat of the Mercedes sedan with his father to Ben-Gurion Airport where their private jet was waiting. Even through the car's windows, they could feel the desert heat melt away the farther they drove north. Just before the highrise buildings of Tel Aviv came into view, Paul Hessler had to lean forward to tell his driver to turn the air conditioning down.

"It went well this morning," Ari said, looking up from his laptop computer.

"This early deployment is strictly public relations," Paul Hessler replied, not turning his gaze from the window as Israel slid by beyond him. "We're still six months to a year away from being ready. I don't know what the government is thinking."

"They are thinking that they will finally be safe."

Hessler looked over and studied his son's expression. "I can tell there's something else on your mind."

"I've been looking at the figures."

"And?"

"To get this far this fast has placed us considerably over budget. The cost overruns are monumental. In short, we're deeply in the red. As much as three hundred million dollars."

Paul Hessler's expression didn't change. "Consider it an investment."

"With no potential for return," his son scoffed.

"Really? Then tell me why the Americans agreed to underwrite the Arrow project in the first place?"

"Because they want a missile shield of their own."

"Exactly. But the testing they have done so far was found to be in violation of the SALT treaty. The project stalled and Congress was not about to dedicate two billion dollars for what many perceive as a white elephant anyway. What was the alternative?"

"Develop the project somewhere else," Ari Hessler said, realizing.

Paul Hessler patted his son's face affectionately. "Now you're learning what that business school couldn't teach you. The way the world works."

"We lose money developing the Arrow for Israel . . ."

"But then we sell the technology to Washington once it is proven."

"Very risky."

"You don't beat out Raytheon, General Dynamics, Grumman, or Martin-Marietta without taking risks."

Ari Hessler folded the newspaper in his lap. "I should have figured this out by myself."

His father shrugged, as the car slowed onto the entrance ramp for Ben-Gurion Airport. "You were too busy working on your thesis."

"I've been working on something else I need to talk to you about."

"You're full of surprises, aren't you?"

"This is a big one. A huge one. You're not going to believe it."

"Try me."

"It can wait until we get back to New York. That way you'll have something to look forward to when we get home."

* * *

ARI WAS PAUL Hessler's fifth child and the older of two with his second wife. His first wife had died at the age of forty-six after bearing four children, all daughters. Two of those were divorced themselves now, one had never married, and the four had combined to produce seven grandchildren Hessler doted upon at every opportunity.

He had married his second wife just short of his fiftieth birthday and her gift to him had been two children, miraculously both sons. The younger, Max, would be graduating from college later this year with a degree in theater and no interest in business. But Ari was truly his father's son, sharing his looks as well as his interests.

Ari had turned his attention back to his laptop, freeing Paul to gaze out the window and let his mind drift back to the past. For some reason the memories had been very clear of late, especially those of the day his second life had actually begun in the late fall of 1944. . . .

HE REMEMBERED SLOSHING through the muddy marshland of the Polish countryside north of the city of Lodz as he ran, remembered swinging round to look toward the sounds of the pursuing soldiers only to have his face raked by a low hanging branch when he turned back. The ground had dropped off suddenly and he fell heavily into a gully, coming up with a mouthful of muck. He gagged and spit it out, as the freezing rain slapped at his back and soaked his thin shirt.

Paul heard a branch snap at the top of the rise and clawed at a tree to pull himself to his feet. He could hear the soldiers' muffled voices now, the low clatter of their rifles clapping against the heavy coats that shielded them from the frigid cold.

He pushed on through the mud, feet sinking into the fetid ooze up to his ankles. He lost a shoe, but didn't dare try to retrieve it for the moments it would cost him.

Thunder boomed overhead and Paul's heart skipped a beat. He could smell his own sweat over the earth's rancid stench, watched his breath misting before him in the icy air. His stockinged foot and remaining shoe were sodden, weighing him down.

I can't go on.

The days and the miles melted behind him. He halted and doubled over, started to sink to his knees when he saw the stout, severed branch before him. He grasped it in both hands, so numb from the cold he could barely close his fingers around the wood.

Holding the branch to use as a weapon, Paul backed up behind a tree and listened for the sounds of the soldiers. He lurched out, sweeping the branch like a bat, when the squish of their boots was upon him. But his chilled, stockinged foot betrayed him. He crumpled face down in mud with another mouthful of it choking his breath.

A heavy kick sent a burst of pain through his ribs. Then a second kick spilled him onto his side where he lay gagging on the muck until a rifle barrel jabbing his chest pushed him onto his back.

He looked up at the uniformed figures clustered over him, faceless shapes shrouded by the rain and the swirling mist.

"State your name!" a voice demanded. Paul could see it belonged to a short, stocky man who had a black patch covering one eye. "Where have you come from?"

Paul tried to speak but his throat was still clogged with dirt.

"I said state your name!"

The one-eyed soldier pressed the rifle barrel deeper into the boy's solar plexus, and Paul gasped for whatever breath he could grab.

"Shoot him, Sarge," another of the soldiers said matter-of-factly.

"Check his pockets first," the one-eyed one ordered.

Paul felt a soldier's hand groping about him, tearing

fabric away until it closed on a thin leather pouch, now soaked with water and filth. He tried to blink the cascading water from his eyes.

"Holy shit," the soldier said. "You better have a look at this, Sergeant."

The one-eyed sergeant removed his rifle from the boy's chest and placed a boot in its place, as he inspected the pouch's contents with his single eye.

"Well, I'll be damned," the sergeant muttered, as he gazed down at the boy again. "The kid's *Jewish*!"

"How the hell he get way out here?"

"Look at his feet: he ran. Must have escaped from one of the camps we're looking for," the sergeant said and crouched down beside Paul, still holding the papers in his hand. "Listen to me, son. No one's going to hurt you, not anymore. All that's over. You're safe now."

B UT NOW, FIFTY-SEVEN years later, Paul Hessler still did not feel totally safe. Not a single photograph of him remained from his tortured youth. Had there been one showing him at twenty-six, he thought as he looked over at his son, it would have been the very image of Ari. Father and son shared the same ridged face and high forehead which combined to cast their expressions in perpetual shadows. Ari had his mother's thick dark hair, and what little of Paul's that remained had long gone gray from its original light brown. But they had the same eyes: deep, dark, and piercing, and the same lightish skin tone as well.

Looking in the mirror, it seemed to Paul Hessler that his skin had begun to slide off his face, shed by the pitched cheekbones and sharp jaw. He was dismayed by the spiderweb of veins that had sprouted across his nose and cheeks, made even more pronounced by the dry flakiness his face had taken on. Hessler didn't like looking in mirrors anymore, much preferred looking at Ari as a reminder of the man who used to look back.

The car finally came to a halt outside the bustle of Ben-Gurion Airport, pulling ahead of the detachment of soldiers waiting for it. Hessler let himself out before the driver had a chance to come around to the door. His knees ached from sitting too long and his ankles felt swollen. He leaned against the car, as Ari, cased laptop slung over his shoulder, helped the driver lift their luggage from the trunk and the soldiers hurried to catch up.

"*Murderer!*"

The cry came from farther down the airport loading zone, screamed in a raspy wail from amidst the clutter of harried travelers jockeying for position. Hessler was still pressed against the car when an old man lumbered forward wielding a pistol. Their gazes locked and in that instant Hessler realized he was the target, the same instant in which his driver lunged away from the trunk, going for his gun, and Ari spun toward his father.

"*MURDERER!*"

A screech this time punctuated by the popping sounds of gunfire. Paul tried to dive to the concrete for safety, but his body betrayed him, refusing to accept his commands. Leaving him an easy target propped against the car.

Maybe I've been shot. Maybe that's why I can't move. . . .

He saw the soldiers and his driver returning fire, draining their clips. Watched the old gunman collapse to the pavement right in the midst of those fighting to flee.

The screaming had just started to subside when a trio of soldiers barreled into Hessler to cover him. They took him down to the pavement and only in that instant did Hessler realize he hadn't been shot at all. Two of the soldiers hoisted him to his feet to drag him to safety and, with great relief, Hessler looked over toward Ari.

Oh, no . . .

Paul Hessler felt trapped between thoughts, between breaths. His son Ari lay slumped on the sidewalk, blood running in several widening pools from beneath him.

"Let me go!" he cried, lashing at the soldiers. "My son! *My son!*"

But before he can tear free, Paul Hessler's legs gave out and he crumpled to the pavement.

CHAPTER 7

DANIELLE RETURNED TO her study of the file on Michael Saltzman, trying to make sense of what she had realized back at his mother's house. If nothing else, the work distracted her from the anxiety she felt over her coming appointment with Dr. Barr. His voice had had an edge to it when she spoke to him earlier, something not quite right hidden in the tone.

Danielle knew it wouldn't be long before Moshe Baruch called to inquire about why the case had yet to be closed. She didn't know what she was going to tell him and was convinced he wouldn't listen to her anyway.

The gun was in his right hand when he shot himself. But Michael Saltzman was left-handed!

The picture on his mother's coffee table of him playing tennis had provided the truth. The question was, what did it mean? He could have shot himself with his off hand, of course, but nothing in the boy's file or anything Danielle had learned from his mother indicated Michael was a candidate for suicide.

He hadn't left a note.

There had been none of the tell-tale signs.

The only notable thing Layla Saltzman had mentioned
was the accidental death of a girl named Beth Jacober she
referred to simply as her son's friend. Danielle made a
mental note to look into the accident, if for no other reason
than to gauge Michael's state of mind in the days preced-
ing his death.

The phone on her desk buzzed.

ONCE AGAIN DANIELLE approached Com-
mander Moshe Baruch's office on the fourth floor stiffly,
prepared for the recriminations he was about to heap upon
her. She wondered if she should voice her suspicions, but
dismissed the idea even more quickly than Baruch would
dismiss the validity of her conclusion. She only hoped Baruch didn't know about her upcoming doctor's appointment. He would goad her about it if he did, and she didn't
need that right now.

"Please sit down, Pakad," he said, sounding surprisingly
restrained, even humble. "I have just received a call regarding you."

Here it comes, she thought to herself.

"Apparently your services have been requested."

Danielle leaned forward.

"You've heard of the shooting today at Ben-Gurion?"

"No, sir."

"You will soon enough; the story was just released to
the news media. In any case, the attack was aimed at Paul
Hessler. I imagine you've heard of him."

"Of course. A Holocaust survivor who is today one of
Israel's greatest benefactors."

"It was Hessler's son who was killed in the attack earlier
this afternoon."

Danielle said nothing. Tragic events had become so
commonplace over the years that she had been desensitized
to them. First her brothers, then her mother, and most recently her father, not to mention her own miscarriage. Each
successive death was greeted with a greater degree of res-

ignation, until it seemed her feelings had been buried too deep to reach. After crying herself out for her own family, it was impossible to shed tears for a stranger.

"Paul Hessler, apparently," Moshe Baruch continued, "was a friend of your father's. Were you aware of that?"

"No," Danielle told him, surprised. She had never once heard her late father mention Hessler.

"In any case, as a result Mr. Hessler has requested that you take charge of the investigation into his son Ari's murder."

"Shin Bet will have something to say about jurisdiction, Commander."

"Not anymore, they won't. Apparently, Paul Hessler's reach stretches into their offices as well. He insisted upon you, was quite adamant in fact."

"I don't even know the man."

"Well, he knows you," Baruch said, the displeasure plain in his voice.

Puzzled as she was, Danielle was still able to enjoy watching her former superior officer in Shin Bet squirm, suddenly beholden to her. One call made on Paul Hessler's behalf had placed Baruch in the uncomfortable position of relying on someone he had determined to destroy. The irony was striking. The same brand of politics that had buried Danielle behind a desk was now offering a temporary respite from Baruch's punitive exile.

"Mr. Hessler has checked into the Hilton in Tel Aviv," Baruch said. "He's expecting you in the next hour, Pakad."

Danielle pursed her lips and checked her watch. Her four o'clock appointment at the doctor's was just an hour off. Meeting Paul Hessler would mean missing it.

"I assume that's not a problem," Baruch continued.

"No. Of course not."

Moshe Baruch tried to make his next words sound meaningless, nonchalant. "I'll send that Saltzman case back to the local authorities."

Danielle felt something prickle the back of her neck. "I'd rather you didn't."

"And why not?"

She knew her hand had been forced. "Certain irregularities have turned up."

"Irregularities?" said Baruch, fighting to keep his voice even.

"It'll all be in my report. It's almost finished," Danielle lied.

The commander's eyes grew uncertain, regarding her differently. Having been forced to assign her to an incredibly high profile case cast their relationship in a whole different light. No choice but to give her his support, even encouragement. How it must have made his skin crawl. . . .

"Then just make sure I have this report on my desk by tomorrow, Pakad. An extra day is the best I can do."

"Of course, Rav nitzav."

CHAPTER 8

"My son was scared," the woman had said when Ben finally got her settled down in a chair in the nearest waiting area on the hospital's second floor. "He was frightened. For over a week now. Always on his computer. Day and night. Hardly ever slept. Jumped when I came up on him from behind. I ask, but he won't tell me, what's got him so scared. He knew he was in danger, but he wouldn't tell me why."

Ben couldn't take his eyes off the woman's pleading gaze. "What happened a week ago?"

"He wouldn't tell me that either. The damn computer. They gave it to him at school. No more soccer. No more friends. Just the computer. Always on the computer."

"What is your name?"

"Hanan Falaya. Shahir was my son's name."

"Do you live far from here?"

"Not very. Why?"

"Because I'd like to see your son's computer."

BEFORE ACCOMPANYING HANAN Falaya back to her home, Ben spoke with the female doctor, an

American volunteer from Doctors Without Borders, who had pronounced Shahir dead.

"Just a formality," she explained, flipping through her notes. "He was dead at the scene."

"Cause of death?"

The doctor's glare mocked him. "I counted over a dozen stab wounds."

"What about signs of resistance? Cuts on his hands and fingers, for instance."

"Look—"

"Did you check or not?"

She slapped her chart closed. "You want to blame someone, blame your own police department for leaving him to roast on the side of the road for hours while they tried to arrange transport. Their report claims the boy was already dead when they reached the scene, but who knows?"

"Were there any defensive wounds or not?"

"No. His hands, fingers, and palms were clean."

"What about the fatal wound?"

"It could have been one of several."

"Your best guess."

"A puncture that severed the aorta. I believe it was the first wound inflicted, so chances are the boy didn't suffer very long."

"Common criminals who cut the heart with their first strike?"

"You're the detective, Inspector. Maybe it was their lucky day."

"It clearly wasn't Shahir Falaya's."

I KNOW WHO you are," Hanan Falaya said softly from the passenger seat of Ben's ancient Peugeot as they drove to her home on the northern outskirts of Jericho. She wore a dark loose-fitting dress called a *jallabiya*, traditional for a Palestinian woman of the old school, but had adjusted the head scarf pinned under her chin so Ben could clearly see a face weathered by the years ahead of its time.

"One of the police you arrested for that taxi driver's murder six years ago was my cousin."

Ben stiffened behind the wheel. "And you still came up to me in the hospital?"

"It's all in the past, but his family misses him."

"The taxi driver's family misses him as well, Umm Falaya."

"He was a collaborator."

"Suspected collaborator," Ben corrected. "Guilty of giving rides to Israelis, of trying to make a living. Nothing more. But for some that was more than enough evidence."

"Including my cousin."

"Your cousin was one of the men who tortured and murdered him."

"My cousin fell in with bad men. It was their fault. *Hal'arsat.* The bastards. And for this he has a life sentence handed down by a military court with no appeal. Even the Israelis would have been fairer."

"Perhaps you would like to talk with them about your son's murder," Ben said, instantly feeling petty for saying it.

Ignoring his taunt, Hanan Falaya stared across the seat, seeming to study him. "You don't really look Palestinian."

"That's what living in the United States for nearly thirty years will do."

"Your complexion and hair are lighter, and your hair is almost straight. You're from Ramallah, aren't you?"

"Yes."

"And yet when you came back you settled in Jericho."

"Because that was where the Palestinian Authority wanted me. Ramallah hadn't yet been turned over to our control."

"Maybe you'll move back there someday. A man shouldn't be too far from his family."

"I don't have family there anymore."

"Too bad," said Hanan Falaya.

*   *   *

M Y HUSBAND IS a refugee currently in exile," she explained minutes later as they sat across from each other in the cramped living room of her small frame house. "He is on a list of those currently seeking repatriation, a list the Israelis must approve."

"You don't sound optimistic."

Her expression looked bled of feeling. "*Mashallah*. Whatever God wills. But the Israelis never approve anyone unless it's political."

Hanan Falaya's voice sounded emotionless and drained of hope. The original home of her husband's parents in Jerusalem, she explained, had been seized during the Six-Day War of 1967 and remained inhabited by Israelis to this day. In between juggling as many cleaning jobs as she could, she was active with a committee determined to see to the return of all confiscated Palestinian homes or, at least, appropriate financial reparations. She seemed to enjoy telling Ben this, if for no other reason than to avoid discussion of her son's murder.

The last few hours had clearly taken their toll. The color had drained from her face, except for her eyes which were drawn and bloodshot. Grief, Ben knew from his own mirror and experience, had a way of accentuating every line and wrinkle, and the plight of Hanan Falaya was no exception. He could imagine her as she must have once been: a vibrant, hopeful woman with a family to tend to. The house full of sweet and spicy smells from the nightly dinner she would lovingly make. Now, instead, the unpleasant smell of stale and soured food hung in the house's air, leaving Ben to wonder if tonight's dinner sat spoiling atop the stove, to remain forever uneaten.

"You said you thought your son was frightened of something," he started.

"I'm certain he was," Hanan Falaya said, squeezing the arms of her chair.

"Do you have any idea of what?"

"No. He wouldn't tell me."

"When did this start?"

"A week ago, ten days. Maybe a little longer. Who knows anymore with kids when they get to this age, they're so busy. You have children, Inspector?"

"No. Not anymore."

Hanan Falaya's eyes prodded him.

"They were murdered six years ago."

Hanan Falaya swallowed hard and something changed in her gaze, looking at Ben now instead of past him. "Here?"

Ben shook his head. "In America."

"Evil is everywhere, isn't it?"

"Yes, Umm Falaya."

"I'm not a mother anymore," she said, looking down. "One boy dead and two in prison."

"Israeli prison?"

"One there and the youngest, who was arrested three months ago during a street battle, here." She grasped a flap of the chair's fabric and squeezed it. "He's only fifteen. I told him not to go. I told him!"

"What's the name of your son being held in Palestine?"

"Farouk. Why?"

"Just curious." Ben leaned over and took her hand. "You're certain the change in your son's behavior began as little as a week ago, as much as ten days."

She squeezed his hand tightly. "Something like that."

"Do you remember him receiving any phone calls or mail around that same time?"

"Nothing out of the ordinary."

"No visits from friends or strangers?"

"I don't know his friends. I don't know if he has any. He used to, but then he started with the computer. . . ."

"But he had the computer much longer than ten days."

"Six months. The school gave it to him and let him keep it." Hanan Falaya pushed herself out of her chair and bid Ben to join her. "Come, the computer's in his room. I'll show you."

*　　*　　*

BEN WASN'T MUCH good with computers; he didn't have to be to find there wasn't much to look at on the Falaya boy's computer at all. In fact, there was nothing.

FILES NOT FOUND

"What's it mean?" Hanan Falaya asked, peering at the monitor over Ben's shoulder.

"The contents of the hard drive have been erased."

"I don't know what that means."

"The computer's empty. There's nothing on it."

"My son would never have done that. Not to his computer."

"I didn't say it was something he did, Umm Falaya."

Something changed in the woman's expression, resignation retreating in favor of mild surprise. "You believe me?"

"I believe all aspects of this investigation should be looked into. You said your son was scared of something. You said he had been spending a lot of time, too much time, on his computer. Do you know where he keeps his back-up discs?"

"I don't know what a back-up disc looks like," Hanan Falaya said, embarrassed.

A quick check of the desk drawers revealed no discs whatsoever. Ben wasn't surprised. If the Falaya boy had reason to erase his own hard drive, or if somebody had done it for him, he or they wouldn't have left backup discs behind. Still, the boy would never have destroyed all his discs, only the pertinent ones. By all appearances, though, there were no discs present anywhere.

"I would like to take this computer with me, if you don't mind," Ben said to Hanan Falaya.

"Why?" she snapped, resisting as if holding on to the last tangible part of her son.

"Because it may be possible to reconstruct the contents of the hard drive. I'd also like to hear more about your son's school and about his job in Israel."

"The school is how he *got* the job. They made all the arrangements, secured all the necessary papers and passes."

Ben shook his head, wondered if he had heard the woman correctly. "Arranging jobs? Lending computers? What sort of Palestinian school is this, Umm Falaya?"

"An experimental school for both Palestinians and Israelis," the woman told him. "Outside Jerusalem near Abu Gosh. My son was the best student."

CHAPTER 9

"I'M SORRY I'M late, Mr. Hessler," Danielle said, when she was introduced to Paul Hessler in the living room section of his Tel Aviv Hilton suite.

Shin Bet, Israel's internal security service, had posted guards throughout the lobby and along the floor on the chance that Hessler's life remained in danger. His son's murder at Ben-Gurion Airport was already being labeled the worst security disaster since the Rabin assassination. Clearly, Shin Bet couldn't afford to take any further chances. The suite he had been assigned had been designed for visiting heads of state and other dignitaries. Paul Hessler technically qualified as neither, though in actuality he was much more.

No one had done more for his homeland, Danielle knew, than the old man seated before her. A steady portion of his multi-billion-dollar fortune reaped from computer software, oil exploration, and biotechnological research was either granted outright to various components of the government or reinvested in Israeli industry. Hessler had built factories and plants to bolster the country's often sagging economy. He put thousands of people, primarily immigrants who would have otherwise become burdens of the state, to work even though the costs of operating in Israel were excessive and the country's laws restrictive in promoting real foreign investment.

Danielle knew the Hessler legend as well as anyone. How he had escaped from one of the hundreds of Nazi labor camps based in Poland just before the camp was dismantled and the remaining prisoners slaughtered. History had known little of this sordid chapter of the war until relatively recent days, and what it knew now made Hessler's tale of survival all the more incredible.

He had been found by American soldiers while fleeing through the woods days after his escape from the camp outside of Lodz where he had watched both his parents die in the ghetto. His feet were bloodied, blistered, and scraped raw. He had not eaten, had drunk little water, could only mumble incoherently when he was at last rescued. But he was carrying a tattered, worn set of papers that were enough to get him placed in a resettlement camp and later on a boat of Jewish refugees bound for Palestine.

An orphan, like so many others. Including her now. *Alone.*

D ANIELLE HAD DECIDED to keep her appointment with the doctor before meeting Hessler even though it meant fighting rush hour traffic to reach Tel Aviv. She knew the news was bad as soon as Dr. Barr walked into the room, not so much from the way he looked as the way he was holding the file containing her test results. He was a small man with thinning gray hair and a dour face. His smile, when it came, always seemed forced.

"I'd like to talk to you about the results of the latest test we did," he opened, after they were both seated, his forced smile nowhere to be seen.

"The ultrasound?" Danielle asked, trying not to shake.

"The prenatal series." Dr. Barr leaned back and his chair creaked. "I'd like to do a follow-up."

"Why?"

"Some of the blood work was inconclusive."

"Is that cause for concern? Should I be worried?"

"You asked for the full genetic spectrum, Pakad."

"I thought I was playing it safe."

"You were and I'm not saying you're wrong to, not at all. But ten years ago these genetic markers hadn't been identified and today, lots of times, the pattern results remain inconclusive."

"What are we talking about here?"

"Nothing yet."

"Can't you give me some idea?"

The doctor's expression didn't change. "The testing of genetic predisposition and tendencies remains an inexact science. Discussing things further at this point would alarm you for reasons that will probably turn out baseless. Today I'd just like to draw some more blood and we can discuss the results tomorrow morning. Until then, I don't want you to worry," he finished in an effort to sound comforting.

WAITING FOR THE blood to be drawn had made Danielle even later than she had counted on for her meeting, but Paul Hessler didn't seem overly bothered. His gaze was so distant it looked out of focus. His eyes were red and puffy, and his hair stood straight up where he had forgotten to comb it back into place. He sat stoop-shouldered before her with the folds of his slightly protruding stomach hanging over his belt.

"You look like your father," Hessler said, suddenly paying attention to her.

"Did you know him well?"

"We met in a camp in Greece, made the trip here together." Hessler sounded as though the past was a much better place to live in for now. "Fought side by side for the Haganah with the other madmen. We parted ways briefly when your father joined the Irgun, then met up again . . . later. Anyway, he was a great soldier, but a lousy politician."

Danielle tried very hard to smile, but the lump in her throat made it hard.

"I was a poor soldier mostly, but a very good business-man. Always negotiating. Making deals for the weapons men like your father could use." Hessler sank further into his chair. The drooping skin around his chin and jowls seemed to slide down his face, as if his bones had lost hold of it. "I had not seen your father for ten years when I learned of his death. I have been following your career ever since. He would be very proud."

Then you must not be following my career very closely. . . .

"What did you say, Chief Inspector?"

"Nothing."

"My hearing is not what it used to be; little is."

Danielle leaned a little forward. "I know how difficult this must be."

"The bullet was meant for me, Chief Inspector. It should be my death you are investigating, not my son's." Hessler took a deep breath that ended as a sigh. "It is a terrible thing to lose a child. As a woman, you can understand that, I'm sure."

"Yes," Danielle said, "I can."

CHAPTER 10

"THANK YOU FOR coming to see me, Inspector," John Najarian said after Ben had him paged outside at the Jericho Resort Village's pool area. The sun beat down harshly, baking the concrete even in places where soft cushiony layers of padding had been inlaid to prevent cracking and expansion. Given the weather, Ben had expected the resort to be more crowded, but few of the chaise longues set around the pool area were in use, and stacks of towels remained piled beneath their umbrellaed stands.

"I'm sorry I'm late," said Ben.

"Something important, I'm sure. That's why I'm so interested in you. Come, we can sit at the bar. Are you thirsty?"

"This time of year in Jericho, I'm always thirsty," Ben said.

Najarian smiled. A wealthy Detroit businessman with vast holdings in real estate, Najarian wore a terry-cloth robe over his bathing suit. Ben's page had pulled him from the largest of the three interconnected pools in the complex where he was dutifully completing his laps. Najarian had the look of a man who worked hard to stay in shape. A few years older than Ben, he had a rich tan that hadn't come in his few days in Palestine.

They sat down at the pool bar and Ben took a chair that gave him a clear view of the sparkling fountain that crowned an assemblage of covered tunnels connecting the three pools. Various Jacuzzis rimmed them as well, and from this angle Ben could see the volleyball court that had been set up on a fake beach. From the nearby tennis courts, camouflaged by wind screens, he could hear the steady pop of balls being solidly returned and the occasional clang of one striking the fence.

The Jericho Resort Village, with its expansive rooms, villas, and townhomes was the first of its kind in Palestine. A lush, tropical oasis for tourists, built to compete with the better known resorts in Israel's Eilat and Tiba, which now belonged to Egypt. It boasted competitive prices and a location easily accessible for the wealthy of Jordan and, ultimately, Syria, not to mention Americans like John Najarian. But the return of armed hostilities in the region had doomed occupancy rates, except for police recruits relocated here by the Palestinian Authority after Israelis shelled the academy outside of Jericho.

"I have a confession to make," Najarian started, sipping his Bloody Mary. His terrycloth robe had opened and Ben could see his torso was hairy, thick, and bearlike—a match to his bushy eyebrows. "I don't have any business in the West Bank."

"Oh?" Ben said. He had ordered an iced tea garnished with fresh mint leaves and rolled the frosty glass between his hot palms.

"I came strictly to meet you, Inspector. Or should I say, 'Detective.' "

"Only if we were back in Detroit."

"You're from Dearborn. I'm from Auburn Hills. We're practically neighbors."

"I haven't lived in Dearborn for a long time."

Najarian leaned slightly forward. "I'll get right to the point. You've heard of my firm, Security Concepts?"

"Vaguely."

"We handle private specialized security for businesses and individuals throughout the Midwest, and we've got plans to expand to both the East and West Coasts. Private security, I tell you, is the wave of the future, Ben. May I call you Ben?"

"Feel free."

"Our bodyguards are strictly ex-military and Secret Service. Our surveillance and security equipment is state of the art."

"I don't need any."

Najarian forced a laugh. "Your former superiors say you were one of the best cops they ever saw, and the work you've done over here has gotten some great coverage back home."

"My mother sends me the clippings."

"I'm Armenian, Ben, and our two cultures have got plenty in common. Personally, I don't give a shit what a man is. I care about what he does. That's why I'm here. To offer you a job."

Ben's throat tightened as he swallowed some tea.

"As I said, Security Concepts is expanding. I need good people to head up individual departments. People who can function autonomously and not hear from me unless they fuck up. I'm talking about a couple hundred thousand in salary, plus incentives, a generous stock option, not to mention profit-sharing."

Ben laid his glass down on a coaster. "Are you sure you've got the right Ben Kamal?"

"The Ben Kamal who doesn't take shit from anyone in Palestine or Israel. The Ben Kamal who closed every case he was assigned back in Detroit."

"Except the most important one."

Najarian took a gulp of his Bloody Mary, keeping his eyes on Ben the whole time. "You shot the Sandman dead, Ben."

"Not before he killed my family. In my own home."

Najarian set his drink down on the wrought iron table

top. "I wasn't lying before. I *do* read those articles. I know why you left Detroit and what was waiting when you came back to Palestine. I know what you've been through. I figure maybe you stayed because you didn't have anything to go back to. That's what I'm offering."

Ben let himself think about the money, about living in more than three small rooms. About going after happiness for a third time. He'd had it once, and almost again. But it was never going to happen here; that had become abundantly clear lately.

"I'm flattered, Mr. Najarian."

"Look around you, Ben. The Mideast is going to hell again. It's inevitable; it always was. The dream's finished, but that doesn't mean yours has to be." Najarian stopped, his point made. "I don't expect an answer from you today. Take your time. I'll give you my card. You can call me anytime, day or night. But I want you to promise you'll think about it. Give it some serious consideration."

Ben looked at him noncommittally.

"Hey," Najarian said, leaning back and folding his hands behind his head so the hair on his chest sprouted from his terry-cloth robe, "it isn't like you'd be leaving anything behind here."

CHAPTER 11

HOW MUCH DO you know about me, Chief Inspector?" Paul Hessler continued.

"I know you're one of the ten richest men in the world," Danielle replied, "even though you've given away a huge portion of your wealth to almost any charity that asks for it."

Hessler shrugged humbly. "All have their needs."

"Like Israel."

"I owe my life to Israel, Chief Inspector. It's the least I can do."

"And, from what I understand, Israel owes a great measure of her life to you. Through your real estate and business investments, along with gifts from your charitable foundations."

"Do you have any idea," Paul Hessler asked Danielle, "how meaningless all that seems to me now?"

"A little," she replied honestly.

"I thought I had experienced the worst horrors, the ultimate degradations," Paul Hessler continued. He shook his head sorrowfully. "I was wrong. None of those years could prepare me for this." Danielle could see Hessler's eyes glistening with new tears. "Ari was the only one of my children who cared about my work, who was capable of taking over the business. Now I feel I have done all this for nothing. All because Ari stepped in front of me." Hessler's gaze hardened. "Do you know why you're here, Pakad?"

Danielle leaned forward. "To find out why an attempt was made on your life."

Paul Hessler gritted his teeth. "The why is not important. There are many whys, many reasons why people want me dead. It's the who that matters. The man at Ben-Gurion was not acting alone, Pakad. Someone sent him and your job is to find out who that is. Then you will turn that information over to me."

"With all due respect, sir—"

"That's not the way it works, is it? That's not the way you were trained to do your job. But you often disregard protocol and channels, don't you? Your reputation is well known to me. It is one reason I requested your assignment to this case."

Danielle started to stand up, then changed her mind. "Perhaps you have misjudged me."

"You are called 'pakad' when it should be 'pakadet'— the feminine. Why?"

"My name and title were misprinted on my original National Police identification. They corrected the name. The title stuck."

"Did they misjudge you as well? You see, Chief Inspector," Hessler continued, before she could respond, "I knew you would never have been assigned to this case unless I had requested it. It was imperative for the powers-that-be to understand my desire. For obvious reasons, of course."

"You wanted me to know you could."

"I never spoke to Commander Baruch myself," Hessler resumed, as if Danielle had said nothing at all. "I believe he received a call from the minister of justice. You're right, I wanted you to understand that procedures and channels don't matter here. What matters is I learn who sent the gunman to Ben-Gurion Airport today."

"You might not like what I find, Mr. Hessler."

Hessler's eyes blinked rapidly, slowly losing their intensity, as if they'd tried to hold it too long. "And why is that, Pakad?"

"It seems strange to me that an old man was sent to kill you. The kind of enemies you spoke of would have retained a more seasoned assassin."

"And this one wasn't?"

"He screamed something at you before he started firing, according to witnesses. He called you a murderer and drew attention to himself in the process. That's not what I would call the mark of a professional killer."

"What would you call it, then?"

"A crime rooted in passion, committed by someone who believed himself wronged by you. In business, perhaps. If that is the case, the why would explain the who. There would be no shadows out there for us to chase."

"I have many enemies, Pakad."

"I would look for a disgruntled employee, a bitter rival, someone who thinks he was wronged and has reason to hold a grudge."

Hessler smiled just wide enough for Danielle to see the gap between his front teeth. "When you've been in business as long as I have, that is very likely a lot of people."

"But this man knew he was going to die himself when he started pulling the trigger. And he must have had some reason for calling you a murderer. Or . . ."

"Or *what*?"

"Have you considered the possibility that your son may have been the target?"

"You said—"

"I said the gunman yelled out 'Murderer!' and started shooting. I never said it was demonstratively clear which of you he was aiming at."

Hessler pushed himself out of his chair and lumbered to the suite's bar. He grasped its edge so forcefully the blood was flushed from his knuckles, leaving them visibly white.

"We would have celebrated tonight back in New York," he droned, his back to Danielle. "The missile defense system we built for Israel is being deployed. This morning we witnessed the second consecutive successful test." Hessler cleared his throat and resteadied his thoughts. "In any case, my son was new to the company. Don't waste your time, Pakad. Ari wasn't the target."

"But you said yourself that he would have taken over Hessler Industries someday." Danielle walked across the room and faced him from the other side of the bar. "That is reason enough why we must consider the possibility that your son was the real target."

Hessler dropped his hands from the shiny wood. "Because killing him would be worse than killing me."

"Yes," Danielle nodded.

Hessler looked at her contemplatively. "I selected you for another reason, Pakad. I wanted someone who knows what it feels like to lose a child."

Danielle tried very hard not to react. "That's irrelevant."

"Is it really? Maybe you don't understand the point I was making."

"That you know just as much about me as I do about you."

"Very good."

"I think you chose me for the wrong reasons, Mr. Hessler."

"That remains to be seen, Pakad, doesn't it?" Hessler again grasped the edge of the bar for support, suddenly unsteady on his feet. "When you find who was behind my son's death, then we'll know I was right."

CHAPTER 12

BEN KAMAL WALKED between the adjacent playing fields built in the shadow of the soccer stadium where he had shot a man earlier that day. Two games were going on simultaneously, school boys rushing up and down the field in the steaming air, dueling for the ball. The youth soccer league was new to the West Bank and not terribly well organized.

Despite this drawback, Ben was impressed by the skill level the nine- and ten-year-old boys were displaying, especially those on one of the teams playing on the field to his right. Their coach stood serenely in his green Nike warm-up suit on the sideline, barking an occasional order. As Ben approached him, a perfect cross resulted in an elegant header and another goal for his team. The coach clapped and sent in some subs to relieve the starters at midfield, then turned when he saw Ben approaching.

"I would have thought you'd had enough soccer for one day, Inspector," said Colonel Nabril al-Asi, head of the Protective Security Service. One of fourteen separate police-type Palestinian agencies, it was easily the most feared since it functioned under the direct authority of

President Yasir Arafat. As such, al-Asi was answerable to no one else.

"Believe me, I have." Ben paused and watched several excellent touch passes.

"Impressed, Inspector? My Israeli counterpart at Shin Bet arranged for the captain of their national team to help out, give the boys some pointers."

Ben watched al-Asi's team setting up for a corner kick, continuing their dominance. "Apparently, they listened."

"We're undefeated, Inspector. Normally I wouldn't care about such a thing, but it was hard enough convincing my son to let me coach as it was."

"He doesn't trust your soccer skills?"

"He didn't believe I actually intended to show up for the games."

The corner kick sailed well wide and the opposing team readied a goal kick.

"This is unusually visible of you, Colonel."

Al-Asi turned from the game long enough to give Ben a piercing look with his dark, heavy-lidded eyes. His thick, salt-and-pepper hair didn't so much as stir in the breeze. He looked just as good in his stylish warm-up suit as he did in the expensive European attire Ben was used to seeing him wear.

"Most of my enemies are now in jail, Inspector. The rest are under constant surveillance. I thought it was time to give my children at least the pretense of a normal life."

Ben smiled and said nothing.

Al-Asi frowned. "But now my daughter asks me when there will be a team for her to play on. She watches the World Cup on television, kicks the ball around in the yard like she's an American soccer star. But she doesn't understand our culture is not progressive enough yet to allow for women athletes. I tell her someday it will be and she cries. Children are not too interested in tomorrow."

"In any case, they must be glad to have you around more."

"We're living in a real neighborhood with other children now. They like that, too."

The referee blew the whistle, signalling the end of the game. Al-Asi walked toward his players, clapping dramatically.

"You did a splendid job this morning, Inspector. Tell me, how is the officer who was wounded?"

Ben kept pace alongside the colonel. "He'll recover."

"*Al hamdu lillah*," al-Asi said, his voice unusually reverent. "Praise God."

"Luckily, we recovered the disc and, because of it, we now know Mahmoud Fasil's network."

"Not exactly."

"Mayor Wallid told me—"

"The mayor told you what I told him, Inspector. But I'm telling you the truth: The disc is gibberish. Makes no sense at all."

"Encoded?"

"No," said al-Asi. "Just nothing that seems in any way associated to the terrorist network we were hoping to identify. It's also in English. Maybe you could take a look at it sometime, tell me what you think."

"So what was Fasil doing with it?"

"We're hoping the incarcerated soccer star Abdel Sidr can tell us that, but he hasn't talked yet. I'm going to see him first thing tomorrow. Then I think he'll change his mind."

"Maybe we screwed up somewhere," Ben said, wondering himself. "Maybe you shouldn't have passed Fasil on to us, Colonel."

"You think I made a mistake by trusting your men with the assignment?"

"Only because your men are far more adept at handling such situations."

"You didn't believe my cover story?"

"Not for a minute."

Al-Asi stopped. "I thought it would be good for you, Inspector. A real assignment instead of more training. Following cops around like they're school children."

"One of them almost ended up dead because I wasn't clear enough with my orders."

Al-Asi shrugged the statement off. "I understand you emptied your clip at Fasil. Fifteen shots. Three hits. Not bad, under the circumstances. Someday we'll go to the range. I'll give you some pointers."

"I'm here for something else right now."

"What can I do for you, Inspector?"

Ben hurried after al-Asi onto the field. The grass was soft and full, brown in only a few stray patches thanks to the Israeli irrigation experts who had designed an underground sprinkler system to compensate for the lack of rainfall.

"I have a computer in my car," Ben said. "Its contents have been erased. I was hoping your office could help me reconstruct them."

"And whose computer might this be?"

"A teenage boy, the victim of an apparently random street crime."

Al-Asi slapped palms with his players as they passed him in neat, single file. "When you use the word 'apparent,' I get worried. You don't think the crime was random, do you?"

"The boy's mother doesn't."

"I imagine my wife wouldn't either, if it helped her deal with things."

"The mother insists her son had been acting strange for a week or so. Something had frightened him."

"Where was he killed?"

"On his way to Israel. He was going to his job."

"The boy worked in Israel?" al-Asi asked, surprised.

"In Tel Aviv, I think. The job was arranged by the experimental Israeli-Palestinian collaborative school he attended outside of Abu Gosh."

"I looked into that school for my oldest son. Decided I had enough trouble keeping him safe from other Palestinians, never mind Israelis under the circumstances. I thought it had been shut down."

"Not yet. The school supplied the victim with his computer as well."

Al-Asi stopped in the middle of the field. "Is this an official investigation, Inspector?"

"What do you think?"

Al-Asi slapped Ben's shoulder, regarded him fondly. "You know what I could really use? An assistant coach. There are so many plays to practice and teams to scout. I find myself strapped." The colonel's son ran up and hugged him briefly before dashing off to rejoin his teammates. "Especially now that I have taken on these added responsibilities. Are you interested?"

"I don't know much about the game."

"I can teach you."

"It's a lot to learn, the rules and all."

Ben and al-Asi started walking off the field together.

"My team plays on a number of fields. You adapt according to the size and circumstance. Sometimes you don't know what to do until you get there."

"I'll have to think about it. There's something else, Colonel. The mother of the murdered boy has another son. He's being held in a Palestinian jail."

"What's his name?"

"Farouk Falaya."

"Never heard of him."

"Good, because I would like to see if his release can be expedited."

"Why?"

"So he can go home to his mother."

"A good reason." Al-Asi veered toward the parking lot where his team clustered outside a trio of dark SUVs, each manned by one of the colonel's bodyguards wearing matching warm-up suits. "Come join us, Inspector, we're going for ice cream."

CHAPTER 13

At night the city of Old Jaffa south of Tel Aviv burns with harsh naked light shed from buildings otherwise ensconced in their colorful past. Shoppers and strollers abound, moving through the famed flea market better known as *Shuk Ha-Pispheshim*, ignoring most merchants' calls while paying keen attention to others. Out for bargains instead of the bare necessities of years past. Using their American Express cards to pay merchants selling out of rickety storefronts and pushcarts.

As darkness fell, two men utterly disinterested in all forms of merchandise ambled amidst the grilled falafel stands and cluttered kiosks overflowing with knickknacks, authentic Persian carpets, and leather goods. One was slight with a limp that became noticeable only when he tried to quicken his gait, an older man with an ashen face no amount of light could brighten.

The younger man, dressed in a long black leather coat, towered over him, swallowing the older man in his shadow. Thick dark hair covered the younger man's skull like a bushy cap. He had a sturdy, muscular, almost youthful frame. But deep lines ran out from both his eyes and splintered into a patchy network of furrows and creases. The eyes themselves were tired and bloodshot, the pupils small and the edges of the whites slightly yellowed. A dark shirt clung to the powerful torso contained beneath his coat.

A car with open windows drove by and the older man waited for it to pass before responding. "Why have you come to *me* with these allegations?" Abraham Vorsky asked.

"Because of your past," Hans Mundt, the younger man, replied.

"You mean as head of Mossad," Vorsky said, referring to Israel's Secret Service, "or something else?"

Mundt's eyes dropped to the numbered tattoo exposed on the old man's forearm. "You tell me."

Vorsky pulled his arm back to his side. "Even assuming what you are suggesting is true . . ."

"You've seen the proof."

"I've seen what you've chosen to give me. That's all."

The two men stopped speaking when a toothless salesman shoved an enormous *nargilah*, or waterpipe, in Mundt's face. Mundt snapped a hand forward so fast that the salesman never saw it until impact knocked the waterpipe from his hand and sent it crashing to the pavement.

"You said you didn't want to attract any attention to yourself," Vorsky warned

"Sometimes it can't be helped," said Mundt.

Vorsky looked around to make sure no one was paying attention to them. The smell of *al-ha'esh*, barbecue, hung in the air and the sizzling sounds of meat roasting on open grills followed them wherever they walked. The sounds and sharp scents made him long for food denied him by a restrictive diet he'd been forced to follow for years now.

"And assuming your information is correct, what exactly do you expect me to do?" Vorsky continued.

"That's your decision. I've done my part by coming here and sharing it."

"You could have sought out more traditional authorities."

"I didn't feel that was in anyone's best interests. If this ever became public . . ."

"What about *your* interests?" the old man interrupted.

The way Vorsky looked at him made Mundt wonder if the former head of Mossad knew of the last trip he had made to Poland a few weeks before, the one that had finally yielded what Mundt had long sought. . . .

O VER HERE! I found something!" Mundt heard the workman he had hired call out, as they searched through a section of the woods north of Lodz near the town of Leczyca.

Mundt rushed over and found the man gesturing toward something he had just unearthed three feet down.

"There!" he said to Mundt who had drawn even with him. "It is what you seek, yes?"

Mundt rested his own shovel on the ground and stepped down into the jagged hole, the edges of his long leather coat at once crisped by ice and frozen dirt. Then he crouched and brushed his hand across an object that rose diagonally out of the ground, its color a pale yellowish white.

"It's a bone, isn't it?" the workman demanded excitedly. "This must be the grave you've been looking for! It must be!"

"Yes," Mundt said, his voice empty. "It just might be."

"You spoke of a bonus if—"

The man stopped speaking when Mundt stood up, so tall that they were almost eye-to-eye even though he was standing knee-deep in the depression. The workman, who knew this part of the countryside better than anyone, who had listened to his own father tell stories of the ghosts that had been roaming these woods since World War II, leaned on his shovel and swallowed hard.

"Just whose grave is this?" he asked.

Mundt grabbed his shovel and sank its blade into the ground. "Help me finish digging," he ordered, as his first thrust revealed the tattered threads of what might be an overcoat. "And maybe we'll find out."

I'M ASKING YOU again what your interest in this is?" Abraham Vorsky, the former head of Mossad, repeated. "What you're after."

"Perhaps I am trying to make amends," Mundt offered.

"For your people? Give it up. It's all history now."

"Not this, not what I've brought for you. The security of your country may be at stake here, very likely is."

Vorsky tried to appear unriled. "You still haven't said what you want from me in return."

"Access to your files."

"Impossible!"

"I only ask to see one."

Vorsky's eyes flickered thoughtfully. "I'm still listening. What do you propose?"

"I give you three names to start with. If my story checks out, you give me the access I want in exchange for the rest."

"How many names are there in total?"

"More than three."

With that Hans Mundt slowly and carefully withdrew a set of folded pages from his jacket, making sure to keep both hands in view at all times. Abraham Vorsky took the pages but hesitated before pocketing them, holding the sheets between them in limbo.

"You understand once you start down this road, there's no going back," the old man cautioned.

"I've already been back," Mundt said, thinking of the grave he had found in the woods north of Lodz, Poland, just over two weeks before. "That's why I'm here tonight."

DAY TWO

DAY TWO

CHAPTER 14

"THANKS FOR COMING," Danielle said in greeting when she entered the doctor's office to find Ben already waiting.

"Thanks for calling me," he said, taking both her hands in his. "What's wrong?" They were alone in the waiting room, but he hoped she would have let him hold on anyway.

"I don't know. I had some tests. The doctor wouldn't tell me anything until he saw the results."

Danielle liked the feeling of Ben's hands over hers. They were softer than those of most Israeli men she had known, evidence of a man who had lived his life inside instead of out. She had made the decision to call Ben the night before, her interview with Layla Saltzman weighing heavily on her mind. How sad it was to have no one to help you through the bad times, share the good.

"I thought you had a right to be here," Danielle continued.

"I appreciate that."

"I'm glad you didn't shut the door on me, Ben."

"Because of the way you shut it on me?"

"We've been over this."

"You know I won't give up," he told her. "Strictly not in my nature."

Danielle had learned she was pregnant nearly four months ago, but waited several weeks before telling Ben. Waited because she had decided to raise the child herself. After all, any child with a Jewish mother and Palestinian father would be an outcast, a pariah, from birth. Part of both races and accepted by neither. It wouldn't be fair, to any of them.

Ben and Danielle had met during the first-ever joint investigation undertaken by the Israeli and Palestinian governments. Their animosity quickly turned to mutual respect and, later, a strange kind of dependence that led to them becoming lovers. Both acknowledged the long-term impossibility of their relationship, though, and they reluctantly parted. Entering an ill-timed liaison with an Israeli army officer, Danielle became pregnant soon afterwards. By the time she learned of her pregnancy, she had broken with the officer and he was out of her life. A few weeks later a miscarriage claimed the baby as well.

The sense of loneliness and depression that followed had sent her back to Ben. Neither had any illusions about where their relationship could go, but both desperately enjoyed one another's company nonetheless. Danielle came to look forward to their once-weekly rendezvous more than anything else in her life.

Her current pregnancy had been unplanned as well. At least, that was what she told herself, but even now she wasn't sure. She clutched hard to her second chance to have a child, seeing it as the solution to the woes of her solitary life. With all in her family dead save for a single aunt and uncle, the baby obsessed her so that even her affection for Ben suffered. She knew how badly she had hurt him with her decision to raise the child alone but the excitement and purpose that flooded her life made her oblivious to his needs. She hadn't seen him for six weeks until today and suddenly found herself wondering if her decision was indeed best for all concerned.

Because the truth was, ending up like Layla Saltzman terrified her.

"I'm here for you," Ben said, when the inner office door opened and a nurse poked her head out.

"Ms. Barnea, the doctor will see you now."

D R . B A R R W A S seated behind his desk when Danielle entered his office, Ben just behind her. His hair was prematurely gray and his face always looked sunburned to her.

"Good morning, Pakad." The doctor rose from his chair. What started as a polite gesture changed to pointed interest as he looked at Ben. "I don't think we've met."

Ben extended his hand. "Ben Kamal."

"You're . . ."

"A friend of Danielle's."

Dr. Barr hesitated, then offered them the twin chairs set before his desk. "Please, both of you, sit down."

A clipboard lay atop his desk, the pages upon it creased and rolled from being awkwardly pinned back after they were studied. The doctor flipped back to the first page and tried to straighten them out.

"Pakad Barnea," he started, focusing only on Danielle, "testing the fetus for genetic markers is not an exact science, as I discussed with you earlier. But what I'm about to tell you I can state with great confidence . . . and regret." He leaned forward and crossed his hands over the clipboard, squeezing them tight. "The latest series of fetal blood tests we ran detected a genetic anomaly in your baby."

"Anomaly?"

"A rather serious one, I'm afraid."

Ben looked over and reached to take Danielle's hand again in his, but she pulled both her hands from the chair's arms and wrung them in her lap.

Danielle felt as if the breath had been kicked from her lungs. "Anomaly. That means . . ."

"Something out of kilter. A negative indication."

"What are you saying?"

"Have you ever heard of ornithine transcarbamylase deficiency, or OTC?"

"No. That's the anomaly you're referring to?"

"It's a very rare metabolic disorder that can sometimes be treated with a restrictive low-protein diet and drugs. But the strength of the marker we uncovered indicates your fetus is suffering from a severe form of the disorder." The doctor held his breath for just a moment. "I'm afraid it's fatal."

CHAPTER 15

*F*ATAL...

The word struck Danielle like a sharp body blow. Her heart seemed to stop beating, her breath checked, the entire moment utterly frozen in time.

"I'm very sorry to be so blunt . . ."

. . . fatal . . .

". . . but at this point we should consider genetic termination as an option."

Danielle felt heat building behind her face. Ben reached over into her lap and, this time, took her hand in his.

"You mean abortion," she said.

"In this case I don't believe that's the correct term, no."

"As opposed to genetic termination."

"Because the issue is not really in doubt, unfortunately. We are discussing something that is merciful."

"To whom?" Danielle demanded.

"How sure are you of your findings?" Ben asked the doctor.

"Very."

"Can you repeat this test, whatever you called it?"

"We already have. The genetic markers were identical."

"What about a second opinion?" Ben continued. "There must be a specialist somewhere."

"I consulted with a specialist on the results of both tests and he was the one who made the diagnosis. But you would of course be free to seek out another one on your own."

"I just don't—" Ben stopped when Danielle pulled her hand from his grasp and stood up, walking around to the back of her chair.

"I won't do it," she insisted to the doctor. "Abortion, genetic termination—whatever you call it. I won't do it."

The doctor nodded with genuine sympathy. "You'd be putting your baby through a great deal of pain. Even if he survived—"

"There's a chance, then?"

"Slim, yes, but death would be almost inevitable in the first year of life. Two at the most. OTC's mortality rate in these concentrations is one hundred percent."

"There's no cure?" Ben asked.

"No more than there is for cystic fibrosis or Down's Syndrome. The only advantage we have now is the ability to identify the genetic predispositions in advance."

Danielle squeezed her hands into the chair's back. "Identifying a problem you can't solve isn't an advantage."

"If it saves the child—and parents—needless suffering, I believe it is. And, you must understand, Pakad Barnea, that this does not at all affect your ability to have children in the future. The odds of a second fetus having the OTC genetic marker are no greater than the first."

"And what's that?"

"Forty thousand to one."

"Who's the carrier, the man or the woman?"

"The genetic mutation occurs on the X chromosome, so women are typically carriers, while their sons typically suffer the disease."

Ben swallowed hard and found his throat clogged. He tried to feel relieved that at least it hadn't been his fault. But all he could think of was the fetus—a boy. His son.

He'd had a son before, but a serial killer named the Sandman had slain him just short of the boy's seventh birthday. Ben had found his body just after putting ten bullets into the madman who had terrorized Detroit for months, murdering entire families as they slept. Ben had uncovered the Sandman's true identity close to the very moment the killer had entered his house, returning home moments too late to save his wife and two children. The next months had passed in a blur that cleared only marginally when he returned to his homeland of Palestine, in search of something he could not identify until he met Danielle.

She had given him his life back, only to take it away again by denying him the right to raise his own child. But he would accept that now, he really would, if only that child could be born healthy.

"There's nothing more you can do?" Danielle asked hoarsely, defeated.

"No experimental programs or procedures?" Ben added.

The doctor sighed and leaned back. "OTC deficiency is a urea-cycle disorder. The urea cycle is a series of five liver enzymes that help rid the body of ammonia, a toxic breakdown product of protein. It then accumulates in the blood and travels to the brain, causing coma, brain damage, and death."

Danielle steeled herself before asking her next question. "How long after birth?"

Dr. Barr seemed to have thrown all pretext of tact aside, sparing nothing to make his point. "Typically, newborns slip into a coma within seventy-two hours of birth. Most suffer severe, irreparable brain damage. Half die in the first month, and the ones who don't are often paralyzed or permanently disabled. And most of these will die before the age of five." He realized his bluntness and tried to soften his demeanor. "I just want you to understand the depth of what we're dealing with here."

"Is there any risk to the mother?" Ben asked.

"None," Dr. Barr replied. "Other than the misery that

comes from the moment of the delivery." He shuffled his chair forward. "Medical science has given you a great gift here, Pakad Barnea."

"And what exactly is that?"

"The ability to avoid a heartache and prevent the terrible agony of another from ever occurring. You can get on with your life. Have another a child."

"No," Danielle said, starting for the door. "No more."

Her trembling hand had trouble with the knob until Ben turned it for her.

"Thank you, Doctor," he said, as Danielle disappeared into the waiting room that was filling with patients. "I'm sure she'll be in touch with you soon."

CHAPTER 16

I ALMOST LOST it in there," Danielle said, sitting across from Ben at a table in the Bracha Bakery.

"I don't blame you," Ben told her. She had reminded him to look for the yellow awning in Jerusalem's Hurva Square. Finding a parking space had proven next to impossible, but the smells of fresh baked rolls quickly relaxed him once he was inside. Ben used to come here often when he was in Jerusalem, usually with Danielle on the pretext of business. The bakery smelled the way his mother's kitchen in Ramallah had when she started preparing for family gatherings the day before.

"I'm going to get a second opinion, as many opinions as it takes."

"Until you hear what you want?"

"That's right. Do you blame me?"

"Not at all."

She studied the mug he had brought her, along with a sweet smelling basket of bakloua and ketaify. Neither of them had touched a morsel yet, focused as they still were on the doctor's news. "I guess I don't have to worry about caffeine anymore."

"I got you decaf," Ben told her.

Danielle tried to smile. "You think I'm wasting my time?" she asked him.

"Do you know how many times I've relived the night my family was killed, Danielle?"

"You don't have to talk about this."

"Yes, I do, because it helps. I've relived that night a thousand times, wondering what I could have done different, what would have happened if I had gotten home just a few minutes earlier. Those few minutes could have meant everything, and I'd give anything to have them back. But I can't."

"What are you telling me?"

"That you've got to exhaust every resource you can. Tragedy is bad enough. Thinking you could have done something more is worse."

Danielle shook her head, her eyes dry with unspent tears. Her expression was bleak, colorless. "At least I have my career." And she sipped her coffee which tasted as sharp as the bite in her voice.

"Things are not going well with Moshe Baruch then."

"No, things are going fine so long as I continue to close all cases involving dead children."

"The son of a bitch . . ."

"He wants me to quit."

"So why don't you?"

"And do what instead?"

"Go back to Shin Bet."

Danielle felt the anger simmering in her again, careful not to turn it on Ben. "Not with Baruch's former superior still in charge."

"The army?"

She shook her head. "I won't look good in a uniform much longer."

Ben studied her. "I want to tell you something. If things . . . don't work out." He struggled again for words. "And you want to—"

"I know what you're going to say."

"Then let me say it."

"There's no need."

"What about a future for us?"

"We've been over this."

"Things have changed now."

"Not that," Danielle said.

"I don't want to lose you *and* the baby."

Danielle lowered her cup to the table and looked at Ben accusingly. "You agree with the doctor, don't you?"

"I'd like to ask some questions, educate myself."

"But you agree with him."

Ben nodded. "I agree with him, yes."

"Would you feel the same way if we had planned to raise the child together?"

"What I feel is that you need to explore all the alternatives. But you can't lose sight of reality."

Danielle pushed her elbows forward on the table, the old fire and life back in her eyes. "Reality tends to change very quickly in modern medicine. Dr. Barr evaluated my case based on what is known and available today. But what about six months from now, a year? With the advances medicine is making, they might uncover a new treatment, a new drug to treat this awful thing. How would we feel then? Why do we have to rush into this?"

"We don't," Ben said, echoing her use of the plural. "That's what I've been saying."

"I need to have hope. I need to hold onto this. Exhaust all our options."

"I agree."

"Alternative medicine, faith healing, Romanian gypsies— whatever it takes."

"I'm not sure about the faith healing," Ben said, waiting for Danielle to smile before smiling himself.

"You know Baruch assigns me these cases of dead children because he wants to make me squirm. But I refuse to give him the satisfaction. Instead, I close each case as ordered."

"Since when did this kind of crime become the realm of National Police?"

"Since Moshe Baruch took over and I didn't quit." She sipped her coffee. "But yesterday I actually found a case that hadn't been investigated properly."

"What happened?"

"Suicide of a high school senior. But the pistol was found next to his right hand when he was left-handed."

"Someone trying to make it *look like* suicide?"

"I'm proceeding on that assumption, yes."

Ben drummed his fingers on the table, narrowed his features. "I met a woman at the new hospital in Jericho yesterday who had been summoned to identify the body of her son, murdered in what seemed to be a random crime. But the evidence didn't support that it was random at all. And the woman insisted her son had been terrified of something for over a week before he was killed. He'd been spending a lot of time on his computer, so I thought I might find a clue there. Only the files had been erased." Ben squeezed his features together and shook his head. "I'm wondering if it might have something to do with the boy having attended school in Israel."

"Did you say a school *in Israel*?"

Ben nodded. "An experimental collaborative outside of Abu Gosh."

"Oh my God," Danielle said, nearly spilling her coffee.

CHAPTER 17

THE COOPERATIVE SCHOOL had been
built in the shadow of the dry brown Judean Hills halfway
between the Arab village of Abu Gosh and the Israeli village of Beit Nakufah. A single level, wheat-colored structure with a bunker-style construction surrounded by a
barbed-wire fence and guarded by four Israeli soldiers
armed with Galil assault rifles. Around the rear a pair of
playing fields had been baked dusty brown, the grass dead
in spite of constant efforts of powerful rotating sprinklers.
The lime chalk from white lines marking soccer bounda-
ries and boxes fluttered flakily into the air with each stiff
breeze.

"You'd better let me do the talking inside," Danielle
suggested, the shock raised by the connection between two
dead high school students, Michael Saltzman and Shahir
Falaya, just lifting. Including Michael's friend Beth Jacober, three teenagers previously enrolled in the school had
died in the past ten days. "This may be a collaborative
school, but I doubt they've ever met a Palestinian policeman before."

And, in fact, the soldiers guarding the school at first

balked at allowing Ben entry. It was only when Danielle pointed out that his credentials still permitted free passage in this area and reminded them of the school's cooperative nature that they reluctantly relented.

Inside, the building seemed bigger than it had looked from the outside, composed of a dozen classrooms containing one hundred and fifty high school students evenly split between Israelis and Palestinians. An armed soldier on duty inside the school lobby directed them to the main office where they saw a woman busy stuffing notices into boxes labeled with teachers' names.

"Excuse me," Danielle said and readied her ID, flashing it when the woman turned. "I am Pakad Danielle Barnea of National Police and this is Inspector Bayan Kamal of the Palestinian police force. We would like to speak to the principal."

"That would be me," the woman said, looking at each of them in turn. "Jane Wexler," she added, without extending a hand. She appeared to be in her mid-forties and wore her flaxen hair in a smooth bob. Her lightweight olive skirt and matching blouse were almost the same color as the uniforms of the soldiers outside. "How can I help you?"

"Can we speak somewhere in private?"

Jane Wexler slid a pair of round wire-rimmed glases onto her nose. "My secretary's on break. Someone has to watch the office."

"It's about two of your students," said Ben. "An Israeli and a Palestinian."

"Michael Saltzman," added Danielle, "and . . ."

"Shahir Falaya," Ben completed.

"They're not my students anymore. They completed their semester here and returned to their regular schools two weeks ago." Her face tightened in concern. "Why? Has something happened to them?"

Ben and Danielle looked at each other.

"What is it? Are they in trouble?"

"I'm afraid they were both killed within the last week," said Danielle.

The color drained from Jane Wexler's face. "Killed? Please," she said, gesturing down a short hallway, "let's go into my office."

I CAN'T BELIEVE it," Jane Wexler muttered after Ben and Danielle had finished telling her what had happened, careful to leave out their own unsubstantiated suppositions. She sat back, paralyzed in her chair, holding tight to the arms. "A suicide and a murder. With all that's going on here, with all the students of this school have had to overcome . . ." She shook her head. "It makes everything seem so pointless."

"Did the school provide them with computers?" Ben asked.

"What? No. Michael already owned one. We did provide one for Shahir, as I recall."

"And got him a job in Israel, a most difficult task given the current state of affairs."

"Which makes it all the more vital," Wexler said stridently. "If there's any hope for the future, Inspector, it lies in bringing together the same youths who would otherwise be firing bullets at each other. And a crucial part of that is finding work for young Palestinians in Israel."

"What job did you find for Shahir?" Danielle asked.

"I really couldn't say. We have a placement counselor who handles all that."

Ben noted that on his pad. "We may wish to speak to him later."

"Michael Saltzman's mother mentioned Michael had been despondent in the days leading up to his death," Danielle interjected before Wexler could respond to Ben's request. "She said something about the death of another good friend of his. A girl."

Jane Wexler's mouth dropped. "My God . . . Beth? Beth Jacober?"

"I think that was the name. She attended this school too, didn't she?"

"Yes. Beth was a good friend of both Michael and Shahir. There were rumors she and Shahir were more than friends, but, well, the staff didn't think it was any of our business. This school exists to break down walls, mythologies, the barriers that have kept our two cultures apart for centuries. For six months now authorities on both sides have been trying to shut us down. Do you know how we've withstood them?" Wexler continued without waiting for Ben or Danielle to respond. "By succeeding! Our students are committed to peace, even if no one else is. They will come here every day no matter what, even if we have to hold class in the hills. Can either of you understand that?"

"Go on," Danielle said, exchanging a glance with Ben.

Jane Wexler smiled sadly, her eyes moistening. "I guess you could count their relationship as proof of our success. This is all so terrible. How, how was Beth killed?"

"A car accident, I believe."

Suddenly the principal's eyes turned wary and she dabbed at them with her sleeve. "An accident, suicide, and a carjacking. So what exactly are the two of you investigating?"

"We're not convinced the deaths of these students are what they appear to be," Danielle said, and left it at that. "It would be helpful if you could tell us more about them."

Jane Wexler nodded slowly, sadly. "Within a month of beginning their term here, the three of them were inseparable. Michael and Beth attended the same school in Israel for a time. It was he who introduced her to Shahir after the three boys became friends."

"Three?" said Ben.

"Yes, there was a fourth in their group. The best students in their class; four of the best I've ever seen. What was his name, what was his name . . ." Wexler tapped the desk as she searched her thoughts. "Yakov. Yakov Katavi. From the Golan Heights, I believe."

"Would you have an address?"

"I must, in my files."

"Just those four?" asked Danielle.

"There was a Palestinian girl for a while, as I recall, but something must have happened because suddenly she stopped hanging around with them. It happens often. You know how kids are."

"Of course," said Ben.

"I was sorry when they were rotated out. So bright and vibrant. Absolute whizzes with their computers. Knew more than our technology teacher. I wanted to offer them jobs." Wexler started to smile, stopped quickly. "I missed them when they left. You don't have students long enough to really get to know them, like you do in a regular school. But they were the best we've had in our two years of existence. I often had to chase them out of the computer room myself before I went home."

"Can you get Yakov Katavi's address for us?" Danielle asked her.

"And the name and address of the Palestinian girl," Ben added. "The one who stopped getting along with the rest of the group."

"Right away," said Jane Wexler.

B Y T H E T I M E they were halfway back to Danielle's car, she had received a call on her cell phone from an army detachment sent to check on Yakov Katavi's well-being. "Well, the boy is alive and well and in school as we speak," she told Ben, sliding the phone back into her handbag. "Two soldiers will be watching him for the rest of the day."

"We need to see him," Ben told her.

Danielle checked her watch nervously. "I can't right now. Baruch will have my head if I don't get back to the work I'm supposed to be doing."

"Another of the dead children, Pakad?" Ben asked curiously.

"No, something else," she replied, not bothering to elaborate on her investigation into the murder of Paul Hessler's son.

"Maybe I should go see the boy by myself."

Danielle frowned skeptically. "He lives in the Golan Heights."

"Where my pass does not permit entry . . ."

"Wait until this afternoon and we'll go together. If it makes you feel any better, I can contact the army and have a unit posted near his home."

"It would make me feel better."

"Consider it done," Danielle said. "What about the Palestinian girl the school principal mentioned?"

"From Ramallah," Ben recalled, "where I am permitted to go."

CHAPTER 18

DO YOU ALWAYS keep people waiting, Pakad?" the medical examiner said caustically when Danielle finally arrived. He stood in a white lab jacket sheathed in what looked like a floor-length sheet of plastic with slots for his arms. He still had his goggles on, but not his mask. The goggles could not disguise his annoyed glare.

"I'm sorry," Danielle said, studying his name tag as she continued toward him. "Dr. Ratovsky."

"No matter. This shouldn't take long anyway."

The pathology division of National Police was located in the second sublevel at the organization's Jerusalem headquarters. The autopsy on Paul Hessler's attempted killer had been completed with amazing speed, especially since the department's primary role was to evaluate and analyze data obtained from autopsies performed in the field, sometimes to offer a second opinion but often a first finding.

Each municipality in Israel maintained its own police force which was directly responsible for investigating crimes committed within its jurisdiction. National Police was best known for policing the country's borders and investigating crimes committed in Israeli settlements throughout the occupied territories. The organization also handled cases that cut across districts or were by nature of the larger, more high profile variety. As such, Danielle and others were usually called in after a preliminary investigation was already underway. But in this case Paul Hessler's influence had put them in charge from the very start.

Danielle drew even with Ratovsky, eyeing a lumpy shape covered on the table beneath them. "What can you tell me about him?"

Ratovsky reached for a clipboard that hung from a steel peg built into the table and studied it briefly, as the room's chemical smell continued to assault Danielle: a mild astringent mixing with the unmistakably sour stench of formaldehyde. It always felt colder in here and she wished she had donned a jacket before taking the elevator down.

Ratovsky finally looked up from the review of his notes. "Not very much, I'm afraid. Between the ages of seventy and eighty. An American, judging from the dental work and surgical incisions indicating three gastroenterological operations in the past ten years."

"Gastroenterological?"

"This man had stomach cancer, Pakad. His original stomach had been removed and a new one fashioned in its place. Our tox screens of his blood and internal examination indicated the cancer had returned, a fact his most recent exploratory operation must have revealed."

"How long ago?"

Ratovsky consulted his clipboard again. "Three to six months."

"He was dying, then," Danielle surmised.

"Depends on how aggressively his doctors elected to treat him. But at his age, with a recurrence . . ." Ratovsky shook his head. "There would be little they could do."

Danielle considered the daunting prospects of querying all hospitals in the United States that treat stomach cancer.

"Anything else that might be of help in identifying him?"

"Only this," Ratovsky said, reaching under the blue sheet for the dead man's arm.

He peeled the sheet back from it to expose a tattoo on the dead man's right forearm. That arm now had more bone than muscle and the dried and withered flesh had stripped the tattoo of its shape and bulk.

"You'll want to find a match for this, so I took some digital shots from a number of different angles," Ratovsky continued, and pulled a manila envelope from the bottom of his clipboard. "Scanned and enlarged for the highest degree of clarity."

Danielle unclasped the envelope and withdrew the top shot. The tattoo pictured was much clearer than it was under the fluorescent lights blazing down on the table. It appeared to be some sort of worm holding a knife in one of two thick mandibles fashioned to look like arms. Thin drops of blood dripped from the knife and ran in a splotchy pattern further down the dead man's forearm.

"Anything else?" Danielle asked, eager to be gone from this place.

"Well, there's evidence of a previous bullet wound from forty or fifty years ago."

"His age makes him right for World War II or even Korea," Danielle surmised, "so he could be a veteran."

"Unfortunately, the folds of his skin are too shrunken to determine the exact diameter of the bullet, and it left only minimal scarring. So I can't be any more specific at this time."

"Thank you, Doctor," Danielle said, starting to back away from the table. "Please send me your final report as soon as it's ready."

"There is one more thing I can tell you now," Ratovsky added, when she was halfway to the door.

Danielle turned back toward him. "Yes?"

The pathologist's gaze fell on the sheet-covered form on the table. "I don't know if this matters, but he had a glass eye. You might want to check for an American who lost an eye in one of those wars as well. I'm sure those records exist somewhere."

Danielle nodded, mentally calculating the steps she would have to take to uncover the killer's identity.

Again she considered the man's age: seventy-five or so, and dying of stomach cancer. What turns a dying old man into a killer? Surely something in the past, a past Danielle would have to unearth if she was going to find the reason why someone wanted Paul Hessler dead.

She had almost reached the door when two men barged through it. Danielle had to twist sideways to avoid being struck.

One of the men looked at her, recognition flashing in his eyes before they fell on the envelope the pathologist had just given to her. "I'll take that, if you don't mind, Pakad Barnea."

Danielle held her ground and tucked the envelope behind her hip. "I *do* mind. Who are you? Where are your ID badges? You're not National Police."

"This is no longer a National Police matter, Pakad."

She studied the men more closely: twin statues fashioned out of granite squeezed into sports jackets. Each with close-cropped hair and massive shoulders.

"Commander Baruch is waiting for you in your office," the speaker continued. "He will explain everything."

Danielle kept her eyes on both men, especially the telltale bulges their pistols made in their tight-fitting jackets. "I hope you don't mind if I hear that from him."

"Not at all," the man said and produced a wireless phone. "Press seven and you can speak to Commander Baruch directly."

Danielle took the phone but didn't press the number right away. "What's going on here?"

"That is no longer your concern."

"Who are you?"

"Also, not your concern."

"It's my case."

"Not anymore, Pakad."

CHAPTER 19

"YOU LIVE HERE?" an old woman sitting in the lobby of the apartment building asked Ben Kamal.

"No."

"They send you to fix my stove? It's still broken."

"I'm sorry. I'm not the repairman."

"Who are you, then?"

Ben had been about to knock on the apartment building's front door to draw the seated woman's attention when he saw that the lock was broken and walked into the stifling lobby.

"Who's going to fix my stove?" the old woman persisted, as Ben walked past her toward the steel mailboxes built into one of the lobby walls, in search of the name "Ashawi," family of the Palestinian girl named Zeima who had been friendly with the three dead students from the cooperative school.

He recognized the building on Al-Nahdah Street near the bustling Manara Circle to be one of those built by the Palestinian Authority as an initial demonstration of its intention to provide for the people. The goal in those days had been to construct as much affordable housing as quickly as possible, with little regard for form or function. The result here was four stories with few defining features, and a concrete exterior as dull and shabby as the lobby. Ben knew that much of the funds budgeted for this and other projects had mysteriously disappeared, leading ultimately to fewer being undertaken and a surge in seaside villas on the Gaza seacoast for Palestinian officials.

Easily the West Bank's most progressive city, Ramallah had already been slated to replace Gaza as the administrative center of Palestinian government authority once self-rule was complete. As such, though, it had been the center of many of the worst uprisings in recent months, uprisings that had ravaged the city's landscape, leaving deep scars the recent quelling of violence could not erase.

Even so, the outskirts of the old city looked to Ben remarkably unchanged. The square, flat-roofed buildings here were old and faded, the dust rising continually off them in the dry heat that baked the West Bank. Indications of the modern era were limited to stray television antennas atop decaying flat roofs, haphazardly strung electrical lines, and worn cars squeezed into spaces along the crumbling streets littered with rubble from small arms fire and an occasional stray Israeli rocket.

Approaching the center of Ramallah, though, was like entering another world. Here newly renovated shops, stores, and outdoor cafes dotted the landscape previously occupied by abandoned and run-down buildings. But the renewal efforts seemed to have frozen in midstream. Work that had been suspended months before had never started up again on structures that seemed to exist in a perpetual state of limbo. And those that had managed to remain up and running amidst the debacle of debris struggled for the few patrons who could afford their food and wares.

"Hey," the old woman continued to pester, slowly coming out of her chair, "what about my stove?"

Ben found the Ashawi family's apartment number on their mailbox and climbed the stairs to the fourth floor where they lived. The fire door had been removed and he started down the corridor listening to the blare of televisions and radios emanating through the apartments' paper-thin walls. The stale smell of foods long cooked and eaten hung in the air, and the corridor walls were stained with dirt and whatever vapors managed to leak out through the bottoms of the doors.

Ben stopped at the Ashawis' door and knocked.

"They're gone," a voice said from down the hall.

Ben turned and saw a man with a toolbox emerging from the apartment several doors down. "What do you mean gone?"

"Gone. Left." The man narrowed his eyes and tensed a little. "What's it to you?"

Ben approached, reaching for his ID. "I am Inspector Bayan Kamal of the Palestinian police."

"Is that why they left so fast?" the man asked, disinterested. "Because the police are after them?"

"Who are you?"

"I work here. The superintendent. Something breaks, I fix it." He looked around him, shrugging. "There is much work."

"The Authority pays you?"

"Used to. Then the building was sold to businessmen. Palestinian, I think, but then I hear they're really Israeli. I never met them. They pay me a little more, invest the same amount—nothing."

"You say the Ashawis moved?"

"No, I say they left. Gone." He started forward, fishing on his belt for the proper key. "Here, I show you. . . ."

He tried fitting it into the front door of the Ashawi's apartment, found it was the wrong key, and tried another. Ben waited impatiently before the superintendent was finally able to find the right key and shove the door open, the near side grinding against the doorjamb.

Ben entered the apartment just ahead of the superintendent, realizing instantly what the man had meant. The Ashawis had left all of their furniture behind. He continued on past a galley kitchen with stools set at a counter into a living room with a clear view downtown to a pair of luxury hotels that were under construction. Even more prominent were the naked steel frames of a number of highrise office buildings built by foreign investors hoping to turn Ramallah into a prime center for commerce.

Gazing out the window, Ben tried to remember what exactly had been torn down to make room for all the new construction, but too many years had passed and the memories must not have been important enough to keep. Replaced by the sight of cranes lowering fresh steel into place and the clanging sounds of heavy machinery at work. Ben found those sounds the most striking, because there was nothing like them recalled from his youth growing up amidst the large Palestinian-Christian community in Ramallah. Whatever was built in those days was built by hand with hammers and saws instead of heavy machines.

Strangely, this was one of the things Ben would miss most if he decided to return to Detroit. Watching Palestine grow and evolve before his eyes. He wondered, though, whether this was reason to stay or go. After all, he had come back here because he wanted to embrace the world of his father, to find a life worth living. But in a few years Palestine would no longer be the world of his father. And the change wouldn't be all positive, thanks to the corruption of values and new standards the Palestinians would have to accept.

The opening of markets, tourism, and booming trade would leave entire classes of people out. No longer held in the bonds of brotherhood of a struggling race. Their world would be defined by the contents of their wallets instead of their conscience. Peace was indeed the greatest weapon of war. Skyscrapers would go up. The refugee camps would not come down. People would make a big show about caring, but the anger would be gone, dollars thrown at the same people who used to throw rocks.

Leave now, go back to Detroit to work for John Najarian and Security Concepts, and Ben could miss all that. This world had killed his father. He didn't have to let it destroy him too.

"How many in the family?" Ben asked the superintendent, eager to distance himself from his own thoughts.

"The parents and two children—no, three children. Anyway, I think it's three."

The superintendent kept his distance as Ben entered the largest of three small bedrooms and opened the single closet. Plenty of clothes hung comfortably, but there were also a number of hangers scattered on the floor atop boxes and shoes. Evidence that the Ashawis had packed and left in a hurry, traveling light.

Ben turned toward the superintendent who had remained in the bedroom's doorway. "How long ago did they leave?"

The man shrugged. "I don't know."

"When did you notice?"

"A couple days ago. Three or four, maybe."

Ben started from the room. "Come downstairs with me."

"Why?"

"I want you to open the Ashawis' mailbox for me."

A S IT TURNED out, Ben didn't need the superintendent's services in the lobby at all; the Ashawis' mailbox no longer conformed to its slot and was easily opened without a key.

"Hey," the old woman, who had not moved from her chair, yelled to the superintendent this time, "you going to fix my stove today?"

Mail spilled out as soon as Ben yanked the small door downward. Some smaller envelopes fluttered to the floor behind a number of magazines that landed with a clump. Ben checked the dates stamped across the cancelled stamps. By all indications, the Ashawis had not been here to retrieve their mail for seven days.

The same time period in which Michael Saltzman had

died in an apparent suicide and Shahir Falaya had been murdered on the road.

"I'm guessing they didn't leave a forwarding address," Ben said to the superintendent.

The man shook his head, glad to have an excuse not to pay any attention to the old woman with the broken stove. "Not with me."

"Were they friendly with anyone else in the building?"

"I wouldn't know."

"Is there anyone else you can ask?"

"I wouldn't know who. This isn't the only building I work in."

Ben knelt down and began to retrieve the fallen mail. "Just get me a bag then."

"A bag?"

"I need something to put the Ashawis' mail into. I'm taking it with me."

"Why?"

Ben stood up with the pile neatly in hand. "To deliver once I find them."

CHAPTER 20

"PAUL HESSLER FLEW back to the United States this morning," Commander Moshe Baruch told Danielle when she reached his office. "Apparently he felt his life was in danger."

"That doesn't explain why you're pulling me off the case."

"It's not you, Pakad. It's us—National Police. The matter has been turned over to other authorities."

"Those two men in the basement . . ."

"Just messengers who wanted to make sure they collected all our evidence."

"Mossad?" Danielle asked, referring to Israel's foreign intelligence service.

"What's the difference?"

"A domestic murder shouldn't be of any concern to them."

"Unless it was committed by a foreigner."

"How could they know something I only just learned?"

Baruch's dark eyes seemed to sink even deeper into his skull. "I don't really care. It's not my problem anymore."

"It was Hessler himself who called National Police to

make sure I was assigned to the case. He must have called Mossad to have us taken off it. Why would he do that? Yesterday he was so determined to have me find out why he had been targeted. What made him change his mind?"

"Again," Baruch said impatiently, "I don't care. I care about supervising the cases assigned to my own investigators. The one I gave you to close yesterday, for example. I notice you haven't turned that report in yet."

"You assigned me to the Hessler investigation before I finished the paperwork. Just a formality," Danielle lied. "I'll have it to you as soon as I can."

"In that case, I left another case on your desk this morning. I suggest you busy yourself with it and the Saltzman one instead of a case that is no longer yours." Baruch seemed to be finished but then suddenly resumed. "It is time you learned your parameters, Pakad."

"A difficult task when you keep changing them, Rav nitzav."

D OWN IN HER office, Danielle quickly reconstructed the tattoo on the killer's arm as best she could. Her memory pictured it perfectly, but her drawing skills were not sufficient to re-create anything but a vague outline. In spite of the killer's old bullet wound, glass eye, and possible service for the Americans in either World War II or Korea, the tattoo was likely the best evidence she had to aid her in determining his identity.

Of course, this case didn't even belong to her anymore; the cases that did lay in file folders she had doodled all over in search of a better rendition of the elderly killer's tattoo.

A worm holding a knife dripping with blood . . .

But what kind of worm? And what was the significance of the knife?

First things first.

Danielle slid Michael Saltzman's file aside and quickly skimmed the contents of the one Moshe Baruch had left on her desk that morning: a thirteen-year-old boy who had died in a bicycle accident. Fractured skull. He hadn't been wearing a helmet. Remained in a brain-dead coma for two weeks before his parents were finally able to turn the machines pumping what passed for life into him off.

So he didn't fit the profile of Michael Saltzman and the other dead students who'd attended the cooperative school outside of Jerusalem. Danielle closed the thirteen-year-old boy's file and shoved it aside.

She sat back in her chair and closed her eyes, reviewing the cases in her mind. The first of the students to die, by all accounts, had been the Israeli girl, Beth Jacober, who'd been killed in a car accident. According to Michael Saltzman's mother, the girl's death might have had something to do with Michael's alleged suicide, committed around the very same time the mother of the murdered Palestinian boy told Ben her son began to act frightened, terrified of something.

Another parent, another dead child.

Was that why this whole matter so obsessed her, why she was almost glad to be pulled off the Paul Hessler investigation for the opportunity it gave her to pursue this?

Danielle needed to talk to the parents of the girl who had died in the car crash. Learn the details. Come to know their grief.

Oh God...

She felt like a monster, prying into the lives of others to better understand her own. Taking solace, comfort, in those whose grief was worse than hers. Therapy for her own damaged soul following her meeting with Dr. Barr that morning.

Danielle hadn't prayed in a long time and she found she couldn't start again now. God had already taken too much from her.

But it wasn't just God who killed children. There were three students who attended the same school. All dead. All killed, perhaps, by man.

Why?

Moshe Baruch didn't care about them. Just cases to be closed to assure and continue her misery. Well, Danielle was going to surprise him. She was going to bring him an answer he never would have expected.

If they had been murdered, then why?

Danielle knew she had to find the answer.

For her own child.

For herself.

CHAPTER 21

As INSTRUCTED, BEN was waiting on Amman Street across from the municipal building that housed Jericho's police station when the minivan pulled up to the curb. He could see a number of kids buckled tightly into the seats: a half dozen, evenly split between boys and girls, all looking to be between six and seven. He slid open the passenger side door and found Colonel Nabrial al-Asi of the Palestinian Protective Security Service in the driver's seat.

"Get in, Inspector," the colonel said. He was wearing a cream-colored linen suit and a carefully knotted green Armani tie deliberately left outside the strap of the shoulder harness. "It's my day to drive the car pool. I just picked up my youngest son and the others at school."

Ben gazed back at the three boys, wondering which one of them was al-Asi's youngest son. "You did say you wanted to be around your family more."

The colonel carefully pulled away from the curb. "I have decided to act more like a normal parent. Soccer coaching and now car pooling. I had this American minivan imported especially for the task."

"How many shadow vehicles are watching us?"

"Three. One behind and one in front."

"That's only two."

"Did I forget to mention the helicopter?"

Ben leaned his head out the open window and looked up.

"Who knows what's next?" said al-Asi, sounding genuinely excited. "My daughter's school is having a graduation party. I'm thinking of chaperoning."

"I didn't know Palestinian schools were permitted to have parties."

The colonel cleared his throat. "My daughter attends a private school in Israel."

He continued driving the minivan slowly, clearly unfamiliar with its controls. Ben watched him fiddle with the steering wheel adjustment. Then with the air conditioning controls.

"Were your people able to reconstruct the files on that computer, Colonel?"

"No, I'm afraid not, Inspector. Because there are no files. Someone removed the machine's hard drive."

Al-Asi's revelation caught Ben totally off guard. Clearly, the perpetrator hadn't wanted Shahir Falaya's files recovered under any circumstances.

"Would you like to tell me what's going on, Inspector?" al-Asi asked.

"I did tell you: The boy who owned the computer was murdered in an apparently random crime."

"But you, of course, did not believe the crime was random and now you appear to be right. How is it these things seem to fall into your lap?"

"I don't ask for them, Colonel."

"I didn't mean it as an insult, Inspector. Quite the opposite. You see things other men don't. You should consider a position where your talents would be more appreciated."

"As your assistant soccer coach, you mean."

"Why not? In the eyes of many it's a position you have

already held for some time, given our close relationship these last several years. You might even say it explains why your many enemies in Palestine have not acted against you. I dare say that they fear the repercussions."

"You want to make the relationship official."

Al-Asi shrugged. "You look comfortable sitting there in the co-pilot's seat, Inspector. I ask only that you keep that in mind."

"I will."

"Especially since I understand you are considering another line of work anyway." Something in the colonel's tone had changed. He sounded slighted, hurt. "I'm not sure how well you would fare in the private sector, my friend."

"How did you find out?"

"Your meeting occurred in the West Bank, didn't it?" Al-Asi flashed a brief smile. "An American like John Najarian comes here and I pay attention. I have never trusted the Armenians."

"Why?"

"Because they tempt my friends with career changes."

"Is this a negotiation, Colonel?"

"Everything is a negotiation. But I'm surprised I had to hear about your meeting from someone other than you. Believe me when I say there's nothing for you in the United States, Inspector. Here at least you have me."

"I haven't forgotten your offer."

"What about Najarian's?"

"I haven't had many options to weigh for a while. I'd like to enjoy the feeling a bit longer."

Al-Asi shrugged, letting it go. "In that case, tell me who you think killed the Falaya boy."

"I don't know."

"But this other bit of information you asked me for will help you find out."

"It might."

The colonel waited for a red light and fished a piece of paper from his pocket.

"I'm hot, Daddy," a boy in the rearmost seat said.

Al-Asi's fumbled for the air conditioning switch and started the minivan through the intersection. Then he handed the piece of paper to Ben.

"The Ashawi family is quiet, reserved, of modest means. They're not troublemakers so, unfortunately, we have no recent intelligence file on them. It's a common name, but I believe I've narrowed down their relatives to the three on that list."

Ben studied the names and addresses quickly. "Interesting that you could still come up with this so fast. I hadn't realized your office was so technologically advanced."

"It's not," al-Asi said, switching on his left-turn indicator. "We inherited the files from the Israelis who were quite good at keeping tabs on everyone. Give me until tomorrow morning and I'll have the list narrowed down to one."

CHAPTER 22

E XHUME HER BODY? In God's name, why?"

"Please," Danielle told David and Sheri Jacober as compassionately as she could manage, "I know how this must sound to you. But I wouldn't be here if I didn't have my reasons. The fact is . . . I'm here because the possibility exists that your daughter Beth's death was not an accident."

The Jacobers exchanged an anxious glance. They lived in Saryan, a wealthy, exclusive suburb of Tel Aviv notable for fenced and gated yards that were much larger than what ordinary Israelis were used to. The freshly paved streets were wider than most and a private security force patrolled them to supplement the local army contingent and police.

"What are you talking about?" Sheri Jacober asked.

"I believe your daughter may have been murdered."

Tears welled up in Sheri Jacober's eyes. Danielle recalled a picture of her late daughter from Layla Saltzman's coffee table. The resemblance between mother and daughter was striking. The dark hair and delicate features. An even, natural Mediterranean tan with a slightly red nose for both of them.

"She was driving drunk, Chief Inspector. She left a party at a friend's house and was driving drunk when she . . ." Sobs drowned out the rest of her words.

"I read the report. Her friends said she hadn't been drinking."

"That's what they always say. To protect each other."

"We moved here from the United States to get away from this kind of thing," her husband David added. "We thought it would be different."

"Just as you thought the cooperative school your daughter attended until the semester ended a month ago would be different?" Danielle asked them both.

Sheri Jacober replied after glancing at her husband. "Why is that important?"

"Two other students from that school have died in the past week."

"We knew about the Saltzman boy's suicide, but we didn't go to the funeral. Just couldn't handle another."

"A Palestinian boy from the school is dead too."

"What does this have to do with us, with our daughter?" David Jacober demanded.

"The three were very close friends, inseparable according to the cooperative school's principal."

Sheri Jacober leaned forward, seeming to distance herself from her husband. She had offered coffee when Danielle first arrived, set the machine, and never returned to the kitchen to fetch it. Now the smell of the fresh brew hung heavy in the house's air, swallowing everything else. "What do you want from us, Chief Inspector?"

"Upon your request, for religious reasons, an autopsy was never performed on your daughter. Why bother, when the cause of death was so obvious? But now that it may not be so obvious we need to be sure. Investigate every possibility."

"The crash killed her," David Jacober reminded. "What do you expect an autopsy at this point to show?"

Danielle leaned forward, longing for the cup of coffee—decaf, of course—Sheri Jacober had never brought her.

She had a terrible craving for something sweet as well, a danish or cookie to go with it. It had been that way lately. Hungry day and night. Her stomach rumbled and she thought she might have felt the tiny baby inside her move.

"I don't believe your daughter's car accident was an accident at all." Danielle lowered her voice. "I don't believe Michael Saltzman killed himself, and I don't believe a Palestinian boy named Shahir Falaya's death resulted from an ordinary carjacking gone wrong."

David Jacober's expression hardened, his jaw protruding outward as he took his wife's hand. "What you believe or don't believe is not enough to convince us to desecrate the body of our daughter."

Danielle leaned forward. "Mr. and Mrs. Jacober, police reports indicate your daughter left the party somewhere between ten o'clock and ten-fifteen. But the car's clock was frozen at eleven-twenty when the accident occurred. Now it's only a fifteen minute drive back to your house from the Tel Aviv apartment where the party was being held." Danielle paused to let her point sink in. "That leaves up to forty-five minutes unaccounted for."

Sheri Jacober pulled her hand stiffly from her husband's grasp. "You think something happened to Beth between the time she left the party and the accident."

"Yes, I do."

"This is ridiculous!" David Jacober roared and lurched to his feet, hands placed menacingly on his hips as he glared at Danielle. "Why are you pursuing this when none of the other police saw a reason to?"

"The Tel Aviv officials never bothered to look."

"You would have us believe National Police is that much more efficient, then?"

Danielle turned in the chair to face David Jacober directly. "Mr. Jacober, I believe your daughter was murdered." Rotating her gaze between the two of them now. "I know how painful it must be for you to hear that. But I'm sure if you give it some thought you'll want to be sure, as I do. Because if I'm right, and I truly believe I am, that's the only way we'll ever be able to bring her killers to justice."

"It doesn't make any sense," Sheri Jacober interjected. "Why Beth? *Why?*"

"There's only one way to find out," said Danielle.

C H A P T E R 2 3

HANS MUNDT SAT in the wobbly wooden
chair he'd set next to his bed. He had rented a room in
the Petra Hostel near the entrance to the Arab market in
the old city of Jerusalem. He could have afforded something better but had chosen this for the anonymity it provided. Still, it would've been nice to have a room that had
a desk; the cramped confines of this dingy one forced him
to use his bed, atop which he had spread out his letters
and notes. Instead of a desk, he had a crumbling balcony
facing the Tower of David. Music wafted in at all hours
of the night from a dance club downstairs, so much so that
last night he had slid his balcony door closed and braved
the suffocating heat to shut out the sound.

Mundt had been collecting correspondence from survivors of the Nazi labor camp north of Lodz, Poland, for
years, doing his best to distill their contents into one coherent story to trace the events that had come to dominate
his life. Mundt knew he was close to the truth now. The
tattered interview notes and replies before him held that
truth. Mundt had laid them across the bedspread in chron-
ological order starting nearly a year before the camp was
dismantled in late 1944. . . .

* * *

*T*HE BOY LEANED *over the hole, retching into the stink accumulated beneath it. He felt the gun barrel poke at him again from the doorway.*

"Hurry up! There are others in line out here."

The boy heaved again, his empty stomach spasming violently. He tried to push himself back to his feet but the cramps seized him again and kept him doubled over.

"I said, come out of there!"

The gun barrel jabbed him in the ribs just before a heavy boot kicked him in the rear. The boy crumpled into a ball and felt the shadow of the labor camp commandant, or Haupsturmfuehrer, *Gunthar Weiss, loom over him.*

"You worthless piece of scum! You know the rules, if you don't work, you die. What's it to be, then, eh?" Poking him harder now. "What's it to be?"

The boy tried to move, couldn't. Tried to breathe but Weiss's gun barrel dug deeper into his ribs, closing down his lungs.

"Mundt!" Haupsturmfuehrer Weiss barked.

Seconds later another soldier the boy did not recognize snapped to attention and approached. Although no more than twenty years of age, he was a virtual twin of the Haupsturmfuehrer. The same man, only younger.

"Mundt, you will take this boy behind the building and shoot him," Weiss ordered unhesitantly. "He is a useless piece of shit, and it is time you broke your rifle in."

"Yes, Haupsturmfuehrer!"

"Get moving now! Go!"

The boy felt a powerful arm hoist him brutally to his feet.

"And, Mundt, one bullet and no more. If I hear a second shot, I'll put one of my own in you. If the shot doesn't finish him, use your bayonet or your knife. Are we clear?"

"Clear, Haupsturmfuehrer!"

"Then move!"

The boy lacked the strength to walk and was dragged

by Mundt across the muddy field toward the rear of a former stable that had been converted into a barracks or Pferdebaraken. The intense, bitter stench of glue and tanning dye from the nearby factory made him retch yet again. Behind the old wooden building, its holes patched with strips of blankets and cloth, Mundt let him drop to the ground. The boy cowered there, shaking horribly and racked again by dry heaves.

"Look at me!" came the order.

The boy did his best to gaze up through the tangle of his soiled hair at the young Nazi who towered over him in his boots and warm great coat. The soldier's hair was close-cropped and his features and eyes dark for a German. The boy recognized him as a youthful member of the Waffen SS, which was directly responsible for factory camps, or Judenlager, such as this one.

"You're a Jew, aren't you?" The boy noticed Mundt's rifle was still shouldered. "Answer me!"

"What's the difference? You going to kill me twice?"

"So the little shit has a tongue."

The boy trembled harder and tightened his arms around his thin shirt. "It's not my fault I'm so weak. It's my leg. I broke it before they took me from the ghetto and it didn't set right."

Mundt turned his gaze downward. "Looks fine to me."

"Then just kill me and get it over with."

Mundt knelt down, so close the boy could smell the soap on his skin. "I'm not going to kill you."

The boy looked up, afraid to hope. "What?"

"You're going back inside the factory and you're going to work harder than you ever did before. Because if you slack I'm going to finish the job the Haupsturmfuehrer told me to. Do you understand?"

The boy nodded. "I . . . understand."

Mundt raised his rifle and fired a single shot that echoed loudly in the wind. For a moment the smell of cordite drowned out the stench of the dyes pumping from inside *the factory. Then he knelt down and helped the boy to his feet, almost gently.*

"What's your name?"

"Hessler," the boy managed through his dry, cracking lips. "Paul Hessler."

HUNCHED OVER HIS hotel bed, Hans Mundt found his head was aching too much to continue his review. He gathered the letters and notes carefully into a pile and returned them to the worn briefcase his mother had told him had once belonged to his father, Karl. Karl Mundt, whose first and only posting in the army of the Reich had been as a guard in one of the Nazi labor camps located outside of Lodz.

The names of three men . . .

Last night he had handed them over to the former head of Israel's Mossad, and by tonight, Hans Mundt was quite certain, the men would all be dead.

He lay atop the bed that was now cleared of his notes and letters and waited for the call he was expecting to come any moment from Abraham Vorsky.

CHAPTER 24

PAUL HESSLER ONCE again scanned the autopsy report his contact in Mossad had delivered that morning, still not believing it could be right. And yet his son's killer could be no other man.

After all these years, Paul thought to himself, *why had the man resurfaced after all these years?*

It didn't matter. The investigation had effectively been shut down. Paul Hessler knew what he needed to know. The involvement of the National Police was now superfluous, so he'd had the case closed as quickly as he had opened it. He tried to tell himself he was doing them a favor, but in reality he feared Danielle Barnea would be clever enough to uncover the truth. He had chosen her for the case because he knew she was the best, and now he was dismissing her for the same reason.

Hessler's high-placed contacts also helped him expedite the arrangements to have his son's body returned on the same flight with him to the United States. He insisted on making all the travel arrangements himself, anything to keep himself busy and focused on something other than yesterday's tragedy, even if it was just for a moment.

Paul was set to leave his fortified suite at the Hilton for the flight home when his phone rang.

"Yes," he answered.

"Mr. Hessler? This is Burnstein in New York. I worked for your son. I'm terribly sorry, sir."

"What is it, Burnstein?"

"Well, I'm sorry for the intrusion, but I just wanted you to know that I went ahead and cancelled all the plans for next week."

"What plans?"

"The reception your son arranged a few days ago."

The phone felt suddenly heavy in Paul's hand. "What reception?"

"Er, I assumed you knew."

"Well, Burnstein, clearly I don't."

"He never told me the specifics, sir," Burnstein stammered. "Just that you were going to be celebrating something."

"We won't be anymore."

"I know that, sir. I'm sorry."

"Then I can assume we're finished," Paul said and hung up the phone.

But Burnstein's words lingered in his mind. Why had Ari planned a party and why had he kept it a secret from him? His son had been acting strangely as of late. Almost too happy and energetic. Always seeming on the verge of telling Paul something, right up to their last conversation in the back of the car when Ari said he had a surprise he would share once they were back in New York.

Paul wondered if that surprise had something to do with this party. Now, caught in the firm grasp of grief once more, he realized he would never know.

CHAPTER 25

IS THIS ALL you really want to discuss?" Ben Kamal asked Danielle Barnea, as she drove toward the Golan Heights.

"You said you wanted to compare notes."

"And we have. You're having a body exhumed for autopsy without a supervisor's permission, and I'm searching for a family that disappeared suddenly from their home. I'm also having police officers canvass all Shahir Falaya's neighbors." "Why?"

"Because someone went to great lengths to break into his house and remove the hard drive from his computer. A neighbor might have seen something without realizing."

"And what do you think we'll learn in the Golan, Inspector?"

"You're avoiding the issue."

"No, I just don't want to talk about it."

"With me or at all?"

"Who else could I possibly discuss this with?"

"My point exactly."

Behind the wheel, Danielle sighed. "I don't like thinking about what the doctor said."

"You have to. *We* have to."

"It's only been a few hours. I need time to let what the doctor said settle in."

"It won't help. Believe me. News like this never settles in. It only festers until it totally obsesses you. Something I know about."

"Is that supposed to make me feel better?"

"There's nothing I can say that will make you feel better."

Danielle hadn't really intended to say anything, but the words spilled out anyway. "It feels worse this time than the first. The first time I lost a baby it was earlier on in the pregnancy, and it happened so suddenly I didn't have time to feel as bad as I do now."

"Because this time you have a choice."

"Do I really, Ben?"

"It's not fair to do this to yourself, Danielle."

"You're telling me to have an abortion."

Ben's voice lowered. "I feel as if I've lost this baby twice: first when you told me you wanted to raise him alone and then again this morning when the doctor explained what he had found. I don't know how many more opportunities I'm going to get to be a father. Without you, probably none. But I know I'd rather take that chance than let a baby come into the world with the kind of problems this one is likely to have."

Danielle smiled sadly. "You know, it's funny. This case we've stumbled onto seems to be about murdered children and I feel I can still do something for them. They're dead and yet I want to help them so bad. But I can't do anything for my own baby who's still *alive*."

"I have a confession to make," Ben said, and she looked over at him in the passenger seat. "I was glad when Moshe Baruch was named commissioner of National Police. Glad because I thought he might fire you, and you would come to live with me in the United States."

"You'd leave Palestine?"

"For you and the baby? Just say the word. I wouldn't even bother to pack."

"Even now?"

"Even more."

Danielle slowed her car for the checkpoint leading into the Golan Heights. "I don't deserve you, Ben."

"You've got me, all the same."

THE FAMILY OF Yakov Katavi lived among the seventeen thousand Israelis who have settled amidst the scenic lush hills and streams of the Golan Heights. Their settlement in Mevo Hama was composed of white stucco-faced ranch homes situated on a flat stretch of wide-open ground that afforded a comfortable amount of land for each family. From this section of the plateau that formed the Golan the residents of Mevo Hama near the Syrian border had a clear view of the fenced-off minefields and ruins of Syrian villages and army bases that had been overrun during the Six-Day War of 1967.

Rain clouds were lifting off the cliffs high above the Sea of Galilee and the settlement when Danielle edged her car along a narrow road toward the Katavi home. The best wine in Israel came from vineyards planted in the Golan, and the thick vines that filled the fields for as far as she could see convinced her that the Katavis must be among those who grew and harvested the grapes. A well-known hot spring was located in Mevo Hama, accounting to a great degree for the character of the soil. The air smelled of the fresh, sweet grapes that dominated the plateau in marked contrast to the stench of car exhaust that seemed to perpetually hover over Tel Aviv, and even Jerusalem now. Danielle was so accustomed to the polluted air she scarcely noticed it, until the Golan reminded her what fresh air smelled like.

She turned off the main road and angled down an even narrower one that sliced through a tunnel of ripening vines. The Katavi home appeared in a clearing up ahead, set well back from the road. Upon Danielle's instructions, a pair of soldiers had been posted here since that morning, although only one was visible now. That soldier raised one hand, while keeping the other fastened menacingly on his Uzi submachine gun.

"Can I help you?" he said, coming around to the driver's side of the car once Danielle had come to a stop.

Danielle showed the man her identification. "You should have been told to expect us."

"Of course, Pakad."

"Yakov Katavi is home from school?"

"Inside with his mother right now."

She turned to Ben. "Let's go have a talk with the boy, Inspector."

The soldier tensed as he stood beside the door of Danielle's car, eyeing Ben suspiciously. "I have clearance for you, Pakad. No one else."

"This is Inspector Bayan Kamal of the Palestinian Police. He is here on my authority."

"You can discuss this with the sergeant posted inside the house with the family, while I stay out here with Inspector Kamal."

"Fine," Danielle said, obviously annoyed, then climbed out and headed up the walk toward the home's front door.

The soldier kept his eyes on Ben while Ben followed Danielle's progress up the pressed-gravel road to the front door. She knocked briefly, then turned the knob.

The door started inward and Ben watched Danielle freeze just inside instead of proceeding. She had started to swing back toward him when the door slammed closed behind her, and Ben saw the Israeli soldier posted at the car window bringing his Uzi around.

C H A P T E R 2 6

BEN HURLED HIMSELF across the front seat of Danielle's Jeep, just managing to jerk the barrel of the Uzi aside before the soldier opened fire. The submachine gun's bullets stitched a jagged design through the Jeep's upholstery and shattered the rear window.

Ben's scorched hands continued to cling to the Uzi's stock and barrel, as the soldier caught him under the chin with the gun's butt. Stars exploded before his eyes and Ben's teeth mashed together. His jaw ached as much as his chin, his eyes filling with water that stole his vision.

But he didn't need totally clear sight to see the soldier had pushed too much of his upper body into the Jeep, sacrificing balance in the process. Ben managed to jerk his own body upward and slammed the soldier's skull hard against the roof. Still holding the Uzi down, Ben snapped the side of his head up into the soldier's face.

He felt, actually *felt*, the man's nose crush on impact. The bones compressed like an accordian, only they didn't ease back, and Ben heard the soldier gasp in pain. He could smell blood now, heard the man's raspy breathing all focused through his mouth. But the man held enough presence of mind to cling to his Uzi, fighting to twist the barrel into Ben's midsection.

Ben tried to smash the soldier with his skull again, missed, and felt the force of the lost blow shove both of them against the door. One of their flailing arms struck the latch and popped it open, leaving both men to spill out into the road.

I F DANIELLE HAD gone for her gun upon seeing one of the real Israeli soldier's bodies lying across the Katavis' foyer, she knew she'd be dead now. Instead she had dropped to the floor, her momentum slamming the door closed as bullets split the air above her. Flecks of wood and plaster flew in all directions, coughed up with the thumps of impact.

Danielle rolled and managed to free her pistol, firing in a wide arc toward the figure in a soldier's uniform that hurled itself over a couch in the home's living room. Danielle fired into the fabric, watched puffs of stuffing jump into the air. The gunman popped back up over the rear of the couch, firing. His barrage obliterated a trio of family pictures hanging on the wall, and Danielle felt glass and pieces of the Katavis' memories rain down upon her.

She glimpsed the body of a woman lying just to one side of the couch, while slumped in a chair with a neat bullet wound in his forehead sat a boy she was certain must be Yakov Katavi. Next to him a table had been spilled over, the computer upon it smashed into oblivion.

But it was the pictures of the Katavis that bothered her the most, just as they had in the Saltzman home. Frozen moments of happy times, now lying torn and tattered between two of the subjects who would never smile for the camera again. The pictures of mother and son more alive than they were.

Danielle felt bile surge up her throat. She had just slammed a fresh clip home when the gunman leaped over the top of the couch, firing straight for her.

* * *

BEN LANDED FACE-TO-FACE on the ground with the man dressed as an Israeli soldier. The man's warm, reeking breath coated Ben's face as they struggled for control of the Uzi. The soldier landed a knee in Ben's groin, and a series of flashes, brighter than the stars in the Jeep, exploded before his eyes. He felt the breath catching in his gut, pushed all his strength into his fingers to maintain his hold on the Uzi.

The soldier tried kneeing him again, got only the inside of his thigh, but twisted so he ended up atop Ben. Still eye-to-eye, Ben strained his neck to push his head upward. The man's breath assaulted him again and Ben could feel the Uzi being wrenched slowly from his grasp. The man's eyes bulged confidently, his finger ready to dart for the trigger. Ben visualized him pressing it, launching a river of hot lead into his belly. Then he heard gunshots coming from the house and thought of Danielle fighting for her life inside just as he was out here.

Ben didn't dare strip a hand from the Uzi. The man's hot breath smelled like spoiled food and his ruined nose leaked blood that ran down Ben's cheeks. Ben followed the blood trail, lurched forward with his mouth open and bit into the man's nose. Bit hard, like he was tearing a stubborn piece of chicken off the bone.

The screech that followed was the loudest one Ben had ever heard, as he clamped his teeth tight and twisted his jaw. At first he thought he must have bitten his own tongue. Then he realized the the marble-sized chunk of grizzle in his mouth was the tip of the man's nose. Disgusted, he spit it free in the same instant the man jerked away from him. Pain tore the man's thoughts from his Uzi long enough for Ben to push him over backwards, landing with his thumbs jammed into the eyes that had radiated confidence just seconds before.

The man's scream was hoarser this time and the Uzi clattered to the ground between them. Ben kept pushing his thumbs home until the man raked his face with his fingernails. Ben twisted away from the pain, and his assailant used a desperate burst of strength to shove him back. Ben's shoulders thumped hard to the ground and what was left of his breath pinballed against his ribs. He climbed back to his knees, just as the man yanked the Uzi off the ground and leveled it.

THE CLIP JAMMED on its way into her nine-millimeter pistol and Danielle knew she'd never be able to right it before the gunman's bullets found her. A pole lamp teetered by her side and Danielle used a sweep of her arm to knock it over into the gunman's path just before he loomed over her.

The man tripped and slammed his chin into a coffee table which toppled under his weight, leaving him between the dead Katavis and atop the pictures his barrage had knocked from the wall. Danielle wasn't sure whether the crunch she heard was bone or wood shattering, but she had the presence of mind to spin aside and scamper back toward the foyer.

The man started shooting again in the same moment she dove to the floor and groped for the sidearm still holstered on the dead Israeli soldier's belt. Her hand closed on the butt and she gazed back to see the killer staggering to his feet. His eyes were glazed, the right side of his face hanging lower than the left. Blood gushed from a gash under his chin as he stumbled forward and tried to level his pistol.

The dead soldier's safety strap was undone, allowing Danielle to draw his pistol in one swift motion. She steadied it on the man advancing upon her and opened fire just as his bullets started anew.

Glass shattered behind her. A vase exploded to her right. Then the shooting stopped. The man halted, dropped his gun and crumpled to the floor, three dark holes widening in his chest before he fell over onto his stomach.

* * *

OUTSIDE, THE FAKE soldier opened fire with his Uzi. Blinded by Ben's assault on his eyes, though, his shots flew wild and high, as Ben launched himself forward.

Impact threw both men back to the ground, the Uzi sent flying to one side. The fake soldier turned onto his stomach and crawled fast for it. But Ben threw himself onto the man's back and clamped both hands on the back of his head, holding his face in the dirt. The man heaved and struggled desperately, feet kicking and hands thrashing in all directions. They flailed backwards for Ben, but Ben arched his back to stay clear of their grasp. Pushing harder, visualizing the man's face being driven into the ground—*through* the ground.

Finally the man's fingers clutched at the air, then dropped in frozen half-made fists. Ben kept pressing long after the assailant had gone still, kept pressing until he realized inside the house the gunfire had ceased and pushed himself up to go after Danielle.

INSIDE, DANIELLE LET the pistol drop from her grasp and stayed on her knees. The room seemed to be spinning. She felt dizzy and tried to steady herself with deep breaths.

It was no use. Her position in the hall gave her a direct view of a dead boy seated in a chair, looking up as if to gaze at the wound that had killed him. A boy who would never do his homework or go out with his friends again.

Whoever had murdered Yakov Katavi's friends at the cooperative school had killed the soldiers Danielle had dispatched to guard the Katavis and then the Katavis themselves. She wondered if the father lay dead somewhere else in the house.

Danielle leaned over and vomited. She was still dry heaving when Ben burst through the door holding an Uzi coated with dirt.

"Are you all right?"

Danielle managed to nod, wiped her mouth with a sleeve. Ben bent over and extended a hand to help her up.

And the window over his right shoulder exploded under a fresh fusillade of fire, showering both of them with glass.

CHAPTER 27

"GIVE ME THE gun!" Danielle demanded, lunging to her feet. She stripped the Uzi from Ben's hands and gave him the pistol she had taken off the dead Israeli soldier in its place.

More gunshots sent glass raining into the house, followed by the sound of footsteps rushing over gravel. Danielle spun away from Ben and fired a burst from the Uzi out one of the shattered windows. Spent shells bounced off the wall and rolled across the wood floor.

"The back!" Danielle said.

None of the enemy was visible through the windows overlooking the house's rear. Ben moved to the door first, prepared to open it while Danielle covered him. The first steps outside would be the most dangerous; if an ambush had been set, that's when it would come.

Ben emerged holding his breath with pistol ready, realizing he had no idea how many bullets remained in its clip. Satisfied no one was lying in wait, he signalled Danielle to follow.

She joined him outside and scanned the open ground up to the field line where the vineyards began, searching for any signs of their attackers. Suddenly a series of thuds sounded inside the Katavi's home.

"Come on!" she rasped, realizing the enemy had concentrated their attack from the front.

She grabbed Ben's arm and yanked him on toward the thick vines of the fields, which they immediately saw were crisscrossed with vehicle-sized paths between the rows. The rustling of the vines sounded like the quiet sweep of trees on a fall day, loud enough, Danielle hoped, to disguise their footsteps and presence once the gunmen now inside the house offered pursuit. As an added advantage, darkness was descending quickly, the rain that had seemed in the offing holding off for now.

The sweet scent of ripe grapes rose into the humid air, while stray stalks and the sharp branches of the vines raked their faces and arms as Ben and Danielle rushed amidst the rows. They continued running side by side until they heard a quick thump that seemed to resonate from beneath them.

"What could—"

Before Ben could finish his sentence the overhead irrigation system snapped on, drenching them thoroughly with a misty blanket of moisture, but failing to wash the blood and death from the air.

"Your damn Israeli water experts," he muttered to Danielle.

"Masters of modern technology."

They trudged on, clothes soaked and footprints instantly more noticeable in the damp ground.

"Wait!" Danielle said, seizing Ben's arm.

"What's wrong?"

"They're coming! I can hear them!"

Ben gazed back down the path that had brought them this far. "We've got to make a stand."

"I've got a better idea," Danielle said, and veered to the right.

They passed into one of the open paths that ran between the rows and found themselves in a huge swathe of land that was in the process of being cleared. At the near edge loomed a massive combine that Danielle had glimpsed a few moments before between the rows of vines. As Danielle led the way toward it, she and Ben could hear its heavy engine still idling. On the ground alongside the combine lay the body of a man.

"Yakov Katavi's father," Ben concluded grimly. "The killers must have found him out here."

"Quick!" Danielle said, starting forward.

"What?"

She didn't respond, just led him in a sprint toward the idling combine, its dagger-sharp steel teeth stretching nearly thirty feet across. Before they reached it, Ben could hear the sounds of running feet sloshing through the freshly watered ground.

Danielle handed him the Uzi and climbed up behind the controls of the combine, testing the pedals and shift as she gripped the wheel.

Ben looked on in disbelief. "Do you know what you're doing?" he asked, squeezing himself into the seat next to her.

"I spent three summers working on a kibbutz. You're damn right I do. Just stay down."

The smell of gasoline from its powerful idling engine was thick enough to taste and she feared the machine might stall out and flood as soon as she jammed it into gear. But the combine lurched forward when she engaged the transmission, sputtering once but then gathering speed across the open ground. Hesitating not at all, Danielle quickly located the controls for the cutter and threw a switch which started the machine's steel teeth churning.

The sounds of the pumps driving the irrigation outlets disguised the combine's engine enough to keep the gunmen from realizing Danielle's gambit. Rows and rows of grape vines were chewed up in the combine's wake, but the gunmen never saw the huge machine until it burst from a row almost directly before them.

Ben watched their eyes bulge in terror. One or two managed to get off a few errant shots while the rest turned to flee. The bullets clanged off the heavy steel of the combine as the machine swallowed the world in its path. It seemed almost surreal when it finally caught up with the first men, drawing them into its churning teeth and giving nothing but a red-stained ground back. The combine sucked them in and ground them up with a crackling sound like wood being fed into a chipper. The combine never slowed or even buckled, just rolled on effortlessly with whatever was left of the gunmen spread in red streaks over the earth in its wake.

Danielle spun round in her seat, gun ready, to see if any had managed to escape the churning blades. But there was nothing to the rear but a series of moist, pulpy splotches coating the ground.

"I guess we can forget about interrogating them, Inspector," she said.

Ben held his gaze on the gunmen's remains. "Who were they, Pakad? Who the hell were they?"

CHAPTER 28

CAPTAIN ASHER BAIN was waiting when the car pulled through the security gate and curled round the circular drive that fronted the house. It was one of the largest of the many magnificent homes built on the shores of the Mediterranean in the affluent suburb of Herzliya Pituah twelve miles from Tel Aviv.

"Good evening, ma'am," Bain said as he opened the car's right rear door.

The woman slid out high heels first, her long legs and hips clad in tight-fitting black pants. "My, you're a chivalrous one now, aren't you?"

Bain looked her over carefully. "I don't believe I've seen you here before."

"Special order, lover. What the general wants, the general gets." She gazed about her. "I thought this house was on the beach."

"We're two blocks away. More privacy back here."

"I can see why," she said with a wink, suddenly distracted. "Nice breeze. Hey, I can hear the sea."

"I'm glad," Bain said, stiffening. "You've been briefed, I assume."

The woman nodded. "What about you?" She wiggled her fingers before him. "Cash in advance, honey."

Bain handed her an envelope. The woman leafed through its contents, eyes gleaming, before depositing the envelope in her handbag.

"Come this way," Bain said, after the woman had clamped the bag shut again. He detested these nocturnal binges of General Efrain Janush, but the general, who was deputy chief of staff for the Israeli army, insisted upon them. Bain revered the man too much to voice his displeasure. Besides, he understood. Understood that the general's position ruled out all pretext of a private life. Understood the madness that festered just beneath the surface of the great war hero's psyche. If this was what it took to keep that madness at bay, then so be it. Certainly the general had that much coming to him.

Bain had attended all three of the funerals of the general's children. Two of the boys had been lost to war: one in Lebanon and one to a suicide bomber targeting a barracks. But it was the death of his daughter to cancer that pushed the general over the edge. His unmitigated hatred and mistrust of the Arabs was legendary, had been responsible for him being denied the position of chief of staff when he was up for it. The general fretted briefly, then continued about his business, resolved to do the job of protecting the nation of Israel that he had sworn to do.

Only Captain Bain, his chief aide, knew how he kept his hate at bay enough to do so.

Bain led tonight's woman through the foyer and up the staircase that circled toward the second floor. She walked behind him but Bain was careful to keep his pace such that she was never totally out of line of his peripheral vision. He'd been a member of the Israeli Special Forces long before accepting this post and some things stuck.

On the second floor he stopped at the third closed door they came to. "This room leads directly into the study. The door is on the left side."

The woman winked at him. "Been briefed, lover, like I told you."

"I'll be outside the whole time."

"That's up to you."

"When he's finished with you, you will leave straight-away."

"Just the way I like it," the woman said and disappeared into the room adjoining the study.

Bain assumed the stance of his silent vigil, regretting he could not move far enough from the study to obliterate the sounds that would soon be emanating from within.

Inside in the inner room the general sat stiffly in the leather chair set two yards away from a thirty-five-inch television. He heard the woman enter the adjoining room and raised the remote control device that had been set upon the chair's arm. He knew the placement of buttons by heart and went through the proper sequence without even glancing down. The first button turned the room to black, the second activated the television whose blank screen lit the room a dull gray. A third sent an unseen VCR whirling and brought the screen to life.

For all the technical wizardry, the quality of the television picture was notably poor. Grainy and ill-defined, too much contrast. The picture focused on a young woman lying naked on a bed of crimson sheets masturbating feverishly. The camera drew shakily closer to her, locked on her face.

The woman was Arabic, that much and only that much was clear.

The general's fists clenched briefly and then he groped for the pair of small headphones perched upon the other chair arm and fitted them over his ears. The sounds of her moaning filled his ears. Janush smiled in anticipation of what was to come.

Seconds later a pair of masked figures strode into the shot. Surprise filled the woman's face. They grasped and dragged her from the bed where the camera followed them to a chair. The men thrust her naked form into the chair and strapped her arms and legs to it. The woman was still struggling. Her protests filled the general's ears through his headphones. Better that way, he thought. The camera zoomed in on one of the masked figures whipping forth a knife, then panned to the bulging eyes of the woman who now lay still in hopeless terror. Her screams must have been too much for the microphone because they dissolved into static at their crescendo.

The general's thoughts burned with visions of his children. Pictures of them lined his study. Their deaths had ruined his life, filled him with a hate he was powerless to relieve and control until he happened upon this rather unique means. The psychiatrists the government had insisted he see as a matter of policy said he had to put his grief out of his head, to displace it onto something else. How right they were. The pain of others proved the only way to vanquish his own. And the pain of an Arab, well, that stretched far beyond relief to the onset of ecstasy.

On the screen the masked man sliced off the woman's right nipple. Her wail filled his ear. The sound drove Janush to moan with pleasure. As if on cue, the door from the room adjoining the study opened and the nude form of the woman emerged. She slid forward through the dark, her path illuminated by the dull haze of the television. She took her position in front of the general and crouched down. The picture's dull light splotched over her as she slid her fingers over the general's crotch and found his zipper. His hands were working through her dark hair now. Whether she was Arabic or not he could not say. Close enough, though.

On the big screen, the Arab woman reeled agonizingly back against her binds as her left nipple was severed.

The general enjoyed the irony. One of them slowly dying while another provided him pleasure. Slaves to the whims of his mind just as he had been turned into a slave of grief by their fanaticism. To live with what they had done to him, General Efrain Janush had made this the part of his life that allowed him to endure the rest of it.

The woman took him in her mouth as on screen the masked figure drew the Arab woman's head back to expose her throat. Blood slid down from the right corner of her mouth. Terror and pain had silenced her terror but her whimpers were delicious in the general's ears. The camera drew in close to capture her pleading face and then pulled back to include the knife poised for its next thrust. The general's hands dug into the head sliding back and forth over his groin.

The woman drew her hands upward, smiling to herself. Men were weak creatures, truly weak, so vulnerable to pleasure, so lost in it. How fitting that this assignment would allow her to make use of the most special skills she had developed over the years.

And the special weapon.

The idea had developed while she was watching a television commercial for artificial fingernails. A bit of glue, press on, and *voila*! The woman made her own nails, frosted the tips with melted steel, let them harden, and then filed them razor sharp. A glancing twitch to any major artery was all it took.

The woman waited, the gray shadows from the television shimmering on her naked back. She could follow the action on screen from the general's responses, his moment sure to mirror that of the blade being drawn across the Arab woman's throat.

The general watched the blade's steel touch the throat of the woman on the film, her bleeding chest lost to this angle. In his ears her final pleas emerged weakly, hopelessly. The general saw the knife begin its sweep, saw the spurt of blood lunge toward the camera as the woman's gasp filled his ears. His pleasure in that instant was so great that he felt only a slight twinge at his own throat. It was the screen again that showed him the truth because the next instant found it splattered with blood, seeming to mix almost with the dying woman's in the shot.

The general's final thought was that he must force up the air bottlenecked in his throat. At last he realized the dying gurgle in his ears was his own, since the sounds of the Arab woman dying on the screen had already been stilled.

The dead Arab stared blankly at him just as he stared at her, his corpse lit only by the pulsing glow off the television screen which had turned to static with the end of the tape.

Captain Bain didn't enter the study until he was sure it was the sound of static that filled his ears. His key swept the door's deadbolt aside and he burst inside. What he saw shocked and stunned him at the same time.

The general was sitting in his chair, blood pooling bib-like down his chest from the neat tear in his throat. His eyes bulged open, seeing nothing.

Bain saw the open window. His soldier's mind took it all in, prioritized his actions, realizing instantly that the assassin he had allowed into the house was gone.

DAY THREE

CHAPTER 29

PAUL HESSLER HAD dreamed once again of the labor camp. Every time he thought the memories were buried too deep to gnaw at him, they resurfaced with a fury and rage that made it seem like yesterday. His conscious mind had learned to control them. But Hessler enjoyed no such control over the unconscious that took over when he slept, especially in times of great stress.

Upon his return to New York, he had been met at the airport by Franklin Russett, an ex-FBI agent who currently headed up security for Hessler Industries. Russett came accompanied by a phalanx of armed men with tiny earpieces showing in their ears.

"What is this?" Hessler demanded.

"Precautions, sir," Russett reported. "Under the circumstances, I have ordered your personal security stepped up."

"Good. Now order it stepped down to the normal level."

"Sir—"

"Listen to me. I'm not going to change the way I live. I've already had to do that once in my life and I don't plan on doing it again. I'm going to do the things I always do, keep to my regular schedule. Take my walk in the morning and visit the schools every Wednesday. As much as possible, anyway."

Hessler arose as dawn was breaking over the Manhattan skyline. He had not shared his bed with another woman since his second wife divorced him, and had no desire to. But he wanted, desperately at times, to share his life with his children. Other than Ari, though, they had their own lives with no desire to follow the path he had worked so hard to fashion.

He had once envisioned a life in which all his children and grandchildren would settle in Manhattan, close enough for him to see whenever he desired. He had seen them yesterday as the family gathered in New York for Ari's funeral. A few days more, a week at most, and they would scatter again. Promises made, sure to be broken. Offers to reconsider past decisions. But the truth was none of his other children cared about the business. Only Ari.

And Ari would be buried this morning.

Hessler drew on his slippers and robe, then sat on the edge of the bed, watching the sky brighten beyond the naked windows. He thought of the camp again where the sun seemed to shine only in summer, baking the fetid ground and drawing a rancid sewer stench from it. Inside, the factory would reek of chemicals and astringents. At night, whenever possible, Hessler would scrub himself with a pilfered bar of soap. No matter how much he washed, though, he could not rid his skin of the stink like sour iodine and sulphur. At times, even today once in a while, he fancied he could catch a whiff of it rising through the fancy soaps, colognes, and silk shirts. Climbing out of his pores to remind him that it was no more gone than the memories that had produced it.

The forecast for the funeral day was hot and dry, stifling by midafternoon. The neatly trimmed cemetery grass would smell clean and the flowers fresh, but Hessler had no doubt the camp stench would rise to his nostrils before the day was done. Carve its way through skin moisturized and powdered. Lingering forever beneath the surface to remind him of how little actually separated himself from those years and that life.

Ari's death had reminded him of that, the killer's identity as impossible as it was unavoidable.

How could this have happened?

Just when Paul Hessler's life was at last coming together, the past fled and gone, and the future bright with Ari at the helm of his vast empire.

Ari had been the one since birth, taking an interest in his father's business almost from the time he could speak. Trying to spell the names of Hessler Industries' vast holdings on his alphabet blocks. Asking his father for a list as soon as he could read it. Reading the daily reports and stock quotes before he had learned to multiply.

Paul Hessler's shoulders slumped. He sat on the edge of his bed and sobbed. The past held nothing but pain and now the future, just days before so promising, held the same. Paul knew all too well what it was like to live without hope and now he would know it again.

Perhaps he should care more about who the killer at Ben-Gurion Airport had been working with, let Chief Inspector Danielle Barnea do the job he had chosen her for just two days before. But he couldn't take the chance. Better to let whoever was really behind his son's death remain free than to risk destroying the legacy that would have been his.

Hessler knew Franklin Russett was right about the need to increase security. He didn't believe for a minute that the attempt on his life in Tel Aviv was an isolated incident. Someone had looked into the past and found the truth. And Hessler knew such things tended to become more complicated rather than less.

But today, for now, none of that mattered. Today the ghosts of his past would walk by his side, bringing with them the nose-curdling chemical stink that had hung like a weight in the air of the labor camp outside of Lodz.

Today he was burying his son.

CHAPTER 30

DANIELLE ARRIVED AT her office to find the door locked. She searched her chain for the proper key, inserted it, and turned.

Nothing happened. The key wouldn't budge.

She turned, forcing a smile and trying to appear nonchalant. A few subordinates, *Mefakeah misneh* and *Sgan mefakeah*, sub and deputy inspectors, turned away to avoid meeting her glance. Danielle slid past them to the elevator where she pressed 4.

On the top floor of National Police headquarters, Moshe Baruch's assistant wasn't at his desk, but the commander's door was open. Danielle approached it to find him sitting comfortably behind his desk, his expression just short of a smile.

"I've been expecting you, Pakad."

"I can't get into my office."

"I know. I had the lock changed."

Danielle felt heat rising inside her, a furnace switched on.

Baruch leaned forward and studied her. "It looks as if you've been in quite a scrap. Finally met your match, eh?"

Danielle looked him square in the eye. "No, not yet."

The commander suddenly turned from her gaze. "Would you like to tell me what happened, Pakad?"

Danielle hesitated. "I was going to. In time."

Baruch rested his thick elbows on the blotter. She hated seeing him behind the desk used by her mentor Hershel Giott for so many years, listened to it creak from the strain of his bulk. "And whose time would that be? Yours? Mine? Your Palestinian friend's?"

"You'd be wise to listen to what we uncovered."

"Totally against protocol in a time when contact with Palestinian officials is strictly prohibited without official authorization."

"I did what I had to."

"And finally pissed your career away in the process."

Danielle could see that Baruch was actually enjoying himself. But suddenly his huge jowls puckered and tightened, lips quivering as his eyes seemed to dip deeper into his head like an animal ready to pounce. He picked up a two-sided piece of paper and let it flutter back to the desk.

"This is an exhumation and autopsy order on a deceased girl named Beth Jacober that's been given a level one priority." Baruch picked the paper up again, as if to study it anew. Then he flapped it before her. "It is signed by your superior, the *Rav pakad*, superintendent, who never saw the order until I showed it to him. Who do you suppose forged his signature?"

Danielle could do nothing but stand there.

"You have an explanation for this, Pakad?"

"I was following orders."

"You were? Whose?"

"Yours."

Baruch shook his head disdainfully. "So now, Pakad, you are reduced to lying."

"You gave me the files of two deceased children to close."

"Neither of which has crossed my desk . . ."

"Because I have elected to keep open one of the files, that of Michael Saltzman."

"But it wasn't his body you ordered exhumed and autopsied under level one status."

"No."

"It was the body of this teenage girl on a case already closed by the police in Tel Aviv. Routine driving accident. The girl's parents are very, very irate. They were, in fact, quite adamant about filing civil charges against you and the department, when I spoke with them this morning."

"You sound like you hope that they do, Commander."

"You understand I would have no choice but to testify on their behalf, Pakad. To tell the court you were not acting on my orders or performing within the acceptable limits of the investigation given you."

"Investigation?" Danielle's head was burning now, and there was a pressure building behind her eyes. Static bounced between her ears. "You call following up the routine deaths of children an investigation? How many more of these cases were you expecting to give me, Commander?"

"As many as it takes."

"To what? Make me quit? I won't, you know."

"You no longer have a choice."

Danielle's cheeks sizzled. "I'll file a grievance."

"Because I treated you so badly?"

"You're damn right."

"You had just completed an especially difficult case when I was named head of National Police."

"So what?"

"And you were pregnant."

"And that's your excuse for locking me out of my office?"

"I'm sorry you have misinterpreted my intentions, Pakad. I gave a pregnant investigator who had nearly been killed a series of simple assignments so she could maintain her rank and standing. I see that providing you such a consideration was a mistake."

Danielle could only look at him. Baruch had her and she knew it. "Then let me do my job."

"The job you never completed?"

"Michael Saltzman didn't commit suicide. Beth Jacober's accident was anything but. Order the autopsy. It will prove that."

"Prove what?"

"That she was dead *before* the crash. She and Michael Saltzman were friends, classmates. They attended the same school for a time—a Palestinian-Israeli collaborative outside of Jerusalem. And at least two other students from their class are dead as well, all in the past week or so, including a boy named Katavi living in the Golan Heights. His entire family was murdered yesterday and this time the killers didn't bother to make it look like an accident."

Baruch seemed to be studying her bruises. "And how do you know this?"

"Because we were there!"

"We?"

Danielle tried to wet her lips, but her tongue had turned dry.

"National Police is actively investigating the killing of this family," Baruch resumed.

"What about the bodies?"

"We have them."

"I'm talking about the bodies of the killers."

"We only found the murdered family."

"The killers were there. Check the fields. Check for blood."

"We intend to, Pakad. And when we do will we find any of your blood at the scene?"

"Yes."

"Anyone else's I should know about?"

Danielle tried not to hesitate. "Ben Kamal's."

"So you saw fit to involve a Palestinian in your investigation?"

"It's not just my investigation. There's at least one Palestinian student from the same school who's been killed as well. All the students were friends."

"The Israelis and this Palestinian?"

"You find that very hard to believe, don't you, Commander?"

Baruch shook his head disparagingly. "Where have you been these last few months, Pakad? Open your eyes. Face reality. There is no longer any spirit of cooperation between our peoples; there never was really. It was all just a myth and you fell for it."

"That has nothing to do with this investigation."

"It has *everything* to do with it. You have committed an act of gross insubordination. Grounds for suspension, even termination, if not actual arrest." Baruch lowered his voice and laced it with a false ring of compassion. "I'm not going to do that, though, under the circumstances. Instead, I'm going to reassign you to administration on the first floor. We will discuss your future in more detail following the maternity leave I'm sure you were about to file for. Do you find that fair, Pakad?"

"And my investigation?" Danielle asked.

"Murdered children here and in the West Bank? There is no investigation."

Danielle swallowed hard, feeling her pride forced down with the air. "Just check the results of Beth Jacober's autopsy, the real cause of her death."

"I have."

"You . . ."

Baruch pulled a manila folder from his desk and let it flop to the blotter where his elbows had worn thick indentations in the cardboard. "It's right here. You can read it yourself if you want, but I'll save you the trouble: Beth Jacober died of massive head trauma caused by the single car accident she was involved in. Her blood alcohol was one-point-five. Satisfied?"

Danielle looked at the folder sitting on Baruch's desk. "But . . ."

"You're due in administration in twenty minutes," Baruch said, holding back a satisfied grin. "Don't be late."

CHAPTER 31

"**I** HOPE YOU'RE hungry, Inspector," Colonel Nabril al-Asi greeted, waiting until his wife and children had boarded the cable car before ushering Ben inside.

"I didn't know you were bringing your family," Ben said, uncomfortable, as the colonel's youngest two sons and daughter pushed each other for the best view of the Mount of Temptation they would soon be ascending.

"Relax, Inspector, this is part of my resolution to spend more time with my family. The reason I never had any time for them before was because I was all business. Now, sometimes, they accompany me on my business."

Ben realized the car was empty except for himself and al-Asi's family. The colonel's wife was doing her best to make peace between his children. She was younger than he had guessed and more attractive, dressed in Western-style clothing every bit as fashionable as her husband's European designer suits.

"And sometimes my work accompanies them," al-Asi continued, leading Ben to the opposite end of the twenty-passenger cable car. "Have a seat, Inspector."

Ben had barely sat down when the cable car jerked forward and then settled into a smooth ride up the barren, rocky slope. He knew the Mount of Temptation got its name from being the place where Christian theologians teach Christ withstood temptation by Satan after his baptism in the Jordan River. On the terraced cliff directly above the cable car, hidden by caves where Jesus purportedly fasted for more than a month, a French restaurant was now in operation.

"You know," al-Asi said, reading Ben's mind, "this was all made possible by the Authority negotiating a deal with the Greek Orthodox Church which controls the Mount. I wonder if they realized what they were getting into. Another ten years and our little district of Jericho will have ten thousand hotel rooms and enough tourists to fill every one of them."

"Something to look forward to . . ."

"Have you eaten in this restaurant, Inspector?"

"Not yet."

"You must try the *musakhana*," al-Asi said, referring to a popular Beduoin chicken dish. "Or the *mansaf*."

Ben recalled the sweet smell of seasonings that would linger in the house for days after his mother made that spicy meal. "It's a little early in the day for rice and beef, Colonel."

"Precisely the reason why you can look forward to crepes, fancy egg dishes, French pastry—all yours for the asking."

"I didn't know the restaurant opened for breakfast."

"It doesn't. The proprietors generously made an exception today."

Before them the perfectly beveled and shiny face of the Mount drew closer. Up close it looked like dark, dull ice thirsting for the sun. Untouched by man and barely hospitable to his presence, if the grinding of the car's cables overhead was any indication.

Al-Asi turned his gaze back to the front of the cable car, where his children had at last made peace. "You've never met my wife, have you, Inspector?"

"No."

"Then this morning will be the perfect opportunity for us all to become better acquainted. A pity Pakad Barnea couldn't join us. I should have given you more notice."

"It wouldn't have helped."

"Problems between you, I gather."

"Just the usual."

"And which usual is that, Inspector? The usual where you visited each other regularly, or the more recent usual where you don't see each other at all?"

"You've been keeping tabs on me."

The boyish glint flickered in al-Asi's grayish eyes. "For your own good, of course. And Pakad Barnea's. We wouldn't want any enemies to take advantage of a perceived vulnerability."

"And have they tried?"

Al-Asi shrugged noncommittally. "If you haven't noticed, then what's the difference?"

The cable car squealed on, halfway to the summit now.

"Anything new on the disc recovered at the soccer stadium?" Ben wondered.

"You mean the disc *you* recovered. Sometimes you are much too modest, Inspector."

"Fasil's hand-off was obvious."

Al-Asi frowned. "I wish the contents of that disc were equally obvious. But unfortunately they still don't seem to make any sense. The disc certainly doesn't seem connected to the most wanted terrorist in Palestine."

"Not anymore, Colonel."

"Thanks to your expert marksmanship. I haven't forgotten our trip to the shooting range. We'll go next week. The Israelis have sent us a new shipment of pistols I've been wanting to try out."

Ben gazed out the cable car's window to check their progress up the mountain. "What more have you learned about the Ashawi family, Colonel?"

Al-Asi slid a little closer to Ben on the seat. "They have not left the West Bank and the only relatives they have live in the Aida refugee camp in Bethlehem. Their family has no history of operations against Israel or links to Hamas. Not a single registered arrest by either us or the Israeli authorities."

"What about their daughter Zeina?"

"Pretty much what you told me. An honor student who's already won scholarships to a number of American universities. First in her class and perfect attendance in school until eight days ago."

"When her friends from the collaborative school she attended for a semester started dying."

Al-Asi frowned. "I can't tell you whether the Ashawis have moved in with their relatives at Aida; I'm afraid my contacts in refugee camps are not what they used to be. When the fences came down, my informants went with them. In any case, you will set off with a full stomach this morning, Inspector. Which is more than I can say for the residents of Aida."

Ben's cell phone rang and he snatched it from his pocket, hoping it was Danielle on the other end of the line. He excused himself and slid away from Colonel al-Asi.

"Hello."

"Good morning, Inspector," a husky voice greeted.

"Mr. Najarian?"

"I hadn't heard from you, thought I'd give you a call before I headed back to the States."

"How did you get my number?"

"I'm in the security business, remember?"

Ben stole a sidelong glance at the colonel. "Next time just ask me for it."

"Have you given any thought to my offer?"

"I haven't had time yet."

"I'm thinking about you to head up our Special Investigations unit. A private force of detectives paid to solve crimes botched or ignored by local authorities. I could show you the projections. Do you have some time?"

"Not today."

"Oh well. You have my number in Detroit, yes?"

"Yes."

"Let's talk soon."

Ben pressed the end button and turned back to al-Asi. "I'm sorry, Colonel."

"For what, Inspector?" Al-Asi smiled contently. "You haven't taken the job yet."

CHAPTER 32

DANIELLE'S NEW OFFICE was a single prefabricated desk squeezed in among dozens of others like it, lacking even the wood veneer of her former one upstairs. Administrative workers at National Police held no rank and were generally poorly paid.

A male supervisor with a bird's nest of curly hair and a mouthful of gum who looked all of twenty-five had escorted Danielle to her desk and promised to return presently to brief her on her duties. He wore a white shirt with faded tentacle-like ink stains running down the left side in spite of his plastic pocket protector. He had left her almost an hour ago now, during which time Danielle had busied herself by carving neat patterns with a pocket knife on the underside of her top desk drawer. She was amazed by how much the juvenile response, like that of a wrongly disciplined child, satisfied her. But that made her think of her own child again and sadness quickly engulfed her emotions.

Again and again she replayed her conversation with Commander Moshe Baruch in her head. He had finally gotten the upper hand with her; Danielle had made it so easy she began to wonder if he hadn't set this whole scenario up. More likely he had just waited for her to make the kind of mistake he knew would be inevitable, because he knew her.

Somehow it was the autopsy results on the exhumed body of Beth Jacober that Danielle kept coming back to. Baruch said he had read the report and insisted it had shed no new light on the girl's death. Danielle was certain he'd been telling the truth, just as she was certain that Beth Jacober *had* been murdered. The autopsy report *should* have shown that, which meant it had been altered.

By whom?

Someone with a powerful reach, that was for sure. Someone with a very good reason to want the systematic execution of high school classmates to remain unnoticed.

The phone on Danielle's desk rang, startling her. She cleared her throat and reached for it, then pulled her hand back, having no idea of what she might be asked and what she was supposed to say in return. She made a mental note to call Dr. Barr and give him her new work number.

The phone kept ringing. Some of Danielle's coworkers began to turn her way.

Finally she picked it up.

"Hello?"

"Chief Inspector Barnea?"

"Not anymore."

"I know. I'm sorry."

"You *know*? Who is this? How did you get my number? I don't even know my number."

"I need to see you."

Danielle gazed around the room. Workers everywhere with their dreams tucked into the brown lunch bags they hauled to work with them.

"Does this have something to do with an administrative problem?"

"You were investigating the murder of Paul Hessler's son, yes?"

"I'm afraid I can't—"

"Please, this is for your own good."

"All right. I was assigned to that investigation for a very brief period, a single afternoon. Until someone else took over."

"That's what we need to talk about."

Danielle leaned forward. "What do you know about this murder?"

"That it's connected to others."

Danielle reined herself in, imagining Moshe Baruch listening on the other end of the line biting his fleshy lip to hold back his laughter. Danielle Barnea, the old investigative fire horse, charging off at the first sound of a bell straight into professional oblivion.

"How is it connected?" she posed tentatively.

"I told you, we need to meet."

"Not until you tell me who you are."

"My name is Asher Bain. Until last night I was chief aide to deputy chief of staff of the army, General Efrain Janush."

"What happened?"

"He was murdered."

Danielle looked around the room for the gum-chewing, wild-haired supervisor and spotted him checking items off on a clipboard, having forgotten she existed. "Where would you like to meet?"

For paul hessler, the funeral of his son passed in a blur. The hordes in attendance, overflowing the temple auditorium, were of no comfort to him. Many of them did not even know Ari, or knew him only cursorily through business. They had flown here from far and wide, not out of grief so much as an obligation to Paul himself. Their condolences were expressed honestly behind warm, dry handshakes. But most were here because they worried what their absence might look like.

The truly grieving, Ari's lifelong friends and fraternity brothers from college, the young people he worked with in the company, were the ones Paul wanted to be around. They truly knew his son; the loss they suffered, thus, as real as his own. Paul came almost to detest the numbing recitals of regret; there would be nothing but these for the next three days and nights of shiva, the Jewish memorial tradition.

Ari's mother Elaine, whom Paul had not seen since they divorced, seemed at first to have changed, enough so Paul had to wonder if she had given up drinking. But at the gathering after the funeral she downed wine glass after wine glass, the red and white mixing in her head to leave her in the dull fog he remembered all too well. She leaned on her new husband through the reception's final hour, the man constantly checking the Rolex watch that Paul Hessler's money had bought him.

Paul's other children, meanwhile, provided a sense of solidarity and many obligatory smiles and hugs that left him smelling of whatever perfume his daughters had donned. He found himself concentrating as much as possible on the grandchildren he seldom saw, wondering if there might be an Ari among them, a namesake to whom he could someday entrust the future of Hessler Industries.

In a room jammed with milling, well-meaning people, Paul Hessler had never felt more alone. The only thing that rivaled the last few days for desperate loneliness was the trek he had made through Poland after his escape from the labor camp outside Lodz near the end of 1944. He remembered each moment and mile with a clarity that had never faded with time. Always pushing on, telling himself another hour, another mile, before he could rest.

While he could escape the labor camp in the war's final days, though, he could not escape the death of his son. At night, when sleep wouldn't come, he tried to apologize out loud to Ari for being responsible for his death. There were some things a father never shares even with his son and the greatest of these had come back to haunt Paul Hessler.

An old, arthritic man coming at him outside Ben-Gurion Airport. A ghost who hadn't given up breathing yet. After all these years . . .

Why? And how, in God's name, had he found out?

Paul had intended to explain everything to Ari in time, had even planned the time and place.

At the castle. Upon its completion.

Over three years ago, Paul Hessler had struck a deal with the State of New Jersey to lease for one dollar per year a large tract of land in the cliffs of Palisades State Park overlooking the Hudson River north of the George Washington Bridge. On this land he had reconstructed a medieval castle that would be open to the public and, perhaps, someday turned into a museum modeled after the Metropolitan's Cloisters located across the Hudson.

Every time Paul saw the nearly completed castle, he viewed it as it had been fifty-seven years before when finding it in the woods beyond Leczyca, Poland, had saved his life following his escape from the camp. That was how he would have started telling the story to Ari, with the part that was already known. The part that was a prime component of the Hessler legend.

Upon learning that the Polish government was about to raze its crumbling structure, Paul Hessler bought the castle and had the limestone blocks that formed its walls taken apart, numbered, and crated for shipping to New York, and then reassembled along the cliffs of Palisades State Park. Much of the original structure was gone in the late fall of 1944; even less of it remained today. The surrounding wall had collapsed into piles of rubble and the inner gardens had been a memory since the castle was abandoned during the Protestant uprising of the sixteenth century. The ancient structure constructed in the fourteenth century originally had six towers, but only four remained in any shape to rebuild. The pink marble pilasters and carved stone columns were crumbling yet still could be restored for a price only Paul Hessler was willing to pay.

He had returned to Poland personally to supervise the initial process himself. Trucks had ferried the vast amount of disassembled materials, all carefully labeled and photographed, to chartered cargo planes. Hessler had ordered the four remaining towers, though, to be removed intact, using state of the art laser equipment to shear them from their bases. Cranes then lowered the towers into huge flatbed trucks for the trip to the airport.

Once in New Jersey, Hessler paid to build a complex of roads wide and sturdy enough to allow the towers and the rest of the pieces to be carried by cargo trucks to the construction site in Palisades State Park. And even then those roads had proven barely wide enough to accommodate the heavy-duty cranes required to safely raise the towers back into place upon the cliffs.

Paul Hessler hadn't seen the castle in over a month, since he had left for Israel to oversee deployment of the Arrow antimissile system. He knew the final stages of the massive effort were nearing an end, including the renovations and reconstruction aimed at creating a fully functional replica. To accomplish that, he had hired a dozen artists to re-create the fresco paintings of various landscapes that highlighted areas the castle's original owner had visited, and stonemasons to repair the walls and rebuild the cracked and broken stone benches that rimmed many of them.

In the soon-to-be-re-created gardens, Paul would have begun to tell his son what had really transpired within those walls over a half century before. The secret he had shared with no man. The secret that held the real reason why he had rebuilt this piece of his past so close to his New York City home.

"Sir?"

Paul turned to see an attractive woman standing at his side, cup of coffee extended toward him. In the camp prisoners had been allotted two cups of coffee per day, though it was never hot. That, just over two hundred grams of bread, and two servings of barely a liter of soup had constituted his entire daily ration.

"Thank you," Paul said, accepting the cup from the woman in a hand he willed not to tremble. He was certain he knew her, but couldn't place her exactly. "Thank you, er . . ."

"I'm Tess Sanderson, Mr. Hessler. I work for you or, more accurately, I worked for Ari."

"Have we met before?"

"Not officially, no. I just wanted to say how sorry I am."

Paul shrugged, waiting for the woman to drift away as all the others did.

"There's something I need to speak to you about, sir," she said instead, lowering her voice. "Concerning Ari."

"Of course. As soon as I get back to the office."

"Mr. Hessler, I think you need to hear this as soon as possible. That's what Ari would have wanted. I know he planned on telling you himself, as soon as the two of you got back to New York. He wanted to surprise you."

"Surprise me?" A memory fluttered through Paul Hessler's mind, of words that had been among his son's last—something he promised to tell his father when they returned to the city. And there was that phone call Paul had received in Tel Aviv from an associate telling him about a celebration that Ari had arranged. "Does this have something to do with a party he was planning?"

Tess Sanderson cleared her throat. "It has to do with Lot four-sixty-one."

"The project I terminated."

"Ari ordered testing restarted."

"Without my approval?" Paul asked, mystified and almost angered by his son's actions.

"He believed in the project, sir. He believed as I did that we were close. He allowed us to move forward in preliminary trials."

Paul Hessler smiled, wondering how he would have reprimanded Ari if he were alive. "Go on."

"It works, sir."

Paul blinked his eyes rapidly. "Did you say . . ."

"That's right, sir," Tess Sanderson acknowledged. "Lot four-sixty-one works."

CHAPTER 34

"A SHAWI," THE AIDA refugee camp administrator repeated, flipping through a box of file cards. "Ashawi . . ." Ben noticed an old IBM computer on his desk that wasn't even plugged in. "Just give me a moment, please."

In the complex dichotomy that Palestine had become, Ben found Bethlehem to be the most complex of all. Where Christian pilgrims used to gather in view of Manger Square, the finishing touches were being put on a controversial Israeli housing project. Not far away, a former Palestinian girls' school that had once been a sultan's palace built in the first millennium was now the Inter-Continental Bethlehem, a luxury hotel crammed with suites, gourmet restaurants, bars, and a fitness club. It was almost directly across the road from the refugee camp where Ben's investigation had led him today. Construction of the hotel had been slowed repeatedly by frequent clashes between Israeli soldiers and Palestinian youths, which often resulted in tear gas wafting across the property. It was the only project of note, Ben thought, where the workmen wore gas masks clipped to their belts.

Just beyond the hotel's lavish swimming pool, a high concrete wall was all that stood between the Inter-Continental's grounds and the Aida refugee camp where the relatives of the missing Ashawi family lived. Depending on the wind, Ben wondered if the pleasant scents of the hotel's abundant flowers and smells of gourmet food being cooked might drift into the camp. And, also depending on the wind, whether the stench of spoiled mud and overflowing sewage might disturb the hotel's wealthy guests.

Ben had parked his car outside a slipshod building that housed the Aida refugee camp's headquarters. The Palestinian Authority symbol had been painted near the door, battling that of the United Nations and the International Red Cross for supremacy. There were other smaller symbols that Ben didn't even recognize, as if the logos of international relief and support organizations had become like those of consumer products in sports arenas back in America. The West Bank was nothing if not ironic.

"Yes, of course," the camp administrator said, his hand finally emerging from the file box with a card. "I directed the other two officers to their home just a few minutes ago."

Ben felt a thud in the pit of his stomach. "Other officers?"

"What have the Ashawis done? Administration should be informed, you know," the man called after him, as Ben hurried through the door. "We are the ones in authority here!"

D ANIELLE ARRANGED TO meet Captain Asher Bain at the Holyland Hotel southwest of the city—outside the hotel, actually, near the miniature re-creation of the ancient city that adorned its grounds. Intricately reconstructed of marble, stone, wood, copper, and iron—the materials of the time—the model was an exact replica of biblical Jerusalem. Danielle was walking along the shrunken version of the great wall that had once protected the old city when a man approached her from the opposite direction.

"Pakad Barnea, I'm Captain Asher Bain."

He offered a hand and Danielle took it, feeling a powerful, callused grip. Asher Bain was only slightly taller than her own five-and-a-half feet. He was dressed in comfortably fitting clothes that could not disguise the vast bulk of his upper body and ramrod stance. He had almost no neck and a face so furrowed and angular that it seemed an artist might have taken a chisel to it one night as he slept. His slightly receding hair was cut military-close and he had the look of a man who'd be much more comfortable wearing a uniform. Holding a Galil assault rifle under his arm instead of a brochure that made him look as much like a tourist as he could.

"How do you know me, Captain Bain?"

"I've seen your picture, Pakad. On television and in the newspaper."

"I was talking about the Hessler investigation. How did you know about my brief assignment to the Hessler investigation?"

"General Janush spoke of it. He was planning to make a condolence call, considered even flying to the United States for the funeral, before . . ."

"I'm sorry about his death."

"Thank you."

"But from what I've heard he died of a heart attack."

"It's not true. I was there."

"You said he was murdered."

They walked slowly around the outskirts of a tiny ancient Jerusalem carved out of limestone with an accuracy that included even microscopic writing on a temple's doorway.

"The details don't matter," Bain told her, clearly uncomfortable. "What matters is that General Efrain Janush wasn't the only one: Two others were murdered yesterday."

"Generals?"

"Just men," said Asher Bain. "Old men with something in common."

BEN CUT THROUGH the narrow yards between houses in the camp to reach the Ashawis as quickly as he could. His instinct told him whoever had arrived ahead of him looking for the missing family weren't from the police. But there were two of them to only one of him, and based on the proficiency of their murderous work thus far, those were odds to be avoided.

By the time he was halfway to the Ashawi relatives' lot, his feet were covered in mud and manure from the gardens he had cut through in his mad dash. Ben was just two narrow, cluttered streets away when he nearly collided with a pair of uniformed Fatah representatives assigned to the camp by the Palestinian Council.

His close encounter compelled him to notice the multiple contents of their utility belts, including a flashlight, small medical pouch, walkie-talkie, and more.

"I need your help!" Ben told them, finding his breath.

The two young men looked at each other, startled.

"I'm a Palestinian policeman!" he said, shoving his identification at them. "And this is an emergency!"

"What can we do for you?"

"Just follow my lead and don't say a word." He led them on. "This way! Hurry!"

AN ELDERLY SCHOOLTEACHER killed in a bicycling accident, a prominent businessman poisoned in the course of a routine medical procedure, and General Janush, of course."

"All three died *yesterday*?"

Bain nodded. "That's right, Pakad. All men in their early to late seventies."

"Is that all they have in common, Captain?" Danielle asked Asher Bain.

"No, Pakad. All three were Holocaust survivors, just like—"

"Paul Hessler," Danielle completed for him.

S TAND TO THE side so they think you have a gun," Ben instructed the young Fatah officials as they neared the home of Abdul Ashawi's brother.

"Why?" one of them asked, hedging.

"Because it might keep you alive. Now keep moving. Hurry!"

Ben led the young Fatah officials to the shack-sized structure where the Ashawi family lived. They had just passed through the warped chickenwire fence enclosing the modest yard when a ramshackle door too big for the frame banged open.

A pair of men dressed as Palestinian policemen emerged holding between them a teenage girl whom Ben recognized from her school picture as Zeina Ashawi. Sobbing, protesting family members trailed the officers down the crumbling steps and passed out of the meager shade provided by a tattered awning. The officers ignored their pleas and their presence, stopped only when they saw Ben and the Fatah officials standing in their way.

"I'll take things from here," Ben said, making sure the two men could see how close his hand had moved to his pistol.

The imposters glanced at each other, weighing their options. Without the Fatah officials on either side of him, Ben had no doubt what option they would choose. As it was, the moment remained frozen. The family holding their ground behind the fake policemen. The fake policemen still considering their next step.

The Fatah man on Ben's left began to shake badly.

Ben moved a hand to his elbow, looked back to see one of the imposters starting to reach for his gun.

CHAPTER 35

"**H**OW DID YOU figure this out?" Danielle asked Asher Bain.

"My suspicions grew after the general was murdered and I read more about Hessler's near-murder. That made me do some checking. What I found was too striking to ignore."

"Go on," Danielle prodded.

"All four men were among the original refugees who settled here after World War Two."

"Could they have known each other since then?" Danielle probed, in search of some stray connection.

Bain shook his square, angular head. "The general knew the businessman and he had met Hessler, but he didn't know the schoolteacher who was killed in a traffic accident."

"They couldn't have met as refugees?"

"No. According to what I've been able to piece together none of the four came to Palestine on the same boat or even at the same time."

"So the only thing we know they have in common, besides being survivors, is that three of them are dead and the fourth is alive only because his son got in the way of the bullets meant for him."

"That's right."

"But why contact me?"

"Because of your connection to the Hessler investigation."

"It's been severed, Captain."

"Not before you had a chance to interview Paul Hessler himself, though. I want to know if he said anything that might relate to this. Did he act strange? Did you notice anything unusual?"

Danielle shook her head. "Not a thing." She hesitated briefly. "Not about Hessler anyway."

"Someone *else*?"

Danielle nodded very slowly. "His would-be killer."

B EN LET HIS hand drop to the butt of his pistol and steeled his eyes. In the very last instant before one of the fake policemen drew his gun, the other imposter laid a hand on his arm, restraining him. Slowly they moved away from Zeina Ashawi who looked no less terrified.

"Thank you, gentlemen," Ben said measuredly. "I will see that your commander learns of your cooperation."

Ben held his eyes on the imposters as they started forward out of the yard, passing on either side of him. When they were out of sight, the smaller of the Fatah representatives he had enlisted in the charade tried to light a cigarette but failed because he was shaking too hard. Ben lit it for him.

"Thank you," Ben said, and removed a small pad from his lapel pocket. "Give me your names. I am going to send a personal note to the president himself to inform him of your bravery."

The young men looked at each other. "Will he actually get it?" one asked.

"I know an official who will make sure that he does."

The Fatah officials nodded and gave Ben their names

before turning to leave. He had barely slipped his notebook into his pocket again when a man Ben guessed was Zeina Ashawi's father, Abdul, stormed forward.

"What is going on here? What do the police want with my daughter?"

Ben held a hand up to calm the man. "Those two men weren't really from the police, Abu Ashawi."

The man's face dipped into uncertainty. "They *weren't*? Then who . . ."

"I need to speak to your daughter inside," Ben said. "Then everything will be clear."

THE HOT SUN baked Danielle's flesh, frying the miniature city at her feet, as she tried to recapture all she had learned from the autopsy on the old man who had shot Paul Hessler's son.

"He carried no identification, not even any money."

"Because he knew he was going to die," Bain said. "This was a suicide mission from the start."

"The killer had suffered a reoccurrence of stomach cancer. He didn't have long to live anyway. But he was an American; the pathologist was sure of that much. His only distinguishing features were a glass eye and an unusual tattoo."

"What kind of tattoo?"

"A worm of some kind holding a knife in what looked like small hands with blood dripping down the blade. And there was a name written across the tattoo: NIGHTCRAWLERS."

"A common earthworm that feeds at night."

"I didn't know you were an expert on worms, Captain."

"I'm not. But the term 'Nightcrawlers' has other connotations."

"Such as . . ."

"I don't want to say until I'm sure. You say the dead man was in his seventies?"

"Yes, probably an American veteran of World War

Two. Or the Korean War, both even, but from the age of some old scars the pathologist felt almost certain he fought in World War Two." Danielle tried to gauge his reaction. "But what does something that happened back then have to do with this?"

Bain's expression remained stoic, stonelike in its rigid cast. She was about to press him when her cell phone rang. Thinking it might be Ben she snatched it quickly to her ear.

"Hello."

"Pakad Barnea?" A woman's voice.

"Yes. Who is this?"

"It's Layla Saltzman—Michael's mother." The words emerging between uncomfortable breaths.

"Yes, Mrs. Saltzman?"

"I don't mean to bother you. It's just that, well, I found . . . something in Michael's room and I, well, I don't know who else to call."

"What did you find?"

"You need to see it, Pakad. Trust me, you need to see it."

CHAPTER 36

MY DAUGHTER IS ready to speak with you now, Inspector," Abdul Ashawi said finally, leading his daughter out from an inner room after she had taken several moments to compose herself. "She will answer any questions you may have."

Zeina looked thin and pale, reluctant to leave her father's grasp. She let her dark brown hair tumble freely over her shoulders, a western style Ben thought she might have picked up at the cooperative school. Her eyes of the same dark shade were jittery and evasive.

"Come, Inspector," Abdul Ashawi told him, "over here."

Ben had decided not to rush the girl into talking. Instead he busied himself with getting to know the family better, earning their trust. This house in the Aida refugee camp belonged to Abdul's brother. It was three small, dark rooms which made for a tight squeeze even for the two adults and three children who normally lived here, never mind the five guests who'd been hiding out for a week now. The women moved into the tiny kitchen to prepare tea and pastries, relieved Zeina was not being taken into custody. What Ben had not figured out yet was how to guard against the probability that more men, dispatched by those who had sent the fake policemen, would be coming back for her.

A half hour later the teenage girl was finally ready to tell her story, sipping warm tea from a paper cup because her aunt had run out of the few ceramic and glass ones the family owned. Ben noticed none of them matched.

"It is all right if I join you?" Abdul Ashawi asked.

"I insist that you do," Ben said, even though nothing currently in Palestinian law provided for parents being present during the questioning of minors.

A place was made for the three of them on small chairs squeezed before an ancient soot-colored stove that smelled of rust.

"Did you enjoy the school for Palestinians and Jews you attended last semester near Abu Gosh, Zeina?"

She smiled slightly, relieved by the nature of his question. "Yes. Very much. It was a good school. I learned much."

"I understand you made some very good friends."

Now she stiffened slightly. "A few."

"Michael Saltzman, he was one of them?"

"Yes."

"And Beth Jacober?"

A nod this time.

"And Shahir Falaya."

Another nod.

"What about Yakov Katavi?"

Zeina Ashawi turned pleadingly to her father.

"Is this really necessary?" the man asked Ben.

"You moved your family here without telling a soul," Ben replied, focusing on him. "Why did you find that suddenly necessary, Abu Ashawi?"

The man said nothing.

"I believe you came here to hide after three of your daughter's friends died within a week of each other." Ben looked at Zeina Ashawi again. "I'm sorry to report that

Yakov Katavi was added to the list yesterday."

"*Mish mumkin!*" Zeina moaned. "That can't be!"

"It was not made to look like an accident or suicide this time. The boy was murdered in his home, shot, along with his parents." Ben leaned forward, and the tiny chair creaked under his weight. He looked to Abdul Ashawi. "If I hadn't arrived when I did, those men pretending to be policemen would have taken your daughter and you never would have seen her again. I want to protect her, Abu Ashawi. I want to protect all of you. But I need to know why four of your daughter's classmates—and friends—are dead."

Abu Ashawi looked at his daughter and nodded.

"I didn't have anything to do with it!" she pleaded to Ben. "I stopped being friends with them, I swear!"

"I believe you," Ben said. "Just tell me what was going on."

Zeina Ashawi nodded and began to speak.

L AYLA SALTZMAN OPENED the front door as soon as she saw Danielle coming up the walk of her house in the Jerusalem suburb of Har Adar.

"If I've done something wrong by calling you . . ."

Danielle thought of her supervisor, barely in his twenties, reporting her disappearance to Commander Moshe Baruch. "You've done nothing wrong. Just show me what you found."

The house looked and felt unchanged from two days before. The same smells hung in the air, a bit staler now.

"I thought it was time to start going through Michael's things," Layla Saltzman explained. "Nothing else helped me. I hoped that might."

They reached a doorway to a bedroom and Layla Saltzman flipped on a light, revealing the room of a typical teenage boy. A stereo and television battled books for space on the shelves. A Fender guitar and a set of Alpine skis leaned against each other in one corner. A pair of jeans with one leg turned inside out lay on the floor just in front of the closet. A tropical fish tank rested close enough to the window to capture a portion of the afternoon light, its filter humming softly.

Layla Saltzman moved to her son's twin-sized bed, the covers rumpled and the mattress still holding a faint impression from where the boy used to lie upon it. A storage drawer built into the bed's underside was open, revealing a clutter of what must have been Michael's shirts and jeans.

"The drawer was stuck," his mother explained, voice cracking. "And when I yanked it, it came all the way out. I put it back as soon as I saw."

"Saw what?"

Danielle watched as Layla Saltzman pulled the drawer forward off its runners, on purpose this time.

"That," was all she said, indicating what was revealed behind the storage compartment.

Danielle crouched low and shined her pocket-sized flashlight into the darkness. Blinked rapidly, unable to believe what she was looking at.

I WANTED TO be friends with them," Zeina Ashawi said, looking mostly at her father instead of Ben. "I liked them and they liked me. They knew I was smart, good with a computer. They had this . . . plan."

Ben remained silent, letting the girl tell the tale at her own pace.

"I don't know whose idea it was—Shahir's, I think," she continued finally. "But it had to do with money. They were going to make a lot of money."

Ben was taken aback by the revelation. He had assumed the students had been innocent victims of something they stumbled upon or become involved in coincidentally. The possibility that their own actions had precipitated their deaths, as their friend's assertion seemed to indicate, was the last thing he had expected to hear.

"Go on," Ben prompted, hiding his surprise.

Zeina Ashawi gazed at her father again before resuming. "I don't know everything. I don't even know a lot. I stopped hanging around with them when I realized what it was all about, what they were really up to."

"Which was?"

DANIELLE REACHED INTO the darkness under Michael Saltzman's bed and pulled the backpack toward her, confirming what the glimpse of its contents her flashlight had revealed:

The backpack was full of money. Neatly wrapped stacks of American twenty dollar bills were packed into it, spilling out from the top. So much the bag couldn't even be zippered closed. Between fifty and a hundred thousand dollars, Danielle judged.

"I'd like to tell you that was Michael's Bar Mitzvah money," Layla Saltzman said, but the joke failed miserably. "I thought maybe it had something to do with his death. I never believed it was suicide. I told you that."

There was a strange hint of hope in her voice, in search of some minor consolation that her son's death had been something truly out of her control.

"When was the last time you looked into this space?" Danielle asked her.

"Oh, years. Probably not since the bedroom set was delivered." Layla Saltzman's eyes teared up and she swiped at them with her sleeve. "Yes, years. And there's something else," Layla Saltzman told her. "That backpack-it's not Michael's."

Danielle noticed the initials on it were BKJ.

Beth Jacober.

Danielle tried picturing the four classmates as a kind of adolescent crime ring. Up to something that had led to their deaths. Drugs were the first thing that came to mind. An increasing business in Israel, she knew.

Yet the killers she and Ben had encountered in the Go-

lan Heights yesterday did not behave at all like drug deal-
ers. And those involved in the drug trade never resorted
to the kind of subtleties whoever killed these high school
students had initially exhibited. A suicide and a car accident in Israel. A random carjacking in Jericho. Only the
killings in the Golan had been different. But if she and
Ben had not shown up when they did, who knows what
the killers would have painted the scene to look like? A
Syrian raiding party, perhaps.

Not drugs. No.

What then?

BLACKMAIL," ZEINA ASHAWI said after try-
ing to settle herself with a deep breath. "They were going
to blackmail people. Big, powerful, important people."

"How?"

"I don't know. I told you I didn't get involved after I
found out. I stopped hanging around with them. But I
didn't tell anyone else. It was none of my business." The
girl sat back, as if she was finished.

"What else?"

"They were planning to make a lot of money. I know
that."

Ben recalled the missing hard drive from Shahir Falaya's computer.

"A couple of them were good with computers. Could it
have something to do with that?"

Zeina Ashawi shrugged. "Maybe. Or . . ."

"Yes?"

"Maybe it had something to do with Shahir's job in
Israel."

"Why do you say that?"

"The way he talked sometimes. About how this after-
school job was going to make him rich. I didn't pay attention. I thought he was kidding. You know how boys
talk."

"Of course. Do you know what this job was?"

"The school got it for him. I know that. It must have been with some big company. I think he found something out while he was working there. That's possible, isn't it?"

"That's all you can tell me about who your friends intended to blackmail?"

She stiffened again. "They weren't my friends anymore. I told you."

"And it was just these four."

Zeina Ashawi hedged a little. "I think there may have been someone else."

"The others never mentioned a name?"

"No, but they said things. I don't know. I can't be sure. But I think another student was involved. Not right away—later."

"So you severed your friendship with the murdered students before they actually got started," Ben concluded.

"I don't even know who they intended to blackmail. Or how they found out whatever it was they knew. Or how much money they made. After awhile, right up until the term ended, they didn't bother with me anymore. It was like I wasn't there; the whole rest of the class wasn't there. It was just the four of them and now *they're dead!*"

Zeina Ashawi lurched off the chair into her father's arms. The chair toppled over and clanged against the stove.

"They came for me!" she sobbed. *"Those awful men came for me!"*

Abdul Ashawi stroked his daughter's hair, his eyes finding Ben's. "You saved my daughter's life. For this, my family and I are forever in your debt."

"Then let me protect you," Ben said, rising. "All of you."

"Inspector?"

"You need to be hidden someplace safe where they can't get to you. They'll come again otherwise."

Abdul Ashawi hugged his daughter tighter. "But she told you everything she knows. She can't hurt them, whoever they are."

"They don't know that."

The man's pockmarked face reddened. "Who murders children, Inspector?"

"Someone who believes they have a reason, Abu Ashawi, and now I have to find out what that reason is."

CHAPTER 37

W HAT'S THE MATTER?" Abraham Vorsky asked Hans Mundt. "You don't like the food?"

Mundt stared at the hummus platter with pita, falafel,
onions, and pickles set before him. The restaurant Abu
Shukri was located a few hundred yards from Damascus
Gate, on the left as the Via Dolorosa breaks to the right
in Jerusalem. The restaurant was too crowded and noisy
for Mundt. Bare wood tables packed on top of each other
with conversations drifting into the air to join the cigarette
smoke, caught by the ceiling fans and spun lazily about.
Mundt found himself wishing he had told Vorsky to
choose a simpler place.

"I thought you would approve," the old man said.

"I'm not hungry."

"I was talking about the setting. Plenty of activity and
people." Vorsky glanced around in search of their waiter.
"I don't know what's happened to our next course. . . ."

"I assume the men whose names I provided you have
been dealt with."

Vorsky continued to look for their waiter. "That is no
longer your concern."

"Since you wanted to see me, though, I take it you were satisfied with the reliability of my information."

Vorsky stopped looking for their waiter and looked across the table at Mundt. "I am not satisfied with what it forced me to do." He munched on a pickle, crinkling his nose as if it tasted bitter.

"But you would still like the rest of the names, wouldn't you?"

Vorsky swallowed the last of his pickle and leaned across the table. "I would like to know how you came by this information, Herr Mundt."

"The same way I came by the other names I'm sure you'd like to have in your possession."

"Might it have something to do with a trip you made to Poland recently, to an area outside the city of Lodz, I believe?"

Mundt knew the statement was a veiled threat, meant to emphasize the resources and capabilities Vorsky still possessed. "That is not your concern."

"And I should take your word on that?"

"If you want the rest of the names, yes."

"Have you brought them with you?"

"Have you brought the database you promised I could access? Quid pro quo, remember?"

"How many more names are there?" the old man asked, scratching his thin beard.

"You will get none of them until you live up to your end of the bargain."

"What are you looking for?"

Mundt remained expressionless. "Certainty."

"A difficult commodity to come by these days."

"Do you want the rest of the names or not?"

"What would you do with them if I said no?"

"The international press would be most interested in this story."

"You believe I would allow you to do that?"

"Maybe it's already been done. An e-mail programmed to be sent at a certain hour unless I'm there to cancel the command. If I'm dead, I wouldn't be able to do that. And you wouldn't kill me and risk leaving the rest of the men on my list out there in your country."

The old man calmly smeared some hummus over pita and took a small bite. "You seem to know my intentions better than I."

"I understand obsession."

"This is about duty, Herr Mundt."

"For both of us."

Vorsky weighed the intent of the German's words and pushed the hummus tray back to the center of the table. Then he reached beneath his chair and produced a laptop computer.

"The file for the database you're interested in has already been opened," he explained. "Press enter to proceed."

Before Mundt could do that, the old man fastened his hand around the huge forearm before him. "The machine has been programmed to allow you access to one name and one name only. Try a second and it will automatically shut down. You will copy nothing onto a disk. You will take no notes. You will view half of this file and be done."

Mundt tensed. "Half? That wasn't part of the deal."

"The deal is changed, Herr Mundt. Access to the second half of the file will be yours once we are sure the rest of the names you promised weren't pulled from the phone book."

Mundt slid a CD storage disc across the table, following the same path the old man had taken with the laptop. "When?" he asked.

Vorsky quickly pocketed it. "Is tomorrow soon enough?"

"I suppose it will have to be."

"There's something else," Vorsky said. "The late General Janush's chief aide has been asking questions, apparently making connections between the three victims."

"Why does this concern me?"

"Because it occurs to me someone may have leaked information to him, someone with an interest in putting added pressure on us to suit his own needs."

The big man tapped the portable computer's screen. "I have only one interest."

"It doesn't bother you that the general's aide met with a National Police inspector to enlist her help in his investigation?"

"*Her* help?"

"She is one of their very best."

"Then it seems you have a problem."

"And we intend to deal with it. Just so long as it is not of your making. I would hate to think you would want to implicate us to improve your own situation."

"And why do you imagine I would do that?"

The old man pointed at the laptop. "In case you don't find what you're looking for."

"Let me see," the big man said and pressed ENTER.

CHAPTER 38

P AKAD ?" BEN SAID through Danielle's open car window.

She came alert with a jolt, realizing she must have dozed off while waiting for him. "You're late."

"Are you all right?"

"It's been a long couple of days, that's all. And I've been waiting for you for, I don't know, too long."

For some reason, Danielle had decided to wait in the car for Ben at the Palestinian-Israeli school outside Abu Gosh instead of inside the building. With the afternoon burning away toward evening, she had called to ask Jane Wexler, principal of the school, to please wait for them to arrive.

"Let's go inside."

"I want to hear about this girl you found in the refugee camp first."

I CAN'T BELIEVE this," Danielle said, after Ben had finished relaying his interview with Zeina Ashawi. "Is she under guard?"

"It took some time, but Colonel al-Asi has arranged for the entire family to be moved to a safe house. I stayed with them until his people arrived. That's why I'm late. What about you?"

"I've been reassigned to administration. Commander Baruch did not take kindly to me pursuing an unauthorized investigation."

"That bastard . . ."

"Not to worry. I gave myself the day off and spent part of the afternoon with Layla Saltzman," Danielle told him, leaving out mention of her meeting with Captain Asher Bain for the moment. "You won't believe what she found under her son's bed. . . ."

IT MAKES NO sense," Ben said, after listening to Danielle tell him about the money stuffed into a bag belonging to another of the murdered students. "The students handle everything so discreetly, careful to cover their tracks, and then they take the risk of withdrawing that amount of cash. Why?"

"As you said, it doesn't go along with the rest of how they carried out their plan."

"But they must have had their reasons, Pakad."

"Are we going to tell the principal the truth?" Danielle asked, after both of them had contemplated what those reasons might be for a few moments.

"That her best students were running a blackmail ring? No, we just tell her we need the details on the job the school secured for Shahir Falaya. Then we dig deeper to see if another student was involved, as Zeina Ashawi suggested, on the chance that student might be able to tell us more."

"Before he or she is killed as well, of course. Where do you think all this is going to take us, Inspector?"

Ben shrugged. "I don't know. Maybe the Falaya boy gets a low level job at a major corporation, an international conglomerate maybe. At some point he sees or overhears something, finds out something the company cannot afford to let go public."

"And then what? He enlists the help of these other students? Why?"

"To cover his ass, Pakad. Each takes on a role. The details remain for us to uncover."

"And then this company the boy worked for decides to kill him and his accomplices," Danielle said, not sounding convinced. "Again, it doesn't make sense."

"Then we find what does make sense and maybe we find their killers."

THANK YOU FOR waiting for us," Ben told the school's principal Jane Wexler, while Danielle sank into a chair in her office.

"You said it was important."

"We need the details of the job the school procured for Shahir Falaya," Danielle informed the principal.

"Just a moment," Jane Wexler said, and switched on her computer.

She brought up the proper file and scanned the information briefly. IBM had opened a major corporate headquarters in Tel Aviv, Ben thought, and there were any number of large banks, brokerage houses, and insurance companies that would have made prime fodder for a blackmailer of any age.

"Here it is," from the principal finally. "Yes, I remember now. Tel Aviv."

Ben and Danielle waited expectantly.

"Abasca Machines," said Jane Wexler.

Ben leaned over the principal's desk. "Excuse me?"

"Abasca Machines. Would you like the address?"

"What kind of corporation is that?" Ben asked her.

Jane Wexler almost laughed. "A very small one, I would imagine: They fix business machines."

Ben looked over at Danielle who had started to rise, using the arms of the chair for support. All the color had drained out of her face and she leaned on the top of the desk suddenly, looking dizzy.

"Pakad?"

By then, though, she was falling backwards, the floor coming up fast when Ben caught her.

CHAPTER 39

TESS SANDERSON REMAINED at Paul Hessler's apartment long after the other mourners had left. Together they sat out on the spacious balcony, gazing into the Manhattan night.

"I don't understand," Paul said, fingers squeezed into his cheeks. It was the first opportunity he'd had to continue the discussion they had begun earlier in the day. He liked the young woman's company, especially after realizing how much time Ari must have spent with her these past few months. "How exactly did a project I ordered terminated successfully pass its preliminary testing phase?"

"Ari never followed through on your order," Tess Sanderson explained. "He thought the project was too valuable."

"Valuable?" Paul Hessler challenged. "We had already spent half a billion dollars developing Lot four-sixty-one with nothing to show for it."

"Ari believed strongly in its potential."

"Potential, Sanderson, is the folly of the young."

Sanderson smiled, her pearl white teeth flashing in the moonlight. "Ari knew that was exactly how you felt.

That's why he rerouted the research money from another source and changed the project's protocol altogether at the Hessler Institute."

"So I wouldn't know."

"Ari believed he was looking at what might be the greatest discovery in the history of medical science."

"Potential again," Paul scoffed. "What was your role in this, Sanderson?"

Tess didn't hesitate. "I was responsible for the diversion of funds into a phantom project so Lot four-sixty-one could remain under development."

"Grounds for dismissal."

"We *both* understood that."

"You're telling me my son was willing to sacrifice his career for this project?"

"That's how much he believed in it."

"Then by all means, Sanderson, tell me how this belief of his was finally justfied."

"A closed and blind study, meaning the recipients had signed up for any and all measures. They never knew whether they even received Lot four-sixty-one."

"When I terminated the project," Paul Hessler recalled, "we were at Lot four-fifty-two, and every test patient had died."

Both of them knew and accepted that the purpose of such blind studies was not to determine so much if a new drug worked, as to see at what point its toxicity stopped becoming terminal and a safe dosage approximated. Only then were formal clinical trials undertaken.

"Eight more lots failed after Ari took over the project," Tess Sanderson explained. "But Lot four-sixty-one achieved results in eight of the ten patients who were given the drug."

"Eight of ten? That's unheard of!"

Sanderson nodded enthusiastically. "And all patients had reached so-called terminal levels. Seven of them are still alive today."

Paul Hessler's eyes widened. "Why didn't my son tell me about this, for God's sake?"

"He was going to. But he wanted all the data in hand first so you wouldn't be mad."

"Mad? I probably would have smacked him." Paul started to smile for the first time in days, but it faded quickly and he felt the prick of tears brewing behind his eyes again.

"He was planning to show the test results to you as soon as you returned from Israel, once the Arrow anti-missile system was finally deployed. Ari didn't want anything to distract you before then."

"That's what this party he was planning was about, wasn't it?"

Sanderson nodded sadly.

"You know what this means, Sanderson, don't you?"

"We can only begin to imagine."

"Try. I want to share my son's vision."

Sanderson sighed, clearly uncomfortable with that task. "The revolutionizing of medical treatment practices for the most serious of diseases. The end of suffering for millions and millions of people. Lives extended. Families preserved."

"He didn't raise the possible economic windfall such a drug would bring?"

Sanderson let herself smile slightly. "Actually he had detailed reports drawn up. According to the latest projections, the potential was there to do fifty billion dollars of business in the drug's first year out of the box alone."

She thought that would make Paul Hessler happy, but instead his features drooped, looking exactly as he had while standing over his son's grave that morning.

Tess Sanderson touched the old man's shoulder briefly. "But it was never about the money. Ari saw this as his chance to prove himself to you. When the project succeeded, he knew he had succeeded too." Sanderson waited for Paul Hessler to look her way again before resuming. "You should know that."

Hessler used a handkerchief to pat his moistening eyes. "Tell me, Sanderson, how did the two of you go about this behind my back?"

"It helped that you were so consumed with the Arrow missile shield project for Israel. But all my communications with Ari from the institute were routed via fax or e-mail through our headquarters in Tel Aviv. The breakthrough came while the two of you were over there, a little over a month ago. He told me he was going to download a copy of the report for you, that he couldn't wait any longer." Sanderson let her eyes drop. "I guess he changed his mind."

"All this subterfuge . . ."

Tess Sanderson swallowed hard, as if unsure about proceeding. "Ari knew how closely you watched him, monitored his work. He didn't want to leave you any clue of his commitment to Lot four-sixty-one. I never briefed him in person. We never even ate lunch together, met for only very briefly at a time."

Paul Hessler saw something change in the woman's eyes. "Was that difficult for you?"

"Very much so, sir."

"I suspect it was difficult for my son as well."

"I hope so."

"But it was smart, on both your parts." Ari, Paul Hessler mused, had known him better than he realized. He hadn't given the boy enough credit, which made Ari's loss all the more difficult to bear. "Of course," Paul resumed, trying to distract himself. "There is the matter of the four sixty-one's current status. Someone will have to take over the project and shepherd it through the rest of the process. Are you interested, Sanderson?"

"Of course I am, sir."

"Did you and Ari have occasion to discuss a bonus agreement and structure?"

"Er, no, sir."

"I'll have a proposal for you within forty-eight hours."

"That's not neces—"

"Yes, it is, Sanderson. This is about business, not family or friendship. The sooner both of us accept that now, the better off we will be. I think you will do just fine. I will expect all the reports and data on Lot four-sixty-one on my desk tomorrow morning."

"Yes, sir." Sanderson hedged a little. "Would you like me to bring them here, sir, given the circumstances?"

"No," said Paul Hessler. "I think a stop at the office will do me good."

CHAPTER 40

WHEN DANIELLE OPENED her eyes, Ben was hovering over her and she made out the figure of her obstetrician Dr. Barr standing at the foot of the bed. She realized she was dressed in a hospital gown and recognized the view from Mount Scopus out the window that could only mean she was in Jerusalem's Hadassah Hospital, to her dismay a familiar setting for her.

She started to prop herself up on her elbows. "Was it a . . ."

"Miscarriage?" Dr. Barr completed, when she couldn't. "No. Just a reaction to stress and fatigue no woman nearly four months pregnant should be subjecting herself to."

"You heard him, Danielle," Ben said, restraining her gently and then easing her back down to the pillows. He had ridden with her in the amublance from the school, expediting what would have otherwise been an impossible entry into Israel for him. "Easy does it."

She continued to focus on the doctor. "Then it had nothing to do with . . . the problem with the baby we discussed yesterday?"

"Nothing at all," he affirmed. "Although I believe it is

in your best interests to make a decision in the matter as
soon as possible."

"The baby's fine for now, though."

"Well . . ."

"I mean when I fainted nothing happened to him."

Dr. Barr nodded reluctantly. "The sonogram we took
here revealed no structural damage to the fetus."

"Did I approve the test?" Danielle asked him. "Because
I don't remember—"   "I approved it," Ben interrupted.
"I thought it was something you would want to know."

"The important thing," the doctor picked up, "is that
your baby's present good condition should not give you
false hope. I'm afraid it's not going to remain that way for
long." When Danielle made no reply, he started for the
door. "I'll look in on you in the morning. Get some rest."

"What did you tell him?" Danielle demanded, after Dr.
Barr had left the room.

"To do the sonogram."

"Nothing else?

"I didn't have to. He knows. He saw it on my face in
his office yesterday. Yours, too."

"I shouldn't have asked you to come with me."

"So you can go through this alone?"

"I'm used to it. Can't you see this is hard enough for
me, as it is?"

"It would be even harder alone," Ben persisted stubbornly. "I don't give up easy, Danielle."

"I'm thankful for that. Really, I am, Ben."

"But sometimes giving up is not the worst thing a person
can do."

She turned onto her side away from him. "Why don't
you just go check out Abasca Machines?"

"Because it's in Tel Aviv. I can't go there without you.
And anyway . . ."

Danielle twisted back toward Ben. "Anyway what?"

"Commander Baruch knows you're here."

"Shit . . . How?"

"Your identification card when they brought you in.

They called National Police. I'm sure he's been informed by now."

"I'm surprised I'm not under arrest," Danielle said, not caring as much as she thought she would.

Ben leaned over and kissed her lightly on the forehead. "There's something I have to do. I'll be back in a few minutes."

"Take your time. I'm not going anywhere."

DANIELLE HAD JUST settled herself back into bed when the door opened again and Captain Asher Bain poked his head in.

"I hope I'm not disturbing you, Pakad," he said softly.

"Not at all."

He entered the room, his squat muscular frame filling a considerable amount of the door. "When I heard you were here, I was worried. I thought it might have been the work of whoever we are after." He closed the door behind him.

"We, Captain?"

"If my assumption is mistaken . . ."

"It's not, Captain," Danielle said, looking into Bain's deep, dark eyes that reflected the same emptiness she remembered in her father's and both her brothers'. "I had a small accident. Not the result of hostile action, I assure you. I should be out of here by the morning."

"That's comforting."

"And how did you hear I was in the hospital?"

"I . . ."

"Because it occurs to me that the only way you could know is if you were having me watched."

"A loose tail, Pakad, for your own protection. He saw the ambulance arrive at the school you were visiting outside of Jerusalem. He didn't know what happened inside."

"But he assumed hostile action."

Bain shrugged his huge shoulders. "He's career military, like me. It's what we always assume."

"Don't get defensive. I'm glad you came."

That seemed to loosen Asher Bain up a little. Danielle could see the layered cords of muscle that lined his arms and neck relax a bit. "I have the information you requested on Paul Hessler's assailant. I thought you might be interested in hearing it. Also some other information I . . . don't know what to make of yet."

"Start with what you learned about that tattoo."

Bain clasped his hands behind his back, rigid again. "The 'Nightcrawlers' were a World War Two infantry unit attached to the O.S.S."

"O.S.S.?"

"Forerunner of the American Special Forces, or Special Operations as they are called now. Anyway, the Nightcrawlers did a lot of work behind enemy lines during the closing months of the war. Blowing up ammo and fuel dumps mostly in an attempt to halt the Germans in their tracks and, finally, planning raids to rescue the surviving occupants of the labor camps in Poland after the Russians invaded from the east."

"So that's what these Nightcrawlers were up to when they rescued Hessler." Danielle nodded, impressed. "But how'd you find all this out?"

"A friend at the Pentagon owed me a favor. And according to the records he helped me access, the man who tried to kill Paul Hessler is Staff Sergeant Walter Phipps. That glass eye was the key clue: Phipps lost an eye in the early days of his tour in Europe but refused a discharge. Wore a patch instead."

"Don't tell me, Phipps was among those who found Paul Hessler in the woods."

"Half dead, by all accounts. Phipps and the rest of his platoon likely saved Hessler's life."

"And then, nearly fifty-seven years later, he tries to kill him."

Bain frowned. "I can't make sense of it either. Not yet, anyway. Phipps and his men initially thought they had found a Nazi spy, not a Nazi labor camp escapee."

"Have you been able to find any link between Hessler and the three murder victims?"

"Not yet," said Bain. "But there's something else." Bain remained standing at the foot of Danielle's bed. He held his arms stiff and straight by his sides. "It has to do with your late father, Pakad."

Captain Asher Bain moved around to the right side of the bed, closer to Danielle. She saw a flash of warmth on his expression, expected him to reach out and touch her but he stopped just out of range.

"You need to know that I asked one of our military computers for a list of other men who fit the same profile as Hessler and the three other Holocaust survivors who were murdered." He stopped and swallowed hard. "Your father's name was on the list."

CHAPTER 41

ALL THE MEN were survivors of either labor or prison camps," Bain continued. "I'm sorry to have to bring this up."

"It's all right, Captain," Danielle said, wondering exactly what Bain's discovery meant. "But my father wasn't found in the forest. He ended up in a resettlement camp and came to Palestine as a refugee."

"And fought to create the Jewish state. Your father is a legend, Pakad."

"Thank you."

"But so was General Janush," Bain added. "The murders yesterday were well planned, undertaken by professionals with the kind of skills you often hear about but seldom see."

"Except Walter Phipps was an old, dying man," Danielle picked up. "Not a professional."

"So we must consider the very real possibility that Hessler's attempted murder was unrelated to the other executions."

"If only we knew what Walter Phipps was thinking when he began pulling that trigger . . ."

"The Pentagon's file on him ends after his service in Korea, unfortunately. So we have no idea what may have transpired in the years that followed."

"Years don't matter, Captain. Whatever spurred Walter Phipps to action had to have been recent. Otherwise, why would he have waited so long to kill Hessler? And why try for him in Israel instead of the United States?"

Captain Bain shrugged, reluctant to meet her gaze.

"What is it?" Danielle asked him, sensing he was holding something back.

"Nothing. Not yet anyway," he replied defensively. "There are just some . . . indications I find, well, disturbing."

"Disturbing?"

His steely soldier's eyes lost their confident glow. "Impossible would be a better way to describe it. Otherwise . . ."

"Otherwise *what*?"

"The answers are in Germany. That's where I'm headed from here. A nursing home in Remscheid, not far from Dusseldorf, to see a man named Gunthar Weiss. Weiss was the commandant of the labor camp in Poland where Paul Hessler was interned. After I speak with him, I'm certain I'll be able to tell you much more."

"Be careful, Captain."

Bain smiled for the first time Danielle could remember. "Thank you for caring, Inspector."

They were still looking at each other when the door opened and Ben Kamal entered holding flowers in his hand.

"I thought you might like—" Ben stopped when he saw the powerfully built man standing by Danielle's bedside. He ran his teeth over his lower lip. "I'm sorry, Pakad, I didn't know you had company."

"This is Captain Asher Bain, Inspector. We're working on something together."

Ben didn't offer his hand, keeping his attention completely on Danielle. "Another case?"

"It's unofficial, at this point."

"You're taking on too much. That's why you collapsed."

"I'm telling you, there's nothing to worry about."

"I should be going now," Bain said, stiff again with discomfort.

"I believe the inspector was just leaving too."

Ben held out the flowers. "As soon as I put these in water."

"Really," Bain begged off, trying to slide subtly for the door. "I should be going."

"But you'll stay in touch," Danielle prompted.

Bain looked at Ben, shrugged. "I'll let you know what I find out, Pakad."

And then he was gone, the door closing softly behind him.

"Find out about what?" Ben asked.

"It doesn't matter."

"It does if it's endangering your health. Maybe that's why you're doing this."

"To endanger my *own* health? That's absurd."

Ben held his ground. "Not just yours."

"The baby? You think I'm trying to hurt the baby?"

"I think you're trying to punish yourself for what's happened."

She sat up straighter in her bed. "Listen to me. Captain Bain had some information about Paul Hessler. That's all."

"Information pertaining to what?"

Danielle sighed. She wanted to be alone now, wanted nothing more than to ease her exhaustion with a long night's sleep. "The murders of three Holocaust survivors."

"With Paul Hessler nearly the fourth?"

"Possibly. We're not sure yet."

"You mean, Captain Bain's not."

Danielle ignored Ben's sarcasm. "I guess that's what I mean. Whatever you say. I have my reasons, all right?"

"Fine," Ben said, half-heartedly.

"What did you speak to my doctor about after you left the room?"

"How do you know I spoke with him about anything?"

"I didn't; I do now."

"I asked him about the radical prenatal surgeries being done in the United States."

Danielle nodded. "I know all about them. They're not an option in this case."

"But the doctor also mentioned—"

"I don't want to discuss this. Just get out. Please."

Danielle closed her eyes and didn't open them again until the door closed behind him.

CHAPTER 42

BEN STORMED DOWN the hall toward the elevator. He thought he was over considering the possibility that he and Danielle could be together. But her phone call two nights ago had set off the old emotions rampaging through him. He had hope again and the hope hurt terribly. He had forgotten how much it could hurt.

The only alternative was to shut Danielle out of his life before she had the opportunity to do the same to him. Strangely, before their visit to the doctor's office yesterday morning, he actually thought he could do that. Now everything had changed. Facing the loss of their child had rekindled in him all the contradictory and clashing feelings he had battled since their first meeting. Once he had been able to separate their professional relationship from their personal one. Not anymore. Now he could not work a case with her without lapsing into the old discussions they'd had a hundred times already. Prior to the pregnancy it had been possible to compartmentalize his life. Accept whatever she gave him as all he really had and let himself dream about a future that held more.

But that was done, finished. Tonight had provided ample

demonstration. How many times did he have to prove himself worthy? What more could he do? He had run out of ideas and, finally, patience. Ben remembered how much he had looked forward to the one night out of seven they had spent together for months prior to Danielle's pregnancy, her visits making the rest of the week tolerable. He believed he could survive without her in his life; he did not believe he could survive forever hoping she might still be a part of it.

The elevator doors opened on Hadassah Hospital's first floor. Ben hadn't even remembered stepping into the compartment, or pressing the button. He felt stiff and hot, just wanted to get outside.

A scream shocked him just before he reached the front door. Ben spun, instinctively feeling for the pistol he was not permitted to carry in Israel.

Up the hall a bit, he saw a nurse backing out of a supply closet, hands pressed against her face. She screamed again. Ben rushed to her side along with various hospital personnel and eased his way forward until he could see clearly into a closet packed with trays, linens, and towels.

Blood covered the floor, spreading outward from the severed throat of a man sprawled on his back with his head bent obscenely backward. The thin light caught just enough of the man's face for Ben to recognize him.

He felt his breath catch.

The dead man was Captain Asher Bain.

DANIELLE WAS DREAMING about being tucked into bed as a little girl when she heard the door to her hospital room open. She turned onto her back, half-expecting to see her father. But a nurse approached instead, holding a tray in her hand.

"I have the medication you requested," the nurse said and approached the bed.

Danielle stirred restlessly. She watched the nurse lay the tray down on her night-table, then move toward her with a plastic cup in one hand and a paper pill dispenser in the other.

"I'm sorry," Danielle said. "I didn't—"

"Here you go, miss."

Danielle was about to tell the nurse she hadn't asked for any medication; in point of fact had refused even the mildest painkiller or sedative out of fear it might adversely effect her baby. But the nurse kept extending the cup and pill dispenser toward her. Their eyes met and the nurse smiled, something horribly forced about the gesture.

Danielle started to move.

The nurse threw the water into her face before Danielle could lurch from the bed, and lashed out toward her, leading with her nails. Long and perfectly shaped, only a few of them finished in polish. But her hands and fingers were speckled with drying blood.

Those nails! Danielle realized.

She knocked her first swipe away, grabbed the tray from the nightstand to block the second. The nurse's fingernails sliced through the plastic with a grating, tearing sound. Danielle twisted away from the next blow, and the nails dug deep into the mattress as she dropped to the floor.

The nurse jerked her fingers back out, dragging displaced stuffing behind them, showering Danielle with indoor snow. She saw the nurse leaping headlong toward her and groped desperately for the tray that had dropped to the floor next to her, getting it up just in time for the nails to ram against it.

One of them broke and clattered to the floor. But the nurse kept slashing out with the rest of her nails, both hands now, as Danielle back-crawled across the floor, her adrenaline racing. The tray was her only weapon and she used it to fend off the blows until one launched in a wide sidelong arc knocked the tray from her grasp.

The nurse took a backswing at her and Danielle blocked the blow only to be met with another. She managed to lock her hands on the nurse's wrists, trying to hold her off against the nurse's determined efforts to angle her nails for a killing strike.

Fighting for her life, Danielle planted a foot in the nurse's midsection for leverage and heaved the smaller woman up and over her. The nurse landed behind her with a thump that rattled the floor and shook more stuffing from the bed. The nurse regained her balance almost instantly, giving Danielle just enough time to reach up and tear a sheet from the bed. She brought the sheet down over the nurse's torso and face and twisted the fabric tight to hold her in place.

She tried pounding the woman with her elbows, but at once the nurse's razor-sharp nails ripped through the sheet and swiped blindly. Danielle managed to stay just out of range and twisted the sheet around the nurse's head and neck, hoping to choke off her air.

But the nurse's deadly hands held her at bay. Even at this distance, Danielle felt a pair of nails rake her shoulder and the stinging pain caused her grip on the sheet to slacken slightly. Enough for the nurse to grab a fresh breath and launch another attack that gashed Danielle's left breast.

She gasped in pain and tried for a head butt, but the blow landed on the hard part of the nurse's skull and sent star bursts exploding before Danielle's own eyes as well. The nurse finally shook the sheet off and lashed out with a blow that cut Danielle's ankle when she tried to scamper away on her hands and knees.

Danielle twisted round and kicked the nurse in the face as soon as she tried to pounce. Something in the nurse's jaw cracked and that side of her face suddenly sagged when she launched herself at Danielle again, only to be met by another kick, under the chin this time.

Danielle searched the room desperately for another weapon, then decided to just try for the door instead. But the nurse grabbed her by the ankles and dragged her backwards, angling toward the bathroom.

The door to the room exploded inward before they got

there. Ben Kamal burst in, startling the nurse and giving Danielle enough time to lurch sideways, breaking the nurse's grasp. Ben started to come forward and the nurse turned to face him; a tiny figure wrapped in a tattered, blood-smeared uniform, deadly hands held like spears.

"Her nails!" Danielle warned. "Watch her nails!"

With those nails cutting through the air between them, Ben grabbed the wheelchair resting against the wall and jerked it between him and the nurse. She lunged out at him, her hands whistling through the air, but Ben parried with the chair, maneuvering its wheels to keep fending her off.

He could see the hate and frustration building in her face. The nurse stole a glance at Danielle, hoping to distract him, but Ben wasn't fooled. The next time she lashed out with one of her hands, he slammed the chair into her. Impact stole her balance, doubling her partially over.

From the floor Danielle watched Ben shove the wheelchair even harder and drive the nurse backwards. It looked as if his plan was to pin her against the window. Instead of slowing, though, Ben continued to pick up speed, the wheelchair's wheels grinding against the tile floor as it neared the glass.

The nurse's head slammed against the frame and her torso was forced through the open window into the breeze. Ben still didn't let up. He drove the chair up off the floor and into the nurse, doubling her torso over. Her hands groped for the frame and her legs flailed mightily to stop herself from falling. It was no use. The nurse managed only to rake the glass, deadly nails drawing an ear-wrenching screech before she fell screaming backward into the night. The wheelchair followed her to the pavement below, coughing divots from the concrete that quickly filled with the nurse's blood.

The door burst open again. Three real nurses surged inside.

Ben bent over Danielle. "Get a doctor!" he yelled to them when he saw the blood staining her hospital gown. "Did you hear what I said? *Get a doctor!*"

DAY FOUR

CHAPTER 43

PAUL HESSLER SQUEEZED his trip to the office in before the two hour block of time in the afternoon when mourners could come and pay their respects. Others would come tonight and still more in the two days that followed. Paul would greet them all, accept their words of sympathy, whether honestly expressed or not, and leave them to the coffee and pastry laid atop tables throughout the spacious great room in his penthouse apartment.

He'd had trouble sleeping the night before, both from regret and excitement. Regret because his son Ari had not been able to deliver the news on Lot 461 himself; excitement because the success of the project would be a fitting testament to his son. In death Ari would be responsible for the greatest achievement in the long history of Hessler Industries. And, for the first time in four days, Paul found himself with purpose, a reason to go on.

The massive office towers that housed the headquarters for his global conglomerate had been built on a nine-acre site along the East River near the United Nations. He had won a fierce bidding war to first purchase the land and then beat down the zoning opposition to construct the world's tallest office building so close to the water. Modeled after the famed Petronas Twin Towers in Malaysia's Kuala Lumpur, his bookend pair of ninety-story buildings were unquestionably Asian in design. Palatial structures modeled after the Gothic and often haughty residences of warlords from generations long gone.

Their overall height stretched over one thousand five hundred feet from street level. There were thirty elevators, sixty-five thousand square yards of glass and seventy-seven thousand square yards of stainless steel cladding. More than thirty thousand tons of concrete had been poured as foundations for both towers. To Hessler, though, the most distinguishing feature of his Towers was the skybridge that joined them together at the forty-first and forty-second floors. The skybridge stretched the seventy yard distance separating the twin structures, supported by four two-ton steel brackets that firmly attached it to the Towers.

Without stops, the elevator took only a few soundless stomach-rippling seconds to cover the entire distance to the ninetieth floor. Paul stepped out into the spacious office dominated by glass and Oriental architecture. The lighting was purposely dim except directly over his desk, all chairs, and the conference table. Shoji screens formed dividers between various designated areas of the room, and an extravagant collection of Asian art and memorabilia covered the walls and tables. Everything, of course, was original, one of a kind. Ari had found and acquired most of it during the two months he spent following business school working with Paul Hessler's colleagues in Tokyo, Singapore, and Hong Kong.

Paul had not set foot in this office since his son's death and felt instantly soothed by the quiet and dull, amber light. A large indoor waterfall took up a measure of the room's center, so riveting it seemed the entire structure had been built around it. Water crested over rocks as high as the ceiling and slid serenely into the recycling pool at floor level. He stepped close enough to feel the water's light spray and imagined he could hear his son's voice beneath the machine-made flow. It had been a birthday present from Ari, the last gift ever now from son to father.

Hessler saw Tess Sanderson rise from a chair in the sitting area, and forced himself to leave the memories of his son behind.

"You're right on time, Sanderson," Paul greeted the young woman. "That's good. You haven't been up here before, have you?"

"No, I haven't."

"I see you've brought your notes."

Sanderson's eyes turned back to the pile of folders she had deposited on a mahogany table set between a pair of matching leather chairs. "The reports on Lot four-sixty-one you requested, sir."

"I'd like to hear them summarized in your own words," Paul requested, taking the second chair that provided a panoramic view of New York Harbor. "Start with this blind study you mentioned last night."

"Of the eight patients who recovered after receiving four sixty-one, four had terminal cancer, one had AIDS, one had ALS, one had acute viral hepatitis, and one had cystic fibrosis."

"Which of these later died?"

"One of the cancer patients. But her death is now considered to be tangent to the study."

"Tangent?"

"Caused by conditions predisposed. Side effects of the chemotherapy drugs even Lot four-sixty-one couldn't be programmed to overcome."

"We've been able to keep their stories quiet, I assume."

"They all signed the proper forms. I believe one did try to sell his story to the tabloids but none of them were buying; they didn't believe him."

"I can hardly believe it myself. What about the next round of testing?"

"I'm assembling the data for the FDA right now. Their skepticism will undoubtedly make rapid approval unlikely, if not impossible."

"What was Ari's plan in this regard, Sanderson?"

"Well, sir, he was going to suggest that you go public with the preliminaries prior to seeking FDA approval."

"To put pressure on them."

Sanderson nodded. "That was his thought, yes."

"I'm not sure I share it. How long since the blind study was completed?"

"Just over a month."

Hessler weighed the information. "Not enough time to determine Lot four-sixty-one's short-term effectiveness, never mind long-term. We're not even sure its miraculous powers are going to last, not to mention any possible side effects."

"So far, sir, there have been none to speak of."

"So far, yes, but with so much at stake here we need to be sure before proceeding."

Sanderson uncrossed her legs and shifted uncomfortably in her chair.

"That bothers you, Sanderson."

"It would have bothered Ari, even though he predicted it."

"Always in a rush. Throwing caution and pragmatism to the wind."

"If you'll excuse me for saying this, sir, pragmatism is what led you to cancel the project in the first place."

"Then let me rectify my mistake. I want to see a complete overview and demonstration of Lot four-sixty-one, Sanderson. Say, tomorrow morning at the Institute."

CHAPTER 44

THE POLICE HAD been deployed throughout Hadassah Hospital all night, outnumbering the late shift of doctors and nurses. The Jerusalem police force brought the largest contingent, until Shin Bet showed up on the scene and agreed to work side-by-side with National Police since one of its detectives had been the near-victim.

Ben Kamal stayed through it all, ignoring the caustic stares cast his way. He remained inside or near Danielle's room well into the morning, funneling to her what information he could glean as soon as it reached him.

"The woman who tried to kill you died of a broken neck on impact with the concrete below. She has yet to be identified."

"It doesn't matter; I know who she is," Danielle said, grimacing. The wounds inflicted upon her by the woman's deadly nails proved to be superficial, but no less painful. All neatly bandaged now and certain not to hamper her. "We've run into each other in the past."

"A terrorist?" Ben fought against the urge to scratch at the scabs forming across his own facial cuts, inflicted by the fake soldier at the Katavi home in the Golan Heights two days before.

"Not at all. She worked for Mossad."

M OSSAD?" BEN MANAGED, at mention of Israel's international intelligence service.

Danielle nodded. "She went by the name of Ellie, nothing else. No history or background. A contract killer, an assassin. That simple."

"Who worked for Mossad."

"I'm not saying they sent her. It's been a long time since our paths crossed. She could have gone freelance."

"You have a friend who works for Mossad, don't you?"

"Several. But I'm not sure how much they know about Ellie. Her assignments were never the kind that were on the books. I don't think you'll find her in any personnel files."

"How do you know her?"

"We were recruited out of the army together."

"Not for the same job, obviously."

"We need to find out who Ellie has been working for lately."

"As soon as you've gotten some rest."

"This morning will be fine."

"The doctor wants to keep you a little longer."

"For my health, I suppose. No, I think I stand a much better chance of staying alive on the outside," Danielle said as Commander Moshe Baruch appeared in the doorway.

D ANIELLE WATCHED BARUCH stride through the door. He was every bit as wide as Captain Asher Bain but much taller. His steps were lumbering, even plodding, thanks to two bad knees.

Baruch left the door open and looked at Ben. "Leave us, Inspector."

Ben held his ground until a glance at Danielle showed her nodding.

"I'll be right outside," he said.

"Close the door behind you," Baruch followed, not bothering to look at him.

Baruch didn't look as angry as Danielle thought he would. Instead, he seemed surprisingly calm and restrained.

"You're making things so easy for me, Pakad. You know I want you out of National Police and you seem determined to help me at every step."

"Maybe I just got tired of working for someone I have no respect for."

Baruch looked unfazed by her comment. "I'm surprised it took you so long to say that."

"Your predecessor, my mentor, was a great man. I didn't want to disrespect his office."

"You mean my office, of course."

"The only thing that's yours is the title of Rav nitzav which you never earned and can't live up to."

"But out of similar respect for my . . . predecessor, I can let you go at full pension."

"Half my current salary."

"It's the best I can do under terms of the disability act."

"So I'm disabled."

"Defined as 'no longer able to perform one's duties.' In your case that's clearly true," Baruch gloated.

Danielle could hear his noisy breathing from across the room. His clothes and breath always reeked of garlic and the scent finally drifted over to her.

"You haven't asked me anything about what happened here last night," she prompted.

"I am going to cede jurisdiction to the Jerusalem police."

"Not Shin Bet?"

Danielle could sense Baruch fighting not to smile. "You were officially under suspension at the time of the attack and thus no longer a State employee. Shin Bet won't be interested."

"You don't care someone tried to kill me."

"Since it had nothing to do with your work for me, no, I don't, Ms. Barnea," Baruch said, enjoying the fact that he no longer had to address her as "Pakad."

"You've heard of Ellie?"

Baruch's bushy eyebrows fluttered in recognition, but he shook his head. "No, I haven't."

"An assassin trained originally by Mossad. Not the kind of person someone sends out on any ordinary mission. I'm close to something here, don't you see that?"

"You'd have me believe this is all about those children you claim were murdered, is that it?"

"Actually, it's not."

"What then? Ah, there must be *another* case you've been working on behind my back. Tell me, does it have anything to do with the death of Captain Bain?"

"Would you care if it did, Commander?"

"Why did you contact Bain?"

"He contacted *me*. About the murder of his boss—General Janush. If you probe deeper, I think you'll find that Ellie murdered Janush."

"And why would someone you claim is a former Mossad assassin murder the army's deputy chief of staff?"

"It has something to do with Holocaust survivors. General Janush wasn't the only one; two other old men were killed the same day."

"And Bain came to you because . . ."

"The link with Paul Hessler. Bain knew I had been briefly assigned to Hessler's attempted murder. He thought I might know something."

"Which, of course, you didn't."

"No," Danielle conceded.

"So someone is killing Holocaust survivors . . . and someone else is killing high school students," Baruch droned melodramatically.

"Making light of it doesn't make it any less real."

Baruch's expression didn't changed. He looked toward the door, clearly eager to be gone. "Are you finished, Ms. Barnea?"

"Apparently, Commander, I am."

CHAPTER 45

THAT COULD HAVE gone better," Ben said, when Moshe Baruch was gone.

"It went the only way it could."

"You sound resigned to your career in law enforcement being finished."

"I don't care about my career at the moment," Danielle shrugged. "I know someone out there still wants me dead."

"Because of these murdered Holocaust survivors."

"You were listening."

Ben tapped his right ear. "Pressed to the door as soon as Baruch closed it behind me."

"Then you know I have my own problems to worry about."

"You mean your own case. Three murdered Holocaust survivors."

"That we know of," Danielle acknowledged, choosing to omit the late Captain Bain's mention of her father. "It could be more."

"I suppose I'll have to go to Tel Aviv by myself, then."

"Without proper authorization? You'll end up in an Israeli jail until your friend Colonel al-Asi comes to get you."

"What choice do I have?"

"I'll come with you." Danielle checked the watch lying on her night table. "It's almost eight A.M. We'd better get started now if we want to reach Abasca Machines in Tel Aviv by ten in all the traffic."

"Thank you, Pakad."

"I like to finish what I start, Inspector." She tightened her gaze. "Which is more than I can say for you."

"What are you talking about?"

"Why didn't you tell me you were going back to America?"

Ben felt his stomach drop. "I'm not."

"But you've been offered some big security job back in Detroit."

"Colonel al-Asi told you, didn't he?"

"He found out I was in the hospital and called last night to see how I was doing."

"I had the phone shut off."

"It rang anyway. Your job offer happened to come up in conversation."

"Al-Asi doesn't want me to go, wants me to come work for him instead. He told you so you could talk me out of going."

"Don't let me stop you, Inspector. Go home, if you want."

"Would it bother you if I did?"

"Our child needs a father. We had everything worked out."

"No, Danielle: *You* had everything worked out. All I could do was nod my head because you weren't offering me a choice."

"You wouldn't be leaving if the baby was healthy."

"Who said I was leaving? I haven't decided what to do yet, and when I do the baby's health will have nothing to do with that decision."

Danielle's eyes looked at him the way they had on so many of their nights together. A long time since he had seen that gaze. "I can't do this without you, Ben, not now."

"You heard what the doctor said, Danielle."

"Run away then! Do what you want!"

"I want to stay here. I want us to be together. It's you who—"

"—Wants to raise my child as a Jew who can be proud of his legacy? Guilty as charged. And if you thought seriously about it, you'd know I was doing the right thing."

Ben stared at her intently. "That's not the issue now, and you know it."

"You're giving up," Danielle shot at him.

Ben lowered his voice to the tone he used when he stroked her hair while they lay in bed together. "Sometimes it's the best thing you can do."

"Move on, you mean."

He moved to the edge of her bed and sat down beside her. "Come with me."

"Depending on what I decide to do about the baby?"

"Whatever *you* decide to do." Ben thought of the conversation Danielle had just finished with Moshe Baruch. "It's not like our careers are keeping us in the Mideast."

Danielle let herself smile. "A suspended Israeli cop and a Palestinian detective . . . We make as great a team as ever, Ben. Now let's get to Tel Aviv."

CHAPTER 46

ABASCA MACHINES WAS an Arab-owned business machine sales and service store in the commercial center of downtown Tel Aviv. Ben had learned that the company's main business was a new line of digital copiers and full service office machines it was offering for lease. Apparently the lead provided by Zeina Ashawi, about Shahir Falaya's job in Israel being crucial to the blackmail scheme engineered by four classmates, had been wrong.

That seemed to be even more the case when they finally reached the site. Abasca Machines was located on the ground floor of a three-story building just off Allenby Street in Tel Aviv's bustling financial and business district. Standing on the sidewalk after risking their lives by crossing the traffic-choked street, Ben and Danielle looked through the plate glass window at a neat array of copying machines of various sizes and designs. A few of them took up large portions of wall space. There were both new and remanufactured machines available. The shelves lining two of the walls were filled with the smaller copiers and fax machines.

Danielle flashed her identification inside, knowing it

would not hold up to the scrutiny of a simple phone call to National Police. Commander Moshe Baruch had not requested that she return it, perhaps because he was hoping to catch her doing something as stupid as this.

Tabar Azziz, the store's owner, was a portly man with a tiny balding head that was bright red across the dome. His smile showed a host of missing teeth, and he was dressed casually in baggy blue pants and a white shirt. His chewed-off fingernails were stained by ink.

"Welcome to my store," he greeted, after a subordinate had fetched him from the back room. "Please, please, tell me how I can help you. I like police. I help you any way I can." He gave Ben a closer look. "You are not Israeli."

"Palestinian."

Azziz drew back a little. "The two of you work together?"

"The case we're on calls for it," Danielle explained.

The surprise remained clear on Azziz's face. "You would like some tea perhaps? I just made some, both hot and cold."

"Thanks. Maybe later," Danielle said.

Azziz looked hurt that his offer had been turned down. "Then tell me how I can help. I want to be of help."

"You had a young employee here," Danielle started.

"Shahir Falaya," from Ben.

"Who was found dead outside of Jericho four days ago."

Tabar Azziz nodded, interrupting before either of them could continue. "I know. Terrible news, terrible. A good boy, a good worker."

"You had no problems with him?" Ben asked.

"He was late a few times because of the checkpoints. A few times they would not let him through at all." Azziz went out of his way not to sound critical.

"You should feel free to tell us the truth, Mr. Azziz," Danielle prodded.

"Truth?"

"Did the young man ever ask you for money?"

"You mean, his weekly pay?"

"Beyond that."

"Like a loan?"

"We were thinking more like a demand," Ben said.

"I want you to know, Mr. Azziz," Danielle picked up, "that whatever we discuss here will remain strictly between us."

Tabar Azziz nodded, though it was clear he didn't understand what she was talking about.

"So if this boy found out something about you or your business, you may tell us."

The trust vanished from Tabir Azziz's eyes. "Shahir Falaya was a good boy, I tell you. I take him under my wing, bring him with me on service calls. He had a future here. He had a knack for machines. His father was an auto mechanic, I think, before he was exiled. I don't know what you're talking about, making up this trouble between us."

"What do you know about the boy's death, sir?" Ben asked him.

"It was terrible. Tragic."

"It was murder."

"Yes, terrible. Tra—"

"Not random murder, *sidi*. This boy was killed because of something he knew, something he was involved in."

Tabar Azziz's fat round eyes filled with fear. "You think he was involved *here*? That it has something to do with *me*? That is why you ask me these questions?"

"Mr. Azziz," Danielle started.

"I am good citizen. I pay my taxes, stay out of trouble. All my life I live in Israel. When the other Arab merchants strike, I don't strike. When they call for boycott, I don't boycott. Never am I accused of anything!"

"We're not accusing you," Ben said, realizing there was no longer any point to it. "But another of this boy's classmates told me that his job was a key to something he and some other students were involved in. Something criminal."

"Not his job here." Azziz shook his head. "No, I don't understand how this could be."

"Perhaps if you explain what the young man did for you," Danielle said.

"Why don't I show you instead?" Tabar Azziz suggested.

THE BACK SECTION of the store was filled with boxes and even a few large crates of equipment. Orders waiting to be filled, machines for display, and inventory of some of the smaller machines that sold more frequently.

"Very competitive business these days," Azziz explained, leading them to a work area behind a half wall. "Sometimes we lease machines, other times just provide service contracts. Sometimes is company that pays us. Sometimes, depending on warranty agreement, is manufacturer that pays us. Very competitive. This is where I teach Shahir much of the business."

Judging from the stains beneath the man's fingernails, Ben had expected the work area to be lined with the exposed guts of machines littering the tables, bleeding ink. But everything was pristine, almost antiseptic. Nothing broken in view.

"We can't make repairs here," Azziz said, as if reading his mind, "it usually means we have to send piece to factory or order new one. Most of our work is caused by jammed paper, bad toner, or burnt-out microchip. Even an entire circuit board."

Danielle slid up a little closer. The slight motion felt sluggish, partly from the fatigue she still suffered, but partly from the sudden sensation of carrying extra weight. It was the first time she had noticed it. "Circuit board?"

"The digital machines you were looking at in the display area have dedicated hard drives. Nonvolatile memory instead of the volatile memory of the smaller machines. Makes things easier but also more complicated. Something's wrong, the machine usually tells us exactly what. It doesn't, we have to test all the connections, check the integrity of the vaious chips. Replace the entire board, if necessary. I went to school for this," Tabar Azziz said proudly.

"Did Shahir Falaya go to school for it too?" Ben asked.

Azziz looked at the spotless floor. "This was his school."

"What happens if a chip is bad?"

Azziz gazed at Danielle, clearly perplexed. "Sometimes we replace it. Sometimes, like I said, we replace the entire board. Depends. Warranty policies and sevice contracts are very strict and specific."

Ben moved to a state-of-the-art digital copier/printer that had been unpacked in sections and was yet to be assembled. He noticed a computer screen resting on the counter over it.

"So these machines are digitally based," he said. "But what does that mean exactly, this nonvolitile memory?"

"The older machines, until just a few years ago, they were like big cameras. Pages go through and they take a picture, then reproduce the page. You want a hundred copies, machine has to take a hundred pictures. Not anymore."

"No?"

"Now the machine still takes the picture but instead of making copy, it sends picture to chip. Then the copy is made from the chip and stored in the machine's permanent memory before being copied."

"How?"

"Each user has his own dedicated file. Everybody happy until something goes wrong."

"Then they call you," Ben said.

"If I'm lucky."

"What about fax machines?" he asked, and the agitation in his voice made Danielle turn his way. He didn't look back.

"With bigger machines, you don't need them anymore. With the bigger machines like this one," replied Tabar Azziz, drawing a hand over the latest Xerox model unassembled on the floor before him, "you don't need anything else. Phone lines connect them to every office in company."

"And Shahir Falaya knew how to replace these chips," Ben said, feeling his heart quicken, "and the entire circuit boards."

"I taught him, Inspector."

Ben and Danielle looked at each other, realizing they might well have found exactly what they'd been looking for.

"Apparently," Ben said to Azziz, "you taught him too well."

CHAPTER 47

HANS MUNDT WAS in the Petra Hostel reviewing his notes and letters once again when the door to his room splintered with a thunderous crash. He spun in his chair, thinking of the gun he had left on the bureau, but had no time to lunge for it before the pair of steel-eyed men wielding pistols of their own barged in. Mundt saw they were trailed closely by a tall, dark woman whose face was smeared with thick pancake makeup.

"Do you know who I am, Mr. Mundt?"

"I have no idea," Mundt said and sat back down, making sure to keep his hands in view. One of the men had taken a position directly before him, while the other was careful to block Mundt's path to the balcony and possible escape.

"You should. Apparently, we have quite a bit in common."

"Like what?" Mundt said, noticing the woman kept the right side of her face cocked away from him at all times.

"The three names you passed on to a certain former official in the Israeli government. I would like to know how you came upon them."

Mundt studied the expressionless hulks flanking her. "What interest is it of yours?"

The woman took another step closer, even with her guards now. "You recognize my accent, Mundt?"

"German."

"Like yours."

"Yes."

"And if I told you my reason for being in Israel was the same as yours, what would you say?"

"That I doubt it very much."

"Hans Mundt," she said, still hiding one side of her face. "Son of Karl Mundt, a guard at the largest of three Nazi forced labor camps outside of Lodz, Poland until his death. You were a member of the East German secret police, Stasi, until that organization was disbanded upon reunification. Just what have you been doing with your time ever since?"

"Why don't you ask Abraham Vorsky? I mean, that's who told you where to find me, isn't it?"

"With good reason. He thought you might have spent your time gathering the names you handed over to him last night. Thought I might know you, that you might have worked for me."

"Worked for *you*?"

The tall woman came closer to him still, let him see just a bit of the hidden side of her face. "Do you know who I am now, Herr Mundt?"

Mundt nodded, realizing the truth of her identity. "You're a relic."

"I prefer to think of myself as one who refuses to stop pursuing relics. Just like you. And that's the reason I am so interested in your work."

"It doesn't concern you."

"It concerns me that the additional names you provided last night to Vorsky on that disc in the restaurant did *not* check out."

Mundt fought not to show any response. Vorsky had not been as easy to fool with the second set of names as he thought. Then again, Mundt had not counted on this woman's involvement. Vorsky he could fool, but her . . .

"They are all Holocaust survivors," Mundt insisted. "Just like the first three names I gave Vorsky."

"Not according to my information, Herr Mundt. And my information is most accurate." The woman took another step closer. Dabs of sweat smeared her thick makeup, making her face look spotted. "You would be long gone by now if Vorsky had not made only half the file you wanted available to you. He and I are both curious about your sudden interest in Paul Hessler."

"My deal with Vorsky did not include you, *fraulein*."

"You broke your deal, Herr Mundt, when you passed information onto him you knew to be false. I am here to negotiate a new deal. Why was accessing Paul Hessler's confidential file so important to you?" The woman paused and raised her left eyebrow. There was no break in the hairs, as though it were painted on with an eyebrow pencil. "It strikes me as curious, Herr Mundt, that Paul Hessler was interned at the same labor camp where your father served as guard. Karl Mundt, member of the *Waffen SS*. Assigned to one of the three labor camps outside of Lodz, Poland in early 1944 at the age of twenty, the very same year you were born. According to reports and testimony, your father was shot by Paul Hessler just prior to Hessler's escape in late 1944. His body was never found."

"You know my family history quite well."

"I'm not finished yet. Paul Hessler was found by an American GI detachment days later in the forest well north of Lodz, miles away. One of these GIs was the gunman who tried to assassinate Hessler four days ago: Staff Sergeant Walter Phipps."

"This means nothing to me."

"So you don't know Staff Sergeant Walter Phipps?"

"Never met the man."

"Have you ever spoken to him?"

"No."

"Interesting. Because a week before he flew to Israel, Walter Phipps received a phone call from Germany. We traced the number to a school that had been closed and its phones disconnected for months. Apparently, whoever called Staff Sergeant Phipps knew how to manipulate such things." The woman turned her face enough for Mundt to see the uneven texture of the right side. "What does the attempted murder of Paul Hessler have to do with what has brought you to Israel, Herr Mundt?"

"Am I to consider this an interrogation?"

"Just answer my question."

"Because I am curious to know exactly in what capacity you are operating here."

"I want to know the basis of your interest in Paul Hessler, Herr Mundt."

"And if I don't tell you, you'll kill me, is that it?" Mundt asked, glancing at the two gunmen whose fingers had still not left the triggers of their pistols. "You'd be able to, I suppose, but it would be messy. Can you afford that risk? Can your organization afford it, considering you don't officially exist anymore?"

The woman stiffened. "We never *officially* existed."

"Your time has past."

"Not according to your data, Herr Mundt."

Mundt locked his eyes on the woman's. "Tell your men to put their weapons down, or use them. One way or another, this conversation is over."

"You'll have to do better than that; and better than that phoney e-mail threat of yours made to Vorsky about delivering information to various media outlets."

"But I've added a section since I last spoke with Vorsky, describing him as a Holocaust survivor and Israeli war hero who took the law into his own hands by murdering three innocent people, including the deputy chief of staff of the army."

Mundt could see the rage building in the woman's eyes but the color of her face remained placidly pale and unchanging.

"Innocent?"

"There's no proof of the victims' guilt that would stand up in any court, and you know it." Mundt rose, inviting the gunmen to shoot him. "So kill me and you destroy your friend Abraham Vorsky."

The woman started to back up for the door. "We'll find out what you know, Herr Mundt. One way or another."

"Be my guest," Mundt told her.

CHAPTER 48

Get out of here!" Tabar Azziz ranted. "I don't want to talk to you anymore! I don't like what you insinuate."

"We're not leaving," Ben told him.

"Not until you answer a few more questions," Danielle picked up.

"We believe sensitive information was stolen from at least one of the companies you service," Ben explained. "At this point we have no reason to believe you were involved and every reason to believe that Shahir Falaya was. That could change if you remain uncooperative."

"It's hard enough for Arab-owned businesses to survive in Israel already," Danielle added. "Don't make it any harder for yourself."

Tabar Azziz shrugged. "What is it you want to know?"

"You said the most advanced machines you service now have hard drives," Ben said.

"Nonvolatile memory," Azziz nodded.

"And if these hard drives were faulty?" questioned Danielle.

"We would replace the entire circuit board."

"Would all the memory be lost?"

"Not necessarily," Azziz replied. "It's a simple process really to transfer the memory from one board to another. Usually just one chip or switch that's faulty."

"You're a good teacher, yes, Mr. Azziz?" Ben asked him.

"I am very good teacher, Inspector."

"So good that Shahir Falaya could replace these circuit boards on his own?"

"Of course. There is no great trick to it."

"Even if the board wasn't faulty at all?"

The air seemed to drain out of Azziz's lungs. He slumped visibly and tapped the counter before him.

"How long would it take?" Ben continued.

"Minutes."

"And the company would never know, would it?"

"Not if he did it right."

"You taught him, didn't you?"

Azziz nodded grimly. "The boy would do it right."

"So now he has in his possession the board containing everything that was copied, faxed or printed since the machine was delivered."

"Yes," Azziz nodded.

"Could he learn what those contents were? Print them out or something?"

Azziz nodded reluctantly. "But I never left the boy alone. Always we work side by side."

"You taught him how to identify damaged circuit boards, of course," Danielle said, trying not to make it sound like an accusation.

"It's not that hard. A few simple tests once the office machine is plugged into our system tester. One of these." Azziz pulled a car battery-sized device with a high tech LED read-out board from a shelf overhead.

"And when working together, side-by-side, sometimes you let him work this system tester," Danielle resumed. "Maybe trusted him so much you didn't question his findings."

"Shahir was good boy. Comes in early on Sundays. Stays late during the week."

"Is it possible he switched the boards without you knowing?"

"It's possible," Azziz acknowledged, shrugging his portly shoulders. "But what could he gain by that? He'd still have to access the information. No way he could do that. *Mish mumkin!* Because, because he'd need a machine that takes the same circuit board, an *identical machine*."

Ben felt everything click into place. "Like the models on display in the front of your store?"

O VER SEVENTY COMPANIES ," Ben sighed from the passenger seat of Danielle's Jeep, surveying the list provided by Tabar Azziz of companies serviced by Abasca Machines. "Azziz is a busy man."

Beside them traffic continued to snail past, slowed even more by hopeful drivers thinking the Jeep was about to give up its parking space.

Danielle flipped through her copy with considerably less interest. "Law firms, corporate headquarters, and that's only the start of our problems."

"What do you mean?"

"If blackmail's what this is all about, we can't be sure the target or targets were actually the businesses Abasca Machines served," Danielle explained. "It could be a client at one of these law firms, or a customer of one of these companies. All those copies, all those faxes, all those pages transferred from an employee's desktop computer to his file on the printer/copier." She flapped the pages composing the list in frustration. "Who can tell which one was behind the deaths of these children?"

"I see your point."

"There's more; equally unhelpful, I'm afraid. We have no way of gaining access to the circuit boards Shahir Falaya may have replaced, which leaves us with no way of narrowing down the list. Even if we could, blackmail victims are unlikely to talk—that's why they paid in the first place. And, for the same reason, we can forget about them giving us the kind of access to their records that we'd need."

"One of them is responsible for four murders, Pakad. We can't forget that."

"Even if we could narrow down this list . . ."

"There's got to be a way."

"How?"

"Re-create the steps the four students took once Shahir had the stolen circuit boards in his possession."

"Considering the condition of Shahir Falaya's computer when you found it," Danielle reminded, "that won't get us very—"

She stopped suddenly, the pages crinkling in her hand.

"What is it?" Ben asked her.

She held her copy of the list out to him, pointing at one of the final names. "Look."

CHAPTER 49

AS SOON AS the woman and her henchmen had departed, Hans Mundt sat back and tried to think. He had no memory of his father, knew Karl Mundt only from pictures his mother deposited around the house and from the exhaustive research he had conducted, trying to reconstruct the man in his head.

Beyond that, Karl Mundt lived in his son's mind through the stories Hans had solicited from those who knew him. Much of the time, these tales remained just collated notes on paper or the faded recollections of old men speaking in cracking voices. Lately, though, now that Hans Mundt had come so close to the truth, the tales took on a reality all their own.

*P*AUL HESSLER LAY *on his bed in the camp quarters, pale and shivering. He had lost so much weight he had taken to tying a rope around his waist to keep his pants up but now, his intestines racked by dysentery, he lacked the strength to even knot it.*

He was alone in the rank barracks that had once been

a stable, shared by the camp's workers with rats. At night, when he couldn't sleep, Paul would hear the rats scuttling and pittering about. They didn't scare him. They used to, but they didn't anymore.

He tightened the thin blanket around his shoulders. It smelled of mold and mildew, and had been unpacked from boxes left out in the rain while the inmates worked. He had a mattress and a straw pillow. The sum total of his life's possessions.

Paul Hessler knew if you didn't work, you weren't fed. The penalty for sneaking food to a sick or disabled inmate was death, and the Haupsturmfuehrer, Gunthar Weiss, loved to make examples. Paul knew that now that he was no longer of any use to them, the camp guards would be coming soon to put him out of his misery. Take him outside where the other inmates would be able to see the gun pressed against his head and his brains splatter across the ground. He wasn't sure he cared. Perhaps he should look forward to that moment for the opportunity it would provide to join his parents, slaughtered in the Lodz ghetto before he'd been brought here. If it wasn't a bullet that took his life, it would almost certainly be typhoid or the dysentery that plagued him now.

No! He had to survive for his parents. They had sacrificed everything to keep him alive for as long as they could, including ultimately their lives. Give up and he would render their deaths meaningless.

The upstairs door creaked open and the steps of heavy boots clattered down the stairs.

Paul Hessler didn't turn, didn't move. Couldn't help but welcome the end. The boots clacked closer to him and he began to pray silently.

A hand squeezed his shoulder, eased him around gently.

"I brought you some bread," said Karl Mundt, the young guard who had already saved his life once before. "And some pills too." He sat down next to Hessler on the cot and handed him six pills. "Take two now and the rest *later. You'll have to swallow them dry. I couldn't sneak you anything to drink. I'll try again later."*

Paul Hessler managed with great difficulty to choke down the first two pills and then accepted the hunk of bread Mundt had stuffed inside his jacket.

"Thank you," Hessler said, grasping the young guard's sleeve. "Thank you."

Mundt pulled away, as if revolted by his touch. "Another thing. In the soup line I always notice you fighting to be near the front."

"Of course."

"From now on, wait until the end to be served. The potatoes and solids settle near the bottom of the cauldrons. Wait until the end and you'll find more than just broth spooned into your bowl. Do you understand?"

Hessler nodded gratefully and tore off a hunk of bread. "I'm going to be a rich man someday," he said between chews, his stomach quaking from his first solid food in a week. "And I'm going to pay you back for this. You won't be sorry."

"What makes you think I won't be rich myself?" Mundt asked him.

Paul went back to his bread.

"I guess I could always come to you for a job," the guard resumed.

"Only if I live."

"Oh, you'll live," Karl Mundt assured him. "I'm going to make sure of it."

H ANS MUNDT HAD interviewed a dozen survivors from the camp where his father had served, all of whom related parts of the strange friendship that sprouted between Karl Mundt and Paul Hessler. How his father had nursed the boy back to health and kept him alive through the remainder of the boy's stay in the camp. They spoke of overheard conversations in which the two young men compared their divergent lives. Karl Mundt, they said, claimed he had been forced into military service. Taken right out of a school he loved and later away from the woman he had just married.

Karl Mundt did not learn he was going to be a father until a letter reached him shortly after his arrival at the camp. A letter Hans himself found buried amidst other such material in Germany's National Archives. Coming to know the father he had never met had long been an obsession for Hans Mundt. It had taken up a good part of his life and, more recently, came to dominate it. He was in search of no truth other than what little he could learn of the man whose absence had created a void in his life which became more painful for him as the years went on.

But the truth Hans Mundt uncovered was far different from that which he expected.

Just a few weeks before, his funds nearly exhausted, Hans had at last found the body he had been searching for buried in the woods beyond the camp's site north of Lodz. He'd had suspicions before that, suspicions raised by inconsistencies and too much that didn't fit. All underscored by a dread fear Hans had tried to bury where he couldn't reach it.

The crumbling bones he'd lifted out of the ground, though, told a different story. Hans Mundt had to face a reality that was as horrible as it was impossible. That's why he was here. That's why he had to act.

And he would.

Soon.

CHAPTER 50

BEN LOOKED AT the item on the list Danielle was pointing to. "Hessler Industries," he said, feeling his breath catch in his throat.

"Strange, don't you think?"

"You think there's a connection between murdered Holocaust survivors and murdered high school students?" he said and shook his head. "No, Danielle. Hessler Industries has an advanced digital printing station that Abasca Machines services. Don't look for more than that."

"I thought you once told me you didn't believe in coincidence."

"Sorry, that was Sherlock Holmes."

"Another great detective."

They both smiled. Ben wished it could last.

"What are you going to do with that list?" Danielle asked him.

"Try and figure out which of these companies was the one being blackmailed."

"You can tell me all about what you find when I get back from Germany."

"Germany?"

Danielle nodded. "To pick up the trail Asher Bain was following."

"They killed Bain. They'll kill you, too."

Danielle's gaze was strangely emotionless. "They sent Ellie and they'll send someone else for me whether I go or not, Ben. They'll send someone else unless I get them first. I have to find out what Bain was on the verge of uncovering. I don't have a choice."

"Yes, you do," Ben said suddenly. "We both do."

"What do you mean?"

"I can take the job in Detroit." He held his breath for an instant. "You can come with me."

"Run away?"

"*Get* away. There's a difference."

"Not that I can see."

"Because you're not giving it a chance, Danielle. You're not giving *us* a chance."

Danielle's expression softened, but didn't waver. "Captain Bain told me my father's name showed up on a list he generated. He fit the profile of these Holocaust survivors who've been killed."

"So?"

"Do you remember how you felt until you learned the truth about your father?"

Ben nodded, wishing he could lie.

"Well, these men were murdered because of something they have in common. Something they were involved in. What if my father was involved in the same thing?"

Ben reached over and hugged her tenderly. He felt her flinch, but didn't let go. "Beware of searching for secrets you'd rather not find, Danielle."

Danielle remained undeterred. "Ellie was a Mossad assassin, Ben. That means someone in Israel ordered the deaths of these Holocaust survivors. These men who were just like my father."

Ben left his hand where it was, feeling the softness of her skin. "I can call John Najarian right now. We can be on a plane tomorrow and fuck the rest of them."

"You're not listening to me. We'd be leaving too much behind."

"Not always a bad thing," Ben said pointedly.

CHAPTER 51

I'M AFRAID EVEN my contacts cannot penetrate these companies, Inspector," Nabril al-Asi said apologetically to Ben, holding the list of those serviced by Abasca Machines. "Not with the little information you're able to provide."

Months before, after Israeli helicopter gunships strafed the building in which the colonel's Palestinian Protective Security Services was headquartered, al-Asi had relocated his office here in the back rooms of a building off Amman Street. The front rooms served as a civil marriage hall for Jews, catering to secular Israelis who did not want to be wed by an Orthodox rabbi. Such a rite was required to make a marriage official in Israel, but not in the West Bank where an Israeli businessman ran the chapel and paid a registration fee for each marriage performed. The perfect place to house his office, al-Asi had once explained to Ben, since the comings and goings of unfamiliar faces never received undue attention.

"And if I were able to get more? Say, irrefuteable proof these high school students were murdered by one of their victims?"

Al-Asi scratched his chin. His office was cramped and simply furnished, just a place to meet, apparently, although on a few occasions Ben was certain he heard activity in a floor or floors below. He couldn't see any stairs or access doors, though.

"Tell me about these children again, Inspector."

Ben went through the details of his investigation from the beginning, somewhat reassured by the fact that al-Asi was nodding when he finished.

"A question, Inspector: How did the students contact their chosen targets?"

"I assume by electronic mail."

"Via their personal computers?"

"Possibly."

"I doubt it. If you were going to commit such a crime, would you leave the evidence so readily available?"

"I see your point."

"Of course you wouldn't, because no lines in this part of the world are really secure. My Israeli friends watch *everything*."

"You mean electronic correspondence can be traced back to its source, like a phone call."

Al-Asi nodded. "In essence, it *is* a phone call, Inspector. Now, it is possible to confuse the issue by bouncing the signal around a bit. But even that can be tracked down, assuming one is patient."

"The way threats over the Internet are tracked down."

"More or less."

"So what's the alternative?"

"Thinking like a criminal, Inspector?"

"No, Colonel, like a high school student."

"You've just answered your own question."

"What?"

"A site with multiple outgoing lines and multiple users would make the tracing procedure much harder to manage and, even if successful, the target wouldn't necessarily know which computer it came from or what person was logged on at the time."

"A bank of computers."

"That's right."

Ben felt as if someone had just given him a hard shake. "The kind you'd find, say, in a high school . . ."

"Very good, Inspector," al-Asi complimented. "I think you're learning."

DAY FIVE

CHAPTER 52

A LIGHT FOG COATED the German countryside as Danielle drove the rental car toward the only nursing home in Remscheid, Germany. It was located in a residential neighborhood on Hanastrasse and comprised two interconnected buildings.

Danielle followed the signs in German toward the visitor parking lot which at this hour of the morning was virtually deserted. From her car, she walked down a small stone stairway to a second driveway that led to the nursing home's lobby. The huge glass double doors slid open automatically as she approached them, and Danielle moved toward a reception booth behind a long counter on the left.

"Do you speak English?" she asked a receptionist garbed in white.

"Yes," the woman replied.

"I would like to see Herr Weiss. I trust he's still a patient here."

"Gunthar Weiss?"

"That's right."

The receptionist regarded her suspiciously. "You're not a relative, are you?"

Danielle withdrew her National Police identification and handed it across the counter. "I am here on a matter of some urgency."

The receptionist stiffened as she inspected Danielle's credentials. "Is Herr Weiss being investigated by your country?"

"Not directly, no."

"Because it is our job to protect our patients here. We don't want them bothered nor do we wish to have their pasts dredged up."

"What makes you think this is about the past?"

"With men like Gunthar Weiss, it's always about the past," the receptionist said, her final words emerging through a condescending sneer.

"If you don't mind, I've come a very long way."

"I don't mind at all." The receptionist slid a clipboard complete with two-page form across the counter. "Just fill this out so it can be reviewed by our administrator. Make sure you leave your contact number in Germany so we can contact you as soon as he gets to it."

Danielle turned the clipboard around and pushed it back across the formica. "I'm here as a representative of the Israeli government," she bluffed. "If you want, I can return with a member of our embassy here along with my contact at your National Bureau of Investigations." She leaned forward over the counter. "That way we can check up on some more of your residents at the same time."

The receptionist returned the clipboard to its peg and reached for a clip-on pass in its place, but the displeasure lingered in her expression. "You won't get anything out of Gunthar Weiss anyway."

"What do you mean?"

"You'll see."

THE VISITOR'S PASS flapping against her jacket, Danielle rode the elevator to the third floor and stepped out into a large, open area. Before her, residents loitered in wheelchairs or walked about dragging IV poles at their sides. Some leaned awkwardly against a wall. The sounds were quiet and muffled, save for an occasional misplaced cry from somewhere down the hall. The air was sour and spoiled, and the pungent stench of oversprayed Lysol was powerless to do anything but cling to the furniture and walls.

Another receptionist pointed her toward a small lounge off to the side and Danielle approached to the sounds of German blaring over a television in an overlit, windowless room furnished with three rows of interconnected chairs. A solitary man sat in a wheelchair looking up at the wall-mounted screen. His legs were covered by a plaid blanket. He smiled toothlessly at the morning cartoons, lacking enough breath to laugh. His mouth hung open, not changing. His eyes didn't blink.

"Herr Weiss?"

No response.

"Herr Weiss?"

The eyes finally blinked as he turned her way for only as long as it took for him to realize he might be missing something better in the cartoon. Danielle walked out in front of his wheelchair, planting herself between it and the television. Weiss looked agitated, swiping at her as if she were a bothersome bug. Giving up, he simply wheeled his chair backwards to regain a clear view of the cartoon which Danielle recognized as an old American show dubbed in German.

"I need to talk to you about what you did in World War Two, Herr Weiss," Danielle said, hoping her words got through. "I have some questions."

A commercial came on the television and the old man's eyes flickered. He looked at Danielle as if seeing her for the first time.

"You're not my new nurse."

"No, I'm from the police."

"Police? I don't like police."

Danielle stole a quick glance at the screen, convinced

the old man would remain lucid only through the length of the commercial break. "I'd like to talk to you about the labor camp outside of Lodz, Poland."

"I wasn't there, don't know what you're talking about. A schoolteacher. I was a schoolteacher."

"You served twenty years in prison for your crimes. It's public record."

"I should have been a schoolteacher. I would have been a good one."

"What kind of labor camp *Haupsturmfuehrer* were you?"

Weiss looked back at the television to see another commercial beginning. The air seem to drain out of his thin face like a popped balloon.

"A long time ago. Too long."

Danielle looked at the frail old man sitting in the wheelchair before her, confronted all at once by the reality that she had no clear idea of what to ask him. Captain Asher Bain, before he died, had said only that Weiss was the key. Key to *what*? What else had Bain uncovered about this case and Danielle's father?

On the screen angled down from the wall, the second commercial was winding down.

Gunthar Weiss looked up at Danielle suddenly. "You've come to ask me about him, too."

"Who?"

"Karl Mundt. The bastard. Thought he was so much better than the rest of us, too good for labor camp service. Never trusted him. Should have known, should have figured out what he was really up to earlier."

"And what was that?"

Just then the morning cartoons returned to the television and Gunthar Weiss slipped back into his dreamlike trance with his eyes locked on the screen.

CHAPTER 53

BEN KAMAL FOUND Jane Wexler, principal of the Palestinian-Israeli cooperative school outside of Abu Gosh, busy with a stack of student files when he appeared in her office doorway.

"What are you doing here, Inspector?" she asked, clearly annoyed by his unannounced visit.

"I was hoping you could help me with something." He hadn't expected the Israeli soldiers outside to let him in. Having recognized Ben from the other day, though, they had grudgingly granted him entry after making sure he wasn't armed.

Wexler looked around, as if expecting to see Danielle Barnea just behind Ben. "You don't have any authority in Israel. I shouldn't even be talking to you."

"Even if it's in your own best interests and the best interests of the school?"

"Get to the point, please."

"Do you want to help me find whoever killed your students or not, Ms. Wexler?"

Jane Wexler pushed her pile of folders aside. "Go on."

Ben nodded. "I found Zeina Ashawi. She's alive and

under the protection of the Palestinian Authority."

"Thank God."

Ben closed the door to the principal's office behind him. "She told me something you're going to find extremely unsettling, Ms. Wexler. She told me the murdered students were involved in some kind of blackmail ring."

"Blackmail?" Jane Wexler posed incredulously.

Ben nodded. "Shahir Falaya used his job as a business machine technician to steal sensitive information from major companies. I believe one or more of these companies were then extorted under threat that this stolen information would be made public."

Jane Wexler's face widened with fear and realization. "Then it was someone they blackmailed who killed them. That's what you're saying."

"I need to find out who—which company it might have been."

"I told you, Inspector, I didn't know what they were up to, I can't possibly help you."

"Yes, you can," Ben said, holding her gaze. "Because you were involved in the plot."

CHAPTER 54

TESS SANDERSON AND Paul Hessler entered the Hessler Institute just after noon, hoping to keep recognition of their visit to a minimum. Security and laboratory personnel still on the premises couldn't believe their eyes; Paul Hessler had spent extraordinarily little time in the institute that bore his name, especially as of late.

"You're walking too fast," Paul said, feeling his hips begin to ache.

"I'm nervous, sir."

"I told you to call me Paul, and there's nothing to be nervous about."

Sanderson swiped her card to gain access to the secure laboratory area and then keyed the proper combination into the pad next to the door marked CLOSED FOR CONSTRUCTION.

"Your idea, Tess?" Paul wondered, impressed.

"Actually, it was your son's."

Paul felt a familiar heaviness in his stomach as he proceeded through the door into the antechamber. "This is my son's legacy," he said somberly. "All I have left of him."

Tess Sanderson turned toward Hessler and nodded understandingly before approaching the inner door to the project lab. She scanned her iris and heard the door click open.

"I built this institute to find cures and treatments for diseases that continue to plague humanity," Hessler said to her before they entered. "Diseases that attack both genders, all races. Diseases that do not discriminate among classes, that don't care about the size of our wallets or our hearts. I considered myself a man of vision, Tess." Hessler's voice faded a bit. "But somewhere along the line I must have lost that vision. Thank God Ari picked it up."

Tess Sanderson's eyes moistened and she tried to blink them dry. "The world will thank him too, sir."

Hessler pushed out a smile. "Paul. Now show me my son's legacy. Show me Lot four-sixty-one."

CHAPTER 55

DANIELLE COULD DO nothing but wait for another commercial break in the cartoon show Gunthar Weiss sat watching. As soon as the next one came, and the old man's dull gray eyes flickered back to a semblance of life, she resumed.

"Herr Weiss, you said you should have figured it out. Figured *what* out? What were you talking about?"

The old man's lips quivered, his eyes swimming in fear. Danielle realized she had come at him too hard, too fast. She made herself back off.

"You were talking about someone named Mundt."

Weiss smacked his dry lips together. "Yes, Karl Mundt; the bastard. Never trusted him from the day he came to the camp. Knew he was up to something."

"Up to what?" Danielle asked, one eye following the television commercial's progress.

"I caught on finally," the old man rattled, looking more through than at her. "He didn't think I would, but I did. He knew the war was lost. He knew our time was almost up. I guess I knew too, not that I admitted it. But Mundt was ready for it. He was *prepared*."

Danielle saw the screen briefly go dark before a second commercial, thankfully, replaced the first. "How, Herr Weiss, how was he prepared?" she posed gently.

"You are a stupid woman."

"Why?"

"Because it's so obvious. Can't you see it?"

"Why don't you explain it to me?"

Weiss's eyes began to stray back to the television screen, perhaps sensing the imminent return of his cartoons. "Karl Mundt was a traitor. All along he was a traitor and I didn't realize it until it was too late. Until I saw him . . ."

The expression on Gunthar Weiss's face became as blank as the screen with the end of the second commercial. Danielle grasped his shoulders and turned his wheelchair toward her.

"Saw him *what*?"

The cartoon filled the screen again, but Danielle stayed planted before Weiss's line of vision, shaking him.

"Talk!" Danielle crouched and grabbed Gunthar Weiss's knobby arms. She shook him again to hold his attention and felt the bones rubbing against each other beneath her grasp. "Until you saw him *what*?"

"Die." The old man's dry voice had turned grating, painful to listen to. "Until I saw Mundt die."

CHAPTER 56

JANE WEXLER DIDN'T bother to deny Ben's shocking allegation, just stood frozen between him and her desk.

"How did you know?" she asked him finally.

"Zeina Ashawi thought there was someone else involved in the scheme, but had it been another student he or she would have been killed with the others."

"I guess I was lucky," Wexler frowned.

"Not lucky enough to get your money. Nearly a hundred thousand dollars in cash was found under Michael Saltzman's bed, withdrawn apparently by Beth Jacober. It didn't make sense the students would have taken such a risk, unless another partner was expecting her share."

Jane Wexler trembled slightly. She swabbed her eyes with her sleeve, but came away dry. She should have looked regretful, mournful even, but her eyes flashed indignation, her gaze harsh.

"I've got it wrong, don't I?" Ben asked her. "The students didn't need you at all. They would have done this, were doing it, all on their own until you found out. Then you blackmailed *them*."

Jane Wexler said nothing.

"Why?" Ben demanded. *"Why?"*

"You think I want to be here, Inspector? I ran away from some . . . problems in America, left one hell for another. The money was my chance to get out of here before this country explodes, go home and set things right. I asked them for the money I needed, not a penny more."

Ben didn't bother hiding his disgust. "How generous of you."

She looked at him defiantly. "So are you going to arrest me? Hand me over to your Israeli lover?"

Ben remained calm. "It's not me you've got to worry about. Whoever killed your students will figure out your involvement before much longer."

Wexler swallowed hard. "What do you want from me?"

"The evidence indicates that all contact was conducted via computer, up to and including transfer of the extorted funds. But the students never would have used their own computers, since the risk of the messages being traced back to them would have been too great. A bank of computers with numerous outgoing lines, like this school's, would have been much more secure from their vantage point. And you must have caught them in the act."

"Let me walk away from this and I'll help you any way I can," Wexler promised, trying not to sound pleading.

Ben lowered his voice, trying to keep the loathing he felt for this woman from it. "I need to find out who it was they contacted from here. What information they exchanged. Help me, and I won't report you. That will give you time to run from the killers who'll certainly find you eventually otherwise."

Jane Wexler looked down and stared blankly at the desk top, not speaking for a few long moments. "A noble experiment this school—don't you think?"

"In better hands, yes."

"But, you see, we're still in Israeli territory and to get our joint program approved we had to make certain . . . concessions."

"No more games, Ms. Wexler."

"*Security* concessions, Inspector. The government insists we maintain detailed logs of every website accessed by every student."

"Monitored by you, of course."

Wexler nodded.

"Which means you must have erased them, destroyed the evidence."

She shook her head very slowly. "No, Inspector, I didn't."

CHAPTER 57

TESS SANDERSON HAD made sure only Will Nakatami was present for the review of Lot 461 Paul Hessler had requested. The three of them closeted themselves in the small conference room located between prefabricated, soundproof walls and a dropped ceiling.

"Will," Tess began, "I've told Mr. Hessler that as project director you're the one best able to explain the particulars of Lot four-sixty-one."

Nakatami nodded nervously between rapid breaths. He turned to Paul Hessler, eyes wide and anxious. "I'm told, sir, that all you know of Lot four-sixty-one is from the project's initial stages."

"You heard right, Will."

"Then you are aware that the biotech division of Hessler Industries has been at the forefront of what is now called gene therapy for years."

Paul shrugged. "I don't profess to understand very much of it."

"All you need to know for background is that most of this research initially centered on tissue and organ regeneration. We were not alone in this pursuit, of course, and found ourselves lagging well behind some of the larger companies that deal exclusively with this sort of advanced biotechnical research."

Paul nodded. "And as a result the entire division was on the verge of being scrapped when my son and I met with an Israeli scientist who sold us—Ari, mostly—on the concept that would become Lot four-sixty-one."

"Yes," Nakatami acknowledged. "This Israeli scientist had taken gene therapy to the next level, a level that until his discovery was thought to be far beyond our current technological capacity. Something he called the biological computer."

"That's where I get lost," Paul Hessler said humbly.

Nakatami seemed instantly more relaxed, in his element. "You're not alone, sir. Imagine a computer the size of cellular components that could interact with the cellular apparatus of the human body. Instead of microchips, these organic machines would be composed of living molecules that react the same way as microchips. That is, they would be programmed to perform certain tasks once injected into the body, providing doctors with the theoretical means to give direct *in vivo* aid."

Nakatami picked up the remote control device he had practiced using right up until the time Tess Sanderson and Paul Hessler arrived. He touched a button on the pad and all the lights in the room faded out, except for a dull glow emanating from the ceiling. The touch of a second button projected a three-dimensional picture in the center of the conference room. Created through virtual reality technology, the picture fluttered and waved like a floating pool of water. Swimming within it were thousands of elliptical shapes, the dark ones overtaking and consuming the lighter ones.

"What you are looking at," Nakatami explained, "is a virtual depiction of how cancer invades the human body. The dark cancer cells consume the light healthy ones until the body becomes corrupted."

Nakatami touched a third button on the screen and red

circular shapes flooded the scene through an invisible gap.

"The red shapes represent Lot four-sixty-one's biological machines, programmed to seek out and destroy the cancer cells." As Nakatami said that, the red circles began attacking and devouring the dark cancer cells. "Notice that our organic machines concentrate their efforts on the cancer cells and leave the healthy cells alone. Selective destruction, Mr. Hessler, something cancer researchers have believed was theoretically possible for years.

"Theoretical, because no one had actually created the means to accomplish it until Lot four-sixty-one. On paper everything checked out, but our Israeli scientist needed vast amounts of capital to bring the project to fruition. That's where Hessler Industries came in. We built the scientist his lab in this institute and equipped it with everything he needed. I won't bore you with the details or the expense. Suffice it to say that both were extreme. But the initial results, over the course of several years and several hundreds of millions of dollars, were not impressive."

Paul Hessler nodded as if this part was old hat to him. "Yes, yes. And then the scientist in question died and the project seemed doomed. Not wanting to risk the additional tens of millions it would take to continue, I ordered the project cancelled. But obviously my son Ari did not share my pessimism. He believed we were on the threshold of the greatest medical discovery of all time. He couldn't let it go. Without my knowing, he ordered the project continued in this lab."

"With good reason," interjected Tess Sanderson. "Ari saw the end of cancer. He saw the potential eradication of all inherited and acquired life-threatening illnesses. He saw the cure, not just the treatment, for heart disease and arthritis, just to name a couple. And he was right. It should be him standing here giving you the news." Now it was Tess who was breathing hard, barely able to muster her next words. "Go on, Will."

"All of this sprang from the previously untested theories of nanotechnology, which I'm sure you are at least vaguely familiar with. In nanotechnology circuits and diodes are replaced with biomolecules, ribosomes, and polymer elongation and ligation. I'm sorry, sir," he added, when he saw the perplexed look on Paul Hessler's face.

"Don't be, please."

"But—"

"*Living* machines. That's what you're talking about, isn't it? Living machines."

"That's right, sir," said Will Nakatami. "Exactly.

"And now," Tess Sanderson picked up, "we are prepared to enter the first formalized stage of human testing with Lot four-sixty-one. What Dr. Nakatami has just described is potentially the greatest discovery in the history of medical research. With proper assistance and cooperation from the Food and Drug Administration, Ari believed we could be at market readiness with Lot four-sixty-one in slightly less than two years and have it available under experimental protocols in half that. After which . . ."

"After which *what*, Tess?"

Sanderson steadied herself with a deep breath. "After which we will see the end of the worst diseases known to man."

CHAPTER 58

"HESSLER SHOT MUNDT," Gunthar Weiss explained, as soon as the next commercial came on.

Danielle went numb. "Paul Hessler was in your camp? You're telling me he shot this Karl Mundt?"

"Mundt was the guard I once assigned to kill Hessler. I knew he wouldn't do it. I knew from his eyes he didn't have it in him. But he knew there was nothing I could do about it because he was SS and from a well-connected family. His family must have arranged the assignment for him to make sure he survived. But, you see, Mundt had other plans."

"What other plans?"

Gunthar Weiss took a deep breath before responding.

YOU WANTED TO see me, Haupsturmfuehrer?" *Karl Mundt asked from the doorway of the office in the factory Gunthar Weiss had commandeered for his own.*

"Come in, Mundt. Close the door behind you."

Weiss waited until Mundt was standing at attention before his desk before he continued.

"I've been reviewing your file. You have a wife who is expecting your first child."

"I do, Haupsturmfuehrer."

"That was the reason someone arranged this duty for you, I imagine, believing it was safe and simple."

"I reported to this post as I would have reported to any other, Haupsturmfuehrer."

"I applaud your sense of duty," Weiss said, with a slight hint of sarcasm lacing his voice. "Why do you think I am here, Mundt?"

"I don't know, Haupsturmfuehrer."

"Do you suppose it is for the same reasons you are, because it is a safe and simple duty?"

The younger Mundt remained at attention. "It is not my place to say, Haupsturmfuehrer."

Weiss snapped out of his chair and circled round his desk. "What is it we make here, Mundt?"

"Boots, Haupsturmfuehrer."

"And how do you suppose the war would go if the armies of the Reich did not have boots, or if those boots wore out too quickly?"

"Very badly, Haupsturmfuehrer."

Weiss stopped close enough to Mundt to speak directly into his ear. "So they sent me here to make sure the job gets done right. They sent me here to supervise young men, boys really, like you to ensure our quotas are met so the armies of the Reich do not lack for what we are supposed to be producing for them. Do you think I have an easy job, Mundt? Well, do you?"

"No, Haupsturmfuehrer."

"Then why do you make my job more difficult by not obeying orders, by giving special treatment to one certain prisoner?"

"We cannot afford to lose a single worker, Haupsturmfuehrer, for the reasons you just described."

"And that explains why you disregarded my orders to kill that boy some weeks ago?"

Mundt didn't so much as flinch. "I knew you were testing me."

"So you purposely failed. I could have had you summarily executed. You know that."

"I do, Haupsturmfuehrer."

"And yet you still failed to shoot him as ordered. Why, Mundt?"

"I believe you acted without fully evaluating the consequences of your action, Haupsturmfuehrer. The workers here who make the boots work themselves to the death because they cling to the hope that as long as they work they will survive. Kill indiscriminately and you take that hope away. You defeat your own purpose, Haupsturmfuehrer."

Weiss squeezed himself between the desk and the young member of the vaunted SS. "When I first met you, I expected big things. I saw you as a Strosstrupp, a unit commander—at least a Wachteurrer, commander of the guard. But how you have disapppointed me, Mundt. I know what you're up to here—don't think I don't. You believe the war is already lost. You listen to the rumors from the front, the propaganda spread by our mortal enemies. So you are worried about what they will do to you as a war criminal, how you will be judged. You want to go back to your wife and baby, and you put that desire above your service to the Reich. Is that correct, Mundt?"

"It is incorrect, Haupsturmfuehrer!"

"Then, please, set me straight. Explain to me the nature of your relationship with the Hessler boy."

"Each worker is responsible for producing four-point-two pairs of boots per day, Haupsturmfuehrer. If he is unable to work, how will his quota be made up?"

"But you have not given such special attention to other similarly sick prisoners. I didn't see you crying when we buried the bodies of the last lot to die."

"Even more reason why we cannot afford to lose any more good workers."

Weiss glared into Mundt's eyes, nose to nose now. "Do you think me a fool, Mundt?"

"I do not, Haupsturmfuehrer."

"Then don't you think I realize something else is going on here, between you and Hessler?"

"There is nothing, Haupsturmfuehrer."

Weiss nodded his head knowingly. "He's a good looking boy, eh, Mundt?"

Mundt's granite-like face broke for the first time. "Sir?"

"All the time you've spent alone with him . . . Is that what this is about?"

"No, Haupsturmfuehrer!"

"What would your wife think if she learned of this? How would your child feel, growing up in disgrace?"

"I assure you that—"

"If you are not fucking the boy, then what are you up to? What are you after?"

"I already told you, Haupsturmfuehrer."

"So if I ordered you to kill Hessler now, you would do it?"

"I would, sir. But I would be forced to make a report to the Reichstag to question your judgment and adminis- tration of this camp."

"Is that a threat, Mundt?"

"It is a duty, sir. I care only about the Reich. Everything I do is in the Reich's best interests."

Weiss clasped his hands behind his back. "I know you're up to something here, Mundt, and I'm going to find out what it is. You have become a challenge for me. That is why I'm not ordering you killed right now, instead of Hessler. Everything you do, Mundt, beware: I will be watching."

Months later, just after orders came to dismantle the camp and execute the remaining prisoners, Weiss was looking out his window when he saw something startling. He saw Paul Hessler shoot Karl Mundt in the head. The Haupsturmfuehrer *might have intervened at that point, if he wasn't preparing to flee himself. But he also took great pleasure in the fact that Mundt had kept Hessler alive for almost a year, only to be killed himself, and by the very person he'd done his utmost to save. This was how all his efforts had been rewarded. This was how his clever plot had ended.*

As Weiss looked on, Hessler hung a small rucksack over his shoulders and began dragging Mundt's lifeless body into the woods beyond the factory where, Weiss assumed, he intended to bury the corpse. A thick mist was rising and almost at once it swallowed the boy and his burden—the last time Gunthar Weiss had seen either one of them.

Rather than stay to oversee the dismantling of the camp, Weiss tried to flee too, only to be captured by a Russian platoon he dared to execute him on the spot. Instead he was arrested and tried before a War Crimes tribunal. He was yawning when the decision was passed down: Life in prison.

It took twenty years for the world to forget enough so that his release could finally be secured. Ironically, the only job he could come by was as laborer and later foreman of a factory that made shoes. Gunthar Weiss knew the smells of dyes and raw leather well; alone among everything else, these had not changed.

DANIELLE KNEW FROM the receptionist downstairs that Weiss had been a resident for over six years now after a brief retirement from the factory job he had just described. Asher Bain's interest in this old man must have had something to do with Paul Hessler. Hessler was the only conceivable link. But Weiss's story had merely filled in empty spaces in Paul Hessler's life the great man understandably did not want to discuss. Too painful. Too much heartache.

So what was Danielle missing? Hessler was the link to everything here. He had survived in 1944 by escaping the labor camp outside Lodz after killing the guard who had befriended him. Could that be the key to whatever Bain was on the verge of uncovering? Only Weiss would be able to fill in the rest of the missing pieces as to why. What had gone on in the those last days of the war?

"I want to hear more about Paul Hessler, Herr Weiss," Danielle prodded the man in the wheelchair before her. "We're not finished yet."

But the old man's attention was no longer on her. A new cartoon had begun on the wall-mounted television and he craned his neck to find a viewing angle around Danielle. When this failed, he tried to shove Danielle aside with his frail, bony arms.

"That will be quite enough, Chief Inspector Barnea."

Danielle recognized the voice of the receptionist from downstairs and turned slowly. A pair of men were standing just behind her in the doorway.

"These men are from the police," the receptionist said. "They would like to inspect your credentials further."

Danielle knew they weren't police, wished for the gun flying to Germany had made her leave behind. The receptionist cast each of the men a glance.

She knew them, had summoned them to the nursing home before. . . .

"If you would just come downstairs with us," the taller of the two men said, "this shouldn't take too long at all."

Danielle weighed her odds, cursed herself for telling no one besides Ben of her trip here. She moved slowly away from Gunthar Weiss, leaving him to his cartoons. Danielle approached the door, ready to spring as soon as she drew within reach of the smaller man. Disable him and take his gun, while she still had some measure of surprise on her side. Almost there, almost ready, Danielle's gaze drifted beyond the men down the hallway to plan her escape route.

Another pair of men stood on either side of the elevator, hands held inside their jackets so still and stiff they looked like department store mannequins.

"Now, Chief Inspector Barnea," said the taller man, taking hold of her forearm, "if you would just come with us. . . ."

CHAPTER 59

HERE IT IS," said principal Jane Wexler, standing in front of the computer in her office. "All the e-mail correspondence originating at the school since the beginning of the year."

Ben peered over her shoulder. "You're telling me no one else has ever checked this list?"

"It was strictly precautionary, as I said." Then, with a touch of irony, "No one ever had any reason to check it."

Ben kept his eyes on the screen. Somewhere amidst this volume of material would very likely be the extortion targets of the students, one of which had later murdered them. But how was he going to identify those targets?

"What's next?" he asked. "Don't change your mind now, Ms. Wexler, or you'll force me to change mine."

Jane Wexler went back to working the keyboard. "We can start by eliminating any messages since the students' deaths and before their term at the school began." She waited while the computer did just that.

"And now?" Ben prodded.

"You have the names of the companies you suspect might be involved?"

Ben tapped the pocket in which he had tucked the list obtained from Tabar Azziz at Abasca Machines.

"Okay, I'm going to conduct a search for those names."

"I think I can handle that myself, Ms. Wexler," Ben said, not bothering to disguise the obstinacy in his voice. "I think you've done enough."

BEN WAITED UNTIL Jane Wexler had left the room before beginning his search. The process went much more smoothly than he had imagined. He had never understood computers much and used them as little as possible, annoyed by the nasty habit they had of freezing up on him. Ben could only figure he must constantly be hitting a wrong key; found hitting no keys at all to be the best solution.

Today he encountered no problems whatsoever. He performed a wide-listing search to ferret out the companies the murdered students had targeted.

It took a matter of seconds for the computer to complete the search, so fast Ben didn't even realize that the answers had already appeared on the screen.

WHAT'S IT MEAN?" Ben asked Jane Wexler when she returned.

She studied the results of his search: electronic addresses for four companies, none having an accompanying message.

"They must have installed a tapeworm to make sure no one could steal their messages en route."

"A tapeworm?"

"Something that scrambles the message an instant after it's sent."

"But the addresses are intact. Their tapeworm must not have worked entirely."

Jane Wexler frowned, clearly unsettled by the damning

evidence she had not expected Ben to find. "I guess this is your lucky day, Inspector."

Ben stood up and faced her. "I'd get going now if I were you, Ms. Wexler. Your students' killers won't be far behind."

CHAPTER 60

PAUL HESSLER DROVE to the castle as soon as the meeting was over. His travel and work schedule had kept him away for nearly a month, and he was amazed at the progress the work crew had made in that time.

The structure looked virtually finished, every brick and stone meticulously reassembled down to the last detail. The guard at the gate leading into the fenced-in site along the cliffs of New Jersey's Palisades State Park moved to deny entry until he recognized Hessler and apologized profusely. Paul simply walked on, leaving behind his driver and the bodyguards whom Franklin Russett insisted accompany him everywhere he went.

Ten yards inside the fence stood the sandstone wall that protected the castle's perimeter. It had been little more than rubble when Hessler first climbed the hill to the castle in 1944. But his workmen had magically reconstructed it, using a mixture of the original stone along with perfectly matched replicas to restore the wall to its original medieval specifications. The main archway and gate had not been completed yet, to allow space for the heavy equipment that continued to come and go.

Paul walked through the large gap into a courtyard that would someday house a lavish garden. He sloshed about in the mud, sinking into a deep rut left by one of the massive front loaders that remained on site. Looking up at the castle, he could see that the top floors of the four surviving towers were all in place now. These were the sections he had ordered removed and shipped intact from the castle's original site and explained the presence of the massive cranes; only such a machine could possibly manage the task of setting the sliced off sections in place. But the massive cranes were gone now, evidence that only the fine finish work remained. Within six months, right on schedule, the castle would be opened to the public, allowing patrons to take a journey into a past they would never understand.

Paul Hessler entered the castle through the huge oak door whose heavy hinges had been expertly reattached. If it weren't for the *thwack* of hammers and the occasional hum of power tools, Paul could have convinced himself it was 1944 all over again. The air inside was surprisingly cool on this warm spring day, as if his construction crew had managed even to retain that feature from the castle's original setting. He remembered how amazed he'd been when he learned the castle was only thirty miles from the labor camp outside of Lodz. It had seemed so much farther at the time.

He wanted it to be 1944 again, wanted a chance to start from scratch. Get things right this time, beginning with the night he had come upon this castle for the first time. Since the day he had learned that Polish officials had ordered the castle destroyed, it had taken six years and more millions than even Paul Hessler cared to count to transplant the structure here to New Jersey. Of course, it had been easy for Paul to convince people, especially the media, that he was acting on a whim. An old man reluctant to let go of such a vital part of his past.

He had them all fooled.

The truth was he cared nothing for the castle itself. He

had changed the night he came upon it for the first time and not for the better. He would just as soon see it demolished on the muddy, rancid ground on which it had been built in the fifteenth century by an exiled Norman prince. Maybe even operate the wrecking ball himself.

But he couldn't, because of the secret that still lurked within the castle's walls. A secret he had to protect above all else.

Paul Hessler shuddered from the chill when the door closed behind him. Work lights hanging from the ceiling cut through what would otherwise have been the impenetrable blackness he remembered from his first visit fifty-seven years before on the night he happened upon the castle in the midst of the storm.

A gift from God—that's what this place had been. Paul was certain he would have died if not for the shelter it offered in late 1944. His clothes were drenched, his food and supplies lost miles back to the wind and torrential rain. The only light for those miles had come from lightning bursts, and it had been one of these that illuminated the castle at the top of the hill.

Initially, getting out of the storm seemed goal enough. He had collapsed against the wall inside the castle's door, listening to the rain batter its stone façade and smelling the castle's cold, lonely stench for the first time.

But, suddenly, another scent invaded his nostrils. At first Paul Hessler couldn't believe it. A trick of the mind, the imagination, he told himself. Still the smell persisted and at last he sprang back to his feet.

What happened over the next few minutes was the real reason why Paul Hessler had paid the incredible sum to purchase this castle and have it disassembled brick by brick and piece by piece, so it could be reassembled halfway across the world where his secret would now be safe forever. Paul Hessler wondered what would happen if the world learned the truth about the night he had first come upon the castle.

The possibility set him trembling.

CHAPTER 61

DANIELLE CAUGHT GLIMPSES of the German countryside flashing by the car windows, as the drive that had begun at the rest home stretched deep into the night. She sat squeezed in the backseat of the second car between two lean and sinewy men who did not seem to be watching her. That they had not bound or cuffed her hands was a lesson in itself: the men were not concerned about the threat she posed. She had seen their look before, mostly in the army when she served with the Israeli Special Forces. But these men weren't Israelis; she could tell that much.

They were Germans.

None of the car's occupants spoke a single word to her through the long drive that seemed aimless until they reached the small city of Monchengladback. Continuing on for another fifteen minutes, they neared the Bokelberg, a hill with several off-streets featuring mansions both large and small called *villen*. The farther up the hill, the larger and more separated the residences became. Several of these had tall fences encircling properties layered with thick foliage making the homes themselves invisible from the street. Danielle saw the brake lights in the lead car come on and felt her car slow near a villa surrounded by a ten-foot wall made of brick instead of an iron fence.

The cars had barely come to a halt when an electronic gate opened, and they passed up a winding drive adorned with lavish landscaping toward a huge house set well back from the road. The mansion was built of fawn-colored brick that gleamed in the spill of floodlights spaced about the circular drive. The windows were all closed in spite of the night's warmth, and a pair of men stood rigidly at the top of a granite staircase leading to the entrance.

Danielle watched the men pile out of the car at the foot of the staircase. One grasped her arm so tightly he pinched her skin, and she tried to pull away in anger. But his grip was like iron and she relented, letting the man draw her out of the car and then lead her up the steps.

The double-doors were already open when they reached the top, and Danielle stepped inside. Whoever these men were, they had clearly been summoned by officials at the nursing home. And just as clearly, Gunthar Weiss must be someone they were keeping their eye on.

An old man who did nothing but watch cartoons still under some form of surveillance . . . Whatever Weiss hadn't gotten the chance to tell her must be very important indeed. She thought again of her father, of the list of old men, Holocaust survivors, his name among them.

What am I going to find at the end of this road?

Four of the men who had made the drive here with her escorted Danielle through an elegant marble foyer, covered with an Oriental runner, to an open door on the right. They prodded her to enter and then followed her inside an expansive library, its walls lined with leather-bound books set in exquisite built-in, dark wood shelves. The shelves and the paneling gave the room a dark, shadowy appearance even the well-apportioned lighting could not change. The source of the lighting was invisible, emanating from the corners and gaps in a recessed ceiling. In fact, the foyer had been similarly dark, bathed in shadows as if the villa's resident preferred them to the light.

Danielle stood still in the middle of the room. Beneath her feet was a thick carpet that added to the library's richness. She noticed her four escorts had mechanically taken up posts they must have been well used to, indicating she was not the first visitor to be brought to the villa against her will.

Danielle heard heels clacking intermittently on the exposed portions of the marble foyer seconds before a woman entered the room. Tall, even taller than Danielle at nearly six feet—more than that in her heels. She wore a dark dress that clung to her every curve like paint. The woman's hair was dark, cut fashionably short to frame her long, angular face. Danielle couldn't see her eyes because the woman kept to the shadows, careful to avoid the random splashes of light.

"Leave us," the woman ordered the four men at their posts.

The men hesitated, as if not used to hearing such an order.

"Now," the woman said, with added emphasis in her voice.

The men reluctantly obliged, the last one out closing the door behind him.

"Chief Inspector Danielle Barnea of Israel's National Police," the woman announced, after the latch rattled shut. She had stopped at the very edge of the carpet on which Danielle was standing. "Currently under suspension for gross insubordination. Not expected to return. A pity, given your stellar career and background."

"I suppose I should say thank you."

"Do you know who we are, Chief Inspector?"

"Not a clue."

"I'm disappointed. I thought your conversation with Gunthar Weiss would have given it away."

"It didn't help."

"Have you ever heard of the Gatekeepers, Chief Inspector?"

Danielle hedged, feeling suddenly cold. "Yes."

"My question surprises you?"

"Because the Gatekeepers don't exist anymore."

The woman bristled at her comment. "And when they did?"

"A group of Germans who dedicated themselves after World War Two to tracking down and ferreting out Nazis living under aliases around the world. They worked closely with the Israelis, often behind the scenes."

"My name is Anna Krieger, Chief Inspector Barnea. My parents founded the Gatekeepers. My mother's father was in charge of military ordnance for the Nazis. My father's brother was a guard in Auschwitz. Their one desire after the war was to atone."

"And they did—exceedingly well, by all accounts—until their services were no longer required."

"The death of my parents did not leave the world free of Nazi war criminals, Chief Inspector. But their deaths made those remaining criminals feel safe . . . until I took it upon myself to reestablish the Gatekeepers; guardians committed to assuring Germany does not repeat her mistakes of the past at the same time she atones for them. All of us are relatives, sometimes even the children, of Nazi war criminals. Some of these Nazis you would have heard of; others you would not." The woman spoke emotionlessly, her words sounding almost rehearsed. "And some of these escaped punishment and remained free. Most were very young men during the war and some are left alone after careful investigations of their pasts. Others are too old and infirm to bother with anymore."

"My father survived Dachau," Danielle said, raising the issue that had brought her to Germany in the first place.

"Did he? Are you sure of that?"

"What are you talking about?" Danielle flared back at her in anger.

"Of course, you are sure."

The indifferent way the woman named Anna said that knotted Danielle's stomach. She made herself remain calm, determined to seek out the truth that had sent her to Germany. "What do you know about my father?"

"That is what you have come all this way to learn, isn't it?"

Danielle pulled herself back, trying not to appear too eager. "I came here on the trail of the murderers of three old men in Israel."

"Holocaust survivors."

"Yes."

"And this trail took you to Gunthar Weiss."

"Where your people found me."

"Then you came to Germany for nothing."

Something in Anna's voice, and her eyes, left Danielle unsettled. Gnawing at her in a place she couldn't identify.

"You need an army to hunt down a few remaining old men?"

Anna shook her head. "We need that army to keep the mistakes of the past from repeating themselves. The rise of neo-Nazi movements throughout Europe for years now has been as staggering as it is frightening. We infiltrate these groups and mark those deemed most dangerous."

"You're murderers—that's what you're telling me," said Danielle.

"Saviors is the way we prefer to regard it," Anna Krieger said, and brushed a hand across the left side of her face.

"So why bother with me?"

"Your conversation with Herr Weiss, *Haupsturmfuehrer* of the largest of the three labor camps outside of Lodz, was taped. We need to know exactly what led you to him, how you came by what you learned."

"I haven't learned *anything*! I came to Weiss for information, but he told me nothing. If you taped our conversation, you know that."

"You asked him about Paul Hessler and Karl Mundt."

"I asked him about Hessler. He brought up Mundt."

"You had never heard of Karl Mundt before?" Anna Krieger asked her.

"No."

"And your interest in Paul Hessler, this came about from the case involving his son's murder you were briefly assigned to. Am I right?"

"At first, yes."

"And then you became aware of these other murders you mentioned that seemed to be linked to the attempt on Paul Hessler's life and linked to your father as well."

"What do you know about my father?"

"The connection between him and the three apparent Holocaust survivors who were murdered."

"Apparent," Danielle echoed. Anger surged through her, held back only by an increasing level of uncertainty. "Tell me what you mean!"

A new expression flickered on Anna's face, still partly hidden in the shadows to which she clung. "On the table to your right, there is a picture. Please pick it up."

Danielle stepped to the edge of the rug and saw lying on a small side table a black and white eight-by-ten photograph of a rugged, hard face framed by by a mass of thick hair that belied the man's age.

"Do you know this man, Chief Inspector?"

"Never saw him before in my life."

"Then you have never heard of Hans Mundt?"

"I thought Weiss said his name was Karl."

"It was: Karl is Hans's father. Hans is the man in the picture. He learned his trade years ago with Stasi, the East German secret police. Hans Mundt is the man who provided the names of the three men who were murdered in Israel three days ago, along with a number of other names."

"My *father's*?"

"Your father's already dead. There would have been no point."

"Why? Why did Mundt want those three men killed and why should you care?"

"Because they were Nazis, Chief Inspector."

C H A P T E R 6 2

BEN LEFT THE school, expecting that Jane Wexler would leave very soon after his departure.

Driving his ancient green Peugeot back into the West Bank, he considered the results of the computer's cross match between companies e-mailed through the school and companies serviced by Abasca Machines. There had been *four matches*. Not one, but *four*. This hadn't been a simple one-shot exercise that had ended tragically for the murdered students, no game gone wrong. And, if the targets chosen were any indication, they were after big money. Who knew how much had been wired into accounts the students would have opened electronically and then drained as soon as the deposits were made? The money Danielle found beneath Michael Saltzman's bed, extorted by Jane Wexler, was likely only a small portion of what the scheme had brought them.

That's where the students had made their greatest mistake. Beth Jacober must have withdrawn the cash to pay off Jane Wexler from the account they had opened electronically. Only someone was watching. Such large withdrawals of cash, extremely easy to keep track of, would have alerted the killers. And when they checked out Beth Jacober they must have realized they had found at least one of their blackmailers.

Ben recalled the discrepancy Danielle had turned up between the time the girl had left her friend's birthday party and the time the alleged accident had occurred. More than enough time for the killers to question her about the identities of her accomplices. Drugs or torture—such a young girl would have quickly submitted to either. That would have given the killers the names of all four students, five including Zeina Ashawi, and explained why Beth had been the first to die.

Jane Wexler's extortion had caused it all, forced the students to expose themselves. If not for her, he was convinced, they would still be alive today.

Ben considered returning to the school now and arresting Jane Wexler himself. While she had caused the students' deaths, though, she hadn't been the one who killed them, and Ben reviewed the list of possible suspects once again.

All of their targets were well-known firms and businesses, one of which stood out for its size and power: Hessler Industries.

The link with Danielle's pursuits was unavoidable, too much so to be considered coincidence. Where, though, could the connection possibly lie?

Ben tried to plan his next step. He had the names of four companies, serviced by Abasca Machines, that he felt certain were the ones the murdered students had contacted. There was a law firm, a Palestinian investment consortium, a brokerage house, and, finally, Hessler Industries' corporate offices in Tel Aviv.

Ben had to work out some way to gain access to the companies on the list, but the task seemed futile. Even though they were all suspects, he lacked the evidence he needed to launch an official investigation. And none of the companies would cooperate willingly, since that would indicate they had acceded to extortion demands. Whatever the high school students had uncovered was undoubtedly so sensitive their blackmail victims would still go to extremes to protect it.

Four companies; three in Israel and one in the West Bank. He needed to find out which one was behind the deaths of four children. That meant confronting them with what he knew and bluffing them with what he didn't.

Starting in the West Bank.

He would begin with a Palestinian business consortium that might have some reason to fear him, while the others had none.

CHAPTER 63

IT TOOK SEVERAL moments for Anna's words to sink in.

War criminals! The old men who were murdered, including the army's deputy chief of staff, had been Nazi war criminals!

What about her father? Danielle wondered. How could he possibly be included on such a list?

"We have learned that some months ago Mundt interrogated a dying German," Anna continued. "We believe this German gave Mundt the names of ex-Nazis still living, incredibly, as Jews in Israel."

"You believe there could be more than three."

"I fear that, yes."

"And that my father might have been one of them."

"We're not sure. I can only tell you he certainly fit the profile."

"Profile?"

Anna raised her eyebrows. "What better guise for a former Nazi than that of a Jew, especially a refugee and concentration camp survivor?"

"You're saying this was *widespread*?"

"We don't know. The problem is we're not talking about an organized network here or an organized plot. Taking on the identities of Jewish prisoners was carried out on an individual basis by soldiers or guards who were usually of relatively low rank. It wasn't hard—so many of their victims were alone, the remainder of their families wiped out. Disguising themselves as Jewish refugees was a perfect fit for Nazi soldiers who wished to avoid prosecution."

Danielle swallowed hard. "Tell me what you know about my father."

"I already have."

"Nothing! You said nothing!"

"There's your answer."

Danielle pushed her words through the lump in her throat. "A few years before he died, before a stroke incapacitated him for good, a sniper put a bullet in my father's head. He was never the same."

"The shooter was not ours, Chief Inspector. But that doesn't mean such an action wasn't considered. In his case there were too many . . . irregularities."

"Like what?" Danielle asked, the words feeling like nails as they emerged.

"The money, for instance."

Danielle could feel heat building behind her cheeks. "What money?"

"Over a million dollars deposited to an account in his name in the United States."

"He never even lived to enjoy his pension, for God's sake!"

"No, he didn't. But such a large sum, hidden away, is one of the flags that has alerted us over the years to possible targets."

"I never knew anything about this money."

"Another flag. Targets often keep their stashes secret from even their children. To avoid unwanted questions, of course."

"Stop calling my father a target."

"As I said, we lacked sufficient evidence."

"But you didn't clear him."

"Nor did we kill him, Chief Inspector."

"Why? Because he was lying in a hospital? Or was he already dead by the time you made your decision?"

Anna looked unmoved by Danielle's accusation. "Finding Hans Mundt is our concern now."

"Why?"

"Because he has some . . . information that we seek. Information we hoped he might have shared with you."

"I've never even heard of him before now."

"That's too bad. For you and the future. We will atone for the acts of our fathers and grandfathers. It will never happen again. Not here or anywhere else. Not so long as we stand as keepers of the gate."

Danielle shook her head disparagingly. "The world has caught up with you, Anna. Your targets, these neo-Nazi leaders, are pariahs. It's all self-justification now. You've wiped out all your old enemies so you've got to come up with new ones to perpetuate your own existence."

"You think that's all there is to it?"

"That's exactly what I think."

"You're wrong," Anna said, and stepped into the light, removing the wig that covered her scalp.

Danielle gasped. The right side of her face all the way to her ear was covered in scar tissue. The mottled flesh curled around her exposed dome. Anna turned slightly and Danielle could see the other side of her scalp was smooth, shaved clean to allow a neat fit for her wig and slightly darker than the pale, thick makeup with which she had covered her entire face.

"My parents made their share of enemies in their work, Chief Inspector," Anna explained calmly, holding the wig by her side. "Odessa, the organization charged with resettling escaped Nazis, was foremost among them. One night they blew up our house. They found me on the lawn with half my face on fire. I was rescued. My parents were not."

"I'm sorry," Danielle uttered.

"You don't have to be. It is not for you that we do this.

It is for Germany, and the legacy of our names."

"I'm sorry I can't help you find Mundt."

"So am I."

The menacing intent in the scarred woman's voice was clear, and for some reason Danielle felt more angry than scared.

"This isn't just about Mundt, is it?"

"It no longer matters."

"You thought I had information about something else, some*one* else. Who? What is it that you're really after here?"

"Can't you figure it out for yourself?"

"No."

"Mundt did. It's behind everything he's been doing in your country. But that doesn't matter now, because we're going to act with or without the proof that he's found."

"Proof of what?"

Before Anna could reply, the lights in the house died and all went black.

CHAPTER 64

THE DOOR TO the grand library burst open seconds later as the guards Anna had dismissed surged inside.

"Fraulein!" one called.

"Right here," Anna managed to say before Danielle closed a hand around her throat.

Danielle's plan was to use Anna as a hostage to gain safe passage out of the house. To Danielle's surprise, though, her hold didn't last for long. She heard Anna's dress tear as the taller woman twisted from her grasp.

"Don't shoot her!" Anna ordered, her voice hoarse from the brief pressure Danielle had applied to her throat.

Two more guards rushed in wielding flashlights. Their beams sliced through the huge room, searching for targets. Suddenly the glare of muzzle flashes erupted from the balcony of books that covered the entire far wall. The flashlights hit the floor, one shattering while the other's stubborn beam continued to illuminate the floor.

Anna shouted orders desperately in German and her remaining guards scrambled around the room, caught in the revolving spill of the surviving flashlight as it rolled across the floor. More silenced shots accompanied the now familiar blueish muzzle flashes. Danielle heard grunts, screams, bodies hitting the floor like axe-toppled trees.

Seeing an opening, she started for the door.

"No!" a male voice ordered, suddenly behind her, an amazingly powerful grip fastened around her midsection. "Reinforcements will be coming through there!"

"Who are—"

"There's no time! The window! *Now!*"

The huge casement window before them overlooked the grounds and the figure charged toward it with Danielle in tow. She finally glimpsed his massive size, felt even more clearly just how strong he was.

He fired a series of shots at the window that shattered the glass, easing their crash through it. Danielle and her rescuer hit the ground running, barely breaking stride. More glass shattered and almost immediately footsteps thumped behind them, trailed by gunfire echoing in the night.

Danielle's sprint barely kept her even with the man at her side. She watched him discard a pair of lightweight night-vision goggles, explaining why he had been able to aim and maneuver so adroitly inside the blackened house.

Danielle focused on the brick wall enclosing the grounds just ahead now. Ten feet high and nearly impossible to scale, unless she could grasp one of the vines hanging off it.

The big man heaved himself over the wall several yards ahead of her, never looking back to check on her progress. Danielle clambered after him. She grasped a vine and propelled herself upward, not stopping when she reached the top. She let herself tumble over the wall and dropped onto a thick bush that cushioned her fall. She felt a surge of exhilaration at being free of the property, as she rolled off the bush and reclaimed her feet.

Where was the man who had saved her?

A car screeched into reverse, seeming to appear from nowhere, braking so it stopped right before her. The passenger door swung open, as the first of the villa's gunmen dropped over the wall to give chase.

"Get in if you want to live!" said her rescuer.

Danielle jumped inside. The car tore off before she had time to close the door all the way.

She looked at the driver behind the wheel, recognizing him from a picture she had seen just minutes before.

It was Hans Mundt.

CHAPTER 65

AN IZNAK," BEN repeated to the construction foreman at the foot of the huge steel superstructure. "Excuse me. I need to see Max Price."

The foreman turned away from his badge again and Ben sidestepped to stick it back in his face. "Mr. Price is an Israeli, Inspector," the foreman said finally. "You have no authority over him."

"But last time I checked the city of Nablus was under Palestinian control," Ben reminded. "And, unless you help me, you will experience the scope of my authority first-hand."

The foreman sneered and thrust his finger toward the top of the steel skeleton. "Mr. Price is up there. You want to see him, be my guest. *Allah yisallimak,*" he added sarcastically. "May God make you safe."

Ben climbed into the open elevator and pressed a button on the control panel marked UP. The simple platform, enclosed by rails, jerked upward and then settled into a wobbly climb up the structure's side. When finished this would be a twelve-story Marriot Hotel and Resort. Undertaken by a consortium called Partners for Peace, it was located in the exclusive Rafiddiyah district just a few blocks from the fledgling Palestinian stock market.

Partners for Peace was also the only target of the murdered students well known to Ben. The consortium was made up of Israeli and Palestinian businessmen and devoted to economic expansion in the West Bank. A final peace agreement, if it ever came, would lead to an incredible building boom that would make lots of people very, very rich. But a few businessmen, risk takers by nature, chose to get the jump on things and begin construction while prices on prime real estate were still low.

With peace further off than ever these past few months, that gamble now seemed terribly ill-conceived. Construction continued sporadically, in fits and starts, often contingent on the events of the day. Ben had learned from the consortium's headquarters that this was one of the better days and that a prime Israeli member of Partners for Peace, Max Price, was currently on-site.

Ben held fast to the safety rail, as the car climbed the side of the exposed, steel skeleton. He felt the elevator platform jolt to a halt a few feet short of the top floor where high steel workers, wearing leather safety belts that fastened them to the structure, were busy spot-welding. A man in a hard hat and loosened tie noticed Ben and walked agilely across a makeshift catwalk no more than a yard wide toward the elevator.

"I'm Max Price," he announced, glaring down at Ben. "I heard you were looking for me."

Ben held his ID in one hand, while keeping the other locked on the platform's nearest safety rail. "Inspector Bayan Kamal of the Palestinian police, Mr. Price."

"You want to climb up?"

"Not particularly."

"So what can I do for you?"

"Actually," Ben said, returning his ID to his pocket, "there's something I can do for you. I can keep you out of jail." Ben made sure none of the workers were in earshot before he continued. "I have information that you and your consortium were being blackmailed. I'm working on the case."

"What case? There is no case."

"That's not what the media is going to be told when I have this project shut down."

"You don't have the authority."

"The blackmailers were murdered. That makes all their victims potential suspects, and as such I can temporarily seize all assets."

Price used one booted foot to leisurely scratch his ankle. "I'm Israeli, remember?"

"And this is Palestine. We play by our rules here."

"All the more reason why you should back off, Detective."

"It's Inspector. And I'll back off, once I'm sure you're not guilty."

"Assuming what you say is right, *we're* the victims here. We were the ones being blackmailed."

"You paid."

"Maybe we didn't have a choice."

"I'm not going to ask you what the blackmailers uncovered. I'm guessing it might have something to do with the sources of your funding, something that would upset the Palestinian and Israeli authorities deeply, like maybe your Palestinian partners are just shams. That maybe this, and other projects undertaken by Partners for Peace, will benefit only Israelis."

"Who told you that?"

"If it were true and became public knowledge, you'd be ruined, so of course you paid," Ben continued, instead of responding. "Of course you had no choice."

Price grabbed the exposed rail of the elevator and shook it slightly. "That's only a guess. You'll never be able to prove it."

"For now."

"And I don't know anything about these blackmailers being dead. We never knew who they were—we didn't want to know. They wouldn't tell us how they found out, and we certainly were in no position to press them. Just don't expect me to feel sorry for the bastards."

"They were high school students."

The color drained out of Price's face. "We paid a hundred thousand dollars to a a couple of high school students?"

"Four of them, actually. All dead now, killed by one of their victims."

"Not me. Not us." Price leaned forward, his toes precariously close to the edge of the catwalk. "I don't think I should be talking to you."

"The alternative is the Israeli authorities."

"You're not working with them?"

"Not yet. Cooperate and we can keep it that way."

Price edged closer and leaped gracefully down into the elevator car. It shook and wobbled, left Ben clinging to the rail for dear life.

"You can talk to me on the way down," Price said simply. "We hit the ground, we're done." He grasped the control box from the floor and activated the down mechanism. The platform started downward, leaving Ben to cling to the railing once again. "The blackmailers—these kids, according to you—knew things nobody could have known. I figured it was an inside job."

An inside job . . . Of course it was, Ben reflected, since the students had access to Partners for Peace's most sensitive information, thanks to Shahir Falaya's prowess with digital copying and printing machines.

Ben shifted his weight to better balance himself. "How did you pay them?" he asked Price.

"Electronic transfer into a bank in Zurich."

"You trace the account?"

"It was closed by the time we did."

"They contacted you by e-mail."

"Five messages. We dismissed the first two. Three and four revealed them to be in possession of extremely sensitive information. Five gave us instructions how to pay."

"No address you were supposed to respond to?"

Price shook his head. "Nothing that could lead us back to them. They knew what they were doing. High school students . . . I just can't believe that."

The exposed compartment picked up speed, rattling past each floor.

"Look," said Price, "I've told you everything I can. We even destroyed all the e-mails to make sure there were no links whatsoever to what had taken place."

Ben nodded. He decided Price and Partners for Peace weren't behind the murders; the man had been too forthcoming, too shocked by Ben's revelations. That left three other suspects and, if nothing else, at least now Ben knew the precise methodology the students had used, knowledge that would help him once he somehow gained access to the three companies in Israel.

"You want to tell me how the kids found all this out about us?" Price asked when the elevator thumped to a halt on the sidewalk.

"Sorry," Ben said, opening the gate. "We just hit the ground. We're done."

CHAPTER 66

"I KNOW WHO you are," Danielle said, as Mundt rotated his eyes between the speeding Audi's rearview mirror and the road ahead.

He broke his concentration long enough to gaze across the front seat at her. "What did Anna tell you about me?"

"That you were looking for Nazi war criminals who assumed the identities of Holocaust survivors after World War Two."

Mundt shook his head. "Not quite true. I'm only looking for one."

He screeched the car round a hairpin turn that left Danielle clutching the car's overdoor handle.

"Yet you still found time to rescue me," she managed.

"I came here to Germany to kill Anna."

"Why?"

"To stop her from finding out what she was after in Israel."

"Anna was in Israel?"

"She has a friend there." Again Mundt glanced across the seat. "A former head of Mossad named Abraham Vorsky."

"I know Vorsky."

"You should: he was the one who sent Ellie to kill you."

"My God . . ."

"You were getting too close to the truth I had brought him," Mundt told her.

"About these Holocaust survivors. . . ."

"Once Captain Bain shared his suspicions with you, Vorsky dispatched Ellie."

"To kill both of us. But I ruined his plan. I survived and picked up Bain's trail all the way to Gunthar Weiss."

"Which made Anna believe you were working with me."

"This all goes back to your father's connection to Weiss, doesn't it? To the fact that they served in the same labor camp."

"There's actually a lot more," Mundt said and then screeched into a right-hand turn, heading in a direction perpendicular to the main road that ran downhill away from the Bokelberg.

"I still don't understand why you bothered saving my life back there."

"Because of our fathers, Pakad Barnea. Because of our fathers."

The car thundered on into the night.

T HIS IS ABOUT Paul Hessler," Danielle managed to say. Her breath felt bottled up in her lungs. She was so tense forcing out those few words almost left her gasping. "He killed your father and now you're after revenge."

"Did Anna tell you that?"

"No—Gunthar Weiss. In so many words."

"One of the *Haupsturmfuehrer's* more talkative days, then."

"Getting anything coherent out of him was no easy task." Danielle hesitated. "Tell me about my father."

"How much do you know?"

"Assume nothing."

"The money?"

"Anna . . . mentioned that."

"Did she say where it came from."

Danielle shook her head, then said, "No."

"He got it from Paul Hessler."

Danielle felt her heart skip a beat. "He never told me he knew Hessler, never even mentioned his name."

"It was a long time ago. A time old men try very hard to forget."

Danielle looked at Mundt with a mixture of shock and revulsion. "How do you know all this?"

"I have spent a good part of my life investigating Paul Hessler. Scouring reports, accumulating files, both classified and otherwise."

"Like the one you obtained in Israel. Traded names to get."

"Yes."

"The three men you gave the old Mossad chief were killed the next day."

"But I was never granted access to Hessler's entire file."

"Why?"

"Because the names on the larger list I gave to Abraham Vorsky didn't check out. He didn't take the bait. I thought the first three would be enough to convince him."

"You couldn't have anticipated his contacting Anna Krieger. She must have confirmed that the second list you provided contained the names of *innocent* men!"

"No, only men we can't be sure of."

"Like my father?"

"He's dead. You could leave it at that."

"No, I can't; not any more than you can."

Mundt looked pleased by her response. "I was hoping you would say that. Because I need your help . . . and if you want the truth about your father, you need mine too."

"You expect me to help you kill *Paul Hessler*? Revenge for killing your father before the camp was closed? I learned that much from Weiss."

Mundt jerked the car to the left and slammed it to a halt

on the side of the road. "You learned nothing! I had hope for you, Barnea. But it turns out you're as foolish and misguided as the rest of them."

"Am I? If there's something else going on here, just tell me."

"It would be better if I showed you."

CHAPTER 67

PAUL HESSLER HAD stayed much too long at the chilly castle. Past the time the workmen had left. Past the time he had anything left to remember.

He had sat for most of his visit in the top floor of the largest of the castle's towers upon a stone bench meticulously re-created by European masons. Paul had them flown over to help with these parts of the reconstruction, old men like himself who still remembered the ancient secrets of stonecraft. He sat on the bench staring at the fireplace, which someday, he was assured, might even work again. He stared at it until his mind numbed with thoughts of all those years ago, the hell of the camp and the stranger hell that had followed it. Then he turned to the past week, a time so sad and tragic, made no sweeter by the news of the Hessler Institute's miraculous discovery.

Lot 461 should have been the crowning achievement of his life. His final atonement for the secret he had kept these many years. Because of Hessler Industries, millions upon millions would be spared endless suffering. Children would not lose parents to insidious diseases that struck cruelly and randomly, nor would parents lose children. Cancer, AIDS, ALS ... The list went on and on. The potential of Lot 461 was unlimited.

For this, though, Paul did not feel worthy of accepting credit. How could he when he had ordered the entire project cancelled? No, the credit lay with his son Ari who had not lived to claim or enjoy it.

Paul thought he finally understood the grand scheme of it all. He was just beginning to wonder if he had done enough, atoned enough, to waive the final punishment for his sins when the gunman appeared outside of Ben-Gurion Airport.

Paul rested his shoulders against the rough stone wall and thought of the expense and labor that had gone into reconstructing this castle. It was too bad lives couldn't be remade as easily. Taken apart and put back together, their original magnificence restored.

The wind whistled through the castle walls, sounding like a mournful spirit. Before him the ancient chimney seemed to rattle. Paul Hessler coughed dust from his mouth and lifted himself up.

He knew the time was coming when he must tell the world his tale, tell it before the assassins Franklin Russett feared were coming found him at last. But right now he just wanted to be gone from this place that held the deepest of his secrets.

The bricks lining the narrow staircase that spiralled downward felt cold and brittle to the touch, the mortar binding them gray with age. The winding steps were cracked and blackened in the worn places where most feet had fallen. Hessler descended them carefully, leaving his memories behind, one hand propped against the wall to keep from falling.

But the real fall, he knew, was yet to come and there was nothing he could do to stop it.

DAY SIX

CHAPTER 68

WELL AFTER MIDNIGHT, Ben was still behind his desk at police headquarters in Jericho's Municipal Center, mulling over his next move. He needed access to the three companies in Israel who made up the remainder of his suspects. And for that he needed help.

He needed Danielle.

But she wasn't answering her cell phone. Could be the Israelis were punitively jamming the Palestinian transmission towers, as they had been apt to do lately. He hoped that was the case because he didn't want to consider the alternative: that something had happened to Danielle in Germany where she'd gone on the trail of murdered Holocaust survivors. Ben knew she was terribly frightened by the possibility her father was involved in whatever Asher Bain had uncovered. He had advised her not to go, but Danielle wasn't going to be denied, even though she was in no condition right now to pursue anything.

Deeply worried about her, he kept dialing her number even after it became clear there would be no response and began to blame himself for letting her leave in the first place.

Ben finally opened a folder lying on the edge of his desk. Inside were the field reports from the officers he had assigned to canvass Shahir Falaya's neighborhood on the chance someone might have seen the person who removed the hard drive from his computer. Ben expected nothing as he began to read the reports, surprised then to see that three witness reported seeing *the same man* lurking about the day the boy had died. The man must have made little effort to disguise his presence, since their descriptions matched almost perfectly.

Wait, he knew this man!

Ben read the descriptions again, letting them paint a picture in his head. His officers had asked the witnesses all the right prodding questions. He had trained them better than he thought and as a result the person spotted near the Falaya home was clear in his mind.

It didn't seem possible! Of all the people . . .

Ben thought quickly of how to proceed from here. Al-Asi, he needed to speak to Colonel al-Asi!

"Inspector Kamal," a voice called from the doorway, startling him.

Ben looked up to see a pair of well-dressed men staring in at him. He had seen them before somewhere, but couldn't place it.

"We are sorry to disturb you, Inspector," the speaker continued, "but Colonel al-Asi wishes to see you."

Al-Asi's men . . . Is that where Ben recalled them from? "I tried to reach him before. There was no answer. Where is he?"

"We are not permitted to say. There have been some . . . problems this evening."

"Problems?"

"Please, Inspector, if you'll just accompany us we have a car outside. The colonel is waiting."

Ben's gaze fell briefly on his phone. "Why didn't he call?"

"As I said, it has been a difficult night. I'm sure the colonel will explain everything once you are with him."

"And the phones," the second man added, "they cannot be trusted."

That's when Ben realized where he had seen them before. Five days ago, in the soccer stadium.

The terrorist Mahmoud Fasil's bodyguards, who had escaped in the panic!

He doubted that they recognized him; his glance had been fleeting and their eyes had never been directed his way.

"I can't leave now. I'm sorry," Ben said.

"We have our orders, Inspector. The colonel was very clear."

"This is for your own safety," the second one added.

"Why don't we contact the colonel, and I can explain everything to him?"

"I'm afraid that's impossible."

Ben thought of the pistol holstered on his hip. The two men in the doorway seemed on the verge of action. If they moved, for him or their guns, he would have no choice but to go for his pistol.

"Ah, there you are, Inspector," a familiar voice said from the hallway, just behind the two men who claimed they had been sent by Colonel al-Asi. "Excuse me, please."

The two men separated sheepishly to allow Fawzi Wallid, acting mayor of the district of Jericho, to enter the office flanked by two pairs of uniformed Palestinian policemen.

"I'm sorry to be so late, Inspector," Ben's former captain told him. "Come, we must be going now if we are to make the meeting with the president." Wallid turned back to the two men clinging to the doorway. "Arafat works best in the late hours, schedules most of his meetings then when he can work without interruption."

The two men in the doorway could do nothing but nod.

Ben rose and made sure his shirt was tucked in.

"You look fine, Inspector," Wallid told him. "Our president does not stand on ceremony. Now," he continued to the two men who had backed slightly off, "if you gentlemen don't mind . . ."

T HE COLONEL ASKED me to personally watch over you, Inspector," Wallid explained when they were outside, waiting for the two imposters to drive off before resuming the conversation. A few seconds after the imposters' van left, a pair of cars slid out of their parking spots in subtle pursuit. "He had concerns."

"I don't recall you and al-Asi being on such good terms, *sidi.*"

"In my capacity as chief of police, he was someone to be feared. As acting mayor, he is someone to be cherished."

"Where is the colonel?"

"Waiting for you. My men and I are to escort you there immediately."

"He's all right, then. His family, too."

"For now, Inspector," Wallid said, grasping Ben's arm the way an old friend might. "You knew those men, didn't you?"

"So did you, *sidi.*"

"Me? How?"

"From the soccer stadium: They were Fasil's bodyguards."

"Incredible!"

"Not incredible at all. You see, Mahmoud Fasil was the man who stole the hard drive from the murdered Falaya boy's computer."

CHAPTER 69

"W EISS WAS RIGHT: Paul Hessler did kill my father," was the last thing Hans Mundt said to Danielle during the five hundred mile drive to Lodz, Poland. They averaged ninety miles per hour in the diesel Mercedes Mundt was driving and would have reached their destination much sooner had it not been for several stops mandated by Danielle's queasy stomach. Fresh air and snacks provided short-lived relief but only the complete rest she craved would make her feel better. The brief naps she snatched on the trip provided meager respite at best, even made her feel worse.

It was late morning by the time they finally reached Lodz. The city, Poland's second largest, remained industrial in character, not tremendously changed since the fall of communism. All of its buildings were coated in soot and grime, and the horizon was dominated by tall, smoking chimneys growing out of red-brick factories. Lodz, dark and gray, seemed forever trapped in a past from which it did not know how to escape.

Mundt bypassed the center of the city and continued north, clearly repeating a route he had taken many times before. Danielle knew the labor camp from which Paul Hessler had escaped in late 1944 was actually located well outside of Lodz proper, on the road to Lecyca to the north. This camp and two others in the area had culled their workers from the ranks of the Lodz ghetto.

Danielle assumed the labor camp would be long gone by now, especially after they passed the last of the boarded-up relics of textile mills on the side of the road. But Mundt continued on toward the marshes and forest of Lecyca along the Bzura River. Much to Danielle's surprise, they stopped before a large decrepit building, situated all by itself in a clearing.

Mundt turned toward Danielle stiffly and spoke at last. "This is what's left of the Lodz labor camp, the most well known of the three the Nazis operated in this region. It was a shoe factory in the years before the war. The Nazis appropriated it to make boots."

Mechanically, Mundt opened the driver's door and stepped out. Danielle followed but kept her distance.

"Nearly two thousand eight hundred Jews worked this factory between the years 1942 and 1944 when the camp was closed," Mundt continued. "They came by transport, mostly from the Lodz ghetto and were easily replaceable. Of these, two thousand five hundred died of starvation, disease, or execution. One hundred managed to escape over the years and two hundred more survived the chaos of the final termination orders that were never fully carried out. Nor was the mandated destruction of the camp, since *Haupsturmfuehrer* Weiss fled before carrying out his last instructions."

As they approached, the decaying condition of the old factory was even more obvious. Portions of the roof had collapsed. Not a window remained unbroken and huge sections of the walls had buckled, seemingly a stiff breeze away from crumbling altogether. It was damp and cold, and Danielle shivered in the dank mist that enveloped her. She followed Mundt through the mist, moving closer to the factory. The breeze carried scents of rotting wood and sour ground.

Mundt stopped before a memorial plaque made of chiselled granite that had been cemented into the ground a hundred feet from the factory's boarded up and chained entrance.

"The names of those buried in mass graves on the camp grounds," Mundt explained. "The Polish government will not destroy this place, but neither do they find it worthy of upkeep. They just left it here to rot. Fittingly, I suppose."

Mundt ran his hands along the engraved impressions of names on the plaque.

"You won't find my father's name here, Pakad Barnea. Just those of the laborers who died here, both Jewish and otherwise. You'll notice that Paul Hessler's name is not to be found either."

"Because he escaped after killing your father."

Mundt responded without turning toward her. "This building holds many secrets, Barnea," he said noncommittally, "one of which I am going to share with you now."

But they moved no farther toward the building. Instead Mundt turned and started slowly off toward the dank woods with Danielle following close behind. A few hundred yards in, they stopped over a rectangular hole that was unmistakably a grave.

"This is where my father was buried. I finally found the body three weeks ago, the bones still covered by an SS greatcoat. Frayed and tattered, but the insignias still in place somehow. It made me nauseous."

"You never knew your father."

"I was born after he left for the war."

"In the nursing home Gunthar Weiss told me your father befriended Hessler. Saved his life on at least two occasions and was responsible for keeping Hessler alive."

"All true. Paul Hessler came here a frail, frightened boy of sixteen following the deaths of his parents in the Lodz ghetto. He was sent here to a different kind of death, a different kind of hell. And if it hadn't been for my father, he would undoubtedly have found it."

Danielle lowered her voice. Her lips were dry and cracked from the wind. "You can't get those years back. You can't come to know your father this way."

"No?"

"You've turned a lifelong obsession into a midlife crisis. You don't have any children of your own, do you?"

"Something we have in common, Pakad Barnea."

"The difference being you never will. You've come to realize that but can't accept it. That's why we're here. That's what all this has been about."

"Who are you to tell me what all this is about?"

"Hessler killed your father—Karl Mundt—in order to escape, and now that you've confirmed that, you're going to kill Hessler."

Mundt's expression became almost benign. "Killing Paul Hessler is not my intention at all."

Danielle felt something like a rope tugging her backwards. "Then why did you send Sergeant Phipps, the old man, to Ben-Gurion Airport last week?"

Mundt shook his head. "I didn't. He wasn't sent by me."

"You deny having any contact with Phipps?"

"No. I spoke to him: to help me fill in some of the final missing details. About finding Paul Hessler near death in the woods weeks after his escape."

"And what did you tell him?"

"Nothing. But he must have figured it out for himself."

"*What* did he figure out for himself?" Danielle asked, exasperated.

Mundt's stonelike expression wavered ever so slightly. "The man he rescued wasn't Paul Hessler. It was Karl Mundt. My father."

CHAPTER 70

"I WANT THIS mess cleaned up. Is that clear?"
Israeli foreign minister David Turkanis made no effort
to disguise his anger directed at the former head of Israel's
Mossad, Abraham Vorsky.

"This is not my mess, Minister," Vorsky said, trying to
sound respectful. "It belongs to history."

Turkanis snorted in disgust. He started to shake his head,
then simply stiffened and sneered. "You blame these murders on *history*?"

"Justice often takes its time."

Turkanis shook his head, kicked the sand of the Negev
Desert about, to vent his anger. They had met here at Turkanis's request because he needed to be present at Israel's
Air Defense Command headquarters for further tests on
the Arrow missile defense system being conducted at midnight. But the location also afforded a degree of privacy
usually not possible in Israel.

"Justice," Turkanis repeated, fighting to keep his voice
down. "If what you say is true, and I'm not at all convinced it was, you should have passed the information
along through the proper channels."

"That is not the way such things are done."

"In your day, perhaps," Turkanis snapped, shaking his head in dismay. "Not anymore. My God, where have you been? Don't you realize that Israel no longer operates in a vacuum? Our actions have consequences, and yours have placed this government in an extremely uncomfortable, not to say dangerous, position."

"If all had gone according to plan, you would never have found out."

"What do you think this is, Vorsky, 1967? 1973 perhaps?"

"You would be wise to remember those times, Minister."

"And you would be wise to remember the lessons learned from them. Did you think the late Captain Bain's conclusions would not reach us? How could you believe we would not figure out who was behind the murders of these three old men?"

"Not just any old men."

"No. One of them was deputy chief of staff of the army. My God, if the truth of what you did ever came out . . ."

"Let it!" Vorsky raged, voice carrying through the desert. "Let the rest of the bastards flee in fear!"

"There are no others, Vorsky. Do you understand that? Your inquiries into Paul Hessler's background are absurd and ill-founded."

"We don't know that yet," Vorsky insisted, in a softer voice.

"That is exactly why I called you here," David Turkanis said firmly. "Paul Hessler is not to be touched. You will end your investigation forthwith."

"Do you hear what you're saying?"

"The real question is do *you* hear what I'm saying, Vorsky? Because the responsibility is yours. Whatever it takes, whatever you need to do."

"I have resources, you know," the older man said lamely, realizing in that instant how stupid he sounded.

"Good. Then use them to deal with whoever might cause

Paul Hessler any harm. The government desires no involvement in this. This conversation never took place."

Vorsky's eyes blinked grimly. "You speak as though something else never took place."

For a moment David Turkanis's features flared. He took a step toward Vorsky and seemed on the verge of grabbing him when he settled himself and churned his feet into the dry ground beneath him.

"I am going to forget you said that, Vorsky. I am to inform you that Paul Hessler's life is now in your hands. His protection is your responsibility. End this absurd vendetta of yours and focus your energies there. You know what I am saying."

"And it disgusts me."

"Then understand that should anything happen to Paul Hessler, no matter what its source, the blame will fall on you."

"I understand perfectly."

David Turkanis shuffled his feet and nodded. "Then I believe you have another meeting to set up, don't you?"

CHAPTER 71

"FASIL'S BODYGUARDS KNEW nothing," al-Asi told Ben after they had shaken hands warmly.

"Your men work fast, Colonel."

"Anger sometimes makes me neglect subtlety. It isn't just these two men we're dealing with, Inspector."

"So I gathered."

They sat on the bed in the back room of a thirty-two-foot Winnebago motor home. Beyond the closed sliding divider, Ben could hear the Walt Disney video al-Asi's wife and three youngest children were watching. Ben had glimpsed the colonel's teenage son seated by himself doing homework when al-Asi escorted him to the rear of the Winnebago. The boy was a younger, more casually dressed version of his father.

"Others came to my house tonight," the colonel explained. He wore a taupe-colored Italian suit, elegant as always even with a mock turtleneck in place of a dress shirt. "They were not selling magazine subscriptions."

"Your family," Ben realized.

"Yes, targeted by the same people behind the murders of these children you uncovered, we believe."

"I'm sorry."

Mayor Fawzi Wallid and his guards had driven Ben to the Winnebago's parking spot in the cramped rear lot of the Jerusalem Hotel on Amman Street. From there it was only twenty miles to the Allenby Bridge and Jordan, should the colonel find the need to take his family across the border for safekeeping.

Al-Asi flashed a slight smile. "It is the killers who are going to be sorry, Inspector. They went to the wrong house, the old one we used before I moved back to the neighborhood so my kids could go to a regular school and play soccer. Did I tell you we made the division finals?"

"No."

"You'll attend, of course."

"As assistant coach?"

"The job is still available, Inspector."

"I'm keeping my options open."

"A wise thing in such uncertain times."

"The men who came to your house," Ben said, changing the subject back.

"They were disguised as Israeli soldiers. There were too many of them for my men to risk taking them on. But the early warning gave me time to get my family moved into this before they found my most recent address." Al-Asi looked about him proudly. "What do you think, Inspector?"

"Anyone with direct knowledge of the murder of these children is being silenced," Ben said. "Someone is covering their tracks."

The colonel chided him with a glare, rested the soft drink in his lap. "I was talking about the Winnebago."

"Oh. The truth is I've never seen anything like it in Palestine, Colonel."

"Of course, you haven't. Our streets are too narrow to maneuver safely." He tapped the nearest wall fondly. "But I couldn't resist. Perfect for outings, camping trips . . ."

"And a way you could be with your family if you had to move them in a hurry."

"Precisely why I obtained it after the peace process broke down. It came in especially handy tonight, since we seem to be facing a determined army. And now you tell me that the animal Mahmoud Fasil was part of it."

"A small part. A messenger, nothing more. His job was to destroy the hard drive on Shahir Falaya's computer and pass the disc containing a certain portion of its contents on to someone else."

"The soccer star, of course."

"I'd like to take a look at that disc we found on him, Colonel. Can we get it?"

"Of course we can: It's right here."

"In the *Winnebago*?"

Al-Asi nodded. "Hidden among my children's video games. For safekeeping."

BEN CONTINUED STARING at the screen long after he had finished scrolling through the contents. He didn't notice that his fingers had stiffened and his breathing had gone shallow.

"The disc is gibberish . . . nothing that seems in any way associated to the terrorist network we were hoping to identify. It's also in English. Maybe you could take a look at it sometime, tell me what you think."

Ben recalled al-Asi's words to him from nearly a week ago, berated himself for not taking the colonel up on his offer sooner. Maybe Danielle would not be in danger. Maybe she would not have gone to Germany and would be here with him.

It's all here on the disc. Everything I was looking for. . . .

The disc contained the information the murdered students had gathered on the companies they had blackmailed. That information constituted the students' proof, their fallback should one of their targets refuse to comply with their demands.

Hidden with the Palestinian student Shahir Falaya, because he had been the one to lift it off the pilfered circuit boards.

According to copies of the e-mails also contained on the disc, the four high school students had extorted a total of *$1.3 million!* Had it routed electronically into accounts they had closed immediately and transferred into others listed elsewhere in the database. A single withdrawal, for an amount slightly less than a hundred thousand American dollars, was noted, reflecting the sum required to buy Jane Wexler's silence.

Ben could see why someone reading the disc's contents with no prior knowledge of the information would be totally baffled. They read like gibberish, nonsense, unless the reader understood the basis.

Ben started over again at the beginning of the computer disc and concentrated on exactly what information the murdered students had threatened to reveal about the four companies in question. The Palestinian-Israeli consortium, Partners for Peace, was exactly what he thought: a sham in which Jewish businessmen like Max Price endeavored to get rich on Palestinian land. Their Palestinian partners in the deal, the students had uncovered, were paid a handsome sum merely for use of their names.

As for the prestigious law firm, the sudents had managed to accumulate a host of confidential affidavits and depositions taken in cases that would never go to trial because the information could not be allowed to go public.

The data concerning the brokerage house appeared on screen next. Here the students had collected memoranda indicating illegal insider trading at the brokerage house surrounding a number of IPOs, initial public offerings, in the European market Hundreds of years of jail time for those responsible if the truth ever came out.

The fourth packet of information Ben found pertained to a potential victim the students had never gotten around to contacting. A small private hospital that specialized in the discreet treatment of alcohol and drug addiction. Listed were the names of prominent Israelis who had resided there for varying lengths of time.

When Ben came to the final batch of information, he quickly realized why the students had skipped over the vulnerable clinic patients. Indeed, they had found something much bigger and more vulnerable to go after: Hessler Industries.

The other victims had all been charged a hundred thousand dollars. From Hessler Industries, the students had upped their demands to *one million*. Ben read on, quickly grasping what the circuit board stolen from the conglomerate's Tel Aviv headquarters had yielded.

Ben's breath quickened.

The e-mails to Hessler Industries in Tel Aviv made it very plain what the students had uncovered and what they planned to do with it. They knew the value of the information.

It concerned a project involving something called Lot 461.

Ben read on, skipping over the specifics at first until he realized what the confidential report claimed Lot 461 could do.

Oh my God . . .

"What is it, Inspector?" Colonel al-Asi asked him.

Ben continued to stare at the screen. Wondering. Was this the miracle he'd been looking for? Could it be he had found it while looking for something else entirely?

"Inspector."

Ben turned to find al-Asi staring at the screen over his shoulder.

"You were mumbling. What is it? What have you found?"

For the first time he could remember, Ben chose to evade al-Asi's question. "I need to see the soccer star Abdel Sidr, Colonel. I need to see him now."

CHAPTER 72

Y OU TOLD ME that Paul Hessler killed your father."

Hans Mundt had not responded to Danielle the first time she spoke those words, while standing over the empty grave.

"Come on," he said instead and started back for his car.

Danielle had no choice but to follow him and they both climbed back into the Mercedes. Mundt continued driving briefly north toward the town of Leczyca, then turned off down a narrow, bumpy road that sliced through the forest and followed the Bzura River for a brief stretch. She lost track of the miles that passed with the silence hanging between them. But the drive took over two hours.

At last Mundt halted the car at the foot of a hillside topped with a flat plain. He climbed out and began walking up the hill, waiting for Danielle to fall into step alongside him before he finally spoke.

"We just retraced a large portion of the route Paul Hessler took west after he escaped from the labor camp."

"Why did you tell me Paul Hessler killed your father?" she demanded.

"Because, in essence, he did," Mundt said, finally responding. "Because on that last day in the camp, my father ceased to exist. Karl Mundt became Paul Hessler." Mundt continued leading the way up the hill.

"Then the grave you found near the factory . . ."

"The man buried there was Paul Hessler, buried in my father's uniform. They must have exchanged clothes before my father shot him. That's why Gunthar Weiss thought he witnessed Hessler shooting my father when, in fact, it was the other way around."

"Then why did you need to see Israel's detailed file on Hessler?"

"Final proof, Pakad Barnea. I was aware of certain scars and birthmarks on my father's body, including one from a bayonet wound he suffered in training. I knew Paul Hessler's confidential file would include mention of all such markings." His features sank a little. "Unfortunately, the portion of the file I was allowed to see did not include what I was looking for."

"Denying your final confirmation."

"That only means I'll have to get it from Hessler himself. Same as you."

"Me?"

"Your father, Pakad. Hessler is the only man who can tell you the truth of his past."

"You keep referring to him as Hessler, not Karl Mundt or your father."

"Because he's not my father; not anymore. He's just another man, a stranger who must pay for what he did to my mother and myself."

"And you need me to get to him."

"I think I might, yes."

"Because he knows me."

"It's in your best interests too, Pakad. You must see that."

Danielle was glad for the steep climb after so many hours of riding in the car. It gave her a chance to digest all these new facts with the others she had already uncovered. She recalled what Gunthar Weiss claimed he had witnessed from his office window in the factory. He had seen what appeared to be Hessler shooting Mundt because the two had already switched clothes. For all these years that was the story the former labor camp *Haupsturmfuehrer* had told anyone who wanted to listen.

When they reached the top of the hill, Danielle planted herself in front of Hans Mundt defiantly. "No more games, do you hear me? I want to know what happened here."

Mundt held his ground. "Fine. Turn around, Pakad Barnea, and tell me what you see."

Danielle hesitated, then turned, angling her body sideways in order to keep a partial gaze on Mundt. Before her the hilltop was barren and desolate, devoid of anything living and dominated by chunks of brick and gray rocks mixing with brown dirt.

"Nothing," she said.

"I see the ruins of a castle," Mundt said almost dreamily as he stepped past her. "One of several in this area and the perfect place to seek refuge. This is where Karl Mundt came to escape a storm that would have otherwise killed him. For some reason the Gods were on his side that night. When the weather cleared, he continued on, rationing his supplies while he made his way west through the valley. He had almost reached the Warta River when he was rescued."

"By the American commando team led by Sergeant Phipps . . ."

Mundt nodded only once. "Again Karl Mundt would have died if they had not come upon him. Perhaps, though, I'm not giving my father enough credit. This was a man, after all, who had planned *everything* from the first moment he laid eyes on Paul Hessler. He knew when he came to the camp the end was near for Germany—that was why my grandfather had worked so hard to keep him off the front. But my father was smart enough to realize what his fate would be once Germany surrendered to the Allies. He would be executed, at the very least jailed for the rest of his life. He knew when he kissed my mother before he left it was for the last time, and learning she was pregnant with me did not alter his plans in the slightest."

Danielle moved closer to Mundt and straddled a cavernous rut in the shape of a huge tread. Other similar ruts lined the hilltop in an irregular, crisscrossing pattern. Clearly, massive machinery had claimed this hill in the relatively recent past, taking the remains of the castle with them, if Mundt's information was correct.

"You don't sound like you blame him," she said softly.

"I've spent my whole life blaming him, but the truth is I might never have seen him again anyway. Or if I did it would have been in disgrace. I hate him for abandoning me, Barnea, at the same time I know it was the only thing he could have done."

"Trade places with a Jew."

"A Jew with no family left, no property, no *identity* other than whatever he took with him from the camp. Kill that Jew and become him. But I don't think he planned on becoming a folk hero."

"You're defending him."

"I don't know. Maybe I am. He left my mother and me in poverty and disgrace, never contacted us through all the years he was alive. I wanted to believe he was a hero but I knew he was a monster like all the other Nazis. I tried very hard to forget him, but how could I when I had no memory of him in the first place? That's what made everything so complicated. There was this vast hole at the edge of my consciousness and my life that I knew I could never fill. I gave up trying years ago."

"Until you found out he was alive, living as Paul Hessler. How?"

"A dying German who gave me the names of the other three true impersonators lived in the same camp as Hessler. He claimed he witnessed my father shoot Hessler after they had exchanged clothes."

"He saw the same thing Weiss saw?"

"Only he got it right."

Danielle hesitated. "And the second list of names you gave Vorsky . . ."

"Fit the same profile as the three I was sure of. Most had already been investigated and cleared."

"Like my father." Danielle had expected an argument, continued when Mundt didn't offer one. "So what is it you're after? Revenge? Compensation?"

"I honestly don't know. I don't think I can decide until I'm face to face with him. I just know I have to do this, that nothing else matters."

Danielle found the irony between them striking: She would do anything to save her child, while Mundt had done everything to find his father. "It doesn't bother you that Hessler has long been the state of Israel's greatest benefactor?"

"I suppose he was after redemption, absolution. You know something? I think Karl Mundt actually *became* Paul Hessler. He didn't just live as a Jew and an Israeli; he was one. One of you," Hans Mundt added, staring at Danielle.

Danielle shivered, finding the strength at last to pose the question that had brought her this far. "What about my father?"

"What did Anna tell you?"

"There was the issue of an account Hessler opened in my father's name, but nothing else. My father was investigated and *cleared* by the Gatekeepers."

"Not cleared—filed."

"What does that mean?"

"Allowed to live pending further investigation."

One of her shoes slipped on a water-filled rut and her foot nearly came out of her shoe. "You believe my father was a Nazi war criminal, just like yours."

"The evidence is too strong to ignore."

"Not enough for the Gatekeepers."

"The question is whether it's enough for you, Barnea."

"He was a great man!"

"So, apparently, is my father."

Something pricked Danielle's spine. "How did Anna know all this? About you, about me?"

Hans Mundt turned away from the scattered remnants of the castle that had saved his father's life. "From Abraham Vorsky. You said so yourself before."

"You're a fool, Mundt. You played right into their hands by coming back to Poland."

"Anna Krieger didn't know what I found here."

"But Vorsky did and he would have told her! They both knew you would be coming back here to prove your case, after you rescued me."

Mundt's eyes widened, his face reddening as he spun around toward the ground-level trees rimming most of the hilltop. Pushed back his coat and went for his pistol.

"No!" Danielle screamed.

She barreled into Mundt and took him to the ground just as the first gunshots split the crisp air, spraying them with dirt.

CHAPTER 73

IS THERE SOMETHING you're not telling me, Inspector?" Colonel al-Asi asked Ben before they entered the former Israeli military barracks that had been transformed into Jericho's lone jail.

"If you need to ask, you know there is."

Al-Asi stopped before the door. "Does this concern Pakad Barnea?"

Ben couldn't help but smile. "No matter how much credit I give you, Colonel, it's never enough."

"I only hope that whatever is going on it has nothing to do with the visit the two of you made to Pakad Barnea's doctor last week."

Ben shook his head in amazement. "Is there ever a time you're not watching me, Colonel?"

"I watch everyone, Inspector."

"Enemies only, I thought."

"Friends are more important."

"But you don't know what happened inside the office."

"My surveillance stops at the door." Al-Asi turned his gaze back toward the Winnebago parked across the street. Here on the outskirts of Jericho, he didn't have to worry about its considerable size blocking the narrow streets. Inside his wife and youngest children were watching another animated video—a present last Christmas from Ben. "But that doesn't mean my concern does," he resumed.

"Thank you, Colonel."

Officially, maintenance of the jail fell under the jurisdiction of the Tanzim, Arafat's paramilitary organization. But al-Asi had not called ahead to alert them of his coming. Ben always enjoyed seeing the shock on an official's face when al-Asi appeared without warning and tonight was no exception. The duty officer jumped out of his chair and knocked over his cup of tea, cupping his hands beneath his desk to catch the spilled liquid.

"What can I do for you, Colonel?" the officer asked, as tea pooled on the floor despite his most determined efforts.

Seconds later, al-Asi and Ben were being escorted to a cell on the third floor where the Palestinian soccer star Abdel Sidr was incarcerated.

"He is the only one up here, *sidi*," the duty officer said nervously to al-Asi. "For obvious reasons."

"Word of Sidr's arrest has still not been made public," the colonel explained to Ben. "He is a folk hero, after all."

The duty officer unlocked the heavy wooden door and yanked it open. The bottom scratched across the floor, resisting. When the door would move no further, the duty officer graciously motioned for al-Asi and Ben to enter.

"Leave us," the colonel said.

Ben heard the man's heels clacking briskly down the hallway and watched as Abdel Sidr sat up on the stone cot built into the side wall.

"You know who I am?" al-Asi asked him.

Sidr looked at al-Asi as if Ben weren't in the room. "Everyone knows who you are."

"Then listen closely to what I am about to tell you. You have refused to answer questions thus far. That must change. Cooperate fully with us today and there may be a way I can get you out of this. I'm not promising anything, mind you, but I am in a position to influence matters as best I can. You may even be back playing for the team again before next week is out. Is that clear?"

"Yes, *sidi*."

"Very good. Now, I believe you've already met Inspector Bayan Kamal of our police."

The soccer star finally acknowledged Ben with a passing glance.

"Inspector Kamal," al-Asi continued, "has some questions for you. You will answer each one fully and truthfully. You will not hesitate and you will hold nothing back. Comply and rest assured my influence will be applied on your behalf." The colonel tilted his head toward Ben, yielding the floor. "Inspector."

"When did Mahmoud Fasil hire you?"

"I saw him for the first time when he hugged me on the field after the game."

"Someone else made the arrangements, then."

Sidr nodded, his back against the stone wall of the cell. "A few days before the game. In a bar where the members of the team are invited to drink for free. I was told someone would approach me after the final whistle and I should act as naturally as possible. But I didn't realize—"

"What were your instructions regarding the disc Fasil passed on to you?"

Abdel Sidr didn't hesitate. "I was to take it with me to Athens."

"Athens?"

"We have a game there the day after tomorrow. We are always taken straight to the plane at the airport in Gaza. They never bring us through the security checkpoint."

"Go on."

"Tomorrow we—the team, I mean—were to sightsee in Athens. I was to bring the disc with me and separate myself from the rest of the group at the National Museum. I would then be approached by someone who asks me for my autograph. When I finish signing, he tells me to keep the pen and I hand over the disc."

"Why have you not told this to anyone before?"

"I was never asked, *sidi.*"

Al-Asi looked uneasy, almost embarrassed, for the first time Ben could remember. "I'm sorry, Inspector. Please continue."

"You don't know who this person will be who's supposed to contact you?"

"He will know me."

"How?"

"We are to wear warm-up suits with our name and number on them, Inspector."

Ben nodded, looked back at al-Asi. "I'm finished here. Let's go."

"Not just yet," the colonel said. "I have another question for the prisoner before we leave." He focused his gaze unblinkingly on Abdel Sidr. Ben had seen that look before, as dangerous as a bullet. "Why did you do it?"

Sidr shrugged his muscular shoulders. "We are not paid to play soccer, *sidi.*"

NOBODY KNOWS ABDEL Sidr has been jailed," Ben repeated thoughtfully when they were back outside.

"His teammates probably, but we are not allowing them to talk to the media."

"So the courier has no reason to believe Sidr won't be showing up at the National Museum in Athens to hand over the disc as planned."

Al-Asi looked perplexed. "You want Sidr to stick to the original plan?"

"Not exactly, Colonel."

CHAPTER 74

"UNDER THE CIRCUMSTANCES, I thought we should meet," Abraham Vorsky, former head of Mossad, said to Anna Krieger, head of the Gatekeepers.

"Why?" she asked him. She had refused his offer to take the chair next to the one where Vorsky was seated, preferring to stand. Her wig clung tightly to her scalp and the pancake makeup she had applied to her face, made especially for burn victims, felt like a Halloween mask she dared not remove.

"Because this situation is complicated."

"Not to us."

"My point exactly."

They had met in eastern Istanbul at the Hotel Princess Ortakoy in Ortakoy Square overlooking the Bosphorus. The view through the lobby windows included the vast Feriye palaces from Byzantine times and the great columns of the Bosphorus Bridge. In centuries past the network of canals winding back and forth to the strait had been the only way to travel amidst the villages that lined it. Though connecting roads had long since been added, the character of this famed section of Istanbul still relied on the waterway that had once been cluttered with boats carrying both people and merchandise. The lifeline of a city for which water was like blood.

The furniture in the Princess Ortakoy's lobby looked more appropriate for a museum's baroque period display than a hotel. Abraham Vorsky's chair and the one he offered to Anna Krieger were salvaged from the Ciragan Palace after it was badly damaged by fire in the late nineteenth century. That palace, now fully restored as a hotel itself, no longer needed the chairs long since appropriated by the Hotel Princess Ortakoy.

"If Hans Mundt's suspicions about Paul Hessler are correct," Vorsky continued, "your people will act."

Anna stood more erectly. "You called me here to tell me what my people are going to do?"

"But this time you cannot let them."

"You intend to stop me?"

"I have my orders."

"And I have my duty."

Abraham Vorsky leaned back, let his shoulders melt into the soft fabric of the antique chair. It was hard looking up at Anna. The thick makeup took the sheen from her flesh and gave her a ghostlike pallor. Vorsky tried not to think what lay beneath that coating. Instead he remembered the tall woman looming over him as a beautiful little girl, full of questions. He remembered the aftermath of the explosion that had claimed the lives of her parents and nearly burned Anna alive, of inquiring as to what would become of her.

"You are too young to be a relic like me, Anna," he said finally, hoping to sound convincing.

"You worked with my father."

"And your mother," Vorsky told her. "They provided considerable assistance to us in those days. But those days are over."

"Not so long as men like Hessler are still out there. Not so long as a single one of them is left alive, enticing others to follow."

Vorsky wondered what he could do to conciliate the tall woman. He thought of taking her hand, but she stood too far away for him to reach. "It is time to let go, Anna. For both of us."

"You didn't feel that way when Mundt came to you with his list of names. You acted within twenty-four hours."

"Those names brought it all back to me, made me feel it was fifty years ago and I was still tracking down the killers of my parents with the help of yours."

"You never found those men, did you?"

"No," Vorsky said regretfully.

"And yet you tell me it is time to let go."

"Of Paul Hessler, anyway. Your mother and father would have done so."

Anna's features flared, emotion stretching her skin in unaccustomed lines. "Because he has bought his penance, his atonement, with billions of dollars of gifts and donations? Because he has lived so long as a Jew, you are willing to accept he has become one?"

Vorsky shrugged. "He was just a guard, not one of the monsters."

"They were all monsters."

Vorsky finally stood up, pushing hard on the old chair's arms to rise. "The decision is not mine alone, Anna."

"But you agree with it, don't you?"

"Under the circumstances, I have no choice."

"So they sent you here to stop me."

"I came to stop you any way I can."

"What about Mundt, will you stop him as well?"

"Once we find him, yes."

"And Barnea, the Israeli detective he rescued?"

Vorsky nodded. "If she has joined him."

"You would destroy me and one of your own to protect a man like Paul Hessler—or, should I say, Karl Mundt?"

"It's the way things are, I'm afraid. I'm sorry, Anna."

She made no move toward him. "I'm sorry, too."

*   *   *

Anna watched through the lobby window as Abraham Vorsky's guards, unseen during their meeting, piled into the car with him. The car drove off, heading along the shore toward the bridge where it would pass to the European side of the Bosphorus en route to central Istanbul.

She barely blinked when Vorsky's car erupted in a burst of flames that sent burnt embers and charred chips of metal raining into the waters below. A secondary blast, the fuel tank probably, sent the husk spinning into the air. It landed off the road, keeling over the rail that separated the street from the sea.

Anna turned to see the guards who had accompanied her here standing rigidly behind her. "Contact the others," she ordered. "We will meet them in the United States."

Her cellular phone rang and Anna grasped it anxiously. The number was changed electronically almost daily and she had given the latest to only one other person.

"It's done," reported the leader of the team Anna had sent to Poland.

DAY SEVEN

CHAPTER 75

BEN KAMAL ENTERED the National Archaeological Museum in Athens closely behind the Palestinian national soccer team. He stayed near enough to them to appear perhaps part of the group, yet far enough back so none of them would notice him.

It was a cloudy, rainy day, which allowed him to cover Abdel Sidr's warm-up suit with a long coat. The warm-up suit had the star's name and number embroidered upon the shiny blue fabric.

"I do not think this is a good idea," Colonel Nabril al-Asi had cautioned yesterday outside the jail in Jericho after Ben explained his plan.

"Why not? Since Sidr's arrest has remained secret, it's safe to assume the courier he was to meet in Athens has no knowledge of it."

"You're also assuming the courier does not know what Sidr looks like, Inspector. Not even a picture."

"True enough, Colonel," Ben conceded. "But Sidr stressed the importance of wearing his warm-up suit. Why would that be so vital, unless the courier was relying on it to identify him?"

Al-Asi had shrugged, unable to refute Ben's point. "I have no friends in Athens, Inspector," he said instead. "You'll be totally on your own."

"I don't expect to be there very long."

Al-Asi hesitated before resuming. "You know exactly who killed those children now, don't you?"

"I think so, yes. I'll learn for sure in Athens."

"Think or hope? Your voice, Inspector, its tone disturbs me. It has the ring of a man who is after more than solving a mystery."

"Only if I get the chance," Ben said cryptically.

Al-Asi left things at that. He helped Ben with the travel arrangements and drove him to Gaza Airport in the Winnebago. Ben took a flight to Cairo and then boarded a jet bound straight for Athens. He carried no weapons, only a small tote bag with the overcoat and Abdel Sidr's soccer warm-up suit inside. The team had arrived in Athens yesterday with the museum visit scheduled for this afternoon, the day before their game against the Greek national team.

Inside the museum, Ben hung slightly back amidst the reporters covering the soccer team's visit before entering a restroom. He left the overcoat hanging in a stall and emerged wearing the warm-up suit with the number seven and name "Sidr" plainly visible. The rest of the team had proceeded well ahead of him and he veered off down a separate corridor.

"I was to separate myself from the team," Abdel Sidr had said. *"The courier would find me to pick up the disc."*

In spite of what he had told al-Asi, though, Ben still couldn't be sure if the courier might recognize Sidr on sight as well as by name and number. If that were the case, his plan was going to fail in a hurry; it might have already failed if the courier was paying very close attention.

The great collection of Greek art and artifacts was spread throughout the sprawling white marble expanse of the National Archaeological Museum. Individual chambers and galleries highlighted different periods, eras, and themes. Unarmed, Ben walked about in search of a chamber that provided a measure of cover in case he needed it. He was likely being watched even now and reached out to grab a tri-folded map of the museum from a reception table.

His intention was to use the map to help hide his face. Then, almost as an afterthought, he began to study the museum's layout. Just past the garden on the ground floor, a new exhibit called "Weapons and Armor of Ancient Greece" had been highlighted with a star.

Ben continued down the long corridor toward it, perturbed to find a sign posted on the closed door announcing the exhibit was not scheduled to open until next week. He tried the knob anyway and felt it twist in his hand. Not looking back, Ben entered the hall and closed the door behind him.

True to its name, the exhibit was composed of weapons and armaments both large and small. From full-scale catapults used in siege tactics during the Persian Wars, to mannequins outfitted in full heavy armor and helmets, to an assortment of swords, spears, javelins, bows and arrows, and sling-propelled pellets, the exhibit offered a complete overview of the Greek war machine.

Ben felt for the outline of the computer disc in his warm-up jacket and moved for the wall.

H E WAS STANDING behind a mechanical stone and bolt-thrower when the door to the hall eased open again. A man in a suit entered, holding a small pistol in his hand. The man closed the door behind him and turned.

Ben fired the arrow from a bow he had pulled from a wall exhibit. He aimed high and well to the right, but the torsion on the string fooled him and the arrow lodged in the wood of the door barely a foot over the courier's head.

"You were supposed to bring a pen, not a pistol," Ben said. "Drop it."

The courier hesitated, swept his eyes about the exhibit hall.

"Do it now. I'm not very good with this thing. Next time, I might not be able to miss."

The courier let his gun clatter to the floor and stuck up his hands even though Ben hadn't told him to. He was shaking; a balding, middle-aged man wearing a dark suit.

Ben stepped out from the cover of the mechanical stone and bolt-thrower, having another arrow secured in place but with no tension on the string. The courier looked at him and narrowed his eyes.

"You're not Abdel Sidr."

"Would you have shot him too?"

"I was just protecting myself! After what happened . . ."

"Why don't you tell me?"

"Who *are* you?"

Ben held the bow and arrow mostly for show. "You go first."

"My name is Kiriakis."

"Who do you work for?"

"The Athens offices of Hessler Industries."

Ben hesitated, aware now which of the targets had been responsible for the murders of their young blackmailers. Not that he was surprised; after viewing the disc now held in his pocket back in al-Asi's Winnebago, Hessler Industries seemed the most likely choice since that company had paid the most and had the most to lose.

By far.

But Ben had something to lose too. That was the bigger reason why he was here.

"You're here to pick up the disc," he prodded.

"Yes," Kiriakis replied.

"Who accompanied you?"

"No one! I swear!"

"You weren't followed?"

"I . . . don't think so."

"You weren't ordered to kill whoever gave you the disc."

Kiriakis's eyes widened. "I've never killed anyone in my life. I just run the office here."

"But you brought a gun with you."

"Because of last week," the Greek insisted.

"Last week?"

"The murder."

"You know about the murders?"

"Only one: Ari Hessler. I hadn't heard anything since then. I wasn't even sure the meeting was still on until I saw your warm-up suit."

"And approached even though you knew I wasn't the real Abdel Sidr."

"That could have been part of the plan. I didn't know, couldn't be sure."

"You thought I might have come here to kill you."

"Yes!"

"Because of Lot four-sixty-one," Ben said, recalling its presence on the disc.

"Because of *what*?"

"Lot four-sixty-one. A new discovery by Hessler Industries' Biotech Division in New York City. But certain correspondence came through the company's headquarters in Tel Aviv."

"I don't know what you're talking about!"

"Four high school students did. They found evidence of Lot four-sixty-one's existence, and its potential, and blackmailed *someone* at Hessler to keep the discovery secret. A discovery worth billions and billions of dollars that they threatened to sell to the highest bidder unless their terms were met."

"This is madness!"

"The madness was killing the students to keep them quiet. I'm a police officer, Kiriakis, investigating those murders. And your presence here today makes you an accomplice."

"But I haven't done anything wrong!"

"You brought a gun to a meeting. That suggests otherwise."

"Because of Ari Hessler's murder. How could I know I wasn't being targeted too?"

Ben could see all the pieces of the plot falling into place. "Ari Hessler was the one who contacted you, wasn't he?"

"Yes, eight days ago."

Which would be the day before Mahmoud Fasil passed the disc to Abdel Sidr at the soccer game. Fasil had to be the man Hessler Industries retained to kill Shahir Falaya and then steal the hard drive off his computer. The information on this disc must have been salvaged off that drive, including a confidential e-mail sent from a Tess Sanderson in New York to Ari Hessler in Tel Aviv. Ari Hessler was the man the students had blackmailed at Hessler Industries. He was the man who had ordered their deaths, but he still would have needed the disc to see *exactly* what the students had uncovered and how.

"You were supposed to give the disc to Ari Hessler once in New York, yes?" Ben surmised.

Kiriakis nodded. "He had already sent me tickets for a flight leaving Athens early tomorrow morning. Everything had been arranged. But after he was killed I received no further instructions."

"You heard from no one else at the company?"

"No one! Nothing! I swear! I stuck to the original plan. That's all!"

Ben finally lowered the bow and arrow and stretched his weary shoulders. "This conversation must remain between us."

"I understand."

"Talk to anyone else at the company about this and you could get both of us killed."

"I have already forgotten I ever met you, believe me! I never heard of this Lot four-sixty-one. I was going to pick up the disc and put it in the company safe until I received further instructions."

"I'll spare you the trouble."

Kiriakis looked confused. "You're going to keep it?"

Now it was Ben who nodded. "There's someone else who needs to see its contents."

CHAPTER 76

W HAT DO YOU expect to find when we get to New York?" Danielle asked Karl Mundt, while they sat virtually alone in the international departure lounge at France's Charles de Gaulle Airport in the late hours of the night.

"Much the same thing you're looking for," he replied. "The truth about my father."

The flight to New York's Kennedy Airport had been delayed again, further stalling the long circuitous route they had opted to take from Poland on the chance that Anna Krieger, leader of the Gatekeepers, caught on to the ruse they had used on her.

Back in the forest, nearly a day earlier now, Danielle and Mundt had hugged the ground as the snipers' bullets continued to split the air all around them.

"The Gatekeepers," Mundt had muttered. "They must be in the trees somewhere."

"I can't find them," Danielle said, trying desperately to pin down the origin of the shots from the sounds. But the echo in the open woods confused her bearings. In any case, Mundt had the only gun and it wasn't capable of handling such a range effectively.

"Maybe we don't have to," Mundt said, starting to push himself backwards through the chunks and rubble, all that remained of the castle that had saved his father's life.

The motion attracted the snipers who fired a fresh barrage, several shots of which just missed hitting both of them.

"What are you doing?" Danielle asked Mundt.

"I've studied this castle," he said, "everything about it I could get my hands on." He swept his thick, meaty hands across the ground as he continued to push backwards, brushing aside all debris in search of something beneath it. "The castle's many toilets, called garderobes, drained down into holes leading to a tunnel that channeled the waste into a common cesspit, accessible since it had to be treated regularly." He stopped and looked up, out into the trees. "Somewhere out there."

"How many bullets do you have?"

"Two clips. Plenty if we can find our way out of here."

Danielle joined him in the task of searching through the rubble for one of the drainage holes they hoped had survived the dismantling of the castle. She had just pushed aside a jagged slab of limestone when her hand sank through a narrow covering of brush.

"Mundt!" she called softly.

He crawled toward her through another onslaught of bullets. By the time he reached her side, Danielle had unearthed a hole that seemed to drop into the very bowels of the earth. Pitched on a steep downward angle and utterly black.

"Stay close to me," Mundt said, dropping in head first.

"I'll be right behind you."

So long as they stayed flat on the ground, the grade of the hilltop would shield their descent from the snipers who would probably assume they were simply digging in to make a stand. Danielle started to shimmy down after Mundt as soon as his feet had disappeared into the hole. She tried to camouflage the hole a bit with a few handfuls of rubble before heading downward. The grade was not as steep as she thought and, actually, quite easy to traverse.

Until the smell assaulted her. It had to be her imagination; human waste from the castle would have decomposed long, long ago. Nonetheless, the ground had a rancid, sour stench to it. A mixture of excrement and spoiled mud.

Danielle forced herself to breathe through her mouth, fighting against nausea and the disorientation that came when all light vanished once they dropped into the tunnel that had been the drainage conduit for all castle waste. She tried to stay on Mundt's heels, relying on her ears to keep track of his progress through the tunnel toward the cesspit in the woods. He must have had a cigarette lighter because a small flame flickered sporadically well before her, as he checked what lay ahead of them.

What if the tunnel collapsed further down the grade? What if the access hatch leading out of the cesspit had been lost to the ages?

Considering those questions was pointless; this was their only chance of survival.

The stench, imaginary or otherwise, seemed to worsen the deeper they drew, reaching its ultimate when the tunnel widened into a large, circular underground ditch.

The cesspit.

Danielle could only hope the few hundred yards they had traveled was enough to put them behind the position of the snipers. The cesspit ceiling was just high enough for them to stand. With his hands outstretched, the six-and-a-half foot tall Mundt was able to easily probe the ceiling, scratching at the dirt in search of the cleaning hatch. Occasionally Danielle saw his lighter flicker briefly to life, breaking the darkness.

He found the hatch after a few minutes of probing. Then it took all of his considerable strength to jar the heavy ancient stone covering loose, and then jostle it from its perch.

Danielle and Mundt emerged tentatively onto the forest floor, shielding themselves in the leaves and brush. Without the sound of gunfire, they had no way of marking the position of the snipers posted around the hillside. And, with only a single pistol between them, there was no margin for error.

"Give me the gun," Danielle whispered.

"What?" Mundt shot back.

"There are four of them: two in the trees, two on the ground. I'll take the ones on the ground out first."

Mundt looked at her sententiously, as if to remind himself she was a woman. "You?"

"What I do best. We can get the snipers together when I'm done."

Mundt shook his head, had to fight to keep his voice low. "You must be forgetting who you're talking to."

"No, Anna Krieger told me of your days with the East German secret police. But those gunmen out there aren't basement-bred amateurs and you don't have a government backing you up."

Mundt began to seethe, had started to shake with rage when Danielle continued.

"Do you want to find your father or not?"

With that, Mundt had snickered and passed her his pistol. Its steel felt warm to the touch, the grip moist with his sweat. Danielle tested the gun's weight, familiarizing herself with its heft and balance before moving off into the woods.

She thought she would feel hesitant, even stiff with fear. But her feet felt light, time turned back a decade to her years with the Israeli Special Forces when this kind of work had made up her world. She slipped back into it as smoothly as she melted soundlessly into the woods.

Time and space became a blur. Two gunmen were out here to be dealt with, the world reduced to that task and nothing more. Danielle tracked them with her ears, listening for the sounds that would give them away while her motions remained no louder than the rustling of the brush.

Thoughts rampaged through her as she sank deeper into the forest. She held a gun in the same hand that in a few months would be cradling a baby, and she knew every bit of the steel as intimately as she would soon know her child's flesh. Was she doing this because of the genetic defect afflicting that child? Was Ben right about her taking on so much to punish herself?

Danielle was spared considering an answer when a muffled voice speaking into a communicator gave the first of the ground-based gunmen away. She tucked the gun into her belt and moved on him from the rear, electing to use her hands. She willed her heart quiet, believed the beating of the baby's growing inside her submitted to the same command.

The first man never heard her, never turned. It was over very quickly, the muffled snap when Danielle broke his neck no louder than a branch cracking. She drew a knife from a sheath around his ankle and used it on the second man, positioned a hundred feet away from the first just as she had suspected. Danielle left the blade there, wiped her hands off on the brush and dirt.

She returned to Mundt with the dead men's guns. They divided the two tree-mounted snipers between them and agreed to reconnoiter in the same spot once they were finished. Danielle heard the sharp crack of Mundt's gun an instant after a short burst from hers dropped a black-clad gunman from a tree.

She found Mundt hovering over the second sniper at the foot of a tree fifty yards from their planned rendezvous. Mundt's bullet had turned the man's shoulder to gristle and the resulting fall had broken at least one of his legs.

"We need to question him," Mundt said, paying Danielle little heed. "What *I* do best."

It didn't take Mundt long to get the information he was after and then to coerce the man into making the call Anna Krieger was expecting.

Danielle watched the man dial and heard him say, "It's done," before Mundt finished him with a single gunshot.

The stench in the tunnel had not been borne in Danielle's imagination at all, as their clothes plainly exhibited. They stopped in the town of Lezcaya to clean up and purchase fresh clothes before beginning the long journey that was currently delayed in Paris.

"The truth won't change anything now," Danielle said, as they continued to wait in the departure lounge.

"Satisfaction, then. That's what we both want, isn't it?"

"You're going to kill Paul Hessler, aren't you? *Aren't* you?"

Mundt stiffened. "He's not Paul Hessler, remember? He's Karl Mundt, the brave soldier who ran away from his wife and child. He sacrificed us to history." He looked at her and his face wrinkled in displeasure at what he saw. "My father ran *from* his family, while yours ran *to* his."

"You don't know that!"

Gloating now. "It's easier once you accept it."

"I'm telling you it's not true." Then, lamely, "I'd know if it were."

"How, Barnea? You think evil brands men with a different color or a different scent?" Mundt shook his head. "If that were true, policemen like you would have an easy job on their hands. But evil doesn't look any different. It hides behind masks and false fronts that allow it to thrive and prosper. The real villains aren't the animals the Gatekeepers exterminate like vermin. The real villains hide in the guise of men no one could possibly believe are anything but good. They are the most dangerous ones. They are the ones only true keepers of the gate can identify."

Danielle wouldn't budge. "Your father. Not mine."

Mundt softened his gaze slightly. "Yours is dead anyway, sparing you the agony of a decision. The agony of knowing."

"Oh, I'm going to know all right," Danielle said, resolvedly. "Just like you told me, I'm going to find out from the one man who can tell me."

DAY EIGHT

CHAPTER 77

PAUL HESSLER STOOD inside the sky-bridge connecting the two buildings of the Towers, looking out over the East River. A simple twist of his shoulders and all of Manhattan was before him. Normally he loved this view, especially from the only skybridge of its kind in the United States. It was his favorite feature of the building he had built and rented out at full capacity. The waiting time for office space in the Towers was estimated to be five years.

But today was different. Today, as dusk descended on the city of New York, Paul Hessler took no enjoyment in this or in anything. Sitting shiva was done. Relatives and friends had stopped visiting and phoning. His grandchildren had returned to school, his ex-wife to her home in Palm Springs, his other children to the worlds they had made for themselves.

Today Paul Hessler was left to face his son's murder alone. To distract himself, he tried to focus on the miraculous success of Lot 461. No matter how many lives Lot 461 saved, though, it could not bring back his son.

But something else plagued Paul Hessler as he stood in

the skybridge in the last of the day's light. Others would surely be able to figure out the same truth Sergeant Walter Phipps, the old soldier who murdered Ari, had. And that truth could destroy him as effectively as a bullet. The only question was which would strike him down first.

"Mr. Hessler?"

Startled, Paul turned to see one of his blazer-attired security guards standing at one end of the skybridge.

"I'm sorry to bother you, sir," the guard continued, "but there's someone downstairs who would like to see you."

"I don't have any appointments scheduled for this evening."

"I understand, sir. But this man is a policeman, a *Palestinian* policeman."

"Palestinian?"

The guard nodded stiffly. "He says he has information about your son's murder."

CHAPTER 78

HE'S NOT ANSWERING," Danielle said, pushing the END button on Mundt's cell phone.

The big man scowled. "You said that was the number Hessler gave you, that you could reach him at it twenty-four hours a day."

"Something has changed, obviously."

Danielle had already tried reaching Paul Hessler through his company's switchboard, identifying herself and then saying she had turned up vital information about the murder of his son. But Hessler was unreachable, having left strict instructions that he was not to be disturbed.

"We'll have to wait, then," Mundt said.

"No," Danielle insisted, "we can't wait. The Gatekeepers must be on their way, if they're not here already. We have to confront Hessler now. Tonight."

"How?"

"We do what we do best, Mundt."

The long circuitous route Danielle and Hans Mundt had taken to reach New York City left Danielle Barnea limp and exhausted. She could tell by the coarse texture of her hair which always seemed to dry out when she overexerted herself. Her pregnancy made the strains of such over-exertion show all the faster. But she tried to reach deep inside herself for the reserves she would need to see this through to the end.

Following the attempt made on his life in Israel, Danielle knew, Paul Hessler would be extremely well guarded. Given this, along with the fact that she and Mundt lacked the resources needed to gain access to his home, they had no choice but to turn elsewhere. Danielle suggested Hessler's corporate headquarters in the Towers he had built held their best hope. Find entry to the building and lie in wait for him to arrive the next morning. Not the best of plans, but their only viable option under the circumstances.

A call by Danielle to the building maintenance department yielded the name of the cleaning company that provided janitorial services. The company's parking lot in New Jersey was unguarded. The night provided the only camouflage she and Mundt needed to steal a van with the company's markings and drive away unhindered. They changed into overalls on the way into Manhattan and parked near a service entrance of the Towers.

They lacked the proper keys, of course, but that proved only a minor inconvenience. Danielle went to work on the door with some tools found in the rear of the truck. Nothing small and edged enough to allow for subtlety, but sufficient to assure them of an entry that would reveal a damaged lock only to the closest observer.

She could sense Mundt behind her watching the street the whole time. Mundt, here to meet the father who had been living a lie for more than half a century after abandoning him.

And I'm here to learn whether my father lied to me my entire life, Danielle thought as the door finally opened with a click.

"Hessler's office is on the top floor," Mundt announced. "There's a private elevator that accesses it on the other side of the building."

"How do you know that?" Danielle asked, falling in step behind him.

"This isn't my first trip here, Pakad Barnea, but it is going to be my last."

CHAPTER 79

BEN KAMAL HAD contemplated several means to help him gain access to Paul Hessler. In the end, though, he had settled upon the simplest: He simply walked into the lobby of the Towers and announced himself at the security desk.

"You'll have to do better than that," the guard had said.

"Just tell Paul Hessler what I told you. He'll see me."

It took a number of phone calls back and forth, and some patient waiting under the watchful eye of additional guards summoned to the lobby, but in the end Ben was proven right. Those same guards eventually became his escorts in an express elevator ride to the forty-second floor where he was led down a hall marked with signs for the Towers' skybridge.

Paul Hessler, a man he had never met, stood there suspended between his twin buildings. In the dull light he looked sad and alone, the life sucked out of him. Ben knew the feeling well from Detroit, from the death of his own children. He wanted to tell Paul Hessler it would get better with time, that it would come to make sense. But he knew it wouldn't.

"Leave us," Hessler order the guards who had accompanied Ben this far.

The men did so reluctantly.

Ben felt Hessler's eyes lock upon him.

"Please, Inspector Kamal, join me over here and enjoy the view."

Ben approached him hesitantly, feeling a rush of vertigo as he padded along the skybridge. When he gazed out over the water, his stomach quivered at the illusion of walking across open air.

"My men have checked your credentials," Hessler continued, as Ben drew closer. "I'm sorry it took so long. But with the time difference and everything . . ."   "There's no need to apologize, sir."

"You've come a long way to see me, Inspector."

"I have my reasons."

"Reasons none of your superiors were aware of, apparently."

"Were you able to reach Colonel al-Asi?"

"We cannot confirm he even exists."

Ben managed a slight smile. "But you still elected to see me."

"Because you said it concerned my son's murder. And your name is not unknown to me."

"Oh?"

"It surfaced in my scrutiny of Chief Inspector Danielle Barnea of Israel's National Police."

"You requested she be assigned to the case. Then, just as suddenly, you changed your mind."

"She took you into her confidence, I see."

Ben nodded. "And now I am taking you into mine. You should know that Pakad Barnea never really stopped investigating your son's murder at all."

"So what are you, her messenger come to tell me what she uncovered?"

"No, Mr. Hessler. What I uncovered I learned myself. Pakad Barnea is not aware of it. *No one* in Israel is aware of it."

Hessler's eyes narrowed in concern. "Is that important?"

"Very, because it is something you do not want revealed under any circumstances. Believe me."

Ben watched Hessler's eyes grow cold. The old man's long, skeletal fingers fastened into trembling fists.

"So that's what this is about," he hissed. "Another person comes dragging my past with him. Congratulations, Inspector."

"This isn't about you, or the past," Ben said, trying to stay focused. "As I told the men downstairs, it's about your son."

Hessler looked confused now, even disoriented. "My son," he said, as if hearing it for the first time. "So you came all this way with information about his murder."

"Not exactly."

"Should I summon my security guards back, Inspector?"

"You don't want to do that. Really."

"But if this isn't about his murder, what does this have to do with my son?"

"Lot four-sixty-one," Ben said, and watched Paul Hessler go ghost white.

CHAPTER 80

THE TWELVE GATEKEEPERS accompanying Anna Krieger into the United States flew into three different northeast airports. Since they were unable to bring any weapons into the country, Anna's instructions were to rendezvous with an American contact in a Connecticut hotel parking lot just short of the New York border. There, the Gatekeepers would meet up with her and three American drivers, then proceed well-armed into New York City to execute Karl Mundt, better known as Paul Hessler.

Anna had obtained some intelligence on Hessler. Not enough to form a concrete plan of attack, but sufficient to enable her to choose from a number of alternatives equally fraught with risk. It was quite by accident upon reaching Connecticut that Anna learned from her source that Hessler had been unexpectedly detained at his office this very night. She had counted on at least the night for planning, but the opportunity to go after Hessler under cover of dark was too much to pass off. A full frontal assault as he left the building later this evening might be the best, and only, option available.

For Anna the long trip had been difficult. She was not used to being among people, even less used to traveling. Worse, the dry atmosphere in the plane had caused her thick pancake makeup to crack, leading a number of the other passengers, she was certain, to look at and notice her. She hated the stares that made her feel like a freak, at the same she welcomed them for strengthening her resolve.

Her face, after all, was a constant reminder of what men like Karl Mundt had done to her and her parents. Whenever she weakened or began to doubt, Anna needed only to recall hearing the terrible screams of her parents even as the pain from the flames ravaged her. She would never forget the stench of her burning hair or sound of her flesh sizzling like bacon before she threw herself from the flames out the window, landing in the moist dirt of the garden below. She was still screaming when some neighbors found her, as much to drown out the cries of her parents as to drown her own pain.

She had become a freak that night; friendless, orphaned, and outcast. But the hate in her had been ignited as well, and no amount of fruitless plastic surgeries could quell that. It was purpose that drove her in the years following. Finishing the work her parents had begun. Wiping out the last of those who had embroidered swastikas on their coats and in their hearts.

The Gatekeepers' targets, though, were dwindling. Just a few old harmless men scattered here and there. The late Abraham Vorsky had been right about that much: Anna's time, and her reason for being, were just about past. She had to let go, move on.

But first there was Karl Mundt, a man who had parlayed his murder of a Jewish boy into a multi-billion-dollar fortune. The reputed benevolence and generosity of Paul Hessler, the man Mundt became, could change that truth no more than Anna could change the face that looked back at her in the mirror as she applied her makeup.

Karl Mundt embodied the very reason why her parents

had decided to become keepers of the gate and ultimately died horribly for it. Anna might die in New York City tonight. Even if successful, she might be caught and arrested, forced to finish her life as the prisoner she had long been anyway.

CHAPTER 81

WHAT I HAVE to tell you," Ben resumed before the color could return to Paul Hessler's face, "isn't going to be easy to hear."

"My son is dead, Inspector. It can't be any harder than that."

"Maybe." Ben continued to struggle for words. "Ari was involved in something you know nothing about."

"I know about Lot four-sixty-one now," Hessler reflected sadly.

"So did four high school students in Israel and Palestine, all murdered in the past month. I imagine your son believed he had no choice."

"No choice? What are you talking about?"

Ben hesitated. "He had them killed."

The old man's expression began to fill with anger. His lips quivered. "*High school students?* That's ridiculous! Why would Ari possibly do such a thing?"

"Because they were blackmailing him."

"*Blackmailing* him?"

"With a threat to reveal the existence of Lot four-sixty-one to the world, and offer what they had learned about it to rival pharmaceutical companies."

Paul Hessler suddenly looked unsteady on his feet. He pulled them together and leaned against the glass for support. "I don't believe you. I believe *you* are the blackmailer, here to extort something out of me with these bizarre claims. Yes, that's what it must be."

"It isn't, believe me."

"I can't. I won't."

"Then believe this: A month ago your son received a confidential report someone named Tess Sanderson, here in New York, sent via e-mail. He downloaded the contents of an attachment onto the hard drive of a digital office machine in your Tel Aviv headquarters. One of these high school students, with a part time job as a technician, removed the machine's circuit board and downloaded its contents. He and the others then threatened to sell what they had learned about Lot four-sixty-one to the highest bidder if their ransom demands weren't met. They thought they would find plenty of takers among leading pharmaceutical companies and I'd say they were right. So your son paid them a million dollars."

"A million dollars?"

"But it didn't stop there. Lot four-sixty-one's existence was still in jeopardy. Your son couldn't be sure the money would keep the students silent and so long as they were alive they remained threats to his project. He must have felt he had no choice. So he had them tracked down and killed, Mr. Hessler. I'm sorry to have to tell you this."

"You, you walk in here and expect me to believe all this, take such a ridiculous, scandalous story at your word? You expect me to believe a . . ."

"A Palestinian, an Arab?" Ben finished when Hessler's words tailed off in a breathless huff. "No, sir, I don't. That's why I brought along a disc which proves my allegations."

Hessler's face had begun to redden. A vein throbbed in his neck. "And does this disc prove that my son had these children killed as well?"

"Not in a court of law. But that's not the court that matters, is it, sir?"

Hessler regarded Ben curiously. "Then I'm right, aren't I, Inspector? Now you've come here to blackmail *me*."

"No. I've come here to make a deal."

"A *deal*?"

"You make them all the time, Mr. Hessler. This is just another one. Bottom line: I'm the only one right now who knows what I just told you. You and your family can be spared the disgrace, the embarrassment of your son's complicity in at least eight murders."

"I don't give a damn about disgrace *or* embarrassment! This is *my* son we're talking about!"

"And his good name. The murdered heir to the Hessler fortune linked to the execution of four children, connected to terrorists and killers he hired to carry out their executions. Is that how you want his legacy to read?"

"It's a lie!"

"Watch the disc, sir. You'll see it's anything but."

Ben could see Hessler's mind working logically again. "And you're the only one who knows about all this?"

"I did take a few precautions."

"Go on."

"The man you can find no record of—Colonel al-Asi—I left a copy of the disc with him. If anything happens to me, he will release it to the international media along with my full report. And since you can't find al-Asi, it's safe to assume you'll never be able to find his copy of the disc."

Hessler nodded slowly, rage under control now. "So you want me to buy your silence, is that it, Inspector?"

"Not with money," Ben told him.

"With what then?"

"Lot four-sixty-one."

BEN STOPPED FOR a moment to compose himself, afraid to show any sign of weakness or hesitation to Paul Hessler.

"I don't understand," the old man said, sounding confused and almost relieved.

"The confidential report your son received from Tess Sanderson was rather specific as to Lot four-sixty-one's remarkable capabilities. Advanced genetic therapy. Nanotechnology. Biological computers. Organic machines. I wish I understood these things. . . ."

"I only want to understand what happened here, how everything went so wrong."

As best as he could, Ben summarized the steps Ari Hessler had taken. From the clever murders of the four students in question, to stealing the hard drive from Shahir Falaya's computer, to smuggling a disc containing the information relevant to him out of the West Bank to an intermediary in Athens who was to deliver it to Ari in New York.

"Impossible! Where would my son find the men, the killers, to do such a thing? He didn't know such people."

"I can't tell you that, sir.

"Then tell me what it is you are getting at, what's brought you halfway across the world to offer me your silence."

"Birth defects," Ben said, taking a deep breath.

"What?"

"Theoretically, Lot four-sixty-one could, *should*, be able to repair them *in the fetus* so the child can be born healthy and whole."

"I suppose you're right. Theoretically. But I'm no expert. I only learned of Lot four-sixty-one's potential myself a few days ago."

Ben chose his next words carefully, stumbling over them a little. "I have a good friend, a very good friend. She's pregnant and her baby has a genetic, er, I think the doctor called it a genetic anomaly." He tried not to sound pleading. "I want you to treat my friend with Lot four-sixty-one. I want you to try and save her baby. I'm afraid this is her last chance."

"Inspector, what you're asking would be extremely dangerous, perhaps even fatal. Lot four-sixty-one hasn't been tested on a person that way yet, not even in the preliminary stages."

Ben remained adamant, undeterred. "My friend cannot afford to wait until it has been, Mr. Hessler. Treat her with four sixty-one and the truth about your son being a murderer remains between us. Refuse and . . ." He let his voice fade out, having said enough.

Paul Hessler regarded him with a gaze that flickered his eyebrows. "This must be a very good friend of yours, Inspector."

"She is."

"It occurs to me how prominently your name surfaced in that report I ordered on Pakad Danielle Barnea."

Ben ignored Hessler's suggestion. "Do we have a deal or not?"

"This drug could kill your friend, Inspector."

Ben swallowed hard. "That will be her decision to make."

"And assuming she says no . . ."

"Giving her the choice fulfills your side of the bargain."

Hessler's face suddenly paled. He looked woozy and once more leaned against the wall of the skybridge for support, his fingers dragging across the glass. "My son should have come to me, told me of the problem with these high school students."

"What would you have done?"

"There are other ways to assure silence, far more subtle ways."

"I'm sorry he didn't give you the chance, sir."

"You're missing the point. He didn't give me the chance because the project was his. He wanted to surprise me, to make me proud. And I would have been; God, how I would have been. He couldn't let anything get in the way of that." Hessler's voice settled into a low monotone. "Perhaps you should arrest me instead."

"I'm not here to arrest anyone. I'm here to save a woman I love."

"Her baby, you mean."

"No, I mean her. She can't lose this baby, sir. You know that . . . and so do I."

Hessler looked at Ben differently, as if they shared something neither quite understood. "And why should I trust you?"

"Because if you agree and I release the disc anyway, there'll be nothing to stop you from killing me . . . and Pakad Barnea."

Hessler frowned, weighing the prospects. "I'll need to see this disc of yours first."

"I expected as much."

"Come, Inspector," Hessler said, raising a quivering hand to Ben's elbow. "There's a computer in my office. I'll make sure we're not disturbed."

THE THREE RENTED Ford Explorers reached New York City after dark, each driven by an American member of the Gatekeepers who was familiar with the streets and traffic laws. Anna Krieger rode in the passenger seat of the lead Explorer, glad no one could see the weariness on her expression. These moments should have been full of fresh resolve and reinvigorated purpose. Instead Anna greeted them with the acknowledgment that her very reason for being was ebbing. An era had past; she was the last remnant. With Abraham Vorsky gone, Anna wondered if there was even anyone else who could recall her parents and the courageous, selfless acts that had cost them their lives.

She knew that Paul Hessler, really Karl Mundt, had to die for *her*, not so much for punishment, as vindication of everything she had always believed. He was no real villain and no great victory lay in his execution. It was over and had been for a long time. So she had greeted Vorsky's call last week summoning her to Israel with a hope of purpose regained, her reason for being restored. Another lie. Anna had done it to herself and this was the price she would pay: after Paul Hessler, the terrible acknowledgment that there were no others.

Anna couldn't imagine how she could live with no one to pursue. The passing years had become a greater threat than all the enemies of the Gatekeepers combined, stealing her targets and filling Germany with a compassionate populace that was forever seeking to make amends. Her country had finally agreed on financial compensation for the survivors of the Holocaust. Had even forced the Swiss banks that had absconded with Jewish family fortunes to make reparations to the proper heirs. There was no longer a reason to deny the past because, finally, it was over.

For Anna Krieger, though, there remained one last task to complete.

CHAPTER 83

"I T ' S ALL RIGHT," Paul Hessler said to his blazered security guards, after leading Ben into his private elevator. "My guest and I are going up to my office."

The guards stiffened, clearly uneasy over not being allowed to accompany their employer.

"Alone," Hessler added for emphasis. "Assuming I agree to this, Inspector," he continued after the elevator door had closed, "Pakad Barnea will have to come here to the Hessler Institute for the treatments."

Ben felt the car racing upwards, picking up enough speed to make his ears pop. "That can be arranged."

"You think she will go along with you? A great detective helping to cover up the murders of three Israeli citizens? Letting their killers go free?"

Ben hadn't considered the prospects of that. "I know how much she wants this baby, Mr. Hessler," he said simply. "She'll go along."

The door slid open into Hessler's office on the top floor, the sound of soft rushing water from an artfully fashioned waterfall replacing the mechanical whir of the elevator. Paul Hessler emerged first and headed toward his desk across the room.

Ben saw there was a computer set upon it, had begun to reach into his pocket for the disc, when a huge shape lunged out from the cover of the waterfall in Hessler's path.

N O!" DANIELLE SCREAMED the moment she saw the gun in Hans Mundt's hand.

Passion, rather than instinct, pushed her forward between the pistol and Paul Hessler. If his long-festering rage led Mundt to shoot his father now, she would never know the truth about her own father.

Danielle had barely planted herself in front of the old man, flinching against the fear of the bullet splitting her own flesh, when she saw Hessler shoved aside by another man who halted abruptly and threw his hands up in the air.

S TOP!" BEN YELLED , realizing with shock that the woman standing before him was Danielle.

"Get out of my way!" the huge man ranted.

He lifted his free hand to brush her aside, but Danielle blocked the swipe and tried to go for his gun hand. Equal to the task, the huge man tripped her up and leveled his gun on Ben now who stood rigid in front of the stunned Paul Hessler.

D ANIELLE BARNEA GLANCED at Paul Hessler and then looked up from the floor at Hans Mundt.

"I need to speak to him first," she said fiercely. "We both do. You know that."

The pistol trembled in Mundt's hand. "I have to do this!"

"You can't. Not this way."

"It's what I came here to do!"

"Look at him. What does he mean to you?"

"Nothing!"

"Exactly," Danielle said, climbing back to her feet slowly.

"Get out of my way!" Mundt ordered Ben. "I'll shoot you too!"

"Who is this man, Pakad?" Ben asked Danielle.

"You two *know* each other?" Mundt posed disbelievingly.

"I guess I should have left you on the case, Chief Inspector Barnea," said Paul Hessler between heavy breaths, "since you've found your way here anyway."

She glanced his way. "This is about me now, too, Mr. Hessler."

"Who is this man you brought with you?"

"You don't recognize me, do you?" Mundt charged, spitting the words at him.

"Should I?"

"No. That's the point. I'm your son."

Hessler's eyes bulged in disbelief. "My *what*?"

"Pakad Barnea," Ben started, struggling to keep his voice even, "I have informed Mr. Hessler of his late son's complicity in the murder of four high school students: three Israelis and one Palestinian."

Danielle tried very hard not to look surprised.

"I have also made an arrangement whereby this information will remain only with us once he performs a certain service on your behalf."

"What the fuck is he talking about?" Mundt demanded. Then, to Ben, "*Who* are you?"

"Inspector Bayan Kamal of the Palestinian police."

"Palestinian police . . ." Mundt motioned Ben away with his gun. "Get out now and you can live."

"I can't do that."

Danielle almost casually planted herself once again in front of Hans Mundt. "We had an arrangement. Put the gun down."

"I don't know what any of you are talking about!" Hessler insisted.

Mundt kept his eyes on Danielle and finally lowered the pistol to his hip. "Ask your questions quickly."

Ben dropped his hands and stepped aside, as Danielle swung toward Paul Hessler. "We know who you are and what you are. What you did."

"I need to sit down," Hessler said, and dropped into one of the chairs in a grouping near the waterfall. He fought to steady himself, resumed speaking even though he clearly was still shaken. "After so many years . . . It was the gunman in Tel Aviv who gave the truth away, wasn't it? The sergeant whose men rescued me in the woods."

"Trying to right that wrong!" Mundt seethed.

"Who is this animal?" Hessler wondered, dumbfounded.

"You call me an animal?" Mundt came forward until he was even with Danielle. "You *still* haven't figured it out? I've been to the grave. I know the truth. I know *everything*."

Hessler looked confused, anguished. "How is that possible?"

"The commandant of your camp filled in much of the story," Danielle told him, picking up where Mundt left off.

"But he's, he's dead."

"Close to it, but not quite."

"I was sure that he was executed. . . ." Hessler's voice drifted off wearily. He closed his eyes and opened them again to find Danielle Barnea standing over him now.

"I want to know about my father," she demanded. "I want to know if he was one of you."

"One of *who*?"

"No more games!" Mundt ordered, storming forward until Ben Kamal stepped before him to block his advance.

Danielle hadn't moved an inch. "Tell me about you and my father. About the money, everything. The truth."

"Your father saved my life, Pakad." Hessler took a deep breath. "That's where the story really begins. . . ."

CHAPTER 84

I N T H E 1 9 5 6 war," Hessler continued, "we were both assigned to a secret detachment sent across the Sinai to infiltrate Egypt and capture Nasser. It was a bold and striking plan, the first embarked upon by those who had grown out of the Haganah rebel force and the even more militant Irgun. We had drilled and trained for months. No one outside of a select few in the military and government knew about the force or the plan. Military records would show that we never actually left our units. Military records would show that the members of our strike force were never even acquainted with each other.

"Our mission failed miserably when we happened upon an Egyptian patrol. Bad timing, coincidence, poor intelligence—the reason didn't matter. The entire Egyptian patrol, nearly forty men, was slaughtered. In this fierce battle there would never be any record of, though, eight of the dozen in our party were killed outright, two mortally wounded and two critically. I was one of these last two and the other was your father who literally carried me out of the desert on his back."

Paul Hessler heaved a long, deep sigh.

"A hundred times I begged your father to leave me behind. But, being the stubborn ass that he was, he was hearing none of it, and days later the two of us were spotted by an Israeli helicopter on a reconnaissance mission and rescued.

"I don't remember any of those final hours myself; your father filled them in for me later. But on that day I swore I would repay him somehow. Years later, once I finally had the financial means to make good on my promise, I appeared at your home in Israel with a check in my wallet. Our mission to take Nasser hostage was so secret we hadn't seen each other in all the years since. Looking at your father made me realize how much older we both had gotten. I met you that day. Your father introduced us, but I guess you don't remember.

"Your father, of course, refused the money, and we parted as lifelong friends never to meet again face to face. As soon as I returned to the United States, though, I opened an account in his name and deposited the money in the hope someday he might change his mind."

Hessler's voice softened.

"I learned of his death after the funeral had already taken place and tried to figure out how to tell you of the gift that now belongs to you. Over a million dollars, if I remember correctly."

"What about before?"

"Before what?"

"Before the Sinai, before the Haganah. I'm talking about Germany!"

Hessler shook his head very slowly. "We met only once before the 1956 war, and that was in a refugee camp in 1947. Then we came to Palestine on board the same boat."

Danielle turned back to look at Mundt.

"He's lying," the big man insisted. "Tell her the truth."

"I have."

Mundt pushed his way past Ben, eyes bulging, pistol tight in his hand. "You've lied all your life!"

"Most of it, yes. But not about this."

"I saw where you buried Hessler."

Hessler climbed to his feet frowning, and stared perplexedly at Mundt. "That's impossible. No one ever found his body. I'm sure of that much."

"You dressed him in your uniform and coat—"

"Uniform and coat?"

"—and then you shot him."

"*Shot* him?" Paul Hessler sounded utterly mystified. He looked dazedly toward Ben Kamal. "Please tell me what this man is talking about. Someone tell me."

"*I'm the son you, Karl Mundt, abandoned, goddamnit!*"

A single quick lunge brought Mundt to Hessler before either Ben or Danielle could intervene. He grasped Hessler by his suit jacket's lapels and slammed him into the faux rock side of the waterfall, hearing the old man's breath escape him in a rush.

"You ran away and left me for dead after the war. To think, this is the first time I've ever seen my father face-to-face. I didn't know how I would feel. But I know now."

Hessler's eyes swam with fear and puzzlement, as he tried to find his breath.

"My mother and I were both dead to you," Mundt continued. "You had a new life to start. You befriended the real Hessler in the camp just so you could kill him and take his place when the time was right. Weiss saw you do it. Weiss knew *everything!*"

"Weiss," Paul Hessler barely managed to repeat.

"The commandant of the labor camp outside Lodz on the road to Leczyca. Remember?"

"No," Hessler said through a grimace, having finally found his breath. He no longer looked scared. "You're mistaken. I wasn't in that camp at all."

"*What?*"

Hans Mundt pushed Hessler hard against the side of the waterfall again, but this time the old man seemed not to feel it.

"I'm not Karl Mundt," he said.

CHAPTER 85

AFTER ALL THESE years, still you refuse to acknowledge me!"

Hessler looked almost calm now. "Because I'm not your father. Your father is dead. I realize that now."

"I don't believe it, not a word of it!" Mundt ranted, still clutching the man he believed was his father by the lapels.

"Then let me show you. I can prove everything I've said. I can prove Karl Mundt is dead."

Paul Hessler felt the big man finally release him, mumbling to himself, trying to make sense of what he had just heard.

Still leaning against the wall, Hessler turned toward Danielle. "I'm sorry about your baby. I hope I am able to help."

"What are you talking about?"

"Tell her, Inspector."

"Lot four-sixty-one," Ben started, wishing he could have chosen a better time to explain. "The reason those four students in Israel and Palestine had to die. . . ."

"I don't understand."

Ben looked toward Hessler before responding. "Ari Hessler arranged their deaths to keep a medical discovery secret," he said and proceeded to explain the existence of Lot 461. He went on to outline the fact that it might be capable of saving the baby she was carrying.

When Ben had finished his story, Danielle was at first speechless. Then she turned back to Paul Hessler. "I'm sorry about your son."

"I am, too. More than you can possibly know. I feel that he is doubly lost to me. But it is his name, and my family, I must protect now, Pakad. You agree to keep this between us, as Inspector Kamal has proposed, and I will do everything in my power to help you save your own child."

Danielle found herself overwhelmed by the prospects. The sudden return of hope after a week of misery set her heart beating faster. Still, she found the thought of letting cold-blooded killers go unpunished revolting. But what had duty done for her? Where had it gotten her besides a suspension at the hands of a hateful superior? Danielle had done so much, always everything she was told without question or protest, and this was how she had been treated in return.

"When can we do this?" she asked Hessler.

"I don't know, Pakad. I'll put experts on your case immediately. We can draw blood tonight at my institute and begin the process. It might take months. It might happen too late to be of any good to you."

"I'll take that chance. The quicker we get started the better."

Paul Hessler looked back at Hans Mundt. "As soon as you have all heard the true story."

ANNA KRIEGER'S FORD Explorer was stopped at a traffic light in view of the Towers when she saw a pair of dark Suburbans emerge from the private underground garage. The powerfully built security men standing on either side of the open bay made sure the vehicles had merged safely into traffic before retreating down the ramp.

Anna felt the hairs on her neck prickle and stand on end, like those of an animal catching the scent.

Could Paul Hessler be inside one of those Suburbans? Why else would there be such a security presence?

Still unsure of exactly how she was going to proceed, Anna lifted the tiny walkie-talkie to her ravaged lips. "I think I have Hessler in view. Proceed on my tail."

HESSLER INSISTED THAT his chief of security, Franklin Russett, drive them himself to their destination, while six of his guards—ex-soldiers, all—followed in the second Suburban.

Hessler sat next to Russett in the front seat, didn't speak until they had pulled out of the garage. "I'm going to ask you some questions, Russett. Answer truthfully and no recriminations will come of it. You have my word. Is that agreeable?"

Russett checked the car's other occupants in the rear-view mirror, seeming to sense where this was going. He nodded in assent.

"Mr. Russett," Hessler resumed, "in Israel did you use your considerable contacts to help my son Ari retain the services of a number of professionals with a certain deadly expertise?"

"They weren't all Israeli."

"Please answer my question."

"Yes, sir, I did."

Paul Hessler fought to remain calm. "These men, I just learned, were retained to murder high school students. Is that correct?"

"They were hired to preserve the interests of Hessler Industries, sir. Each of them top of the line. Very discreet as well, if that's where your concern lies."

"My concern lies with the fact that you helped my son become a murderer."

"In the best interests of the company, sir."

"Ari's words or yours?"

"Both of us, sir. We were after criminals, blackmailers. I reported the fact they were high school students to your son once the first was identified. He ordered the operation to go forward anyway and, for the record, I agreed with him."

"And your killers continued their work even after my son's death?"

"I made sure of it."

"I appreciate your honesty."

"I'm not proud of what I did, sir, but if I—"

"I've heard enough, thank you, Mr. Russett." Paul Hessler swung round to face the others. "I'm sorry. This is something I will always be deeply ashamed of. If there was a way to make things right, if there was anything I could do . . ."

"I hope you're not talking to me," Hans Mundt snapped from the rear-most seat.

"Inspector Kamal and Chief Inspector Barnea just got their answers, Herr Mundt. Yours are coming soon."

"Why can't you just tell me?"

"Did you come to find your father or not, Herr Mundt?"

"You know I did."

"Then you will leave satisfied, too."

Hessler looked toward Danielle. "Once we are finished, we will go straight to the Institute, Pakad, to begin the process. You understand there are no guarantees of success whatsoever and plenty of risk."

"I'm used to those kinds of terms."

"My experts will advise you that Lot four-sixty-one has been tried only on terminal patients for whom potentially fatal doses are not a concern. They will say they have no idea how much of the programmed substance to use in treating an unborn fetus, much less what the side effects might be."

"Whatever they are," said Danielle, looking back at Ben, "they're better than genetic termination."

Ben nodded, happy he could do this for her, all the while wishing he didn't have to in such an underhanded fashion.

Had he become the kind of person he had spent his career hunting, a man willing to do do anything to further his own ends?

But he owed Danielle that much. In spite of their recent estrangement, she had taught him to live and hope again. Now, thanks to Paul Hessler and Lot 461, he had been able to do the same for her.

"You still haven't told us where we're going," Ben noted.

"Just over the New Jersey border," Hessler said, as Franklin Russett pushed the lead Suburban through the night. "Palisades Park."

THE *THWOCK* OF the doors of the two Suburbans closing came one after the other. They had pulled both vehicles through the steel fence enclosing the property on which the castle had been rebuilt, high on the cliffs of Palisades State Park overlooking the Hudson River. Scaffolding remained in place over a large measure of the castle wall so workmen could complete their reconstruction efforts.

Even that, though, did little to detract from the awesome scope of the site. The wall was uneven, high in some places and lower in others, just as it had been five hundred years before. The moonlight and spray of the floods powered by industrial-strength generators was bright enough for Ben and Danielle to see the slitted holes, high up in the topmost battlements, through which arrows could be shot and spears hurled with virtual impunity. Paul Hessler's restoration efforts had been so complete and exacting that the entire group stared in amazement.

The only portion not completed was a gap that would soon be filled by a fully functional gatehouse and mechanical gate that in ancient times would have helped keep enemies from gaining access. Tonight that chasm opened into a spacious courtyard that fronted the castle itself. Hessler led the way across it with Franklin Russett clinging stubbornly to his side. Russett had left the armed guards who had accompanied them posted near the entrances of both the fence and the castle.

Once inside, Hessler ordered Russett to wait for them at the bottom of the narrow stone stairway that spiraled upward through the central tower. Russett protested, but Hessler was adamant and took the lead up the dimly lit stairs as his security chief looked on in consternation.

"I told him if you wanted to kill me, I'd be dead already," Hessler said, setting a slow but steady pace.

"I haven't made my decision yet," Hans Mundt reminded.

Hessler didn't respond. Danielle could see a composed look in his eyes and detected an almost soothing, complacent sound in his voice. She couldn't identify exactly when or why it had happened. But clearly something had changed in Hessler. A weight seemed to have been lifted from him; not enough to compensate for the loss of his son, of course, nor to mitigate the crimes for which Ari was responsible, but considerable all the same.

Struggling for breath by the time they reached the top tower room, Hessler sat down on the stone bench and held its edge with both hands, gazing about the tower almost reverently.

"I remember seeing this place from the forest, coming here to seek refuge from the storm. It saved my life."

"All that is well known," chided Mundt impatiently. "Already part of the great Hessler legend."

"There's one part no one has ever heard until now."

"And what's that?"

"I wasn't alone."

CHAPTER 86

*T*ERRIFIED AND FREEZING, *Paul Hessler first dismissed the sounds as rats, or even larger animals foraging in the floors above. It was only when he listened closer, able to filter out the storm beyond, that he recognized the sounds as the clatter of boots on a stone floor like the one on which he had collapsed.*

Perhaps someone else had taken refuge from the storm here in the abandoned castle, someone perhaps willing to share food and maybe a change of clothes.

His soaking shoes sloshed noisily as Paul began to climb the stairs, and he sat down to squeeze some of the water from them before continuing. He didn't want to give his presence away and risk startling the castle's other guest until he absolutely had to. So he trudged on slowly, careful to avoid a misplaced step in what quickly became near total darkness.

The luscious scent of birch wood flaming in a hearth reached him just before he heard the crackling as the flames ate at the bark. He imagined embers rising through one of the chimney stacks he had glimpsed from beyond and again blessed his luck.

Recharged, Paul Hessler continued on, stopping at the stop of the stairs in a doorway to find a figure roasting what looked like a small rabbit in the fire over a makeshift spit. Paul didn't speak, just shuffled slightly forward and waited for the figure to turn.

"I didn't mean to bother you," he said, when the young man about his own age finally swung around.

"Who are you?"

"It's just that I saw the castle and came in to escape the storm." Paul kept speaking as the stranger strode toward him. The stick in his hand glowed orange, the rabbit upon it still smoking. "I'm sorry if I—"

The stranger shoved him backwards and pressed the sizzling end of the stick against his throat. "You're lying! Tell me who sent you or I'll kill you now!"

"No one! I'm, I'm alone!"

"They sent you, didn't they? Who caught on to my plan? How many others are there?"

"No one, I tell you! Just—"

Paul Hessler never finished his sentence. The stranger jerked his smoking stick forward and Paul felt it scrape across his flesh when he turned to avoid the thrust. The smell of the roasting meat filled his nostrils as he pushed the stranger away and held his hands out in a gesture of peace.

"Please, I mean you no harm. I'll leave if you want."

The stranger screamed and lunged again. Paul managed to rip the stick out of his hand and the smoking carcass of the rabbit plopped to the stone floor still threaded over the wood. The stranger closed his hands around Paul's painfully thin throat and nearly crushed the cartilage with the first savage thrust of his thumbs.

But Paul held to enough breath to knee him hard in the groin twice. The stranger's knees started to buckle, not enough to stop him from holding on, and the two of them hit the floor together. They rolled and the stranger ended up on top, his renewed grasp forcing the air back out of Paul's tortured lungs.

Paul flailed his hands wildly, trying to dislodge the stranger's powerful hands. He felt a numbness spreading through him, his head seeming to expand. His hands flopped to the stone floor and thrashed about, scraping up against the warm soft carcass of the cooked rabbit.

He grabbed the stick, its roasted rabbit still in place, and drove it upwards. He felt it pierce the stranger's throat and a spray of warm blood coated his face. The grip, though, still did not slacken and Paul jabbed and jabbed until at last the fingers went limp, and the stranger collapsed atop him.

It was all Paul could do to lift the body off him and spill it over to the side. He thought he might have blacked out briefly himself and awoke to the feeling it must have all been a dream until he saw the blood running beneath him and felt its slickness against his own face and neck. He checked the young man for signs of life, but found none.

He sprang to his feet, suddenly revolted. He knew he would have vomited had there been anything in his stomach. The thought of that reminded him he hadn't eaten for two days and returned his focus to the still smoking rabbit resting on the floor by the corpse.

Paul Hessler stooped only long enough to retrieve it, and moved toward the fire to finish cooking the meal that would give . . .

GIVE ME THE strength I needed to go on," Paul Hessler finished, pushing himself up to his feet. "After I ate, I exchanged my wet clothes for a dry set I found in the dead man's rucksack."

A pickax left behind by one of the workmen stood in the corner and Paul Hessler picked it up and tested its weight. The pickax looked surprisingly light in his grasp, as he moved toward the newly mortared chimney and measured off his first strike.

"I left here the next day . . ."

As he spoke, Hessler punctuated his words with a series of heavy blows to the fireplace chimney.

". . . wearing the dead man's clothes . . ."

whop . . .

". . . the food he had brought with him . . ."

whop . . .

". . . and his papers which the American soldiers found in my inside pocket five days later."

Hessler launched three more powerful strikes that splintered the chimney in a series of jagged cracks. Then he used the pickax to tear away the brick and mortar, shedding shards and chunks to the floor as his audience looked on in utter puzzlement.

"The papers made them believe I was Paul Hessler, a survivor of a labor camp north of Lodz. But I wasn't. I thought I had *killed* Paul Hessler in this castle and have lived with the guilt over that for all these years."

One last savage thrust opened a gaping chasm in the chimney and the old man stepped back, leaned on the handle to inspect his handiwork.

"Because now the story at last has an end." Sweating and almost out of breath he focused on Hans Mundt. "You came here in search of your father, Herr Mundt."

Mundt started forward, but turned toward the chimney when the man who had lived as Paul Hessler directed him there with his eyes.

A skeleton was plainly visible inside, nailed to the inner castle wall.

"Meet Karl Mundt," Hessler continued. "The man I really killed that night in 1944."

CHAPTER 87

HANS MUNDT STARED at his father's skeleton, barely hearing the man who had become Paul Hessler as he continued his story.

"The papers I took from your father he had already stolen from the *real* Paul Hessler. I'm not Jewish, but I'm not German either. I'm Polish. My real name isn't Paul Hessler *or* Karl Mundt; it's Piotr Dudek. I had escaped from a different labor camp outside of Lodz, near the village of Minsk. I came upon this castle a day or so after Karl Mundt had killed Paul Hessler and assumed his identity. So, for all these years, I thought *Hessler* was the man I had killed. Before tonight only one other man knew the story of that night in the forest." Paul Hessler, born Piotr Dudek, looked toward Danielle. "Your father, Pakad Barnea. I confessed the truth to him as he carried me across the Sinai after the Nasser mission failed."

"What did he say to you?" Danielle heard herself ask him.

"He told me it didn't mean a thing. He told me I had survived because I was meant to, and that was all that mattered. He told me Piotr Dudek was dead. I had left him in that castle and that's where he should stay." Hessler lowered his voice slightly. "Your father told me I had the chance, the opportunity, to do good for myself and my country. I think I've done that. At least, I tried."

"What your son did," Danielle told him, "wasn't your fault . . . *Mr. Hessler*. It wasn't your fault."

"Yes, it was, and I *do* take the blame for it, because he wanted to prove himself to me. Ari wanted for himself exactly what I wanted for him. He was so driven by the desire to succeed, the desire I had instilled in him, he couldn't see the evil of these murders. Or, if he did, he rationalized it. Lot four-sixty-one was the first thing he had done on his own. He could never risk letting these children destroy it. Never."

Mundt was still standing transfixed before the exposed chimney, staring at the bones of his father, the man who had lived as Paul Hessler had hidden away fifty-seven years before.

"So I guess I killed your father, Herr Mundt. I, Piotr Dudek, a poor Polish boy interned at a Nazi labor camp until I was lucky enough to escape after they left me for dead. I survived by pretending to be shot and hiding beneath other bodies in a mass grave they spilled us into. If you want to kill me for that . . ."

Hans Mundt stayed silent and still.

"That's why you had to reassemble the castle here," Danielle said to Hessler. She tried to see him as he had described himself, as Piotr Dudek. But he remained Paul Hessler, hero and benefactor of the State of Israel, to her, just as he had to her father. "To keep your secret safe."

Hessler nodded. "They were going to demolish this castle back in Poland. I couldn't take the chance that the bones of the man I killed would be found, especially with today's DNA testing. Imagine them finding out the real Paul Hessler died more than a half century ago. . . ."

"Only it wasn't Hessler," Hans Mundt reminded. "It was my father, Karl Mundt, whom you buried behind that wall."

"But, you see, I didn't know that. And all these years I lived in fear of being exposed as Piotr Dudek who killed a Jew and assumed his identity. I had nightmares about them coming to arrest me at the Bar Mitzvahs or weddings of my children."

"Instead, they would have come to give you a medal for what you did," Hans Mundt managed.

"Is that a problem for you, Herr Mundt?"

Mundt's face had gone blank, all the emotion sucked out of him. "My father abandoned my mother. He knew exactly what he was going to do the moment he kissed her good-bye for the last time. He had everything planned. All that remained was to choose his 'victim' once he reached the camp." His eyes returned to the skeleton that had been hidden in the tower chimney all these years. "The truth is if you had turned out to really be Karl Mundt, I might have killed you myself. Might have killed my own father. I don't know. So perhaps you did me a great favor all those years ago. I suppose I'm in your debt."

Paul Hessler, who had left Piotr Dudek behind him in this very spot fifty-seven years before, turned toward Ben and Danielle. "As I am in yours for keeping the truth about my son a secret. We should get to the institute as soon as—"

His words were interrupted by the sound of gunfire erupting outside the castle.

CHAPTER 88

THE FOUR OF them stared at each other in consternation for a few moments, before Ben said, "Quick!"

He led the way downstairs with Hans Mundt by his side, Danielle next to Hessler just behind them.

"It must be Anna Krieger," Mundt said to Danielle. He turned to look at Paul Hessler. "The Gatekeepers have come for him."

Hessler's eyes flashed with fear and recognition. "Nazi hunters? Here? *Now?*"

"Executioners of former Nazis who escaped traditional justice."

"They believe they're after Karl Mundt," Danielle told him.

"Then what are we going to do?"

Ben looked at Danielle. "The only thing we can do: fight."

THEY MET UP with Hessler's security chief Franklin Russett just inside the castle at the foot of the stairs.

He was sweating, out of breath, and had one assault rifle in hand and another shouldered.

"How many?" Ben asked him, as the gunfire continued outside.

"Lots. A dozen anyway, and well armed. They shot the two men I posted at the fence before we even knew what was happening."

"What about the rest of them?"

"I've already called nine-one-one," the burly Russett said. "But the police are too far away to do us any good in the time we've got." He looked at Paul Hessler. "We've got to get you out of here, sir."

"What about the back?" Danielle suggested.

Hessler shook his head. "The wall is solid back there. And high."

"Perfect," Danielle disagreed.

"Give me your coat," Ben told the old man, as he eyed both Hessler and Danielle.

"Why?"

"Just do it!" Ben took Hessler's overcoat and turned toward Russett as he pulled his arms through its sleeves. "Mr. Russett, you're going to stay with me, by my side once we move outside."

"I'll do no such thing!"

Ben waited for a break in the gunfire to respond. "Yes, you will—if you want your employer to survive."

OUTSIDE THE AIR sang with gunshots. Hessler Industries' surviving four guards returned the enemy fire from behind the castle wall where the gatehouse would someday be. If only it were in place now, Ben thought. He noted with relief that the four guards wielded assault rifles which evened the odds somewhat. The bodies of two guards who'd already been shot down lay just in front of the fence where Russett had posted them.

The strategy of the Gatekeepers was well thought out. They were firing from the wooded cover that rimmed the castle's cleared site on the cliffs. That made it impossible to get a firm fix on the gunmen's positions, as they set about picking off the guards one at a time.

Ben moved outside, draped in Paul Hessler's overcoat and holding it so his face was obscured. He moved hesitantly, hunched over to appear as an old man. Franklin Russett clung to his side, firing off token volleys into the woods just to keep the opposition honest. They stopped behind a massive front loader that had helped fit the massive stones of the castle wall in place, pressing their backs against its cool yellow steel.

Ben tried to spot Danielle back near the door but she had already disappeared around the side of the castle, Paul Hessler safe by her side for the time being. If Hessler didn't survive this attack, Lot 461 would no longer be an option for her, for *them*. The baby, Ben's son, had to be saved, which meant saving Hessler.

Hans Mundt had volunteered to escort the two of them around to the rear of the castle to make sure it was clear. From that point, it would be up to Danielle to figure out a way to get Paul Hessler and herself over the wall.

Mundt zigzagged back in a dash, camouflaged by the night. His cold eyes stared at Russett behind the loader's cover. "I need a gun. I gave mine to Barnea."

Russett yanked a pistol from his belt and handed it to Mundt, while Ben considered the prospects of Hessler and Danielle trying to scale a wall identical to the one that lay directly before them. Even if they made it, they would have to traverse rough terrain near the cliffs pursued by a dozen or more gunmen.

"We've got to stop the Gatekeepers here," he said to Russett and Mundt.

"We'll be lucky just to hold them off!" Russett insisted, a grimace stretched across his face.

"No, we have to *stop* them. End it now."

"Impossible!"

Ben focused on the castle's front wall, the battlements. "Not if we get the rest of your men up there," he told

Russett as the Gatekeepers' fire continued to pepper the site.

"That's crazy!"

Mundt followed Ben's gaze to the vertical slits through which arrows had flown in centuries past. "No, he's right. He's right." Then, to Russett, "We do it his way or we all die!"

DANIELLE LED PAUL Hessler to the rear wall without attracting any gunfire. "Those stairs over there!" she signalled, veering toward them in the open.

Hessler snatched her arm and restrained her before she had taken a step. "There are none on the other side."

"But there's scaffolding, just like in the front of the castle, isn't there?"

Hessler's eyes widened. "By God, yes."

"We can do this, sir."

Hessler still didn't let go of her arm. "I'm doing this for your father, Pakad. Not just for my son's reputation and to save myself from the disgrace."

Danielle closed her hand tenderly over his. "Thank you."

Then, holding the gun Mundt had provided before her, Danielle started forward in a crouch. She swept the smaller, rear courtyard in search of motion, sound, or stray light, but there was none. She reached the steps and climbed them ahead of Paul Hessler, an outstretched hand signalling him to hold at the bottom until she beckoned otherwise.

He caught up with her on one of the lower segments of the wall, then held his position again. From there Danielle climbed a shorter set of stairs to the higher segment, called a merlon, where the construction scaffolding was still in place against the outside of the wall. Keeping her knees bent to stay low, Danielle signalled Hessler to follow her again. The scaffolding was just a short drop from them now.

She was reaching a hand down to help the old man up when she felt something like a match strike her skin, only with the force of a kick. She had never been shot before and assumed it was just a cramp, a stubborn muscle acting up.

Then, through the darkness, she saw flecks of sandstone spurting into the air all around her.

Bullets!

As Danielle started back for the stairs, her legs gave out and she collapsed atop Paul Hessler, tumbling both of them back down into the yard behind the castle.

CHAPTER 89

N OW!" RUSSETT SIGNALLED, having
given his men their instructions.

As Ben watched, the four guards, armed with assault
rifles, darted from their postions of cover behind the castle
wall up two sets of stairs to positions before the open slats
atop the battlements.

"You've got to draw the Gatekeepers' fire, try to draw
them out into the open," Ben told Russett.

Russett looked at him, as bullets clanged off the loader's
steel skin. "What about you?"

"Let me have one of those," Ben said, gesturing toward
the second assault rifle Russett wore over his shoulder.

Russett gave it to Ben and watched him handle it uneasily, trying to gauge its weight and balance.

"Ever fire one of those before?" Russett asked.

"On the police range once."

"I'll go up there instead of you," Mundt offered, reaching for the assault rifle.

Ben pulled it back. "No," he said, then smiled slightly.
"We need someone who's a better shot than I am to draw
their fire."

Ben waited for Mundt and Russett to rush from the cover of the loader to the castle wall before he followed the path of Russett's four remaining guards up the stone steps to the ancient battlements. Mundt and Russett clacked off shots as they ran, drawing all the enemy fire to themselves and clearing Ben's path.

He stumbled twice on the steps and fell the second time. Ended up crawling to the top of the wall on all fours. Once there, Ben chose a slot in the battlement five yards from the nearest man and studied the way that guard had extended his rifle barrel through the opening in the castle wall. Ben balanced the weight of his weapon comfortably on the sill and considered the effects of the gun's kick once he began firing. But he seemed to remember the M-16 he had fired on a police range in Detroit had barely no kick at all.

Lowering himself to more easily peer through the foot-square slat, Ben waited for the enemy to begin their attack.

DON'T MOVE," PAUL Hessler whispered, trying to hold Danielle still.

"We've got to get out of here. I've got to help you escape." She tried to sit up and something that felt like jagged teeth sank into her midsection. The pain stole her breath and sent a flash exploding before her eyes.

"Easy," Paul Hessler soothed. "Easy now."

Danielle now felt a warmth spreading through her shirt and soaking her pants. "I've been . . . shot."

"You're going to be all right."

"Got to, got to get you out of here."

"Hand me your gun."

Danielle dropped it. The old man picked it up, held it taut.

"You're going to have to kill them," she managed, trying to swallow.

Paul Hessler cradled her against him, recalling how Danielle's father had carried him out of the Sinai Desert.

He remembered confessing the truth, wanting to die as Piotr Dudek, the man he really was.

"That's all right," he said. "I've done it before."

FROM HIS POSITION high on the castle wall, Ben had a bird's-eye view of all the territory in front of him through the night. Though he could not see Mundt and Russett from this vantage point, he heard their fire resume as soon as the Gatekeepers—he counted eight of them—began their deliberate advance on the castle. Although Mundt and Russett's bullets scored no hits, they accomplished the desired effect of concentrating the enemy's efforts on them for now, providing Ben and the other riflemen with what they needed: a clear field of fire from the battlements.

He waited for Russett's professionals to start shooting before he followed suit, the attackers almost to the fence fifty feet from the castle wall. Ben squeezed one eye closed, aimed as best as he could through the barrel-mounted sight, and began firing one shot after another. The sounds stung his ears, quickly lost amidst the cadence of the other shots reverberating around him.

Ben watched the attackers being cut down in their tracks, crumbling or twisting to the ground. A few scrambled for cover until more bullets pummeled them.

Ben kept firing at the attackers who had escaped the initial surprise barrage. The farther away they drew, the more random and less focused his aim became. He wished he had taken Colonel al-Asi up on his offer of a lesson at the shooting range. Ben knew he was running dangerously low on ammo and began to take more disciplined shots.

He heard the spent jackets clacking metallically against the rebuilt wall, spilling off the ledge and pooling on the level below. His mind flashed back to the same sound clicking in his ears eight years ago when he pumped round after round into the madman who had just slain his family. Standing there in the upstairs hall of his home as the shells

402 / JON LAND

clamored down the stairs, he couldn't save his wife and children.

But he could save Danielle and their baby here tonight.

Ben snapped a fresh clip home and fell into a strange, easy rhythm. His targets seemed to brighten before him as he tightened his gaze upon them. He barely felt himself pull the trigger, the slight recoil greeted with a reassurance of another bullet launched on line. Alongside him, bursts from the rest of Russett's guards came nonstop, leaving a tinny echo bouncing about the pit of his skull. Ben's neck ached, but he refused to relax his aim through the rifle's bore-mounted sight.

We can do this. We can win. . . .

Then he heard a whooooosh like the sound of a firecracker jetting into the air. A streak of light flashed out of the treeline for the castle, surging over the steel security fence.

A rocket! It had to be a rocket!

Ben ducked an instant before impact well down the wall to his right. The ancient stone and mortar blew inward, collapsing the entire section of the wall.

Another rocket exploded out from the woods, and Ben dropped back from the wall and curled into a ball. The explosion stung his ears, left them ringing as dust and debris rained down upon him. He plopped down to the next level and heard himself screaming until the third rocket drowned the sound out, ripping apart the battlement directly over him. He looked up to see Russett's guards all gone, lost to the hot smoking debris. Ben started to raise his head and fresh automatic fire chewed up what little cover remained above him.

His primary instructor at the police academy had been a marine combat vet who droned on in a southern drawl about what it was like to be caught in a firefight. Something that couldn't be taught, had to be lived through to understand.

Ben understood now, and the truth was even the marine vet's painful remembrances hadn't done this dread feeling justice. Ben felt his very insides were coming unglued, his guts spasming and seizing up into a tight, twisted mass. He clamped his hands over his ears as chunks of Paul Hessler's reconstructed castle wall smacked and stung him. Covered his head with his elbows and felt arrowhead-sized shards spear his flesh. He could smell his own blood, but clung to his sanity with the realization that he hadn't been hit badly yet.

Not that it mattered, because Ben realized that there was no way now to stop the Gatekeepers' advance on the castle, or their pursuit of the man they believed to be Karl Mundt. He thought of Danielle and pried a hand from his head to feel beneath him for his rifle. Fire the bullets he had left and buy her as much time as he could, if nothing else.

The rifle was gone. He must have knocked it aside off the ledge where it had tumbled to the dark chalky ground below. Still pressed tight against the stone ledge, Ben looked back down into the courtyard in search of his rifle.

His eyes locked instead on a target halfway between the wall and the castle. His mind worked fast, clinging to hope, calculating his chances. If he could reach it, maybe, just maybe he could turn the battle in their favor. He knew he might die in the process but felt strangely resigned to that; death was so close now the fear of it had been stripped away.

Ben saw both Mundt and Russett lurch into the opening in the center of the castle wall, firing wildly at the latest wave of attackers as they burst through the security fence's gate. Russett was hit in the leg and crumpled. Mundt took bullet after bullet, clinging incredibly to his feet until his pistol clicked empty and he keeled over, still trying to reload.

But the two men had bought Ben the time he needed to lower himself to the next ledge on the castle wall and then drop to the ground where Russett was making a desperate effort to drag Mundt to safety.

Ben scrambled past them and rushed toward the one thing he believed might save all their lives.

ANNA KRIEGER HAD anticipated everything perfectly except the enemy's use of the battlements. That was a surprise, and a clever one at that. But she still had three men with her—four including the sniper who reported the real Paul Hessler was pinned down at the rear of the castle. The sniper also reported a hit on a woman Anna believed could only be Danielle Barnea! *Alive!* And since Barnea was here, Mundt must be here too. Obviously they had tricked her in Poland, and now both of them would die.

Like father, like son, Anna thought, finding justice in that.

Once inside the fence, she signalled her men to stop just short of the Suburbans and steadied her rifle on a stocky man who was hovering over another he had just dragged to safety. Before she could pull the trigger, though, Anna heard the roar of a heavy engine split the night and looked up to see a huge yellow loading machine barreling straight toward them.

BEN PUSHED THE loader on, grinding its gears and fighting the pedals all the way to gain maximum speed. It had been twenty years since he'd driven one like it as part of a summer construction job in Dearborn, Michigan. But that had been a much smaller version, and he'd merely worked the shovel under the commands of his boss, rather than actually maneuvering the entire machine without someone telling him exactly what to do.

The cab was a good dozen feet off the ground and barely resembled the smaller one he remembered. The loader had switched on quickly, though, and responded with almost truck-like handling once Ben shoved it into gear.

His vantage point from the cab gave him a clear view

of his targets ahead. The engine buckled, but the huge steel machine lumbered on, gathering speed.

PAUL HESSLER KEPT pressing the balled-up strips of his shirt tightly into Danielle's wound. The blood had slowed, but not stopped and even in the darkness she looked terribly pale. He watched her wet her lips to speak a few times and lowered his ear to listen to words that didn't come.

He had to save her, no matter what it took, save her just as her father had saved him.

Paul Hessler . . .

That's who Danielle's father had saved and that's who he was. If Piotr Dudek hadn't died that night in the castle, he had assuredly died that day in the Sinai. A man was more than a name. Hessler had dedicated so much of his life to Israel because he loved it with the devotion of any Jew. He had been there at the beginning, would help see things through as long as he lived.

His identity lay in his deeds and his accomplishments. He realized he had been wrong to think his life as Paul Hessler had begun the night he had murdered Karl Mundt in the castle. Instead, it had begun the moment he set foot in Palestine and became the man he was today.

Paul Hessler pressed himself against Danielle and kept repeating words of encouragement. "You and your baby are going to live! Do you hear me! You're both going to live!"

THE REST OF her surviving Gatekeepers scattered at the sight of the huge yellow loader surging toward them. But Anna Krieger held her ground, firing a spray of bullets which clanged and flared off the huge shovel. She knew a few had made it into the cab and was certain she'd hit the driver. Anna fully expected the loader to veer harmlessly off, but instead it crashed into the Suburbans, tumbled them over, and kept coming.

CRIMPED LOW IN the loader's cab, Ben glimpsed Franklin Russett crawling desperately aside, dragging the form of Hans Mundt along with him. Then a barrage of bullets struck the machine. Shattered glass sprayed over him, stinging his face and scratching one of his eyes. Ben bit down the pain, but the eye closed, useless now.

He remembered his marine vet police academy instructor opening up one day about how he had won the Medal of Honor by charging directly into a firefight and dropping grenades into a series of Vietcong forward position machine gun nests; four in all, three men in each.

Continuing the loader on through the pain and his ruined vision, Ben realized he was doing the same thing now. His closed eye made it a challenge just to keep the loader heading straight. He hadn't intended to crash dead-on into the Suburbans, and the effect of impact surprised him. The huge vehicles, essentially weightless against the loader's massive power, tumbled not just once, but several times, picking up speed with each roll until they slammed into the fence, buckling it.

Ben's good eye caught a tall woman with a strangely pale face backing off at the last instant, tossing her rifle aside and trying to run. But the thudding roll of one of the Suburbans swiftly caught up and crushed her beneath it, as it came to a stop.

ANNA TRIED TO move, but abandoned the effort when she realized she couldn't breathe. Something pressed against her chest, trapping her. She tried to raise her arm, couldn't. Her chest felt as if she had been caved in, and she realized with a terrible fear that she could feel nothing below her waist.

The numbness was spreading upward now, leaving

Anna powerless to do anything but wait for death to claim her.

THE THREE SURVIVING Gatekeepers, had scattered toward a trio of Ford Explorers parked out of view from the castle. They piled into the lead one, opening fire on the loader as Ben crashed through the security fence and bore down on them.

He couldn't stop, wouldn't stop, realizing these men were the last thing standing between Danielle and safety. He uncoiled himself and rose up fully in the cab, no longer caring if they shot him.

More glass shattered, pricking him, but he pressed the loader onward and struck the Explorer broadside. The loader's teeth chewed through the steel of the door and sank into fabric. It lifted the Explorer slightly up and then dropped it back down again, freeing Ben to ride up and over it, the loader's massive tundra tires crushing the steel frame beneath them. It felt as though he was doing it with his own feet, pressed down hard against the loader's floor that felt sizzling hot.

There might have been screams; the wrenching and screeching of steel made it difficult to tell. His toes tensed and cramps locked up his calves, as the back wheels followed the front ones up and over what was left of the Explorer.

It took Ben a moment to realize the battle was over. He managed to stop the loader and pop open the cab door. Then he climbed down the ladder, collapsing the moment his feet hit the ground.

Danielle!

The thought of her was enough to spur Ben back to his feet, and he staggered off into the night to find her.

CHAPTER 90

THEY WERE IN the Columbia Presbyterian Medical Center emergency room, twelve blocks from the George Washington Bridge, rather than the Hessler Institute. Instead of being given her first injections of Lot 461, Danielle's blood was being typed and matched. An army of doctors hovered over the gurney on which she lay. Ben hung back by the drawn curtain, no one seeming to pay any attention to him. It didn't feel like he was really there. He tried to blink himself back awake, turning the trauma room into a series of frozen still shots. The wrong button hit on the remote control for his vision, as hands and instruments moved in jumpy gaps over Danielle's body.

"Jesus Christ, this is a bad one."

"Get an OR ready and page Dr. Cantrell."

"Forget the OR," another doctor said, his gloves and greens already red with Danielle's blood. "Whatever we're going to do, we've got to do it here."

"Blood pressure dropping, Doctor!" a nurse announced.

"Shit, we're losing her! Get a crash cart in here!"

"Where's that goddamn blood?"

Ben stepped forward, almost surprised when a nurse's

gaze acknowledged his presence. "She's pregnant."

A few of the trauma team members turned toward him, saw his half-closed, bloodied eye. "Jesus," someone said, "this one needs help too."

"Never mind me. You need to know that the woman's pregnant."

"Who are you?" the lead doctor asked him, applying firm pressure to Danielle's wound.

"The father."

"Blood pressure steady, Doctor."

"We're going to have to go in," the lead doctor announced grimly.

A nurse rushed through the curtain with an armful of clear plastic bags full of blood. "Eight units," she said breathlessly. "More on the way."

"Get the rapid infuser over here and give me some room! Christ, I need suction! Somebody get that suction over here!" Working his hands swiftly over Danielle's belly, the trauma doctor glanced at Ben again. "And someone get him out of here! *Now!*"

Ben felt hands close upon him. Then he was being led backward out of the trauma room, his feet not feeling like his own.

T HE DOCTOR FINALLY emerged less than a half hour later, his hospital greens covered in Danielle's blood. Ben looked up at him from his chair, holding his face in his hands. Static pricked the edges of his nerve endings, turning the world slow and dull

"We've managed to stop the blood loss and stabilize her," he reported. "She's on her way up to surgery now. I think she's going to make it."

"What about the baby?" Ben asked, fearing the answer as much as he had ever feared anything in his life.

E P I L O G U E

"So this is the Hessler Institute," Danielle said, looking around her.

At the foot of her bed in Columbia Presbyterian Hospital, Ben Kamal smiled slightly.

"I don't even remember being brought here from the castle. Where's Hessler? Is he all right?"

"Fine. He saved your . . ."

"What?"

"Nothing. Hessler's coming later."

"What about Mundt?"

Ben shook his head slowly, then said, "Only three of the Gatekeepers survived, and one escaped. I don't think we'll be hearing from them again."

"I was thinking about that before, about how their time had passed. They were fighting the wrong enemy. We're the keepers of the gate now, Ben. The enemy's different but not the stakes; they always seem to be the same."

"Otherwise, Danielle, we'd be out of a job."

"What about your eye?" she asked, looking at his bandage.

"Nothing serious. The patch comes off tomorrow."

"We were lucky."

"Yes, we were."

Danielle's eyes flashed wide with hope. "How has the testing gone so far?" she asked, her voice sounding wispy thanks to her dry and cracked lips.

Ben walked over to the side of the bed and took her hand.

"I don't remember any of it, Ben. I guess they've kept me doped up, right? When will Hessler's doctors be able to give me the first injection of Lot four-sixty-one? What do the tests show?"

Ben remained silent.

"We did the right thing making this deal, Ben. We shouldn't feel guilty. There was nothing to be gained from exposing our only suspect, Ari Hessler, already dead. And making the deal could be our only chance to save the baby."

"We did the right thing," he agreed.

Danielle smiled, found his gaze. Suddenly her grasp stiffened in Ben's. Her face went blank. She glanced down toward the surgical dressing wrapped around her entire midsection and the drain protruding from the site of the incision itself. A deep emptiness spread through her as she realized she could no longer feel the baby's presence.

"Danielle," she heard Ben say.

The tears had already begun to spill from her eyes when she raised up toward him. Ben took her in his arms and held her, not intending to let go.

"You're going to be fine," he whispered. "You're going to be fine."

Look for

BLOOD DIAMONDS

by JON LAND

available in hardcover from
Forge Books April 2002

PROLOGUE

Tongo, Sierra Leone, 2000

IF YOU'LL FOLLOW me, gentlemen," Colonel Masio Verdoon said to the representatives from Parliament, as they huddled in the thin shade of their truck, "we'll get started."

The six representatives, personally chosen by President Kabbah, followed Verdoon back into the heat of the midday sun. Tongo was located in the Kono region of Sierra Leone, well east of the coastline's cooling ocean breezes. The representatives walked with Colonel Verdoon up the slight hill through the steamy air, their shoes crunching over pressed gravel and their noses wrinkling at the stench of sun-baked mud rising from the shores of the river beyond. Perspiration darkened their shirts in widening blotches that looked like huge insects clawing their way through the fabric.

"As you now, we retook the Tongo diamond fields from the Revolutionary United Front over a year ago," Colonel Verdoon resumed near the crest of the hill. He wore his coarse black hair cropped close to his scalp, his face dappled with scars and his stoutness further exaggerated by a belly that hung over his gun belt. "This, of course, has nearly crippled the rebels' ability to purchase arms on the black market and has allowed the government to use the profits to make substantial investments in our nation's infrastructure."

The six representatives exchanged frowns. Evidence of such investment remained nearly nonexistent, leading many lawmakers to question the functionality of the once diamond-rich fields. Hence, this tour.

A trail had been flattened at the top of the hill, leading down toward a narrow ribbon of water. Government soldiers stood at their posts all along the river bank, overseeing dozens of workers busily dipping large sieves in the water and scooping up whatever they could. The workers shook the sieves to sift out sentiment and dirt, then inspected whatever lay trapped by the screen. The toilsome motion had a choreographed flavor to it, as if it formed the steps of some well-practiced, synchronized dance.

"These are alluvial diamonds, of course, and the method for mining them has remained unchanged for centuries, with a few exceptions."

As the tour group approached the river, more workers hurriedly collected the contents of the sieves into wheelbarrows and brought them to a conveyor belt on which the stones and rocks were placed.

"The conveyor is covered with axle grease," Verdoon explained. "Rough diamonds, we've learned, stick to such grease while regular stones do not." Verdoon failed to add this had been learned from the rebels who had mined Tongo far more successfully when it had been in their possession.

The conveyor belt ferried the stones scooped up from the river to a central location of tables squeezed amidst several high piles of excavated dirt. There, another group of workers, under the even more watchful eye of soldiers, stored the potential diamonds in wooden pails.

"There have been no incidents here in Tongo since I took over security," Verdoon said proudly. "We believe the rebels have totally vacated the area, but we have placed mines and traps in the surrounding woods in case they return."

Suddenly an uncovered truck packed with men and women clad in tattered shorts and frayed shirts rolled down a service road cut from the surrounding forest. The truck parked at an angle on the street and a pair of soldiers armed with M-16 assault rifles climbed down from the cab.

"The next shift of workers has arrived," Colonel Verdoon told the government representatives clustered around him. "Shifts are eight hours long from sunup to sunset." He checked his watch. "This shift appears to be a little early, but . . ."

His voice tailed off as the soldiers herded the workers from the truck, prodding them with the barrels of their M-16s. Near the back several had collapsed from the heat, and the soldiers mounted the truck's bed to rouse them.

Verdoon cleared his throat uneasily, hoping to be saved the embarrassment of one or more of the workers being found dead. He actually breathed a brief sigh of relief when they stirred; brief because the motion was too sudden and abrupt. Verdoon squinted into the sun and saw the dark gun barrels being hoisted from beneath the workers and tossed outward to be snatched out of the air by those workers who had already climbed down.

Rebels! It was the RUF!

The shooting began as Verdoon struggled to shepherd the government representatives back up the hill to safety. Random and wild, punctuated by screams as the rebels fired across the river banks, downing soldiers and workers indiscriminately. The prospecting workers tried to run from the river. The soldiers who could fled into the woods.

Verdoon drew his pistol, sidestepping up the hill, and fired on the rebels the moment they turned their attention upon him. A pair of the representatives went down screaming. Below, on the river bank, some rebels whipped machetes from sheaths hidden by their shirts and set off after the workers struggling to flee.

Blades whistled through the air. Blood leaped upward. The screams bubbled Verdoon's ears. He realized he couldn't swallow, realized his pistol's slide had locked empty and ejected the magazine in favor of a fresh one only to remember his ceremonial gun belt didn't hold any extra clips.

A wave of rebels surged up the hill, their raised machetes fragmenting the sunlight. Verdoon was still trying to shove the last standing representatives over the hill when bloodied blades split the air around him. He sank to his knees and absurdly raised his hands to cover his head.

Verdoon felt a stinging pain, like ice poking into his flesh, and looked down to see his right arm laying on the dirt. He screamed and gazed up at the tall, lithe figure of a woman looming over him, the machete in her hand soaking the ground with fresh blood.

"Dragon," he uttered, recognizing her as the blade rose skyward and then chopped down toward him. "I spit on—"

A flash exploded before Verdoon's eyes before he could finish, dragging a sea of red behind it that swallowed the rest of his world.